M. M. Misevicius is an artist and a dreamer.

This is the second of several books the author has written, including *A Time of Shadows*, a revealing sequel that wonderfully explores the aftermath of *When Darkness Reigned*.

For my children, the best little people a father could ever hope for.

M. M. Misevicius

When Darkness Reigned

Austin Macauley Publishers
LONDON · CAMBRIDGE · NEW YORK · SHARJAH

Copyright © M. M. Misevicius 2024

All rights reserved. No part of this publication may be reproduced, distributed, or transmitted in any form or by any means, including photocopying, recording, or other electronic or mechanical methods, without the prior written permission of the publisher, except in the case of brief quotations embodied in critical reviews and certain other non-commercial uses permitted by copyright law. For permission requests, write to the publisher.

Any person who commits any unauthorized act in relation to this publication may be liable to criminal prosecution and civil claims for damages.

This is a work of fiction. Names, characters, businesses, places, events, locales, and incidents are either the products of the author's imagination or used in a fictitious manner. Any resemblance to actual persons, living or dead, or actual events is purely coincidental.

Ordering Information
Quantity sales: Special discounts are available on quantity purchases by corporations, associations, and others. For details, contact the publisher at the address below.

Publisher's Cataloging-in-Publication data
Misevicius, M. M.
When Darkness Reigned

ISBN 9781649797698 (Paperback)
ISBN 9781649797704 (Hardback)
ISBN 9781649797728 (ePub e-book)
ISBN 9781649797711 (Audiobook)

Library of Congress Control Number: 2023916172

www.austinmacauley.com/us

First Published 2024
Austin Macauley Publishers LLC
40 Wall Street, 33rd Floor, Suite 3302
New York, NY 10005
USA

mail-usa@austinmacauley.com
+1 (646) 5125767

20250129

Thank you to my mother, Angela, for illustrating this book and contributing her poem: *The Roads We Choose*.

Table of Contents

1. A Boy — 1
2. Moonrakers — 12
3. The Great Unknown — 19
4. Is Nowhere Safe? — 27
5. Khaprayelle — 35
6. A Person of Importance — 45
7. The Road to Selkirk — 53
8. Powerful Alliances — 63
9. Out from Under the Rock — 72
10. Clairvoyance — 80
11. Melancholy — 88
12. The Witch's Jar — 96
13. Sonya Sage's Fork — 106
14. Old Crimsinth. Just Past Killik, off of Ergo's Coast. — 116
15. The New Beginning — 125
16. All Work and 'Some' Play — 134
17. The Curious Case of M.L. Higgins — 141
18. A Search for Nya — 153
19. Physical Education and Practical Magic — 158
20. Another Annihilation — 167
21. Tyrant — 175
22. Seven Years Later — 182
23. Michael and the League of Archangels — 191
24. The Meeting of the Minds — 196
25. Contact — 202
26. The Fall of the First Leaf — 207
27. They Come from All Around — 212
28. The Mighty Rufus of Kersius Seals His Fate — 223
29. At the Height of Battle — 234
30. The High King — 246

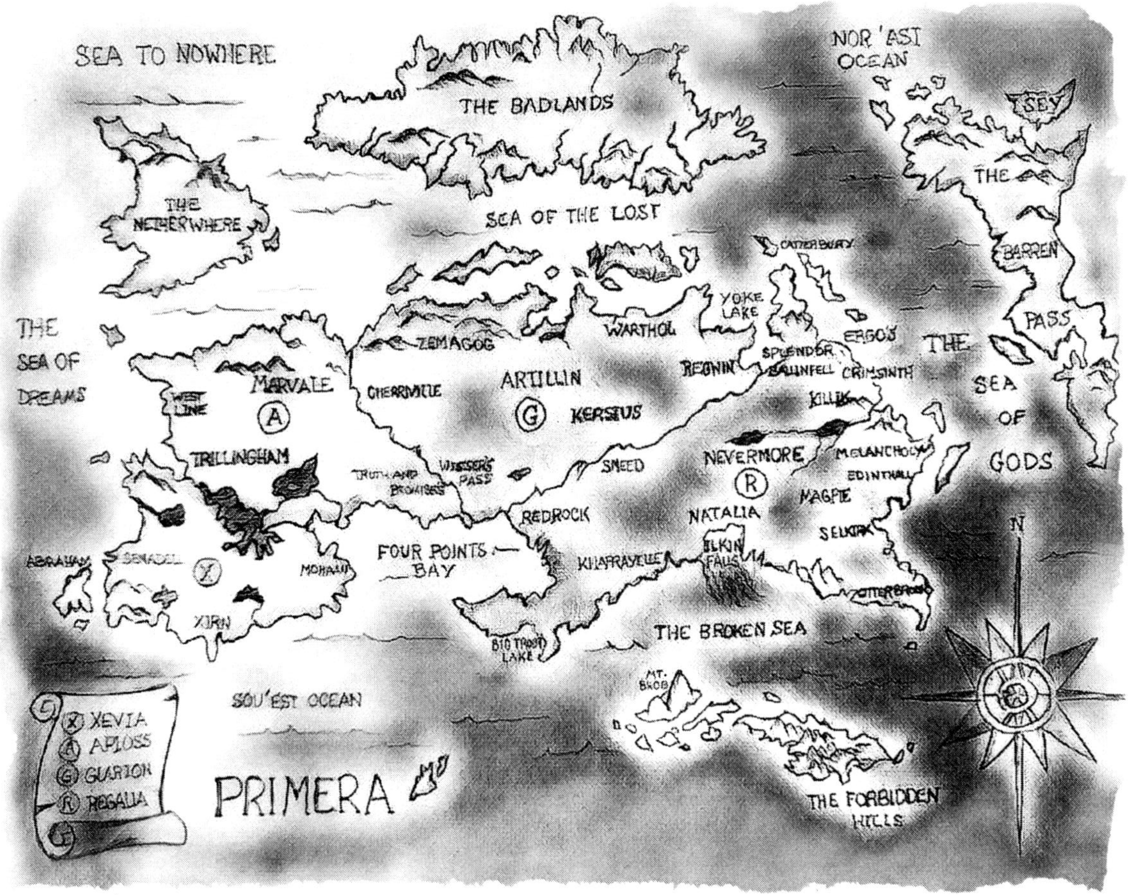
SEA TO NOWHERE
THE BADLANDS
NOR'ASI OCEAN
SEY
THE NETHERWHERE
THE BARREN PASS
SEA OF THE LOST
CATTERBURY
YOKE LAKE
THE SEA OF DREAMS
ZEMAGOG
WARTHOL
ERGO'S
THE SEA OF GODS
MARVALE
WEST LINE
CHERRIVILLE
ARTILLIN
KERSIUS
REGNIN
SPLENDOR
SALINFELL
CRIMSINTH
KILLIK
TRILLINGHAM
TRUTH AND PROMISES
SNEED
NEVERMORE
MELANCHOLY
EDINTHALL
MAGPIE
REDROCK
NATALIA
SELKIRK
N
FOUR POINTS BAY
ABRAHAM
MOHAAN
XIRN
ELKIN FALLS
OTTERBROOK
THE BROKEN SEA
BIG TROUT LAKE
MT. BLOB
SOU'EST OCEAN
XEVIA
APLOSS
GUARION
REGALIA
PRIMERA
THE FORBIDDEN HILLS

He who does not desire power is fit to hold it.

~ Plato

1.
A Boy

A massive, grey cloud passes over the village below, taking the dark shadow with it and releasing the bright, yellow sun from its shroud. It shines brilliantly, high above the small community within the rolling green hills of Little Augustine. It is a hidden place with shacks and huts of all sizes and is filled with good-natured, hard-working people. A thriving village populated at best by merely a hundred citizens. The lush paradise is embedded within the southwestern landscape of its most prominent province, Regalia. It is a part of the biggest, strongest country by far, the great Primera in the continent of Purity…or rather, it once was the strongest. It, unlike the neighboring countries within its oceanic continent, had been badly fractured in almost every foreseeable way and the beloved country has remained that way for a very long time. Although, Little Augustine itself is not among any major trade routes and is well off of any documented map. It is entirely self-reliant regarding its most vital needs. Within the valley, lives every tradesman a small community could want…a farmer, butcher, baker, merchant, doctor, smiths of all manner and several other townsfolk do their part with integrity and pride each and every day. Only once in a moon so blue will men within the community band together to make the long journey to the neighboring cities of Khaprayelle or Red Rock by horseback to barter for luxurious and rare items, beyond what their land and people can readily provide. The surrounding plains make for rich cropland and the southern peninsula of Little Augustine supplies the residents their water via a hard-packed, relatively well-groomed trail that leads a hundred yards to a lake. The path is virtually clear, but small hills that ascend to low-hanging tree branches aid in causing some minor obstructions about midway down. The adolescents of the village never pass up an opportunity to jump and swing forward from them. The lakeshore is a hot-spot and is used by elders and children alike for leisure time but also by men and women of strength for washing and fishing. The lake called 'Big Trout' by the locals provides just that…big trout fish are a staple for the people there as the cool waters of the lake, house them in abundance. Once in a while, should lady luck smile upon you, you may even snag a sinkle-warbler on the end of your snail-wood fishing poles line.

At a closer look, under the newly arrived, bright midday sunshine, a boy runs to his log hut with a straw roof from Little Augustine's center courtyard.

His home is of modest size and is distinguishable from other folk's dwellings. It is the large cast iron weather-vein rooster on its peak, that sets it apart atop the tightly woven, thickly layered straw roof. Before he can run through the heavy, tan, leather-bound wooden door, William's mother comes out. He runs right into her.

"Whoa! My dear child," she says, lovingly.

"Mother! Mother! Where's Nya?" he asks excitably.

"Well, I'm not entirely sure!" replies the beautiful young woman. She has dark hair pulled back to a high bun, with many shiny strays hovering about her face. Her eyes are pastel blue, her features are soft, and she has a fair complexion. The adoring mother smiles at her son with teeth as straight as can be and a love brighter and bigger than that of the warm sunshine above.

Her attire is worn and aged and is topped off with a soiled apron. The thin film of sweat that coats her skin confirms, she's been in her kitchen a while.

"She might be with Dora at the bakery," she adds.

"Great!" exclaims the boy, he turns and heads off running back into the village without hesitation.

"You must find your father too and come back soon for dinner!" calls out his mother.

"Okay, Mama!" shouts the boy.

He passes a few merchant's shacks, enroute to the town bakery.

A man stands on the raised stairway landing of his shop. He is tall and thin with medium-length black hair. It appears wet. He has an equally black moustache, twisted to a point on each end.

He has green eyes that gleam more than is normal and wears an all-white coverall with a heavily bloodied apron.

The man peers out onto the path, as he pulls from his lavishly styled sabretooth pipe. He squints his aged eyes as the boy comes into view.

"Boy!" calls the man…The little boy stops short from his run.

"Yes, sir," he says from the bottom of the stairs.

"What's the bustle about?" he asks, looking down at the boy.

"Going, to find Nya! She's with Dora. But…have you seen my father?"

The man stands under a wooden sign mounted on the roof's edge 'Lars the Butcher' is carved into it. "Not yet, not today," he says. He smiles with his sparkling eyes. Lars is amused as he looks down upon the small, innocent child.

"Thanks, mister!" shouts the boy and with that, he continues on. Lars puffs his pipe one more time, still smiling. He taps the apparatus to the landing's railing to empty it and heads inside. Dora's bakery is just a few places down from the butcher. The boy runs up the rickety wooden steps past a few flowerpots and into the shack. Inside the bakery, the walls are covered with shelves packed with loads of pastries, cupcakes, cookies and just about any other sweet good imaginable. The spaces in between are lined with lace and dried flower petals.

The smell within is a wonderful array. The bakery is beautiful in all its splendor. William scans the area. He hears laughter from the backroom and runs to it to find Dora and his sister.

The room is a peculiar shape and extremely cluttered with sweet ingredients, used cookware and old recipe books. Dora's wares line the walls to the top and hang all over from the ceiling. The baker's books are set all over the room in disarray, some piled low and others up high, some are stacked tightly to the ceiling in crude, untrustworthy columns. There is a large cauldron and kiln-oven at the room's center. It is obvious that they have both been in use for a good, long time.

Dora and Nya sit at a small drift-wood table set in the back corner…They do not notice William standing in the doorway. Dora laughs in her gentle fashion.

The boy studies them through all the obstructing items.

"I gotchya little one!" cheers Dora. She is a heavy set, elderly woman with a simple pale pink dress and has a frilly white apron and equally matching bonnet. She has on tiny, round spectacles that frame her eyes of grey.

"I'm not licked yet!" exclaims Nya.

Nya is tiny, even tinier than her brother and very young at the age of only seven.

She swipes up her share of jacks and bounces a red ball. "Ah, shucks!" exclaims Nya. "It appears you did get me, didn't you Dora," she says in dejection.

"Next time!" says the old woman with a chuckle.

The boy approaches, winding carefully through Dora's intricate maze.

"Oh, dear boy!"

"Good day, Dora."

"Brother!" shouts Nya, as she springs to her feet to hug him. She clutches around him locking her arms and squeezing with an expression of true love and pure admiration.

"You nearly scared the lightning out of me," says Dora with a smile.

"Great time at your birthday party yesterday, so much fun was had! Oh look! You two look like perfect little twins in those clothes," she adds. The brother and sister stand before the old baker. The small boy is ten years young. He is thin and of fair complexion.

A strip of brown hair falls and bounces from under his green bycoket hat and onto his forehead. He has brown eyes and wears a tan leather tunic with a thin, linen, sleeveless shirt underneath and light-brown hemp-cloth pants, stuffed into black boots. He has a blue and black long feather tucked into his left one. Nya is adorned with the same outfit, only the feather is missing. She is also fair-skinned and has long black hair and her mother's deep blue eyes.

"Can I see Rufus? Can I feed him?" asks the boy.

"Why of course! I was waiting for you to say that," answers Dora as she rises from her chair.

It creaks heavily as if on its last legs. She slowly makes her way to the front room. Nya looks at her brother and shuffles her legs quick with excitement in anticipation of Rufus' arrival. Dora comes back to the table carrying a large open-top glass jar and creaks back down into her chair.

"Is he really two hundred years old?" asks Nya with skepticism in her voice.

"Cross my heart," replies Dora. Nya jumps back into her seat excitedly and pulls it forward.

"Which kind today?" asks the boy.

"Hmm…a yellow one," answers the frog's keeper. He turns and works his way to the front.

"My Pa gave this little guy to me for my fifth birthday…The man whom he got him from said he's exceptionally rare…one of a kind," she says of the tiny blue frog in the jar. She carefully slides it to the center of the table among the jacks. "He said, that so long as I feed him well and treat him with respect and include him in daily affairs that he'd never leave me…as long, as I live, and he has been my closest friend ever since. Oh, sure he wanders for fortnights, time and again…but he always returns home," she adds with a tender smile.

"Wow," says Nya in wonderment. The boy arrives at the table with a single fresh flower petal of yellow and a tiny knife and fork. "All set," he announces.

"Uh, uh, uh!" replies the woman in a high-pitched tone of voice, not without a cutting board. She gets up and starts out toward the front again to fetch what they need.

"Wow!" says Nya analyzing Rufus.

"He's great," says the boy.

"Sure is," adds Nya. She is as fascinated as ever by the little blue amphibian before them.

Rufus hops there in the jar, gingerly licking with his tiny purple tongue from one side of his mouth to the next. Nya giggles at the sight. Dora returns and sets down a beautiful teak wood cutting board etched with floral patterns. The boy begins to slice the petal into the smallest of squares as Nya continues to pine over Rufus. The boy picks up the board, sets it back down and looks at Dora. She chuckles with friendly endearing warmth and takes a pair of tiny gold tongs from her apron's front pouch.

The boy smiles, takes them in hand, carefully pinches a square piece of the fresh-cut flower petal and drops it into the jar in front of Rufus. The frog crawls over to it, sits down on his rear end, takes the square into his two tiny, webbed hands and proceeds to nibble the portion with even tinier bites.

"Yayyy! He's so cute!" shouts Nya. As she does, Rufus stops and looks to his admirer for a moment then continues eating. The boy drops more squares into the jar one by one. Rufus takes his time finishing up before gathering a small pile for later.

"I love him!" cries Nya, passionately, as the tiny animal begins to cozy up onto his carefully constructed bed of sheep's wool and raw cotton.

"Awe, time for his nap," affirms Dora. Just then, a woman calls from the front room. "HellooOooo."

"Be right there!" shouts Dora. She rises from the table.

"Well Dora," says the boy. "We should go find our father, it will soon be time for dinner, and we do not want to be late!"

"Aye, enjoy kiddies," returns Dora, with a warm smile.

"B-bye!" shouts Nya, as energetically as always.

The two siblings hurry through Dora's books, below her wares and run quickly by the front counter where the young elvish woman who called out stands in wait.

"Hi, Urma!" shouts Nya, on her way out.

"Hi…bye!" says the woman playfully as the children disappear outside.

"Ah…my fair lady," says Dora, upon her arrival behind the drift-wood counter to greet her newest patron. The young woman, Urma, as Nya had so hastily remarked, is dressed elegantly in a finely crafted dark blue, velvet, form-fitting dress with golden embroidery cascading all along its sleeves and hips. She wears matching blue boots below her knee and an equally matching hair clip that holds up an extremely long, white ponytail. The elf has pale skin, long, pointed ears and a sharply tipped nose.

"What'll it be today dear?" asks the baker as she looks the beautiful young elf in her bright pink eyes.

She clutches her dark leather coin purse.

"One of your scrumptious twinkle-berry pies please," answers Urma.

Dora reaches beneath the counter.

"And how was this morning's worship?" she asks upon setting down the shimmering, open-faced fruit pie.

"Oh fine…fine indeed," replies the young lady, as she dumps out some diamond shaped bits of aubenite and a small piece of bronze She slides the bits and pieces along the counter-top, around the pie and closer to Dora.

Outside the siblings run and jump, weaving their way around this hut and that. They receive numerous calls of greetings from nearby residents as they quickly pass by.

"So, he's at Siro's?"

"Yep," answers Nya. "Haven't quite finished their boat, I suppose."

"The first one there is a dirty rotten scoundrel!" cries the boy as he runs even faster. They sprint a few moments more before arriving to a particularly smaller hut's fenced in backyard, to where their father and his friend are busy putting the final touches on a wooden water vessel of rather impressive size.

"Father! Father!" calls Nya. She ducks underneath the crooked log fence and runs to her dad who quickly takes the twisted-up smoke from his lips, so he doesn't accidentally burn her, as she jumps into his arms. The man stumbles back from the boat upon catching his daughter and is forced to drop his iron hammer to the ground upon impact.

"How's my little Princess?" he asks warmly, as he squeezes Nya in an embrace and shuts his eyes tight.

"I am great, Father!" she says wholeheartedly. The boy is over by the boat, studying it.

"A fine vessel Siro," says the boy as if he were its official inspector.

"Why thank you," says his father's friend.

"Fine children," calls Siro to Marek.

"Yes indeed," agrees the proud papa, as he sets his girl down.

Marek is of average height and weight with brown hair and matching brown eyes.

He wears tan breeches tucked into a darker brown, leather pair of cuff boots, cut just below his knees. He wipes the palms of his dirty hands on his thick, light-grey, high collared long-sleeved shirt. The un-done laces of his open collar sway as he tucks his hair back behind his ears and inhales a puff of smoke. He makes his way over to Siro and his boy. Marek looks a bit soggy from working all day. He wipes some perspiration from his five o'clock shadow. "So? acceptable?" he asks his son, speaking of the boat. "Wonderful, Father, this is just wonderful," replies his boy in a tone of pure authenticity. Marek slides his hand along the bow side of the vessel with the group looking on.

"Yeah, she's alright," he says. He looks to Siro and his friend nods positively in agreement.

"We're coming on her maiden voyage, right, Father?" asks Nya excitedly.

"Wouldn't have it any other way," answers her dad. The four stand in the small backyard, admiring the boat.

It takes up more than half of its vicinity easily, giving the illusion that it's larger and grander than it actually is, within its fenced-in boundary, but it is impressive, nonetheless. In the spaces between, Siro's backyard is chalked full, with tomato plants. He is one of the town's suppliers. They are here and there in no particularly ordered fashion. They stand about two feet tall, the fruit not quite ripe but almost. There are wooden buckets strewn about too, some with rope attached to their handles and some without. Siro is also one of the town's water-hands. He fetches it and delivers it in necessary quantities to the less capable residents from the lake or the town's well at the center courtyard, depending on his mood, how far he chooses to walk or who he's looking to mingle with and like most men of the village, he is also an adept fisherman. A hen flutters noisily by the children and Nya gives chase within the plants.

"It's dinner time Papa and we're probably late," says the boy.

"Well, we had better be going then, we need not keep your mother waiting." Nya darts by. Marek watches her and as she comes back around and by, he snatches his princess up and slings her over his shoulder.

She laughs with vigor as if her whole body were ticklish.

"I gotta bring your Mama her sack of potatoes. So, we had better get home."

"What sack of potatoes?" asks Nya through her laughter.

"This one," he replies. He jumps her up and down as he exits the gate in the fence.

"I'm not potatoes!" shouts Nya.

"You're not?" says the playful papa.

The boy follows closely behind the two…

"See you in the morrow," shouts Marek, as he waves backward to his friend.

"Enjoy your potatoes!" calls Siro.

They arrive home with dusk just beginning to sweep across the land's horizon. It brings with it tremendous, vast smears of pink, orange and gold. The layered colors hang above the trees and lake in stunning beauty, as the evening's sky settles in.

Nya, who is now completely up on her dad's shoulders, points out the sunset.

"It's wonderful, Daddy." The boy jogs up the steps and disappears into the hut.

"It sure is Princess…it sure is." They are still and watch a few moments in silence. The loving Father puts his adoring daughter down and shortly after they enter their home. Inside is laid out thoughtfully so as to maximize space. The kitchen and living room are blended into one larger great room. The main bedroom is set up in the back-corner area and a mounted ladder goes up on a ninety-degree angle to a landing that leads to a small loft bedroom with a bed on each side. There is a hidden hatch in the kitchen floor that gives way to the cold cellar where they keep their provisions and wine. The quaint family sits around their thick, oakwood kitchen table, its surface is filled with ample fixings. There are seared trout fillets, egg-plant steaks, broiled potatoes and mashed squash. There are also a couple of pies, a rhubarb cream and a wild berry. For beverages, there is a pitcher on each end of the table, one has fresh, warm goat's milk and the other is filled with clean, cool water. A large cluster of beeswax candles, of varying heights are at the center. Their flames flicker gently.

"Elsa," says Marek to his wife. "I must thank Jakk tomorrow for his generosity in bringing us this goat's milk."

"Yes, cousin Jakk is always very kind, and his goats are so well-mannered. He brought Susan and Ickabod right up to the door. Darling animals, they are. The kids are steady satisfying their pallets." Marek studies them both.

"They are oblivious and concentrated on their meals. I'll have to thank you as well," says Marek.

"For another fine dinner," he adds, giving Elsa a look only two people so in love could share.

"Aye, you do," she replies with a subtle, suggestive grin, while swiping a lock of hair from her face.

Shortly thereafter, the children are finishing their last bites of dessert.

"I'd like it if I could sleep in the cellar tonight," says the boy.

"Again!" exclaims his mother… "But why? You have a great bed, adorned with straw ground so fine within your mattress, soft pillows and blankets, fit for that of a King, is that not comfort enough?"

"Oh, yes, Mama, it is not any of that, it's the heat. The cellar is much cooler."

"I like you close to me," replies the loving mother.

"He's a big boy Elsa. He is safe there and he could handle himself on his own if need be. You need not worry my love," adds Marek.

"Oh alright…I suppose you are getting big enough."

"Thank you, Mother," says William with a smile.

"Make sure you use a good hide cover down there, after our stories."

"I'm going to skip the stories tonight, Mother. I'm pretty tired out."

Marek looks at his wife across the table in anticipation of her reaction.

"Well, well, well…you really are growing up!" she says, exuberantly.

"I still want stories!" shouts Nya with a dab of cream from the rhubarb pie on the end of her nose.

"Sounds good my dear girl," says Elsa with a chuckle.

The moon shines full and appears close, above Little Augustine. It casts a faint white light onto the lake and village. The community is hush.

On the main level, inside the hut the boy hugs his father and climbs up to the loft, where his mother is reading to Nya.

"I think I will! Do you think we can? together?" says the little elf to the reindeer.

Nya is attentively listening to her mother's story, as the pair lay side by side. There are two large candles between the children's beds on a small hutch, shedding a dim, peaceful, ambiance of light into the room. "I love you, Mom," says the boy.

"I love you," she replies. He lays down beside her and they embrace for a time, while she reads. He moves his arm and reaches to include Nya into the hug, who is now nearly asleep.

The boy releases them and stands up.

"Bye, Mother," he says as he leaves the room.

"Bye for now," she returns, lovingly.

He creeps to the ladder and heads down to the main level.

"William," calls his father.

"Yes," he replies.

The boy's father is seated on his bed, atop the sheets. "Come here," he says. William approaches. "Son, I know you're old enough to take care of yourself." The boy nods in agreement. "You'll need to take as much light with you as you can."

"Yes…I will, good night." The boy walks toward the kitchen.

"I love you, Son."

"Love you too, Dad." William takes a lit candle from the dinner table and sets it carefully on the floor beside a black pelt rug about four square feet in diameter. He curls up one end of it and folds it over in half to reveal the hatch. It is made of wooden layers and hefty with iron hinges fastened into the matching, wood plank floor. He opens it with considerable exertion and lowers himself onto the ladder below. It is a steep ninety-degree incline, like the other ladder, that leads up to the loft, but not nearly as lengthy. He stands there about three quarters of the way down, reaching out and around to the open hatch doors inside handle. It takes great effort as he slowly swings it over and rests the hatch on his head. He reaches in the opposite direction and draws the carpet over top of it, he then clutches the candle in his hand and brings it to him through the hatchway. He lowers himself carefully down the ladder, shutting the hatch gradually so as not to drop the night light or spill its wax. The door closes tight, and the rug lays flat on top. He descends the ladder and walks slowly past shelves of jarred preserves, several wooden crates and barrels, on the floor, along the walls and across the cold cellar's bedrock floor to a nearby spot in the corner where there is a small pile of loose hay about a foot in height. It has a slight impression along the middle from evening's past in which he was able to convince his mother that the cellar was a good, safe place to sleep on overly warm nights. At the foot of the makeshift mattress is a small redwood chest. The boy sets down his candle and settles into the bedding. He reaches forward, opens the wood-box and unfolds a hide blanket. He throws it over himself, as he lays down.

Once he is comfortable and cozy in his new and increasingly favorite spot to sleep, he blows out the candle. With thoughts of his loving family in his mind, he is soon fast asleep.

2.
Moonrakers

The full moon shines bright, casting an illuminated, blueish hue onto the lake's surface, off of Little Augustine's coastline. It glazes the dampened forestry and cascades onto the roofs of all the huts. The only sound to be heard is that of the faint rustling of leaves as a slight breeze, flows through the village. Nightfall has brought with it cool temperatures. A welcome break from the day's heat. Stars twinkle between streaks of clouds above. Colder weather pulls at the accumulating moisture, bringing about a haze that swirls and heavily blankets the lanes and alleys of the sleeping village. It hangs like old smoke and glows white, with the top layer tinged ever so slightly blue. With green, glowing eyes, a creature scurries underneath the mist and into Siro's backyard. The starboard side, tip of the boat breaks eerily through the blue of the haze a few inches, as if sunken within the fog. The curious beast sniffs a tomato plant with its long furry snout before carrying on through to Siro's neighbor's back yard. It disappears into the density of the murk sending it spinning and bounds through Yunessi's pumpkin patch, she nibbles at the leaves of some under-developed bushes. The animal is small in size, about a foot and a half in length. Its fur coat is silver and smooth with significant white blotches around its large, twinkling eyes. It has four clawed fingers on each of her paws and thumbs as well. It scratches and digs a little at the base of a few of the pumpkins. After a short time, she makes her way beneath the lingering haze underneath Yunessi's fence and into an open alleyway. The creature scurries alongside a relatively larger hut than the rest by comparison and stops at an open basement window. She peers inside.

Her shiny tail a bush and her large, triangular, black ears point upward.

Down in the basement on a bed of silk, lays Morbit Len Higgins, fast asleep. He, like little William, must have chosen to be in the considerably cooler lower level this night too, rather than up in the much warmer areas of the residences. M.L. Higgins' home, however, is much nicer than William's family's. Afterall, he is Little Augustine's mayor. The 'go to fellow' as the town's folk would say. He is one of the most important men within the community, if not the most important. He is a former medicine man and alchemist and apart from his main mayoral duties, he is also the village's goods and service organizer, for any parties that venture out of town on trades or purchases and any looking to provide anything for a price. He is a relative newcomer to Little Augustine and for that, his reputation is questionable among some of the citizens of the village. The large, almost round shaped man lay out flat on his back with one leg slumped over and off his mattress, and one arm stretched up over his face covering his eyes, below a tight fitting, crisp, though sweat stained dark grey top hat with a red band around its base. He is wearing a peach shaded, frilly, satin blouse and blue, pleated trousers.

A single flame lamp sets beside a bent, big black long boot on the floor beside the man. It emits a spherical glow illuminating the space around him and his bed. He wears the other boot on his right foot. His left foot, the one slumped to the floor is adorned with a red sock and has yellow patches on its heel and toe. The front patch has failed to do its job and has allowed the big man's big toe to slip the stitch and protrude outward in all its glory. Beside the appendage, is the culprit as to why M.L. is almost fully clothed and snoring rather violently with the exception of the one stray boot and rogue toe, a very large clear bottle lay there empty, on its side. Its label is embossed into the glass and is inscribed simply with three x's, just a few drops of amber liquid is all that remains inside. M.L. is sweating profusely and as he rubs the perspiration from his forehead, he nudges the empty bottle just slightly with his socked foot sending it rolling toward the lamp. It clanks leaving the flame a shudder. The creature jumps just a little and proceeds under the fog and further down the alley way along-side Higgin's hut.

The creature crosses the village's main road to the other side and makes its way up the steps of 'Kirramilly's Herbs.' The animal sends the haze swirling and rising upward, as it reaches the top. On the front deck of the herbal shop, are arrays of pottery and on both sides of the front door, there are thick wooden benches. Underneath one is a ceramic bowl, filled with dried fruit, grains and nuts. She sniffs it out and gets close and cozy and begins to eat. She finishes up inadvertently leaving some for the next animal and hops on to the bench, pushing the glowing fog blanket up even further. She stands on her hind legs and observes the inside of the shop. There are countless shelves all over with hundreds of baskets, pots, jars, cans, cups and bundles of all sorts of herbs. There are plenty of greens, browns and splashes of bright colors in between, here and there. The interior is very cluttered so as not waste any space and to utilize the store area as efficiently as possible. With the fog slowly descending back down and all around her, the curious creature twirls around, jumps off the bench and trots down the stairs and back to the main road. It continues to walk across with purpose until it gets to about the middle, where it stops. Her ears perk up. She spins around and peers all the way down the road beneath the mist to the edge of town at the entrance side, opposite the lake trail. She waits a moment or two before suddenly bolting as fast as she can to the side of the road and back along Mr. Higgins place. The creature kicks up the fog as it disappears to wherever it is it came from.

Little Augustine is and always has been peaceful and in no way a threat to the outside world. Since its earliest settlers had stopped and made what was thought to be a temporary camp by the lakeshore, its group grew and grew, and the community had not been fortified. A town guilty of nothing more than its own ignorant bliss. The hidden valley village is surrounded by forestry and other than its small scale and the sworn secrecy by its people, there has never been anything more done to protect itself. Which is why the entrance way was framed with a large open threshold. It is spacious and unsecure. There are no gates, no fences and no night watch. While it easy to judge…One must consider that the village, until recently had been select to only the utmost trustworthy of folk and things went incredibly well for almost a century…almost. The air feels instantly colder, and the fog is thicker and more blue now than before. A single hooved foot appears below it…then another. Above both hooves, around the ankles, it's legs are wrapped with soiled white bandages. Slowly through the haze walks all four hooves of a black stallion.

    The mist swirls and spins partially revealing the horse and rider above. A silhouette of a figure resembling a large man sits atop the hulking steed. The animal snorts. Twigs snap below his large hooves, as he steps forward a little further and then halts.

The rider on his back is big and muscular in stature. He looks at least seven feet tall on top of the stallion, whose eyes now glow brighter than those of the critter that ran away in fright. The horseman wears dark leather slacks with bandages wrapped around where his pants meet the top of his big black boots.

They are adorned with a sharp horn sticking out from each toe. His hips, thighs and torso are covered with red dragon-scale armor.

His sleeves are leather with forged iron plates on the elbow that match an iron breast plate and thigh guards. Around his neck is a tattered, long scarf that flows down along his back and is equally as red as his dragon-scale. Around his head he wears a steel band, with illegible engravings on its center, each side protrude steel dressings resembling wings from that of a bat. Through the lingering fog and blue moonlight, the mysterious rider seems to be beaming a smile of white teeth from ear to ear.

Upon closer inspection the reality is grim…his face is a skull of pale blue with hollow black eye sockets, they are blacker than the darkest night while surrounding its red glowing pupils. The menacing creature looks forward then left, then right. He pulls a sharply curved hollow tusk from his belt under his hip armor and raises it up. The tusk of bright white turns red as the monster holds it skyward. It illuminates fantastically under the blue moon.

All at once hundreds of beings just like him step gradually through the fog on their horses. They are all over and have encircled the village. The lead rider then lowers his tusk. The light from it fades as he tucks it back into his belt. Not a moment passes before all the hundred plus horsemen reveal themselves fully and charge Little Augustine. Their horse's hooves pound the ground and sound like thunder as they close in. The invaders carry melee weapons of all kinds. Scythes, maces, poleaxes, forked spears and spiked bills. Some have lit torches or bows with flaming arrows. They scramble through town, covering every square inch as they ignite the huts. Some shoot their flaming arrows through windows while others use their torches to light straw roofs. Citizens that make it out of the fire are trampled by giant horses, have their heads smashed in, or their bodies impaled. It is loud, as disturbing screams and shrieks bellow throughout the unsuspecting village. There is a transparent blue wraith, another figure resembling a man. He strides through the scene watching closely as the moonrakers commit their brutal assault and ransack the blind-sided town.

The fog has completely lifted and the black of night has been pushed away since the moonrakers arrived. Little Augustine is now bright in yellow, orange and red flames as the town is pillaged and worse. There are shouts of desperation and terror as the invaders sweep through with an awful evil precision, below plumes of black smoke.

The lead moonraker strides back and forth near the village's entrance swinging a spiked flail around and around, with its chain clanging from its hickory handle the spiked lead ball whirrs as it crushes the heads of those who attempt to breach the boundary through the front.

With him is another rider who carries a brandistock. A retractable three prong sharp blade about two and a half feet long, mounted to a staff.

He impales anyone who is bold enough to try and gain passage. There are riders guarding and set up at the end of the lake trail too, with no intention of letting any potential swimmers go free. Moonrakers wait in the forest as well, around Little Augustine's perimeter. They quickly cut down any person or animal looking to escape. The majority of the village is completely ablaze. The death toll rises all the time. There is blood, bodies and limbs strewn all over. Residents who have survived the smoke and fire are massacred handily in alleys or within the pathways or center court. Women and children are not spared. Nor are the babies, or even the pets of Little Augustine. It seems that no one…not a soul will be spared. The screams of terror are shrill and die down gradually as every last citizen is dispatched of. Soon the rakers have gone and all that can be heard is the popping of embers within the heaps of decimated former homes.

The noonday sun brings with it a sky so bright and beautiful; one would never know what lies beneath it. The scene at the lakeshore is calm and quiet. The water's surface appears to look like an enormous sheet of glass, without even a ripple to give it away. On the shoreline, however, float several mutilated bodies, they sway ever so slightly in the water. The village of Little Augustine has been annihilated…and bodies lay everywhere…Hacked, dismembered, slaughtered. Most are un-recognizable.

Blood spatters, smears and puddles are everywhere as if red paint were spewed about the town. Steady streams of smoke billow up from more blackened piles than not.

Marek and Elsa's home too lays in ruins and rubble. All is quiet as the sun shines down on the devastated remains.

Suddenly, beneath a pile of scorched timber beams and plank floorboards, a noise comes from below. Soon a partially charred, nearby lumber pile begins to jump ever so slightly then harder and soon, evermore prominently until a small void appears within the mess.

The boy…William, climbs out from the cellar hatchway and through the debris, he furrows his eyebrows as he pulls himself up onto his destroyed home. He looks out into the village slowly surveying all that he sees. He seems to be looking right through everything. The place he loved, all he knew is gone, levelled and burned to nothing…All the people too, are gone. It must be a nightmare.

He hopes, as he ponders…the reality sets in…*This cannot be,* he thinks. He is distraught, and fear overcomes him.

"Father!" he calls. "Father!" the boy calls out again, with a tone of voice that could break the hardest of hearts. There is no answer, no reply not a single sound of life…only the embers. The boy carefully steps through the debris and away from his house. He walks to the main road and looks at the bodies but tries not to see them, beyond what is necessary to identify his family. Most of the dead cannot be recognized. He takes his time as he goes, listening for any signs of life within the village. The boy is numb and walks slowly, all over and eventually down to the lakeshore. He returns and walks through the devastated town some more and all the spaces in between. Any hope of finding anyone alive fleeting. It is pure and utter horror. He has sifted through what is left of his hometown for hours. He cannot stay. He must find help. William arrives at the town's main entrance with eyes welled up, a lump in his throat and pit in his stomach. He ignores the especially large pile of bodies near the threshold, he can barely endure the sight of any more mutilated carcasses, so he waits a moment and musters the courage before searching them over. It is bitter-sweet when his investigation is complete. He hadn't found anyone even resembling his family members and can only assume them all dead like the rest. William carries with himself, an extremely heavy heart. His innocence dissolving by the second. The boy stares down the beaten trail that leads away from his village…the one to Khaprayelle. He has never felt more alone in his entire life as he looks out into the lush, green oblivion. William turns around slowly and looks back at what was his home…with a small crinkle between his eyes, he observes for just a moment more, before starting through the open threshold. He is filled with an immense fear of the beyond. He stumbles a little before catching something from his right peripheral. He walks to the stone columns frame and studies it. Rufus crawls steadily down the large cobble-stone pillar until he is eye to eye with the boy. The boy is shocked to find the tiny survivor. He pats himself down as if searching for something…finally he unties the laces of his tunic to reveal a thick cotton shirt with a breast pocket on its left side. He tugs at its slit with his left thumb and looks back at the miniature, blue amphibian. The frog tilts his head sideways for just a second, peers down at the opened pocket and hops in. William and Rufus then take up the trail within the wilds and start out toward the city of Khaprayelle and into the great unknown.

3.
The Great Unknown

William walks the long and winding path for hours. The road ahead appears as if it would be just about eaten up by the forest if it were any more robust, and green. The pathway is narrow but easy enough to hike due to years and years of wear. Indents of reddish brown define it well. The blue sky is visible way up high but just barely. The trees are dense and tall as they scrape at the atmosphere above. It's a warm afternoon with a slight breeze.

Poor William is distraught and confused as he slowly walks while periodically looking all over for whatever might present itself.

Birds chirp from on high when he arrives at a rather straight stretch of the trail. They are comforting, so the boy decides to stop for a rest. He traverses a few yards into the forestry and climbs on top of a large round boulder. He wiggles his rear end into the thick layer of moss atop the giant rock to make himself more comfortable. William pulls at the left side of his tunic further opening it. His tiny companion is fast asleep. He pulls at the front pocket. Rufus is nestled into the left corner at the bottom and slowly awakes as his giant friend studies him. The little frog climbs the pocket's interior, gains good leverage on the upper rim and prepares for launch. William puts his open hand underneath his pocket and extends it in front of Rufus. The frog jumps onto his palm and the boy lowers him to his lap.

Rufus sits on his bottom, crosses his legs and settles his chin into his little hands, resting his elbows on his knees. He looks up to William attentively as if knowing the boy wants to speak or at least prompting him to.

William's nose crinkles up. "I just don't understand," confesses the boy. "Who could have done that, and why…" He pauses.

Rufus lowers his head in agreement to the feelings of pain and confusion, as his keeper ponders aloud. The boy continues…

"They were dead…all of them," says William. His eyes now welled with tears and his demeanor weak. Many moments pass with the boy staring off across the path and into the forest on the other side. His eyebrows furrowed between his eyes with tears flowing steadily down his flush cheeks. The frog stares off too, in the same direction.

"It's…I've just…I never knew such evil," says the poor little one, through his sadness. Rufus looks to William and hops up his leg, climbs his shirt up to his pocket and hangs off its upper rim. With his little blue hand, he pulls and tugs outward, planting his feet on William's chest for leverage and pointing abruptly toward the path, all the while continuing to tug and jerk on the boy's pocket with obvious aggression. William looks down to the trail and over yonder in the direction they've been heading since they met at Little Augustine's threshold.

"I know, I know, we need to find safe haven."

William slowly wipes his tears as Rufus nods excitedly. He jumps from the rock and Rufus lowers himself back into the pocket, clinging onto the top with both hands and peering outward.

"There must be good folks out here somewhere. People who'll want to know of what happened… right?" asks the boy. Inside, he is not so sure.

William looks down to find that Rufus' view of their venture ahead is obstructed every other step by the left breast part of his tunic as he strides. So, he stops and drops down to one knee, he takes off his hat and holds it out in his hand exposing the top. He offers Rufus his free hand.

"Would you fare better atop my hat for this expedition?" asks William. The frog hops to the boy's hand, then to the hat where he crawls to the front. He sits down and clutches the brim.

"You'll be alright…right?" asks William, for assurance. Rufus looks at him and clutches tighter, in anticipation.

"Aye," says the boy. He carefully puts his hat back on, rises to his feet and continues on his way.

"Better?" calls William, looking up… "Oops, better not do that huh?" he says, of tilting his head back. The frog jostles, then collects himself back into position, at front and center of the child's hat. He cocks his little head down toward William as William strains his eyes upward as not to tip his hat up too far and send his little rider for another loop. His eyes cross as they meet the frogs. He staggers his walk just a bit. "Sorry," he says. Rufus nods.

William resumes walking normally again, keeping his eyes straight and level with the trail.

Little Rufus smirks a little sideways smile to himself.

A while later, the boy comes to a point in the road that begins to veer off way to the left, heavily as it winds around. A large branch of an even larger weeping willow pours into the space and hangs about two feet over the right side of the pathway. William is walking with purpose as he goes, so decides to proceed through it rather than move around it, just for a bit of fun. "Hold on to your hat." calls out the boy.

William stops short on the other side of the tree branches.

A bird from up in the sky and out of sight lets out a sound that bellows loudly.

"A woman," whispers the boy.

About thirty yards down the way hobbles what seems to be a very old, very hunched over hag. She shuffles her feet with small, deliberate strides. She has long, thin, greasy grey hair cascading down her back and over a large hood. She wears a thick, dark brown hemp cloak and holds her arms up in front of her with her fingers and hands slumped severely downward at her wrists. Her face looks a century old. Her glassy eyes are sunken into the dark complexion of her wrinkled, weathered face.

Her nose is long, skinny and tapers to a crooked, sharp point. Her lips are pursed inside her mouth tightly.

"I don't know what to do," says William. "I've never seen anyone who doesn't…" the boy stops himself, "…didn't live in Augustine." He waits a minute studying the woman as she approaches before gathering his composure and carrying on ahead.

The boy catches up with the hag rather quickly and attempts to pass without any interaction, keeping his eyes forward and his pace steady.

"To see my daughter!" shrieks the old woman, who is now a few steps behind William. He startles.

"Your daughter?" asks the boy, who feels forced to turn and look at her.

"My daughter, my daughterrr…" sings the hag. William is shaken but doesn't let it show. It helps not, that he has never seen a person quite so ugly in all his young life.

"Good afternoon…umm…Are you going to see your daughter?"

"Haven't in years! Not seen my daughter," she replies. "Must see her, must see her indeed." She shrieks again. All the while never really looking at the boy as she rambles.

"I'd be honored to guide you!" offers William, kicking himself inside for offering such a thing out of pure nervousness. *A terrible idea,* he thinks to himself.

"I do not trusssst sorcerers!" snaps the woman. She then stops and looks right at William. She has one yellow eye, and one is purple.

"I…I'm not anything…I'm just a boy," he says.

"Oh, my daughter, my daughter, have not seen her for so long, farrr too long," cries the woman, now shuffling on past and disregarding William once again.

"Let's get out of here!" whispers the boy. William jogs away from the old woman and keeps a steady stride, looking back occasionally, until the hag is finally out of his rear view. He stops to catch his breath, with his hands on his knees. Rufus struggles for proper footing atop the bycocket hat.

"I hope those are not the only kinds of experiences we can expect beyond home!" says William to his companion. "She's lost her marbles!" he adds. They walk a while more.

"It must be late afternoon," announces William, after scanning the sky. "If only a pony had survived, we'd get wherever we are going a lot faster!" Walking slower now and very hungry, William spots a small puddle within a heavy indent in the trail. "Let us drink."

The two travelers kneel by the clear water and sip using cupped hands as receptacles.

Rufus copies the boy perfectly.

"When the men went on trade missions, they would take days, sometimes weeks. I fear this is going to be a long journey, Rufus." The little frog looks up to his friend.

"We're going to have to eat…and sleep." A moment passes.

"Night fall will be coming soon…I'm glad you're here with me…if not for your company…I don't know if I could do this. I'd be so frightened…You are a great friend."

The frog cups his hands and seems to grin at William before scooping up another drink. The boy laughs. "Let's go!" he exclaims, and they continue.

Shortly after, the pair round yet another bend. A young woman appears quickly from around the turn and comes speed walking up in front of them. "You there! You there!" she repeats with urgency.

William stops. The woman coming straight for them is extremely tall. She wears a long sweeping, dark pink satin dress, that swirls gently below her knees, as she stands there towering. She has straight, shiny blue and black bobbed hair, deep blue eyes and matching blue lips. She has sharp features and a fair complexion. She wears a black string necklace with a simple small black bird pendant hanging above her bosom and has on equally black, thigh-high boots.

"Have you seen an old woman? Where are your guardians? You're just a boy. You must be lost! It is too dangerous to roam out here! Have you seen an old woman? There is something on your hat!" The young woman blurts out all of her questions and comments with a deep voice and without pausing or taking a breath.

She bends over and frantically rubs her thumb over Rufus, squishing him a little, as he rolls over beneath her attempt to wipe him off. The woman does not wait for William's reply and stomps off hastily.

"Mother, MOTHER!" she calls as she goes.

"I turn my back for one minute to fetch your milk and now this! And twice in one day!" she adds, with a sarcastic chuckle.

William and Rufus watch her go in startled fascination until she is out of sight.

"What was that!" says the boy. "This trail is proving to be stranger and stranger."

They walk a few hours more till the sky between the trees ahead turns pink.

"We must stop for the night. We must have supper and take sleep, proclaims William."

"Tomorrow we'll resume," he says as he maneuvers to the right, off the path and into the thicket.

"We cannot wander too far from the trail," he adds. He hikes for a short while, scanning the forest for edible vegetation. Something recognizable and safe enough to eat. With the trail just out of sight and darkness closing in, he spots something.

"Twinkle berries!" shouts William. "I'd hoped we'd find some out here, once it got dark enough!"

Among some bushes at the base of a giant tree trunk, shine hundreds of tiny little berries in all sorts of glowing colors. They blink on and off all over the bushes creating beautiful, fantastic natural light effects. William hurries to the berries and sits cross legged. He takes off his hat, sets Rufus on the ground and puts his hat upside down in his lap. He reaches out to the bush, collecting several of the brightly lit berries. Soon, they dig in. The sparkling cache gets smaller and smaller and as they devour them, it gets darker and darker. William and Rufus are content, as they fill their void from the day's venture. When full and satisfied, they lay in the grass before the glowing bushes. The berries cast an ever-changing array of color among them. The shimmering light is comforting to them both.

Night falls completely. The forest is alive with the sounds of the creatures of the night as they stir. William wakes up with a gasp and quickly sits up. He is left scared by a nightmare. The noise of the woods does not help the negative feelings he has inside. By the light of the berries, he checks on Rufus. He is fast asleep.

The boy sits with knees bent and thighs pressed to his chest and his arms wrapped around his legs.

He is wide eyed when he hears something...something big!

He is certain that whatever it is, it is encroaching upon him and Rufus, closer and steadily closer, though slow in its approach. The anticipation is enough to drive the little boy mad.

"It is nothing," William whispers, trying to convince himself of a lie.

Soon, another rustle in the bushes becomes evident...then another. Just as the boy is about to scream out, there are snapping sounds of twigs and branches behind the trees in front of him. William is paralyzed and does not remove his bulging eyes from the area where the new sounds came from, he is in complete fear as he fixates his vision there. The immediate vicinity gradually begins to light up softly...Slowly a large, white bear comes lumbering out from behind the tree-trunks on all fours.

The great beast is the source of the subtle white glow. The animal radiates internally from a source within. He approaches the boy slowly. The boy is shocked and still frozen in the bear's tracks. It stops just before William and studies him...

"It's not safe here," says the bear, in a deep calming voice. His breath vaporizes as he speaks.

William feels a cool air within the animal's presence. The bear exudes it.

"W-why?" asks the boy in shaky astonishment.

"There are creatures here. They want you gone...I've held them off...for now, but they won't wait much longer."

William is speechless. The bear pauses a moment while scanning the darkness beyond.

"You must go, you must stay on the trail and not venture in here...after dusk."

The bear slowly turns around and heads back toward the trees in which William first saw him, his light fading.

"William is stunned...thank you!" he calls.

"Yes," says the bear, "now go...they won't wait." The white bear disappears into the thicket.

"We gotta move it," says William, to Rufus.

The boy snatches the frog and puts him in his pocket. He slams on his hat, gets to his feet and heads out urgently, trying to find the trail.

It is too dark, and poor William cannot see. Minutes turn to hours. He is lost. "I don't know the way!"

He cries out in frustration. The child runs and maneuvers within the forest as best he can, but it's far too dark to know if the direction he goes is the right one.

"I don't know!" he shouts.

Just then a streak of giant cloud gives way to a bright white, three-quarter moon. It casts a light so bright that it illuminates the forest brilliantly. William stops and looks around for just a second.

Suddenly a large half dog, half coyote steps out from cover and into the moonlight.

Its eyes glow red. The animal glares at William.

"Are you a friend!?" shouts the boy.

The coydog opens his mouth and lets out a long, shrill howl. Instantly five more coydogs reveal themselves. They are growling and drooling and have assumed attack positions. The six run towards the lost boy without hesitation. He drops and cowers. A seventh coydog appears. He runs up behind William, jumps over the boy and lands in front of him. It stands there tall, on all fours. The other six screech to a halt as the seventh stares them down. Obediently, one by one they back up, before quickly leaving the area.

William is seated in the grass. The animal turns around and looks at the boy with its green glowing eyes.

It nudges William with its nose a few times, before burying it under his arm and lifting him to his feet. He then spins the boy around and pushes his upper back, with his bowed head. William takes a few forced steps from his boost and looks back at the coydog. The animal stares blankly at him. It then sits with its four paws together and wraps its tail around them. William dusts off his backside and walks slowly toward the path that has curiously revealed itself through the trees, beneath the moonlight.

4.
Is Nowhere Safe?

"I can't believe you slept through all that!" exclaims William to Rufus, who is now perched back at his place atop the boy's hat. Dawn breaks through the clouds, as William marches with the kind of energy that only a child could possess. He is invigorated to receive the new day, but nonetheless confused by all the recent encounters within the surrounding woods and hopes greatly that they find a refuge before the next nightfall. The path is ever-winding as daylight sets in fully. The day is mild and brings with it a subtle breeze. William walks with a steady pace, until he spots a small shack in the forest, off to the right and up a hill. He stands still awhile and ponders whether or not to investigate the dwelling. "There's smoke coming from the chimney." He points out. Rufus too is also fixated on the shack.

It's a small decrepit structure, with a straw roof. There are no windows...at least not visible from William's vantage point. A long, thin smear of smoke billows faintly from a cobble-stone chimney. There is an old wooden door facing the pathway with long black cast-iron hinges and a matching handle.

"I would knock but...it's *in* the forest..." says William. He thinks a moment... "But it is daytime...it could mean help."

They wait a few indecisive moments more, until the boy makes his mind up. He warily treads the narrow, broken laneway up the rocky hill to the shack.

"Whoever is in here...please be normal," whispers William. They get to the door. He knocks and waits. No one answers so he knocks again. This time there is rustling from within.

After a few clanks from the iron locks on the other side, the door swings open with a loud, palpable creak.

"Ohhh…well, hellooo!" says the old woman in the doorway. "I'm Eleanor." She has white, shoulder-length, thick, poufy hair, it is parted in the middle. She has brown eyes that squint as she smiles revealing her crooked, yellow teeth and the woman wears brown rags and a dark, soiled cloak over those. Her bare, boney feet are blackened with dirt.

William doesn't know what to say. He hadn't exactly prepared for that part, on his way up.

"Good morning, fair lady, I am William and I—"

The woman snatches his arm and hustles him inside, slams the door and shoves him to a table at the shack's center, she sits him down quick.

"I am Eleanor," she says, with a curtsey, "and we are in luck!"

"How?" answers William, before being abruptly interrupted.

"I've been working on my stew a whole fortnight…though I've been short a certain special ingredient…until today it came!" she shouts in delight. The woman walks behind William to a steaming cauldron in the corner of her home and resumes stirring with an over-sized wooden spoon.

William stares at the front door, already regretting having come to the woman's shack altogether.

"It's just been simmering and simmering…but soon…it shall be complete."

William looks around the room. There is cookware all over, and various herbs and animal pelts hung about the ceiling.

The structure is sweltering from the needlessly burning wood stove and hot cauldron that is full of stew…enough to feed a hundred hungry mouths.

"I just—" says William.

"You know what? I'll fix you some tea of my special blend, then…we will be all set and ready," interrupts the cook.

"That sounds nice but—"

"Ah…no, no, don't speak, you will simply drink," orders the old woman, as she fixes the tea on the counter beside her vat of stew.

"Here you are!" she says. She walks over and sets the hot beverage in front of the sweaty and increasingly agitated little boy. The old woman takes a seat at the table in front of the door and across from William. He fidgets.

Rufus lowers his little head exposing only his eyes and fingers as he slumps down lower beneath William's pointed brim.

"Drink!" she says of the bright purple, steaming beverage in front of him.

"Umm, I don't really want a hot drink, m'lady, thank you. I just came here to—"

"You WILL! Drink BOY!" shouts the woman as a thick, clear strand of drool comes out of her mouth and hangs from her bottom lip. Her eyes become vacant, as they change from brown to black. The saliva drops to the grass woven place mat in front of her. William shouts out in fear and springs up from the table. The cup rocks back and forth, almost spilling over. Eleanor jumps quickly from the table too. Her hair floats upward and lingers suspended in air.

"You come here!" she screams. She back hands the tea, sending it in a splash all over the table and floor, and breaking the little wooden mug. The woman grabs William's arm by his wrist and jerks him toward the bubbling cauldron, laughing with a high-pitched cackle.

William tries to plant his heels, but the woman is too strong.

They are not far from the large piping hot pot when finally, his heel catches a warped floorboard.

He stops abruptly and presses his foot further against the protruding plank, he frantically scans the area and spots a rusty, steel butcher knife on a shelf beneath a counter. William manages to reach out with his free hand and grab the large blade. It looks like a short sword in the boy's small hand. The woman struggles to pull him. She screams incoherently and does not notice as he arches back from behind her and plunges the butcher knife deep into her right calf. The old woman releases her grip in a fit. The structure shudders.

William lets go of the blade, leaving it sticking out of her lower leg. He jumps up and holds his hat to his head, as he runs across the shack to the door. He kicks it open. It is dusk. He is astonished, he had only been in there for a few minutes.

William bolts down the broken lane, and back to the trail. He runs as fast as his feet will carry him, only looking back a few times, until finally the woman's screams fade away. Soon, the building is out of view, but still William does not stop. He runs and runs until he cannot run anymore.

The boy finally brings himself to a halt at the side of the road. The sun has begun to set down among the trees far away in the distant horizon. He falls to his knees, catching his breath.

"How did ... What happened?" he blurts.

He takes off his hat to assure that Rufus is still there. "It is like a nightmare! I can't believe this...is nowhere safe?" he asks rhetorically.

The frog shuts his eyes tightly, as if to express his concurring with the feelings of frustration.

They rest awhile. William is left distraught by all the odd occurrences he has been subject to too since his village was pulverized. Before long and as to gain as much ground before nightfall, they are continuing further down the trail. "Look!" exclaims William, pointing ahead. "It's Yawgle!" he says of the orange fungi growing beside the trail. It is a very dense, spongy, safe to eat and very filling type of sweet mushroom. Yawgle commonly grows wild within the area. It is referred to as 'forest fungus', among the locals.

"Oh Rufus! You must have had some of Dora's famous fire roasted Yawgle tarts!"

William runs to the bunch.

"You and I my friend, have found supper!"

He kneels down beside the fungi.

There are four mushrooms, each stand about eight inches tall from thick stocks and are about ten inches around in circumference at their white spotted caps. William sets Rufus on the ground and begins to break off little pieces of food and pile them up.

"This is perfectly ripe! See the pink color inside? That's how you know," asserts the child.

The frog methodically pulls off little bits from the pieces and eats them up. William eats his chosen chunks right from the source.

"We're gonna have to try to sleep in the woods again tonight," says William, popping a Yawgle fragment into his mouth.

"I hate it, but it's our only option," he adds.

Later, amidst the black dark night and after having suppressed his feelings of fear as best he could, William decides to bed down.

"Time for some shut eye," he says, as he slows to a stop. He knows he must keep his wits about himself and sustain bravery as he is forced to wander off the road. "We're not going too far in," he announces. He chooses a tuft of grass for his bed and lays down on his side, facing the trail. Rufus is on his hat beside the tuft.

A while passes, William cannot sleep.

The newly orphaned boy watches the stars in silence... "Nya," he whispers.

He breathes in and exhales slow as a shooting star takes off, and soars through space.

We had better get somewhere soon, somewhere safe, he thinks. He imagines good times with his parents in their home and playing with his sister and their friends at Little Augustine's square. Soon after, he is sound asleep.

In the mid of night, up ahead of William and Rufus, comes the brazen clip-clop of a pair of horse's hooves as they stride along the beaten path. The mysterious night riders come into view under the ample star light. They halt before the boy as he breathes deep and heavy from his slumber, taking a rest, he so sorely needs. The two riders are dressed identically in bronze armor with red under dressings. The rider closest to William lifts his helmet visor to reveal a pale face with a black beard. He is no older than forty. His horse snorts and digs into the ground with his hoof.

The man speaks:

"Boy!" he calls down from his horse.

The men look at one another.

"Boy!" he calls again, this time much louder. William wakes.

The man looks to be up very high among the starry night, from the boy's point of view.

"You shan't be out here," says the man with a gruff voice.

"If you are a stray, you must return to your keeper at once."

"I-I need your help," says William in a soft voice.

The man bellows some forced, obnoxious laughter.

"My home was sacked, burned to the ground!" cries the boy.

"Little Augustine!" adds William, as he sits up, within the cool grass.

"Ha! Never heard of it. We are assassins…contracted to go to Wisser's Pass and take Agnoro's head, for his leadership has been compromised and this little problem of yours shan't disrupt the ongoing predicament or our place there," says the bearded man.

"We are on our way to end the dispute and have been riding for days to oust this particular…problem," adds the second, younger rider.

"Indeed, and besides this thing of yours sounds done with and money is surely not to be a potential with your problem boy," adds the man that had woke William.

"Good luck, young one," says the man and with that, they ride on. William says nothing more. Further perplexed by the strangeness of the new world, he has been thrust into. The boy sits a long time on the tuft, as Rufus sleeps. He feels sad and depressed about his challenging reality and the people lost at Little Augustine, he reminisces some more about his family until dawn breaks. Soon after, William hears something shuffling aggressively from where he is seated. It is still too dark to see just what exactly is coming along the path. He waits a moment.

The mystery encroaches harder and faster, until suddenly...

"YOU ARE MINE!" shouts Eleanor, her hair suspended all around her angry face. William grabs his hat, puts Rufus in his front pocket and is off like a shot, down the trail away from her. She cackles and laughs disturbingly while giving chase.

"I've been searching for you for days!" she calls. Her frenzied eyes, blazing as she pursues her last ingredient. William runs as fast as he can from Eleanor again for what seems to be forever to the boy. He is breathing hard and can't help but slow down, allowing the crazed woman to get closer and closer, until finally his legs give out. He collapses and is numb.

"I never give up!" shrieks Eleanor, as she walks up and towers over her catch. With faint stars all around her from above the tree-tops and streaks of orange and pink in the sky's backdrop, she reaches out to grasp the boy's neck, when a white light begins to glow from within the shadows of the forest beside them.

She pauses as the bright white bear from the night before walks slowly out and onto the road.

Eleanor cries out in terror.

"Curse you! You blasted, terrible beast! CURSE YOU!" she shouts. She backs away from William.

The woman runs back to where she came, shrieking and screaming until her sounds fade once again. William stands up and puts his hat on, he checks on Rufus who is fine in his pocket and begins to speak to the illuminated bear.

"I—"

"You must come with me," interrupts the bear, with his low, hollow sounding voice.

The cold which he exudes feels even better this time on William's skin.

"You won't survive another day here..."

"Where?"

The great bear does not answer.

"Do you have a name…bear?" asks the boy.

"I am Indigo," replies the beast.

"I am William."

"We must go."

"You will escort me?"

"No…I will take you," replies Indigo.

"How?"

Indigo bends his front legs and lowers his head…

"Get on."

William is reluctant but climbs onto Indigo's back and clutches his thick, cool glowing fur above his giant shoulder blades.

"What if I fall?" asks William.

"You will not," answers Indigo.

The boy almost instantly feels safe atop the cool, large bear and surrounded by his white light.

Indigo turns fast and sharp into the forest.

He trots faster and more agile than that of any animal William has ever seen, ridden or been taught about. Much more sure-footed and precise than the common bears of the forest.

Indigo maneuvers the terrain as if following a route, he has ran numerous times before.

Rock, bushes and low-laying branches fly by as he goes. After a time, William slowly starts to lean forward and release his grasp. He lays down limp on his stomach, atop the bears thick, soft back and falls asleep. Indigo does not break stride as he feels William bed down. He grins just a little as he turns back for a second to see William sprawled out and cozy. The cool light barrier that surrounds Indigo keeps the boy pressed on top just so, keeping him safe from falling and shielded from any other danger that may be present itself.

The next morning, the sun is big and bright above the city of Khaprayelle. William wakes up on a steep hill at the outskirts of the forest. He rises to his feet from a bed of grass on the large knoll and quickly looks side to side. Indigo is gone. William checks his pocket to find Rufus looking back at him.

The city before them is tall and wide.

"Wow!" he whispers, "it's like twenty-five Little Augustine's put together. More even!" He says, of the massive, cordoned off, fortified city. It is a condensed place, encircled perfectly by tall, thick limestone block walls.

How long have I been sleeping? The boy wonders to himself. He feels Rufus poking around in his pocket, so he takes him out and puts him on his hat. Rufus assumes his accustomed position.

"Well, my friend, we're here!" says William, in a tone of disbelief. He looks down yonder to the city in the valley.

"I think we'll be safe here," he says with immense relief.
"My father always told me stories of this city…" The boy looks at his toes. "He said he would take me here one day when I was big."

William waits a few moments looking at his feet, then out at Khaprayelle. When he is ready, he heads down the hill and toward the city walls.

5.
Khaprayelle

William hikes down the hill, keeping good footing and grabbing sturdy rooted fragments of foliage every so often for leverage, when the grade draws steeper. He happens onto a broken trail and follows it. All the while the giant limestone walls of Khaprayelle tower higher and higher as William gains ground upon them. Soon the broken trail links up at the bottom of the bushy area with a proper pathway. It is made of bedrock and runs flat and wide, all alongside Khaprayelle's perimeter. The boy takes it and arrives at the main entrance quickly and peers the long way upward. There is a massive stone precipice that carries up at least twenty feet further than that of the rest of the walls atop the extremely tall, closed, wooden doorway. The peak of the precipice is a perfect triangle with a large crest carved into it. The insignia has a Lions head at its center, with the letters 'LL' making up its base with a sword across them, on a diagonal.

"Must be the main passageway," says William, as he diverts his eyes from way above.

"Rufus, this is really something!" exclaims the boy, standing in front of a set of doors at least sixty feet in height and almost twenty feet wide. The Limestone is a hundred feet tall and from the view back at the edge of the forest, at the top of the hill where Indigo had placed the bewildered pair, William appears as but a small spot in front of the enormous entrance.

At a closer view, William examines the oak. The grand doors are etched with a collage of carvings including curious creatures, lush plants and swirling ribbon throughout. About ten to fifteen feet up from the ground are scrapes, dents and gouges in the wood, no doubt from barrages of heavy attacks and onslaughts during quarrels of times gone by. The doors are sullied too, weathered and dull in appearance. "Here goes nothing," says William. He puts out his clenched right fist and only attempts to knock before a tiny hidden door's locks clank below. A door no taller than the boy's hip. Somehow, he had missed it upon investigating prior, but it is well cloaked. William is taken by surprise and jumps backward. Out steps a short, stalky, elderly fellow…A gnome, dressed in black boots, brown slacks, a white blouse and a green vest. He wears a red cone shaped hat on his head and has long curly white hair and a lush, wavy, matching beard. The short, stout, pale-blue eyed man is quite irritated.

"And to what…in this city, do you strive?" demands the gnome. He stares up at the boy and stamps his crooked, wooden staff onto the hard ground.

"I…I am William of Little Augustine, and I am seeking refuge and assistance."

"Ha!" blurts the gnome. "Are not we all!" he proclaims. "Who are you?" adds the guard.

"William, I said so already sir."

"Hmm, maybe…but who are you really?"

"Umm, a boy?" answers William.

"Hmm, you seem like a child, yes, but around here things are not always as they seem."

The short man squints and examines the boy's eyes.

William raises his eyebrows. Excruciating moments pass for the boy.

"Wait here," orders the gnome. He turns, goes inside and shuts the door as aggressively as he had opened it. The boy is tossing small stones at Snidle bushes when the blustery receptionist returns.

"To you, access shall be granted," he announces, before stamping his staff on the ground.

William jogs to the door rather gingerly. There is excitement in his steps.

"Under two conditions," says the gnome, stopping him short.

"The first being paramount to the second," he adds.

"Okay?"

"One…you must visit the mayor in his office! Lucky for you, you picked the right side of the city to enter as his office is but a small jaunt."

"I see…I shall," says William.

"Two…Don't get yourself into mischief."

The gnome grunts, nods and steps beside the small doorway, stamping his little staff and staring straight ahead into the trees opposite the city wall. The boy looks down at the entrance. "Just right through there?" he asks of the opening.

"You, boy, are far too small to garner us going through the trouble of opening the big doors…do you agree?" asks the gnome, still looking outward.

"I do," replies the boy.

"Alright then," he says gruffly and stamps his staff yet again.

William gets down on all fours and crawls through the small entrance way. The gnome then follows.

Inside the city, it is instantly grander than any place William has ever seen. He is in awe by all that he surveys.

"You better get back in my pocket for now Rufus," says the boy, as he takes the blue frog and lowers him inside it. There are lightly colored stone pathways everywhere, leading every which way and beyond those are mainly dust and dirt alley ways. There are stone buildings, two, three and four stories high clustered all over with grand stone columns throughout. Stairways and bridges join them together high and low in a crammed, disheveled network. Most buildings within the commercial district are linked together in some form or another. The city is old and has a rich history. It shows in the architecture. A design that appears hastily built during a period of war and continuously added onto time after time. Men and women shuffle all over. They are loud and consumed by their business. They quickly take brief fleeting moments to greet one another as they pass.

"Now! Mayor Rimpod's building is straight ahead and then the eleventh one on the right. You'll know it by the Khaprayellan blue and orange crest painted on the structure doors. He is on the top floor. You have a little while to report and not a second more or the guards will scoop you up and you'll be back outside quicker than a Primp Fingler can hop!"

William snaps out of his stare. "I shall comply promptly sir."

The gnome grunts. "Someone has taught you the importance of a well thought out set of words lad, haven't they? Now get a move on!"

"I mean no sarcasm. What is your name?" asks William.

"My name is of no relevance to our dealings, but never-the-less, I am Bix Jingling. I am one of the gatekeepers and he…" Bix motions upward with his staff, "is Orion…my associate…We're a duo to be reckoned with."

William is stunned to find a giant man of stone, he hadn't previously noticed before, hulking seventy-five feet high and fifteen feet wide standing at attention beside the inside of the gigantic main door's frame.

He towers there beside the giant doors with large iron loops at their center. Orion is sculpted to the acute likeness of an armored knight, complete with a giant sharpened stone sword. It is at least forty feet long. William starts by looking at the rock titan's gigantic toes then slowly…gradually all the way up along his gargantuan body to his face.

"I don't believe it!" exclaims the boy rather loudly. Orion looks down to William, then back out toward Khaprayelle's interior, with a blank, never changing expression.

"Yes, yes…well, he's my back up, you see…my partner," says Bix, with a raspy chuckle. "Not bad, Eh?"

"How does he…have life?" queries William.

"He is enchanted, no doubt…one of Khaprayelle's longest serving guardians he is. A Champion. The legend goes that he was built to protect this city by legendary mages, the rumor doesn't tell who. Built the same time these very walls were erected of the same rock…almost two centuries ago. When magic was all over…and ran free…but that was before the dark times, before the oppression and near extinction of all that was divine. When the creatures and people all over our world were equal and un-bound by the high king's strangle hold."

William looks intrigued. Bix is in deep recollection and continues.

"Aye…the grasp of the bloody, cursed iron fist."

"Magic," whispers William, to himself and looks back up to the curious stone man.

"Has he been in many an entanglement?" asks William.

"I've seen his full onslaught, only a small handful of times and as sure as he stands tall. He is mighty."

William remains star struck in Orion's fantastic presence.

"Now you need to go," says Bix. "The clock does tick," he grumbles.

"Yes-yes, I shall, thank you Bix, I am off," says the boy, taking a few more seconds to look upon the mighty Orion, before turning and heading into the bustling city.

"Aye!" calls Bix. "If you happen to exit the city from the other side, when you depart…you will meet one of my brothers. He is Zepple but everyone calls him Rooster, his associate is Halen. Zep and I switch ends now and then to keep things interesting. Tell my brother I said, "Hello." They won't cause you any trouble as you'll find leaving Khaprayelle is much easier than entering. Now off you go!"

William waves and continues into the city. The boy opens his tunic as he does…

"I can't believe they have two of those…titans!" he says, looking down at his companion.

William follows the road straight ahead, as directed. He sticks to the right-side. The first building he arrives at is a three-story structure. The bottom is that of a merchant's, a cobbler's to be exact. "Silken's Shoe and Boot." The second story is a hotel, "Fine Morrows Inn' and the third floor is unmarked, with barred windows. William examines the first building before walking on to the next."

He takes his time as he does, peering deeply down the shady alleyway that separates the two.

William feels overwhelmed and slightly anxious what with being in such a large community.

A burly and heavily soiled man walks by, then another.

"Eh! What's a child doing so close to the perimeter?" shouts the man rhetorically. People stir all over. He speaks to answer the man, "I" but the man in less than pleasant garb cares not for the answer, as he hustles on by, all the while glaring at the boy with one good eye.

"A nice encounter," whispers William to Rufus. He looks at the next building. The sign above the door of the stone structure reads: 'Oso's Armament'. There is a large man, a bladesmith out front.

He is forging a sword at an elaborate workstation.

There are two men sitting at a small table atop the short staircase that leads up to the weapons shop part of the lot. They are dressed only in loincloths and burlap boots. The men are barbarians and are of exceptional physical stature. One has long hair, and the others is even longer which is one of the only distinguishable differences between the two. William watches as they engage in a bout of arm-wrestling. They struggle awhile until the less sweaty man with the longer hair wins the tussle. They laugh vigorously, before chugging their mead from large wooden tankards.

William carries on, all the time watching out into the street when he's not closely observing building after building and each curious alleyway that divides them.

The steady flow of people high and low is relentless and so is the banter.

"It's so busy here," whispers William. "If my father were here, this foreign place could prove interesting, fun even...but Rufus, I feel so far from home."

The boy is about halfway to his destination at the mayor's quarters, when a patron on the steps of 'Tully's Treasures' below yet another Inn, calls to him.

"Hey! Young one!" The man is middle in age and dressed rather fine. He is pale and has short dark hair and eyes. William approaches the man and warily ascends the stairs toward him.

"I have some time to use until my meeting with the Lions!"

Whatever that means, thinks William.

"And if you have time as well, maybe you'd like to earn two bits by shining my shoe? I stepped...in...something and am in need of clean footwear!" He motions toward his left foot. It has a mud stain all over its patent leather toe. The forward gentlemen's attire is odd compared with most others of the city, at least so much as William has noticed thus far.

Most seem as if they would not pay any mind to such a stain.

"Well, I could use the monies, but I lack the necessary tools," replies William.

"Yes," says the man. "Over there is a bucket and water too." He proceeds to nod toward a wooden bucket with a red rag slung over its brim. It is by a bench, further down the stone porch of the treasure shop. William goes to retrieve it as the lanky man sets down his oil lamp, he then leans on a stone pillar at the side of the staircase and sticks his dirty shoe forward.

"Okay, here goes nothing," says William, upon setting up. He dips the rag into the bucket and wrings it out. He begins scrubbing. He rinses and buffs the shoe a few times until it is clean to a glimmer.

"A beautiful job, wonderful task!" exclaims the man, who reaches into the breast pocket of his satin coat and hands the boy his earnings.

"With handy work like that, you ought to take that money and buy yourself a shine box. That's how it works, kid! It takes money to make money, supply and demand and all that good stuff," says the man before trotting down the stairs.

William begins to put Tully's bucket back when he hears the man cry out in frustration. He runs to the top of the steps. The man is at the bottom holding up his soiled right foot. William raises his eyebrows.

The man's other shoe is worse than the left one was, before William had tended to it.

"My good lad!" calls the man from just below. William smiles and holds up three fingers.

"Three bits this time!" he shouts, with a clever grin.

Soon after, William is down the street with all five bits of aubenite.

"We can get a wonderful meal and something to drink as well," explains William to Rufus.

"Certainly, we must have a little while longer, before we have to report," he adds.

He walks to the ninth building. "Aurora's Apples and Ale's."

"This looks like a decent eating house."

Stone stairs lead directly up to the entrance, where beside it, there is a man and woman dressed rather poorly and sharing a make-shift pipe of ridiculous proportions.

"A child?" says the woman. "There are no children permitted among the borderlines of Khaprayelle."

"Really?" says William.

"Really," repeats the man, he smiles revealing a yellow smile lacking most of its teeth.

"Why?"

"It is rule…is it not?" the man asks of the woman, as he turns to her.

"You drunkard! exclaims the woman. It definitely is…there are residences and safe havens in the city's center core but beyond that…no children," says the woman.

"I have personal endorsement from Bix Jingling and have an appointment with the mayor."

The man laughs. "Ahh, good 'ole Sully Rimpod! I bet you do!" He doesn't believe the boy.

The woman joins in the laughter.

"You child, speak better than most men I know!" she says.

"Thank you, m'lady. He tips his hat to her, with a shaky hand…n-nice to meet you both." William enters Aurora's through a large birch-wood door. Inside, the dimly lit ale house is about half filled with adults and elders alike.

The ones indulging in meals are seated at tables and booths and the ones over-indulging in ales and meads are at the bar.

The only server in the boy's immediate view is behind the bar, so that's where he heads. On his way, there are several calls and shouts in his direction, all based upon the same context.

"You there! What are you doing here? There are no children allowed 'round here!"

William feels nervous and out of place. When he arrives at the counter, the barkeeper immediately hushes any drunks looking to point out the boy's presence.

"Boy!" says the large man appearing more warrior than servant. "You must have good reason to be here. Tell me you do!" he urges.

"I am hungry," says William, which cues sudden and collective laughter from just about everyone around him, at the bar.

"No! Well…I have clearance from Bix and the Mayor!" exclaims the boy over the noise.

It dies down and tapers off.

"Aha! Okay, now that's more like it!" says the barkeep, with a wink. "You must be someone of importance then…I am Byrn," he adds.

"Yes! I guess I am Byrn…well, maybe. I am William."

"Never guess William," asserts the big man. "What is your business with the mayor?"

"I-I don't really know…I mean…it's a long story."

"I understand, but tell me…you are safe, yes?"

William thinks a moment. "Yes, I-I am for now…is anyone really safe…out here?"

Byrn looks at the boy and searches his eyes. "You're right indeed. What'll it be then?" he offers.

"Do you have swiller meat and sweet potatoes?"

"Yes."

"And twinkle berry pie?"

"Yes sir!" replies the server, with a nod.

"I'll have that! And snibb grape nectar too sir, whichever kind you please, thank you." William's excitement is short-lived. "Wait sir," he says in a low voice… "What would all that cost?"

The man thinks a moment… "Four stamped bronze pieces, or six Aubie bits would do it!"

"Ah…I need to take some things out, I only have five aubenite bits."

"Five bits will do just fine my friend, not to worry."

"Oh, I couldn't, I…I…"

The barkeeper interjects the boy's stammering. "It's okay young one," he affirms.

"Are you sure?" presses William.

"You got it," says Byrn. He smacks his weathered palm against the counter, before disappearing into the back kitchen to relay the order.

After eating at the bar and still surrounded by loud imbeciles and witless drunks, William sneaks tiny bits of scraps and crumbs into his pocket for Rufus. He sincerely thanks and pays the barkeeper.

"I must offer you a trusted chaperone…I insist," says Byrn.

"I am only but a short walk from the mayor's place, I'll be fine," replies William.

"So long as you are certain, friend."

"I am," he confirms. He thanks Byrn again, before exiting Aurora's. This time no one calls out.

William descends the steps, turns to his right and continues down the road.

"Well, we'll be right on time," announces William.

He has gained much needed strength and energy from his generous portion of food and is thoroughly satisfied by the best meal he has had since his last night with his family.

6.
A Person of Importance

William arrives at the eleventh building and makes his way up the stone staircase. It zig-zags all the way to the fourth and final floor. The landing is small and empty. The door is indeed marked with Khaprayelle's crest, just as Bix Jingling said it would be. Embossed into it is a dark blue lion's head with a flaming orange mane and two capitol letter L's at its base make up the top third of the iron door. It is lined with corroded iron rivets. The boy analyzes the sword etched across the double L's.

"I think this man will help us," whispers William, as he knocks. He waits patiently a few moments until the door's locks clank, and it swings wide open.

"Good day young lad! I am Mayor Rimpod of Khaprayelle, respectively," belts the man adorned in the most lavish and flamboyant of garb.

"Good day, fine sir, respectively," returns the boy.

"Come in, come in." The mayor guides William to a chair set before a grand desk. He hops in and shuffles his rear end to the back of his seat leaving his feet to dangle. The mayor sits in his gold framed, blue velvet chair, opposite the boy and begins to nod yes to himself as he exhales slowly with William looking on innocent and anxious. The boy takes off his hat and sets it on his lap. He wipes the hair from his forehead to the side with the back of his hand.

"So, my watchers tell me, you are thee William, himself."

"Yes, I am sir."

The boy scans the room and concludes that it is furnished with less than he figured it would be. A stain glass window allows the day's light to pour a variety of colors inside. They cascade long and narrow across the slate-rock floor. His eyes follow the light and fix themselves back upon the large man across the desk. Mayor Rimpod is clean shaven, with bushy black eyebrows and cool blue eyes. He is of average height and over average weight.

He wears a golden, velvet, puffy hat. It is as equally loud as the rest of his attire.

His eyes turn warm.

"William. What brings you here?"

"Well, sir…it's an awful, terrible story."

"I'm here to listen," obliges Rimpod.

"Thank you," says William, his posture relaxes. "My town…the town I'm from…Little Augustine…well it's…it was sacked and everyone who lived there…was murdered. I don't know by whom or for what cause but…the people need to be…properly put to rest…that's the first thing that must be done."

William begins to choke up and grows frustrated. He puts his head down as a few tears well up and fall to his lap.

"And what else, William?" asks Rimpod, displaying as much empathy as possible.

Anger swirls deep inside the boy. After a moment, he looks up.

"Well, sir…revenge…I mean vengeance must be taken," he says with a fire in his heart and flowing through his eyes.

"Whoa…William…slow it down…there are things you must hear." William looks on attentively, his tears drying leaving shiny track marks on his soft, flushed cheeks.

"The situation over at Little Augustine is going to be handled…a clean-up party is planned to be sent there, over the next few days to collect every soul and give them a proper resting place. The town will then be cleaned up and a memorial will be erected. But as far as vengeance…William, we too do not surely know the cause or who is behind these atrocities that were thrust upon your village…with Khaprayelle being the closest and most prosperous city and Little Augustine's closest ally it is absolutely our duty to do our part and we shall, but revenge? vengeance? that is not in the cards yet, not with so little information."

Mayor Rimpod searches William's face sympathetically for any sign of what he may be thinking.

"How did you know? About Little Augustine? To already have a clean-up party planned."

William sits up in his chair. Mayor Rimpod sits back in his.
"There are many things you will find out and there is a man, a very wise man who can answer all your inquiries. I am deeply sorry for your losses William…I am. Mayor, Morbit Len Higgins had also survived the onslaught that night. He managed to escape and make safe passage by way of horseback. His having survived will help shed great light on some things for us."

"I don't believe it! Were there anymore? Were there any more survivors?" urges William.

"We can't be for certain, but we think not, you are the only two."

"Is it he? Is he the one who will answer my questions?"

"William calm down, just listen; We have received advanced correspondence via raven from the great Argane the Immortal…He has been riding for days to meet you and enlighten you. I on the other hand am sworn to secrecy. You must understand that Argane is the one to help you."

"I do not understand…this…immortal man is coming here? for me?" asks William.

"He'll be in Selkirk, and you are to meet him there."

"I can't go further cross-country! My parents," the boy exhales and continues… "they taught me and educated me wonderfully and I…I always felt inspired by the idea of being independent but I—"

"William, William…" intervenes Rimpod, "We know the delicacy of this situation…more than you can possibly comprehend at this time. I have organized two of my best men to escort you safely by horseback to Selkirk, where Argane will be waiting." A few moments pass.

The boy's confusion grows. He thanks the mayor.

"William," returns Rimpod. "In due time. Argane will be with you; to guide you and you and everything will make sense. Argane is good and righteous to the core of his very soul. He has been around many, many years and his time is never wasted…It seems you are a person of importance."

William's expression goes blank, as he searches the mayor's eyes.

"Tell me young one, how is it you survived the assault on your town?"

"It's nothing valiant, I had simply chosen to sleep in the cold cellar because I was hot. When I awoke in the morning, everything had been levelled."

"Remarkable…sometimes that of which we assume mundane, is in fact a significant part of a divine design…perhaps it's always that after all."

"Well, William of Little Augustine," Mayor Rimpod stands up from the desk. "Across the street from here is a place called 'The Slick Fox'," he continues, "inside you will meet two fellows, Calupa and Jonathan. They will prepare with you for the journey northward."

"Thank you, Mayor."

"Don't mention it, William, call me Sully. And please, take with you the confidence that your town will be properly tended to."

William rises to his feet and manages a smile. He heads out the door and down the steps, feeling overwhelmed and significantly jaded. He arrives at the street and looks across to The Slick Fox. It's on the ground level of yet another three-story building. A large, grey, wooden sign with the place's namesake is carved into it, in bright blue calligraphy. A fox tail is painted on the bottom corner of the letter X. The sign juts out proudly above the front door's frame.

"Rufus…I don't know what we are doing, but here we go." William crosses the street and enters the building. An elderly woman shrouded in a dark shawl observes him closely from the tenth buildings top floor. It is relatively empty inside The Slick Fox. The windowless bar is dim, lit only with red candles at the center of the odd table. The stone walls are lined with large hand weaponry and oil paintings of various foxes are strewn about, here and there.

A young man behind the counter and dressed sharply is conversing with Calupa and Jonathan, who sit side by side with elbows atop the counter as they sip their ales. The door closes behind William with a thump. The two escorts turn and smile. The man on the left in brown coveralls and particularly tarnished silver greaves and matching gauntlets waves the boy to their direction.

William hustles toward them.

"Are you to take me to Selkirk?" he asks, as he stands before them.

"We are…replies the man who had waved. I am Cal."

The other man, Cal's partner, who is dressed in orange and blue under-dressings and covered in chain-mail chimes in… "I am Jon, friend."

"Aye, and I am William, sir," says the boy. He looks to his toes.

The two men could not appear any different from one another. Cal is a man of forty or so years. He has brown hair and eyes and has a dark complexion, with a rather dark five o'clock shadow completing the general tone. Jon is maybe twenty or twenty-five with light skin and yellow, blonde hair, with blue eyes and has a fresh shaved face, if in fact he even shaves at all.

"We've been waiting awhile," says Cal.

"We shan't waste another second," he declares, while rolling up his sleeves.

"Right," agrees Jon.

They down their beverages, pick up their iron long-swords and equip them into the sheaths at their hips and strap their bows over their backs, alongside their quivers.

"So long," says Jon to the barkeeper. The man puts two fingers to his brow in casual salute to the three as they turn to exit the Fox.

They stand outside the ale house a moment.

"Do you carry?" asks Cal, of William.

"Umm carry?" repeats the boy.

"Evidently not," observes Jon.

"Here take this," says Cal as he unbuttons the straps of his left ankle beneath his greaves to reveal a six-inch quartz-rock handled, steel dagger.

"I wonder Cal, though, if marauders may see the lad as a threat, if they spot that he is armed?"

"Pish-posh, Jonathan, if in a pinch the boy can perhaps defend himself."

"I suppose," agrees Jon.

"Besides…I hear this one is a survivor in every sense of the word."

The boy watches on as the men talk and while Cal outfits his ankle with his new blade. It is much more noticeable on William's leg than it had been on Cal's.

"Now, my wee friend. I have names for all my coveted weapons and that one," he says, pointing to William's ankle, "is called, 'Often'!"

"Often?" asks the boy.

"Aye…"

"An interesting name."

"That blade has often saved my very skin, during many a scrape."

The boy laughs and looks down at Often.

"A character you are…you know that right?" asks Jon, to no reply.

"We're off," announces Cal.

They walk around the building and into the alley to where three horses are hitched to a wooden post.

"You ride, yeah?" asks Cal.

"I certainly do," answers William.

"Well, that one is yours," announces Cal, pointing to the small mere on the far end of the three.

She is a dapple grey and has big brown, warm eyes. She looks at the boy nervously.

"She is yours to keep," he adds.

"Mine!" exclaims the boy in astonishment.

"Yes, courtesy of Argane 'the Immortal.'"

"You be sure to give him ample thanks once we arrive at Selkirk."

"Oh, of course!" returns William.

The prestige surrounding Argane grows evermore, and the boy continues to wonder why the mysterious man, with the famed reputation cares so much for his well-being.

Cal mounts his big bay horse and Jon climbs onto his pinto.

"Does she have a name?" asks William as he approaches and strokes his new friend's long neck and muscular shoulder.

"She is yours to give a name," answers Cal, looking down on them. William studies his beautiful horse in fascination.

He whispers slowly moving closer to her face. She looks back at him. He pets her nose reaching up and whispering to her. Cal and Jon look at one another and smile ever so slightly.

Moments pass.

"Norwynn," says William… "she is Norwynn."

"A fine name," says Jon.

"It seems though I may need assistance."

"Ah, yes of course. Maybe Argane thought bigger of your stature, do not hesitate to mention if you are having trouble traversing or are in need of rest or anything," says Cal, as he dismounts and lifts William onto Norwynn.

"A fine saddle as well," says William, as he grabs hold of his mare's reins. Cal mounts his horse again.

"Let's ride," he says. The three trot through the city steadily, as passersby make way.

Evidently Cal and Jon are quite popular as several citizens wave and shout happy greetings as they pass. The riders cross the city steadily.

A time later, the North doors are visible up the way.

"You two are well known to this city." says William, as yet another resident yells a positive bidding toward their direction.

"We William, are serving members of the 'Legion of Lions'…the 'Double L' helped found Khaprayelle and are sworn protectors of it. We protect a select group of allied cities as well. The Lions have a deep, storied history."

"Truth is though," interjects Jon, "this grand city hasn't needed defending in a very long time. But our reach is vast. We partake in missions to aid allied cities in any conflict that Rimpod and Heinridge deem important or urgent enough to intervene upon."

"Heinridge?" inquires the boy.

"Yes, he is Khaprayelle's King but do not repeat that in amongst the wrong company." What's the wrong company, thinks William. "Anyway, he runs the city. Sully answers to him and then represents all matters on his behalf. He then calls the necessary accompanying lesser orders on his own."

They arrive at the gate to the sound of Rooster's 'crow'.

"I see why they call him that," says the boy quietly to his pocket.

"Good day ol' Rooster," calls Cal as they arrive to the gnome.

William stares in wonderment at the Mighty Halen. He is identical to Orion except for a large gouge out of his giant ankle.

"This is the special little guy, eh? Don't be too long boys or the 'Double L' will have fire ants in their britches," says Rooster with bellowing laughter.

"You look like Bix's twin," says the boy. The gnome laughs some more.

"While we are brothers, we are not blood. His is of the Mill-water Bandys," replies Rooster.

"I am Zepple Rooster, Ox." of the Lu-hu Bandys.

"Curious," says William. Rooster laughs some more in his gruff voice.

"Man the doors!" shouts the gnome. Just then eight other gnomes dressed identical to Rooster and Bix exit from two small shanties. Four run from one building to the left of the doorframe and four from the other to the right. They quickly join and form a semi-circle in front of the entrance way, facing the city. They stand guard with their staffs. To William's surprise, Halen begins to move and walks a couple of heavy, long strides forward. He turns and pushes the doors open just enough to let Rooster walk through. Rooster holds his staff out in front of himself in a defensive stance and slowly exits Khaprayelle.

Outside on the hard-beaten path, he looks left and right, then back outward toward the surrounding forest. He stands a moment with suspicious eyes, looking down the road as it disappears within the woods. He goes back inside and halts before Halen. The stone giant looks down at him. Rooster nods.

The ground seems to shake a little as he reaches forward and pushes the doors wide open.

The old doors shutter.

"Ride well!" shouts Rooster.

"Thank you, my good man," says Cal. The three canter by.

The men stop outside the city as the boy turns around to witness Halen pulling the large doors closed from the inside.

William is fascinated by the Khaprayellan titans. He leads his horse around, and the three head out toward the wilderness taking the northward path ahead of them.

The men are mindful to keep young William of Little Augustine in their center. They flank him, just so, with Cal on Norwynn's hind left side and Jon at his forehand right side.

After a few moments, they disappear beneath the trees along the dirt path and into the lush green forestry.

7.
The Road to Selkirk

The trio canter steadily for a time before slowing down to a trot. William breaks the silence.

"Why are not children allowed along Khaprayelle's perimeter regions?" he asks.

"Y'know, you're a well-spoken lad," says Cal. "How old are you, William?"

"Ten and a bit." The men laugh.

"Don't forget the 'bit'," says Jon.

"Well young one, simply put, the reason children are not allowed around there is because it is not always safe and they are kept to the center with their families, for their protection. It also lets the adults keep the more mature and rather boring business of being a grown-up separated."

"To a degree," adds Jon.

Cal continues… "Khaprayelle is laid out with all the residences in the middle and all the businesses around the outside, it's just the way it's always been."

"I see," says William.

Rufus looks on as if part of the conversation from his perch back up on top of the boy's hat.

"That frog simply…sticks with you, does it?" asks Jon.

"Pun intended?" adds Cal rhetorically.

"He sure does…his home was demolished too," replies the boy.

The men's expressions turn solemn.

"So…how long is the journey…to Selkirk?" asks William.

"Well, we'd like to keep a steady pace and that should take what…four days?" suggests Jon with intent for Cal's confirmation.

"Yes, yes, four days at this pace," agrees Cal from in front of the group.

"And what of food…do we hunt it?"

"We have provisions within our packs to last the trip…are you hungry?" asks Jon.

"No thank you," answers William… "and how do we sleep?"

"In shifts, somewhere within the forest," answers Jon.

"But what of the dangers and…the enchantments within the wilds?"

"Most times, we do not encounter any, those occurrences are quite scarce," says Cal.

"You must be joking," asserts William.

The men laugh.

"Sorry to disappoint you, young one," returns Cal, through a smile.

"No, no…it's just…my night in the forest was very, very strange."

"Did you witness oddities within the wilds?" inquires Jon.

"To say the least!" replies the boy.

"Alright, alright, no need to worry William. We are well seasoned in fighting if we must and I assure you, you are safe." William stares into the woods as it passes steadily by and thinks to himself, *how peaceful and ordinary it appears in the light of day.*

Dusk sweeps in. The group stops off to the side of a particularly straight and wide stretch of the road to water their horses and eat their supper. The men dismount and William jumps down from his horse spooking her, but only slightly.

"Time to replenish," announces Cal. Jon ropes the three horses together and leads them to a tree, suitable for attaching them to, as Cal goes through his burlap pack with William at his side. The boy studies the hilt and handle of his protector's weapon.

"What have you named your long sword?" he inquires.

"I met a maiden once, when I was passing through the old village of Dilemma. She was wonderful…at first…but before long William, I learned that she was just as cold as she was beautiful…I named it after her. It has the ability, like she did; to destroy ones very existence with a single encounter…my long sword is Claudia Blackheart."

William observes the black sheath along Cal's side where Claudia lays. "Wow," whispers the boy in fascination, "and how 'bout your bow?"

"Celia," answers Cal, quickly.

"And who was Celia?"

"No one, just like the name."

Jon finishes up tying their horses to the nearby tree, leaving plenty of slack so they can graze.

Calupa and William set down in wait.

"Jon, come…eat!" calls his elder.

William takes Rufus and places him on the ground. Jon joins up with them and sits down. They drink water from wooden canteens and eat their bread and fruit in silence. All the while William looks off, into the forest. He gently lowers a large chunk of red fruit and places it in front of Rufus. "We shall carry on for a while, then we'll make camp," announces Cal. Once done, the two men, the small boy and the tiny frog do just that. They trek a while more until they stop when there is just enough daylight left to rope off the horses and set up their leather hide tarp within the low laying branches of some trees. They build a small fire beneath and seat themselves around it.

"So, William…why so wary of the forest?" asks Jon.

"I…I was attacked by coydogs…with…a relent I've never seen," says William.

"Yes, well we are your sworn protectors and will not let anything breech our defenses," proclaims Cal.

"Fear not William, no harm shall come to you," adds Jon.

The men sit among the fire for a time, sharing stories, keel nuts and snibb grapes. The fire snaps and pops sending an ember flying past Jon and fading into the darkness.

"Jon boy!" says Cal playfully. "You ought to watch those blonde locks 'round such an inferno as this!" he says with a laugh.

William interrupts the banter to press a festering issue. "Have you two…not come upon…any dangers within these woods?"

"It is true William that there are forces within the trees that are… untame and that animals and creatures alike have been known to display an odd might in the strange years past…but these displays are rare," says Cal.

"Besides William, they only show up if they are *really* after something."

The boy stares into the fire as he lays on his side using Cal's pack for his pillow.

"Now…William, enough…time for some shuteye. A man must have all his wits about him if he is to perform at his optimum."

He stares into the fire a few seconds more.

"Thanks for helping me Cal…Jon…I trust you both are great guardians…goodnight."

The two men smile slightly at one another as William closes his eyes. They feel sorry for his situation and what he's been through and though he's just a boy, they respect him greatly.

"There's a good lad," whispers Cal, quietly pointing to William. Jon nods in agreement from across the fire.

"Share a pipe?"

"Sure."

"Then I'm gonna get my rest too," adds Cal, reaching to his front pocket.

"Indeed…been a long day," says Jon shaking his head.

"Shall be an even longer one next morrow."

With the tiny fire fading out before them, the men pass the pipe slowly back and forth and become more and more sleepy, as they do. Soon, they bed-down.

The next morning dawn breaks with beautiful blues, yellows and gold streaks smeared across the sky above the forest.

A large bird sounds off and wakes William as it does. The boy opens his eyes to see Cal and Jon packing their wares into their horse's saddle bags. The tarp is away, and the fire is burnt to just a smolder. William feels better than he has in days. He was finally able to sleep deeper and longer than he had since life in Little Augustine, under the protection of the L.L.

"William!" calls Cal from beside his horse, near the road.

"Yes sir?" shouts the boy.

"Jon has fixed you chicken eggs, pork-meat hash, and corn bread for your breakfast…Eat, while we finish up, then we'll head forth!"

William scans the area afoot to find the two eggs, the hash, and a thick slice of oiled corn bread on a wooden slate with some steel cutlery.

"Thanks Jon! This looks incredible!" calls the boy, before digging in.

A short while later William is sipping from a canteen as the three steadily trot the trail.

"This Argane? has he come from afar to meet me in Selkirk?"

Cal laughs. "If unspeakable miles of vast countryside are far…then yes, I'd say so."

"Wow," responds William with much gratitude.

"Indeed, he is a great man, young one. Argane the Immortal has a reputation unparalleled, and he'll be a proper guardian unto you."

"No disturbances to report, from last night, by the way," announces Jon.

"I had feared I might wake in the night to find you men engaged in squabble," replies William.

Down the way about fifty yards or so come four men on horseback.

"Just keep pace," orders Cal. Jon looks back to him, stares for a moment then nods. They do just that and as the four riders come gradually closer the tension mounts. Rufus lowers himself revealing only his bulging eyes and webbed fingers on the brim's front edge of William's pointed green hat. They glare ahead at the four horsemen. All that can be heard is the collective, steady clip-clop of several hooved feet along the stoney path.

"Well, I'll be," says Jon, looking back at his partner.

"Why it's Stallworth!" cries Cal.

Jon chuckles.

They halt their horses, as the four approach.

"Must have been short order at Natalia," suggests Jon to Cal. The group is jovial.

"Stallworth, you devil! No further business in Natalia, eh?" shouts Cal.

"Just a little bloodletting," announces Stallworth. "Same as Redrock," he adds, as he and his convoy stop before them. They are adorned in matching blue and orange.

"Ah, another success for the L.L.," affirms Cal with satisfaction.

"This must be the orphan?" asks Stallworth. His voice is deep.

"Poor taste, my man!" interjects Jon.

"Aye…apologies," says Stallworth. "Well, you'll be safe with these two, lad!" he continues… "except for maybe this one," he claims, nodding toward Cal.

Cal laughs. "Filthy beggar," he says.

Stallworth laughs too. "Yes, well enough fun for now…we've still got at least a day's ride, and we are plenty fatigued."

Cal winks. "See you fellows back, safe and sound in Khaprayelle."

The men pass one another with a series of nods and salutes. After the group has parted, Cal laughs again… "Stallworth…always a character," he says aloud.

"That man needs to know when to bite his sour tongue," says Jon.

The men ride until sundown. They again, make camp away from the trail.

"We've accomplished much ground thus far," observes Cal as they sit amongst their fire… "two more moons should do it and so far, without a hitch."

Jon concurs. "Aye, we are about halfway, and a good ride so far indeed."

They carry on with eating and talking by the fire. William falls asleep first, with Rufus snuggled beside him and Cal and Jon again share a pipe before their slumber.

In the middle of the night, Norwynn snorts, and spooks, pushing the horses on her sides to thrash around. From within the forest behind William comes a creature with eyes that glow crimson red. The creature is rather large, stands tall and meticulously encroaches the camp on two feet.

The flames of the fire still casting an orange, lowlight onto Cal's face.

The mysterious stalker pushes through some branches. They snap sharply. Cal's eyes flick open in an instant. He searches the woods, from his side where he lays. When he spots the creature's red glowing eyes, he carefully reaches out and grasps his longbow 'Celia'. She is set out just in front of him, there on the ground. Calupa waits as the beast slowly draws itself closer, never taking his eyes off the two, red, luminous circles within the darkness. Cal doesn't blink. A bead of sweat wells up and rolls down from his forehead and along his scruffy cheek toward his chin. When the red eyes are as close, he quickly unloads three arrows just below them, in lightning-fast succession. The beast's eyes go dark as it falls to the ground.

Jon and William don't move a muscle within their slumber. Cal stays awake for the rest of the night, never moving from his spot.

The next morning William again is the last to wake. This time his companions are not within his immediate view, but he notices that his breakfast is. He pulls himself up, sits cross legged and scans the rocky area through the trees.

Calupa and Jonathan are down the way, looking at…something in the long grass and talking low as they do. Their words are inaudible to the boy, and they are too far away for him to read their lips.

"It's a werewolf that's for certain," says Cal.

"Yes, but have you ever seen one so big and so...tall?" asks Jon of the eight-foot, three-hundred-pound brute. Three arrows all in a row stick out from its throat, chest and belly.

"No...I most certainly have not," replies Cal.

The werewolf lay there on its back, sprawled out before them with deep purple blood coagulated and encrusted within the blue-grey fur of its muscular torso. Its eyes are black and are wide open, as is its jaw, revealing long, razor sharp teeth and a long, blue tongue hanging out of its mouth and off to the side.

"We should probably not tell the young one," suggests Jon.

"May aid in his growing strong," counters Cal.

"He has seen his share already, has he not?" asks Jon rhetorically and implying the tragedy at Little Augustine.

"Aye...yes, you are right, of course," agrees Cal.

They head to their horses who are packed and ready, passing William as they do.

"Thanks for the fine meal," says William, as he eats.

"You're welcome," replies Jon.

"So...what's down there?" asks the boy.

"Just...an old saddle," says Cal, as he mounts his horse. "Someone must have just pitched it...weathered old thing," he adds.

Later that day the men are stopped on the road drinking from their canteens. "It's especially hotter than the last two days," notes Jon.

"Here comes something," says Cal. An elderly man with ragged clothing, down the trail is walking slowly toward them. They wait patiently and watch him.

"What is your bidding stranger?" calls Cal as the old man comes near to pass.

"A lovely walk...on a lovely day is all," says the man with a smile exuding warmth.

"Indeed," replies Cal. The man shuffles by and the three riders carry on.

The day comes and goes uneventfully as they make camp a third time and sit around their fire.

"We'll be there sometime tomorrow before dusk," announces Cal of their arrival to Selkirk.

"That's wonderful," says William.

"Aye," agrees Jon.

After provisions, William is asleep first, so Cal and Jon proceed to smoke their pipe, which has inadvertently become a bedtime ritual of theirs.

"We must be on watch from now on," orders Cal… "after last night…no chances."

"I'll take the first watch," volunteers Jon.

The men take turns on watch all night, until the sun finally begins to poke its head through the tall trees.

It brings with it a beautiful array of colors.

It's almost midday when the trio reach a point in the road that straightens out and stretches long and narrow as far as the eye can see, through thick woods. Dense, tall trees loom way above, blocking out direct sunlight and casting a dull, hazy gloom amidst the trail. The air is still.

They trot slowly until Jon raises his hand and keeps it there, from the lead spot. They halt.

Jon sees a rider in the distance.

"Jon, fall back," orders Cal.

Jon circles back around William and Norwynn and takes his partner's place as Cal steps around the boy and up to his front side, taking Jon's place.

"I can't make him out," says Cal, as he stops and squints ahead into the distance. His mates follow suit.

A few suspicious moments pass…

"We will ride on," says the leader of the small convoy.

William grabs Rufus from his hat. "You'll go in my pocket for now friend," he says. "Just for now."

They tread slowly until Cal puts up his hand. They stop.

"He's not moved and he's…" Cal squints… "he's pointing his bow n' arrow at us!"

Not Jon or even William reacts. Though they clearly see it too. More tense moments go by.

"You two stay here, I'll go make peace…maybe," he adds. Cal looks to Jon. "If we should come to blows…protect the boy first," he says, before trotting off.

"Needn't worry William, it's likely nothing," suggests Jon.

They watch as Cal gains ground on the offensive man with the bow pointed outward.

They witness him put his hands in the air and say something uninterpretable. Just then an arrow comes out of the forest, high on the left side of the trail and impales Cal through his temple and sticks out the other side. William cries out in blood-curdling terror. Calupa slumps over and slowly slides off the side of his horse. When he hits the ground, the rider in front of him points and shoots his arrow at Jon and William. The arrow whistles between William's head and Jon's shoulder.

Jon yells a battle cry within the frenzy and grabs William firmly by his back and pulls him onto his horse by his tunic. "Go, go, go!" shouts Jon kicking his horse in its ribs. The man ahead on the trail fires one more missing shot Jon's way before charging ahead. A few more arrows rain down from an unseen vantage point among the trees as the riders get closer to each other. They are going as fast as their horses will allow. It seems the would-be assassin is vying to hit Jon and William head on, with his long sword. Jon pulls out his long sword too. At closer observation, it appears the attacker is more beast than man, hulking and distorted. Jon veers to his left and at the last second jousts the rider right through his stomach, losing his sword in the process. The beast falls backward off his horse. Jon gallops fast with William down the trail, passing Cal's lifeless body and his frightened horse. More arrows rain down. They bounce and stick into the path as they make impact. He goes as fast as possible and intends to, for as long as his steed can handle the wear. He does so for a long time. Jon periodically looks back, to make sure they've gotten away clean.

After a good while and covering plenty of ground, Jon gradually slows up his horse, to give him a much-needed break, and not harm his health. They dismount.

"That's it Veerus," whispers Jon as he strokes his horse's forehead. Jon turns to William.

"I'm sorry we had to leave the other horses. It was a snap decision."

William nods slowly. "I'm sorry about Cal," he says in a low voice.

"He was my foreman," Jon forces a smile… "my mentor."

They stand in silence.

"Quite an ambush," says Jon. They wait awhile more, in silence and share some water.

"I can't believe it, that…man, that…monster, that took Cal…"

Jon winces.

"Looked like…a moonraker…I've never seen one, but its appearance…it matches the rumors…the legend…come young one, we must go." They mount Veerus. Jon keeps William in front of him and they continue down the road as it gradually bends northeast bound.

"Like Cal said before, we shall arrive at Selkirk by dusk, maybe earlier, what with our recent sprint. William, I would like to go quicker than that of days past and don't worry the killers are far behind us now."

"Aye," replies William.

The two ride fast the rest of the day, taking short breaks only for their horse to rest and to drink.

Finally, at mid-day the road comes to a fork with two wooden arrows, pointing in opposite directions, barb wired to a post at the fork's center. The arrow on the left reads: 'Magpie', the one on the right: 'Selkirk'.

Jon eases Veerus right without hesitation and rides on.

"Not too much further now!" he shouts. "Right on schedule!" The path gives way to wide-open fields on either side. Jon follows it quickly as it splits the prairie in two and does so for a long time until Selkirk comes into plain view. John slows up to a trot as they approach the town. It is fortified well with tall, thick, stone walls. The community is small. A place with a population of just a few hundred or so. A wide moat encircles the town's exterior walls, and a drawbridge lays open making up the watery gap.

"Let us take a moment to rest before we go inside," says Jon. He halts his horse, just before the bridge.

"It's been quite the venture," says William. "The way you jousted that moonraker…was…remarkable," adds the boy.

"My practice in the academy had proved fruitful, I suppose."

They set in silence a moment at Selkirk's entrance.

"Are you scared to go back…alone?"

"I would be…probably a little," admits Jon. "But I am to meet up with two other double L's, who are here on business of the more boring sort, and we are to pool back together."

"That is good to hear," says William, with deep conviction. The two stare through Selkirk's open entrance way. "Indeed," says Jon, as he remembers his fallen friend.

8.
Powerful Alliances

Jon and William cross the drawbridge. Once inside, two tall young men dressed identically in leather armor stop them. They are Selkirk guards and stand in front of an aged shack with a large, barred window in its front side. The dark haired, dark eyed and rather weathered man steps forward. He has thrown back hair, a thin goatee and several scars on his face.

"Good day visitor. State your business," he orders plainly.

"I am Jon Hensing of Khaprayelle's L. L," "and am here under official decree from Mayor Sullus Rimpod and in direct ordinance with your leaders, Gritt Ramm and Wesley 'Irongrab' Werriam…respectively," says Jon, with a subtle smile.

"I'll see your decree," replies the guard.

Jon digs around his pack and quickly finds a scroll tied with blue ribbon on each end and adorned with a small orange wax seal at its center. He hands it over. The guard opens and reads it in only seconds and hands it back. He then joins his partner.

"Carry on," he says, as he motions them to head on through. Jon kicks up and canters further into Selkirk. William scans the town. It is modest in scale with stout buildings, no more than two stories high. He can see in the distance to the other end of Selkirk with ease. Cobblestone pathways make up the majority of the grounds. There is grey stonework all over and little to no vegetation. *People are present here and there, but the scenes are not nearly as hectic as those of Khaprayelle,* thinks William to himself.

"This is one of the oldest settlements there is, and the town has fought in many a battle. It has a rich history. Selkirks reputation is illustrious, despite its small size. It is Dwarven, though not exclusively," says Jon.

"I have never heard tell of it…but I haven't heard much about any place outside of Khaprayelle or Redrock. Where are we to me Argane?"

"He is to be in a place called the 'Ivory Tankard'. It is a tavern below the inn he has been staying at, called 'The Rambling Rover'. It's up the way a little," adds Jon.

After a few moments, both the inn and the alehouse come into view on their right side. They approach and hitch their horses to a log fence outside the front door. The stone-block building stands alone and is but a large, two-story cube. Its door is made of polished iron and a large tankard with a mammoth is embossed into it.

Clever, William thinks, as he eyes the door.

"Well, all set then?" asks Jon.

"Yes, I am."

The two pass through the heavy metal door to where inside the tavern, it is well lit by mounted torch light beaming from all four walls and flame lamps at every table. The bar is to their left. The keeper is a stout fellow named Sarrus.

He has big facial features, brown eyes, long matted brown hair and a beard that matches in length.

The only other person in the establishment is a tall, thin elderly man. He is seated at a table to Jon and William's far right, in the back corner. He sits rather comfortably and is wearing a red-wine colored hemp long-robe, that shrouds his whole body. The sleeves are wide and hang well below his wrists and to his knees. The bottom of the robe hovers just barely above the floor.

He has on a wide brimmed hat with a long, bent point at the top. From William's point of view, the large hat hides his entire face. Jon and William approach him and upon closer examination the elderly man has long grey hair that pours out from the hat and down the sides of his face and back. They arrive before the table and Jon begins to speak, "I—"

"I'm sorry for the loss," says Argane, as he looks up to Jon revealing a weathered and lined face. He has modest features and light grey eyes. "So Sorry for Cal."

"How did you?"

"He would be here otherwise…would he not?"

"Yes, he…he would be indeed."

"My personal condolences will be sent to Khaprayelle as soon as I can make it so," says Argane, in a very matter of fact way of speaking. Jon doesn't respond but displays a solemn expression.

"And so…" continues Argane, looking at William. "You are the boy, William."

"Yes, sir…uh…mister…I am William of Little Augustine."

Argane smiles warmly. "The tragic occurrence at your home William, was a terrible atrocity and we feel deeply sorry for you…"

William looks down at his toes.

"But you are safe now…and always will be," adds Argane. William looks up. The elder proceeds…

"Your party, Jonathan, awaits a few doors down at 'The Sabretooth'…you have our utmost gratitude," he says with a smile.

"Thank you," replies Jon, with a slight, nervous bow of his head. He looks at William. "Good luck young one."

He then turns to leave the Ivory Tankard. William watches him go.

"Wait!" he calls, before running to him. "Thank you…for everything," says the boy.

He hugs Jon tightly. I shall never forget you…or Cal.

"My pleasure lad…you will do great things with Argane's guidance. Your future shall be bright! And we will meet again further down the road." and with that, Jon exits the tavern. William walks slowly back to Argane's table and climbs onto the chair across from him. Argane smiles again.

"You wish to avenge your family and your people…and you will…we…will." William perks up.

"But the ones who did this are like nothing you've ever seen or known…and right now you are small…you will grow big in size, no doubt but you must be headstrong too, before you can assert yourself. The physical and mental…must go hand in hand."

"There must be people…others too, who can help me…us…and when they hear of this, they'll—"

"William…William…they are all around…but in the end, only you and you alone can make everything right again…but first…come…follow me. Let me introduce you to Windimere."

Argane rises from the table.

"Who is Windimere?" asks William, as he jumps out of his seat, to join his newest mentor.

"Why, he is your new horse," answers Argane. They exit by the bar and circle around the building to the back. There are two horses, each tied to their own hitching post. Argane's is the large white horse, much whiter than any horse the boy has ever seen. Windimere is light brown and much smaller, with black specks on its backside.

"This…is Legacy," says Argane, of his horse.

"He's beautiful," says William.

"And this…is Windimere…he is yours."

"Wow," whispers William. "He's mine!?"

"Indeed, my gift to you, young one."

"But…how?...why?" questions the boy.

"Well, friend…one does not need a reason to give gifts…to do good…does one?"

"I suppose not sir…thank you, Argane. However, I hadn't even thanked you yet for the mare…"

"It's okay William, it will all make sense soon enough."

"I can already tell you are great. I have heard you are called Argane 'the Immortal.'"

The man chuckles from deep within.

"Yes…I too have heard that from time to time."

"Is it true? that you cannot die?"

"Let me help you onto your horse," offers Argane. "We will have plenty opportunities to converse throughout our journey."

"Our journey to where?" asks William, as Argane lifts him to his saddle.

"Well…we'll speak of that too of course. First, let us be on our way." Argane mounts Legacy upon untying both horses.

"I feel bad having been gifted two horses and not being able to give anything back," says the boy.

"It is alright William; things are given not for what they can derive back in return. Come, let us depart. Ride beside me…always, unless I direct you otherwise," advises Argane, as they head out of Selkirk.

"Are you to adopt me?" asks William, looking over to Argane. The old man chuckles again.

"Sort of," he replies. "Everything shall reveal itself in due time young William, I promise," and with that they exit Selkirk and head Northeast.

At first, the road looks much like it did when William first walked it that miserable morning after the fall of Little Augustine, but soon after, its surroundings change from massive encroaching trees and dense bushes to much more wide-open spaces with rolling green hills, sparsely scattered with giant boulders throughout wavy fields.

"You look tired lad," says Argane, as he looks down to the boy as they trot beside each other.

"I…I am," replies William, reluctantly admitting it. "It's been…a strange time for me of late," he adds.

"Let's stop awhile," suggests Argane, "and you can take rest."

They ride well off-road and choose refuge behind an enormous boulder. The trail is about as far away as the eye can see from the giant rock.

Argane dismounts his horse and helps William down from his. He rummages through a saddle bag mumbling to himself until he pulls out a red and beige wool blanket. He turns and hands it to William.

"Sleep," he says… "and fear not, I will be awake and reading."

"Thank you," says William. He takes the blanket and lays it flat, meticulously pulling each corner one by one until it is in a perfect square. The elder observes in delight in the care the boy displays. William lays down and is asleep almost instantly. Argane further searches his bag. He pulls out a small stack of books and sits cross legged reading his literature. He pauses once in a while to stare toward the forest in the distance, taking time to reflect on what was just read and making sure to absorb it deeply. Soon, he sets his books aside, rises and takes a small roll of material from his bag. He sits back down, unravels the soiled cloth and lays it out in front of himself. There are various pointed shards of charcoal side by side atop the cloth. He then takes another book out from inside his robe. It's a book of rough notes and crude sketches. He opens it to reveal a map and begins shading a water fall above 'The Broken Sea.' with a piece of the coal. It is called 'Ilkin Falls' and is among the south-central region of the Regalian province.

A time later, further down the hills, Argane is fascinated to discover a large herd of Tromplers, way down in the distance. They are traveling East in front of the woods. They are countless in number and all heading in the same direction. Together, they exude significant thumping, though their subtle, muffled steps unfold slowly as they go, across the green landscape. He grins as he watches the stone men, they are very tall, lanky and every one of them, similar in stature. They have large blockheads with long arms, torsos and legs. They are put together tightly from head to toe with perfect square and right angles. The Tromplers walk very slowly and heavily. William wakes from the faint rumble. He stays lying on his side and watches a few moments.

"What are they?" he asks softly.

"Tromplers," answers Argane. He chuckles. "I've not seen any in a long time…You'll never meet anyone who could say a cross word about one of those."

"Wow!" exclaims William in astonishment, as he sits up. They watch the tromps gradually disappear into the heavily wooded area before them, taking long, powerful strides.

"Amazing," whispers the boy. They remind him of miniature versions of Orion and Halen, although these appear more Neanderthal than common man. William then thinks of Bix Jingling.

Suddenly, he grabs his front pocket.

"Phew!" he says under his breath, as he feels Rufus' little body there inside, safe and sound.

"Something wrong?" asks Argane.

"No…no…just checking…something."

"Mhmm, what is it?"

"It's uh, my friend…a pet."

"A pet? May I see?"

"Uh okay," says William. He pulls Rufus gently up and out of his shirt pocket…he holds out his fist and slowly opens it, exhibiting his little blue friend. Argane begins to laugh deeply.

"Oh my…I do not believe it!" he exclaims.

Rufus caulks his head.

"Can it be…? Is it you?" asks Argane in a fascinated, low voice. "The mighty…Rufus of Kersius?"

"Mighty!" shouts William, startling both his elder and his companion.

"You…You know this frog?" Argane takes a little time to collect himself.

"Argane, what is going on?" urges William.

"You must let me see him closer." Argane takes Rufus into his hand and looks the tiny frog over.

"Is it you?" he whispers, curling his lip as he examines Rufus. Rufus nods a distinctive 'yes'.

"I knew it." Argane smiles. There is a twinkle in his eye. He pauses to relish the moment.

"A long-time old friend."

"Old friend!" repeats the boy. "Argane sir, I do not understand. What is the history between the two of you? How is it possible?"

Argane sets Rufus down between them on the blanket.

"Let us ride on and I will tell you."

"Ride! No, no, no, I do not abide, I cannot wait to hear this!"

"Please come, ride, when we get back on the road, I will tell you the story."

With Rufus atop Williams hat they mount and ride toward it. The very moment Legacy's first hoof touches the dirt of the path, William blurts out loudly. "Begin!"

Argane chuckles. "As promised," he says. "What, William, do you know of magic?"

"Magic! I do not know really anything!"

"Had your mother or father ever spoken of magic?"

"Well, I've been taught by Lady Reticent in our school that it is legend, and that man has not wielded it for centuries…that it died out with the generations that came before mine. That it is only mythical now and that though natural enchantments can occur amongst the wild…that some beasts can carry natural magic, it is an extinct ideology, an abandoned way of life."

"You have been taught to speak well. That is true," says Argane, "but with me you will come to know magic."

"Sir, along with teaching the children to speak well, Lady Reticent and our parents also taught us that magic is not to be acknowledged and is definitely not a subject to ever be embraced!"

"And just why not?" challenges Argane, as he halts his horse. William stops his too. They look at one another.

"Because any person who indulges in magical practice will be taken away and jailed…or worse! It is the law of the land. Everyone knows that!"

"Mhm," Argane nods. "Yes, and is everyone from Little Augustine? …with all due respect child, have you been anywhere beyond your home, Khaprayelle or Selkirk?"

"Well…no," answers the boy quietly.

"Ah-so, it is possible then that maybe that it is not what everyone knows?"

"Argane sir…is this a trick? I know that it is unacceptable. I have been taught so my whole life."

"This is no trick. You are not in Little Augustine…that was a place sheltered from that of the real world. It was once a safe haven from all that is evil, but not anymore. This land is untamed and though unfortunately and tragically magic is hidden and suppressed in many places, there are people who use it and can use it quite well!"

"If that ever happened, they would be sought out and put to death!" claims William.

"Maybe," replies Argane… "under the wrong circumstances, it is highly likely."

"William, let me show you something."

Argane dismounts Legacy. The elderly man walks ahead of them, to the middle of the stony pathway. He closes his eyes and raises his arms. His hands are clenched. Nearby winds kick up. His fists tremble. Just then sparks begin to bounce and dance from them. They multiply within his palms as he slowly opens his hands. The bright sparks swirl and gather together until two orange fire balls are spinning intensely above each hand. The energy whirs relentlessly. Argane brings his arms straight out in front of him, guiding the two fire balls, merging them together, combining them into one large sphere. With all his might, he suddenly hurls the fireball from his palms as he strides forward. Flames trail behind, as the ball flies quickly into the path a short distance away.

It crashes fiercely to the ground with devastating impact, biting into it easily and causing a large crater to form there in front of them, as embers, gravel and dirt are thrown high up into the air. The embers float up into the space above, as the gravel and dirt fall back down to the ground, all over with a shudder. William is astonished. Argane turns and walks back to Legacy. He mounts up and looks over at William.

"Now," he says, the crater ahead of them still very much ablaze.

"If seeing is believing?" Argane snaps his fingers and the flames on the pathway extinguish instantly.

"Then what say you?"

The boy searches for words but is speechless.

Argane continues.

"In order for you to hear all that I have to tell you, starting with our little friend Rufus, you must open your mind to all the truths that have been kept from you…from a certain perspective, the boy William died too in the Little Augustine massacre and hence forth, the man William shall emerge."

The boy looks up to Argane, finally understanding for certain that this man will never misguide him.

"Aye," he says, with a nod.

They trot around the deep crater. William examines it closely as they pass.

9.
Out from Under the Rock

Further down the road northeast, the travelers tread slowly as the open fields again close-in tight to the trail with tall trees, bushes and foliage of all kinds.

"Once upon a time there was a war," begins Argane…Artillin, of the Glarion province in those days, was the reigning empire through-out all Primera. It prided itself on providing a great quality of life for its citizens and opportunity for all who would travel there and call it their home. High King Estrich ruled the capital city and was a great king and a good man, all the Artillinian inhabitants were. It was boasted as a place of promise and hope. Naturally when there is good there is evil to counter it, and it came in droves. Queen Hilraguard was a tyrant. She ruled the neighboring Zemagogian kingdom on Artillin's western side with an anger unparalleled after King Rystangaard passed and desired for nothing more than to take the Artillinian kingdom, its people and its land, for little more than control and esteem founded on fear. One day after yet another jealous tantrum, she deployed her army of barbarians to attack the sleeping city. It was a blind-sided assault, occurring in the middle of the night and without declaration. The Zemagogs first blow was extremely effective…crippling the Artillian defenders by almost half. King Estrich naturally was shocked and outraged. Zemagog was miles away and though Queen Hilraguard's reign was questionable and erratic, she had never before dared such a campaign. While her hatred for Artillin had been brewing, no one knew it. The king sent word to allying cities in the hopes of acquiring relief from the onslaught. Armies came in the days that followed but it was nearly too late. The Artillian defenders were almost all dead or captured and its common citizens were in turn thrust into the battle. They toiled to hold the city's core. From the Regalia province, Khaprayelle came to their aid, as did Selkirk and others. With the new arrivals, the battle that had been moving so swiftly in Zemagogian favor, had its tide turned and the shift in momentum brought about a deadlock. On borrowed time, King Estrich and his peers quickly surmised a plan to end the onslaught from the inside and ordered for an unknown assassin to execute the evil queen Hilraguard. And so, the highly affiliated league of red assassins from the rogue village of Kersius deployed their very best to enter Zemagog with the intent to penetrate the castle and take the Queens head.

A 'suicide mission' proclaimed the townspeople's whisperers within Artillin. But an assassin was released all the same…a single young fearless expert was to lay his life on the line for King Estrich, his tacticians, the allying forces and the good of all Primerians.

Legend dictates that the young man was close…and the legend is correct. He raced through the shadows to Zemagog, snuck into the castle there and commenced all the way up to the tower to the evil queen's quarters. But quite unfortunately the innocent townspeople whispered too loudly of the so called 'suicide mission'. Others have suggested the inner workings of a spy or traitor, no one is certain of what happened exactly. When the courageous young assassin stormed the Queen, she changed her form, revealing her true identity. The one appearing as Queen Hilraguard was actually her ally and long-time conspirator. The decoy in the trap was Jezella 'the Nefarious.' Jezella was immensely powerful and had the ability to shape shift and she did just that. All the while Hilraguard was safe elsewhere.

"Who was she, this Jezella?" questions William.

"She was a sinister and cunning, young black witch," answers Argane.

"How do you know all of what occurred?"

"Because I was there…I had arrived from Khaprayelle to render aide. The assassin and I were friends and, it was thought that we could be a powerful partnership in such a daring endeavor. I agreed and was happy to oblige. Artillin was in peril, Estrich and I believed that if we could get to the Queen quick and destroy her, that the rest of the Zemagogian cause would crumble…like a snake, William when you take the head, the rest is lost and left to wither and die without vision. When we stormed the top floor of the tower, Jezella caught us off guard and threw everything she had at us. She was more powerful than even I, back then. She held me against a wall with an unexplainable exertion and toyed with the poor young one. He fought well before joining alongside me against the wall."

"You will be insignificant! For all your miserable days! She shrieked to the assassin as we were pinned there. I watched powerlessly as she shouted out her curious spell. I twisted and turned just enough to break free from her invisible grasp. I charged toward her with all my might, and she still launched me across the room, effortlessly with her awesome power. Blinding light swelled from her being as she continued on with her spell. She shouted to the would-be assassin that within his new state, she had made him immortal, but that if living that way should ever become too much that though she took his voice, he was left with the ability to say three words in succession and three words only. If spoken, they would release him from his living torment, and he would explode profoundly upon succumbing to death. After that, Jezella and I fought so epically that the tower's roof was left blown off and jagged. We traded one magical blow after the other. Then, just before I could not take anymore and I was certain my demise was eminent, she fled…I was astonished. I had gotten to her at least enough to send her off. I fought my way out of Zemagog with my friend in hand and we too fled the area. We stayed in the hills that night and the next day, resting from what we had been through. That was a long time ago…centuries in fact…and the cursed assassin…the young man, well…he is there William…atop your hat sits The Mighty Rufus of Kersius."

The boy gasps!

"Once the most prestigious young assassin in all the land!" says Argane.

"I don't believe it!" exclaims William, taking off his hat, to look at Rufus. The tiny blue amphibian seems to smile meekly. "And after the hills?"

"Well…Artillin indeed was sacked and Warthol, its neighbor to the east after that. Some years later, revenge was taken, Zemagog was crushed, and the Queen was killed. It was in that siege where Sonya Sage took one of her most infamous stands."

"Who?"

"Well," says Argane with a chuckle… "Her story will have to wait 'till another day."

"Well, what happened to you two?"

"We stuck together for a time before I brought Rufus to a very good friend's daughter for her birthday. She wanted nothing more than to have a pet.

She was a good little girl…loving…I believe her name was Dora. The daughter of a working man, a Khaprayellan." Williams eyes widen and his jaw drops.

"I don't believe it. Dora," he whispers. "And you can't reverse the spell?"

"These spells are much easier applied, than reversed, I'm afraid. It is a rare specialty that I do not possess…In all my travels, I've not met anyone who does. I wouldn't even know where to begin and believe me William, I have tried. It is black magic, of the strongest sort." William looks at Rufus with sadness.

"What happened to this witch…Jezella?"

"Well…she continued her evil ways and turned out to be more sorceress than witch. She was only seen one more time…at the fall of Zemagog, she escaped unharmed during that battle and though there was always rumors of her sightings and certain interventions, she nor her wickedness was ever actually seen again."

"My," whispers William. "All I have ever known was Little Augustine. The world beyond with all its complexities, it is so far from my comprehension…so far from home."

"My boy, you are the most perceptive, well-spoken child I have ever met. You are wise beyond your years," states Argane. He smiles warmly.

Later, down the road, as they trot side by side the sky between the tree branches above has turned pink, below the clouds.

"How old are you exactly?" asks William, breaking the silence.

"I am nine hundred, sixty-one, I believe…but after all this time I may be wrong by a number or two."

"That is unbelievable! The eldest man I have ever even heard of was said to be four hundred and even that was urban legend!" exclaims William.

Argane laughs.

"My dear, dear boy…You have entered into a quest…and I shall always be with you, revealing the truth of all things."

They carry on in silence a few moments more. William is amazed.

"I have been told that you are immortal… so what then of your alleged immortality" he persists. Argane gives way to a boisterous laugh, prompting him to halt Legacy to an immediate stop on the road. "I am known as Argane the Immortal…though I am not so immortal at all really."

"I do beg pardon?"

"It depends on which corner of the land you travel. My name will differ. Some folks know I am not immortal, and some folks believe otherwise, it is merely that I've been 'round so long, people begin to cultivate assumptions."

"So, you are not then?"

"When I was young, about seventy-five or so, I was very keen on the practices of alchemy. Have you heard of alchemy William?"

"A little," answers the boy.

"Well, I had scoured the masses. I read and spoke on everything to do with its practice. After many years, I created a potion containing such grandeur that upon ingesting it, one would become immortalized, but!" says Argane, raising his index finger, "though it wards against negative health issues and disease rendering me unable to die naturally. It does not mean I cannot die by common incidents or intentions. I assure you I do feel pain and can be killed. Years later, I searched and studied further. I was unsatisfied with my creation, so I set out to find the mythical…the elusive…the fountain of youth…I found it…I waded in it. I drank from it, but as I did, I learned that it too conjures similar results, only the fountain slowed the aging process, almost to a complete halt."

"Amazing! You truly are great! Who would have thought that one could make such potions? or that there is a fountain of youth? and there are degrees of immortality?"

Argane chuckles and kicks up his horse. William follows.

"You are the only person other than my good friend Be'wick and my cousin Luscious who have ever heard how I acquired such privileges. The recipe to my potion is locked away and the map to the fountain is also hidden…locked away and safe in my mind and on a mountain. See young William if ever this was to be well known, the masses would pine for it, kill for it and I would be responsible for disrupting the course of life and death. No man should bear the burden of igniting such change in the very fabrics of time and nature."

"Everyone would love you! And be happy…and you would be rich beyond count!" exclaims the boy.

Argane stops and looks William in the eyes.

"Would they love me? Would they be happy? and William riches have little to do with money."

A moment passes.

"You are knowledgeable," says William. "I thought I knew so much."

"It is okay not to know everything. You are not meant to, no man is, knowledge comes gradually, with experience, as we grow."

"Could we know everything eventually?" asks William.

"If you picture 'knowledge' as a speck of sand, then imagine a thin glass cube…one that you could…hold in two hands filled with sand and that cube surrounded all around and packed by an infinite amount of more sand in every possible direction. My knowledge would be represented by just a few grains of sand within the cube and maybe one more speck outside of it."

"Surely you would know more than that."

"Alright…two specks outside the cube." Argane smiles and then kicks up again.

"Come William, we must make camp. We will eat and take rest for another day."

Darkness sets in fully as they set up their space. Their horses are tied each to their own trees as they drink steadily from a shallow, narrow creek that winds through the ground. William finishes lining the fire pit with large rocks as Argane drops armfuls of dead wood in its center. When it is full enough with branches, Argane sits down cross-legged with the boy doing the same across from him. He stretches out his crooked index finger and points toward the wood pile. A steady flame streams effortlessly from the tip and ignites their fire.

"Wow! That was much easier than rubbing two sticks together. Is fire your specialty?" asks William enthralled by Argane's ability.

"No, there is so much more."

"Like what?"

"There is almost nothing that cannot be cast. Those without the will to create the power would think it is impossible…like…trying to imagine a new color or shade, one that no one has ever seen and seemingly does not exist. It must be willed from within…generated…or it can never be…there in lays the true power…But for tonight, let us simply eat and be merry. There will be time for more serious matters in the morrow and beyond."

Argane the Immortal, though not so immortal takes a burlap sack from beside the fire and doles out some late-night provisions to William and Rufus.

Soon, after eating their snacks in silence, Argane digs through another pack and pulls out an unmarked book. "Would you like one?" he offers.

William nods. "So long as its…alright."

Argane retrieves a book and hands it to him. "Don't worry...while yes, books are banned under the dark reign...you need not fret here."

"Although limited, we had books in Little Augustine, discloses William. 'Creed, Defiance and Atrocity'?" he reads aloud, upon looking at the cover.

"Too advanced?"

"No...I don't think so, maybe...what are you reading?"

"A book of poetry, by a compilation of authors. Would you like to hear from my book instead?"

William nods again.

Argane flips to a spot in the middle of his thick book of poetry. "They are random William, some short, some longer and not dealing in anything particular."

"Aye," says William, as he lays down on his red and beige blanket and gets cozy.

The fire snaps, releasing a few embers up and away.

Argane reads:

"Though I walk through the rain.

I revel not in disdain but in the comfort of knowing

they will remember my name.

Not for my pain, but for the freedom we gained."

Argane flips the pages again.

"Aha, here's one of length, by my most favorite poet. A lovely woman called Angela, whom I had the pleasure of meeting at a summer festival years ago. As I read her work and spoke to her, it became evident that she had such a warm heart...a true rarity for the times. She could see such goodness and beauty within all things. Most of her work is about love, reflection and gratitude. After meeting her that day, I always knew she would gain admiration and fame for her heartfelt poetry. Years later she did and people all over the land loved her and valued her art. Every single poem is from the heart...a truly creative keepsake. I hold some of them dear in my pack, always. She also wrote books for children with colorful illustrations and made paintings of great detail too. A true artist in every sense. This particular poem is a personal favorite of mine. It is called:

The Roads We Choose

The roads we choose throughout our lives.
Are filled with stumbling blocks
We travel on with battered feet.
Despite its jagged rocks
Life is filled with many questions.
We can't understand just why
Life can cause us so much pain.
No matter how hard we try
Change is a blessing in disguise.
It is there, as is the season
For everything within our lives.
Has happened for a reason
Sometimes the road may seem too long.
No matter what we cannot win
But somehow just when the time is right.
A savior is sent in
Though heartache makes us stronger.
We have so much to bear
If we realize we are not alone.
For he is always there
Faith is a smile worn in our hearts.
When things seem too big a task
He gives us the strength to carry on.
All we need to do...is ask."

Argane smiles and looks up from the text to find William fast asleep. He stares at the boy a moment, keeping his smile. He gently closes his book and sets it down beside himself. He notices Rufus is asleep too on top of the hat in his own spot by the fire. Argane looks up to the stars above, inhales deep, closes his eyes and exhales.

10.

Clairvoyance

Dawn breaks, revealing a heavily clouded, grey sky. It brings with it erratic tempered breezes and scarce drops of cool rain. Thunder rolls off in the distance. William wakes to the sound and finds Argane holding a pewter kettle with both hands. Soon, steam rises out from inside. He pours the hot water into a wooden mug, sets down the kettle and stirs the contents of the cup with a small silver spoon. He holds it out for William. The boy rubs his eyes with clenched fists, sits up and puts on his bycocket hat.

"Thank you," he says graciously, as he takes the mug. "What is it?" he asks.

"Pure goodness," answers the elder. "A blend of keyetta, wobble fruit extract and a bit of fairy dust."

"Fairy dust! You don't…but fairies are just lore!"

Argane laughs… "A fine word…LORE! Well then speaking of 'lore', during our travels today you will hear much 'lore'," announces Argane, quoting in the air with his fingers. "Oh, and I assure you, fairies are very real…Ikaties are lore, Carron birds are lore…"

"And you will tell me of all this lore?" asks William.

Argane smiles as he packs up the last bit of his wares. "I most certainly shall."

William, a little confused having been awake only a moment and then being told of the absolute existence of fairies, fairy dust and then furthermore being instructed to drink something he never has before that's been heated up literally by hand, looks up at Rufus who is observing from his preferred vantage point on the boy's hat, then back over to his mentor.

"Argane sir…I have been pondering something the last while…umm…are you, my savior?"

The old man appears to be caught off guard, even more so than even his inquisitive little counterpart had been only a moment ago.

Argane stares off into the distance. "No child…you are mine."

Shortly after, they are steadily heading down the road which opens up again, as they exit yet another forest.

"So where are we going, asks the boy?"

"Ah, I was beginning to wonder if you would ever ask. To answer the proposed 'where' first we must answer the 'why'," returns Argane.

"I do not understand…so…why then, are we going…somewhere?"

"I know that you have been taught to think 'ill' of magic and those who possess it. That it should be suppressed or even worse, a cause for a death warrant, but William…to understand the 'whys' and the 'wheres', you must forget any of what you have been taught. It is only those with power and the courage to use it that can bring this world back to good, avenge the injustices and bring back freedom."

"What does all that have to do with where? …um…why we are going…where we are going?"

Argane stops Legacy and turns to William, looking deep into his eyes. William does the same with Windimere and returns the stare.

"What powers do you possess?" asks the elder.

The boy's eyes widen. "You cannot be serious! I…I have no powers…I have nothing of the sort!"

"William…it's all right. You must share…you must show me!"

"I have nothing to share, nothing of the kind!" shouts the boy. "Are you to be trusted!" urges William.

Clearly frustrated, he kicks up and strides ahead a few steps, as the rain falls harder.

"Or are you of the very ones I have been warned about all my life?"

"William, slow down…you need to hear me. I am not one who will harm you…I will always be for you, not against you," explains Argane. He trots ahead to meet up with William. The boy looks all around, as if scanning for the best route to make his escape.

"Listen to me William…listen and hear me…Centuries ago…this land was a place where magic ran free. There were more people and races that possessed and displayed magic than those of whom did not. There was true peace! And respect among all. It was a place of love, righteousness and good."

The boy calms as the old man speaks.

"Kingdoms, cities, towns and villages had not war or corruption. There was no pillaging and no injustice…not like today. There was not oppression, hate or fear. People lived harmoniously. Until one day there was a man…a man more powerful than anyone and he would become the king of kings. The Highest King. The one to rule them all. He manipulated everything and everyone and used a massive secret army. His evil black army. He crushed all in his path and when he gained supreme rule and reached the precipice of the grandest authority, it wasn't enough. He came down on these lands with such brutal impact that it shook the very foundation that our civilized world was built upon. High King Thayddeus conquered everything with his un-stoppable power. When he and his regimes strangle-hold on Primera was tight enough, they hunted anyone who opposed him and especially anyone possessing magic. It was mass-murder in every sense. He and his army took and killed anyone they found. It was the darkest of dark times. You see William…the reason you have been taught and trained to believe magic is something to be ashamed of and to be hidden, was because your parents and your community, as most others…wanted to preserve themselves and their people from the great atrocity. It is true that magic is nearly extinct and sacred, but it was not always…many had it, embraced it and wielded it. The world teemed with it…it truly was a spectacle to behold. You see, this high king is jealous and greedy and most of all pure, concentrated evil. He thought that through his authority and his might that he could ravage the land and shape it to his own dark desires…he wanted to be the only one with power…with magic. But there is me, lad…and there is you!"

"Surely the animals and beasts too! I have seen them!" cries the boy.

"Because the King's ambitions did not work…not completely…some fled and hid from his wrath…and so, some still remain spread out across the vast lands but not like before. The animals and beasts who carry are naturally gifted, or direct descendants from the previously enchanted…depending on who you talk to, you will hear varying theories. Some animals thrive in magic because they are not a definite target for the high king, though some too say different. These days, there is far more magic among the wild than men."

"And this high king…he is still the one who reigns?" asks the boy.

Argane nods, "Yes, he is called the high king, but he is more imperial emperor than that, the way in which he rules, so singularly."

"Why had no one taken him? ...like Queen Hilraguard?"

"William this is nothing like that...there has never been anyone in existence in all our known history as powerful as he. Not ever! Not even close. Allied armies including every faction had tried and failed. All manner of races have tried, as well...barbarians, warriors...mages, and wizards. Even the enchanted beasts from time to time. It has been hopeless. He has thwarted mass armies by just himself and himself alone! Ultimately, only one of infinite power must oppose him. He is all powerful but once his space and time are compromised, he will be as mortal as any.. It has been said that one shall come with a limitless, invincible power...a man so strong and so pure of heart, that the king will hardly be a match for him at all."

"I still do not understand what this has to do with where we are going," interjects William. He firmly squeezes Windimere's reins.

"Everything," answers Argane. He continues without skipping a beat. "After all the destruction and murder, the...genocide, a committee of mages and wizards, our circle uncovered a chest deep within Mount Brobdingnagian and inside of it, there were a series of encrypted scrolls. It took our master sorcerer ages to interpret them. The scrolls explained that someone within this land would be born of pure magic and that he would become the most powerful being in all the lands. This man would be the one to finally lead the people to victory over the dark reign." Argane pauses and looks to William, he studies the boy's face as he gently locks eyes with the boy.

"William...the man in those scrolls...the one that it tells of...it is you."

"Surely it is not!" snaps William, sharply.

"Yes, yes, young one, it is!"

"Preposterous! How could it be so? Just because it is written? The one who deciphered it is wrong!"

"The scrolls foretold that the boy would be born within an undocumented village, similar to the very hidden borough where Little Augustine was settled...born pure of heart and intelligent beyond his years. He would have a sister and amidst the warm turn of summer in his tenth year, his whole world would be met with great tragedy, and that only he and another of consequence would survive." The boy takes off his hat to see Rufus. "Two? How could it be so?" whispers William, with tears welling up in his eyes. "It sounds too coincidental, too divine…like…like a fable."

"There is no such thing as too coincidental or too divine and to question those things is for the ignorant," Argane continues, "I understand how you feel…I've been around a long time. William, the weight of the world is no heavier, than when it rests upon the shoulders of a man." The boy forces a slight smirk through his frown.

"We had been watching your village and any suitable community for a long time…since the very day, the scrolls were deciphered."

"You could have stopped it!" cries the boy, growing frustrated at the notion.

"And do what exactly?…just take every boy who is ten? hide each one of them, and set up armies in all the villages of Primera? and then what? maintain occupation for the rest of the time until you came into season? we had to be careful, secretive and wait for the attack, it was our best option…we were ready…but…a problem arose."

"How so?" urges William. He is on the edge of his saddle.

"We had contacts embedded all over. We had one there, at Little Augustine, posing as mayor and he was given a spell, one that would allow him to send instant correspondence to a wizard, one of ours….Instead, he escaped far too easily and rather than send word of the assault and flee to Red Rock as planned, so we could intervene upon the onslaught, rescue you and defend your people, he vanished without a trace."

"Mayor Higgins!" exclaims William.

"The grapevine has proven plenty fruitful thus far for this curious case and our party intends to find him and when we do…I'm sure he will have quite a song to sing."

"This is all so much!"

"We are riding to our hideaway…your new dwelling…and my exile as it were. My peers live there."

"And to where is that?"

"Old Crimsinth. Just past Killik, off of Ergo's coast. We have a small beach with a fortified ruin nearby it, with an undersea network of enforced bunkers below. It was Crimsinth's school of magic before it fell into the ocean."

"Who is we exactly?"

"The seven's circle of wizards and our trusted allies. My people...us. You will be safe there and taught well."

Argane kicks up and trots forward. "Come lad...We will speak more as we go."

William does not follow. Argane guides Legacy around to look back at the boy. "What is it young one?"

William brings up his hands, in front of himself and spreads out his fingers, exposing his palms to the sky. Suddenly a bright blue glow gathers above them.

Bits of thick, liquified mass collect and merge into one. The mass grows brighter and deeper blue, until a peculiar wobbly orb is hovering there, above his palms.

William claps his hands, prompting it to disappear. Argane laughs hard in delight at the revelation and in anticipation of things to come. William smiles and even little Rufus of Kersius is left beaming.

"What was that?" urges Argane.

"I...I'm not sure."

"Do you have more?"

"Aye...many."

Argane is elated. "Come William, let us ride."

They continue on and talk about Primera's current state while riding toward Old Crimsinth.

"How did the evil king know to have Little Augustine ransacked or any communities for that matter?" asks William.

"Years ago, when we started monitoring the necessary locations, so too, did Thayddeus' minions. They did it however, without secrecy, often brazenly attacking small unmapped, unmarked villages and towns, killing most everyone while looking for viable children. It is just one more reason that we are in hiding...we know not how Thayddeus seems to know what we were taught by the scrolls."

"That's horrific! That's...it is terrible...just like that! He does that without resistance?"

"We send warning, as best we can to the leaders of the regarding communities and the possibility of impending attacks, that is all we can do. It is their responsibility after that to do what they will or request defense from allied factions, but the rebellion is too few now and not nearly as organized as before. So, it is highly coveted, and every action must be considered deeply before reacting. What makes the tragedy of your home village so curious is that M.L. Higgins was to have plenty of help from Khaprayelle and the double L all prepared with ours and ready to collaborate with Little Augustine, but word was not sent."

"What about your circle? couldn't you have stopped the assault on Little Augustine yourselves anyway?" asks William.

"Seven," replies Argane. "We are only seven…we are very powerful but even if we could go up against thousands of warriors, countless times and then start spreading magic all around, we wouldn't last very long, we would single ourselves out and become direct targets instantly, perhaps for Thayddeus himself and thus, our very presence would've put you in clear and present danger."

"They knew what they were after. I turned ten just the day before they came."

Argane is silent for a moment.

"There is a bit of a silver lining in all of this though William, if you can believe it."

"What could it possibly be?"

"This 'great' king has seemed to have misinterpreted the prophecy in a few ways."

"How so?"

"They've only ever taken…girls," proclaims Argane.

"Girls?"

"There is more."

"Please go on!" urges the boy.

"They take…seven-year-old girls."

"Nya!" shouts William. "We must go! NOW! We MUST!" he begs. Windimere spooks and stirs upon the boy's exuberant reaction.

"William, William! We know what we're doing and that's why we had to let things unfold as they did. We will do everything in our power to rescue her. It was said that two *children* were to survive, and we will be damned if either of you come to harm!"

"Now! Argane, we must go now!" cries out the boy impatiently. He is exasperated.

"If we went now, we would be going in blind, under-manned and surely vanquished! We must maintain patience and strategy. There is an intricate plan in motion. We will get her back to you! You must compose yourself!"

"What do we do Argane? What do we do?" shouts William as his eyes well up.

"Please, I know this is difficult, but we keep on course to Old Crimsinth, then we all band together and when everything is set, we strike! But we must take it one step at a time. You must trust me…William!"

William freezes a moment…nods yes, in compliance and slouches there on his saddle, with tears falling from his cheeks. He looks at his open hands, they are dirty. He feels empty.

"How do you know…the scroll has not been misread by your friends…and that the high king has it figured properly…You said yourself he is most powerful."

"Ironic is it not? There are seven scrolls that were found in the chest, each one as read have one by one accurately and thoroughly been proven true. They have come to pass, each to absolute fruition. Some even before they were discovered. They have become reality without mistake or misinterpretation. History has shown it every time. The seventh scroll your scroll is the last…and if it had been misread…you would not be here now."

11.
Melancholy

The pair are riding significantly faster than usual when they arrive at a fork in the road. The sign on the post pointing northwest reads 'Edinthall' and the other one pointing northeast says, "Melancholy." Argane, without breaking stride leads to their right, steadily galloping the trail northeast.

"Sounds exciting," calls William. Argane smiles.

"The town of Melancholy is a small delightful little place, with good, hard-working folks. There is no corruption or dishonesty. It is one of my very favorite places to visit whenever I am in the territory. It is a single day's ride from here and when we get there, we shall have a great meal, a hot bath and good a rest," calls Argane.

"Wonderful!" shouts William.

Later that day and after gaining good ground, they are riding at a trot.

The young boy again inquires about the almighty scrolls.

"How is it that you knew I would be the one and not others…There must have been others?"

"The scrolls are quite particular William…They explained the general location, the age of the boy was encrypted, and the season was encoded as well. They even stated that he who survived the onslaught would be forced to trek to his neighboring city. We were confident after analyzing the information that that town would be Khaprayelle. To know with absolute certainty, no matter how unfortunate the repercussions were, we had to wait for certain things to happen as they would and wait for you to wander into Khaprayelle. You see, if we had interfered at Little Augustine, then we would have been meddling with fate and could've risked ruining the destiny therein altogether. This has been a long-time coming William…the greater good is at stake…and rest assured, we feel for you and well acknowledge the horrific losses incurred…we all have made significant sacrifices, all have been in pain…and together, we will make it right."

William nods, as he listens attentively.

"It seems you are starting to believe?" suggests Argane.

"So, it seems," answers the boy. "And what about now? What does it say about the times after our union?"

"It is unclear…the seventh scroll trails off and goes blank after our having met and the period in which we orchestrate our uprising…has yet to be written, beyond inferences."

"Blank," whispers William, "will I be able to see them? The scrolls…when we get to Old Crimsinth?"

"Positively," affirms Argane.

Some time later, the travelers are stopped for a break and provisions.

"It has happened so many times before…it has been such a long time," says the elder, in regard to the carnage of Little Augustine.

"Like the occurrence at Ilken Falls and Regwin or Wisser's Pass and then the incident in Marevale. The king has been relentless in his search…and we were there, amidst the shadows, every step."

The boy stares at his bread after taking a bite. He thinks again of Nya and his mother and father.

"Did you have a wife?" he asks.

"Eh? a wife?" repeats the old wizard. "I did, in fact," he answers. Argane looks off into the distance and beyond…he smiles. "Those were the best one hundred forty-two years of my life," he adds.

"And then…one day, I woke up and it was over, she had left me and was gone…but I still speak to her now and again."

"I see," says William.

"What do you see?" quizzes Argane.

"I…I understand," answers the child and he tries to elaborate. "I just…I see."

Argane's eyes return to focus as if returning from a faraway place.

"I know you do," he says, smiling at his little friend. Upon finishing up eating and watering their horses, the pair pack up and continue riding. The trail soon gives way to open fields. Shortly after, it leads straight through a massive rock formation, made up of grey and red quartz.

"Amazing!" says the boy. The threshold towers above as they approach.

"Wait!" orders Argane from behind William. They halt. The old wizard looks all around and scans the area above. Some rubble falls down onto the road, then some more. Two rather ghastly creatures reveal themselves.

"Blyssers," says Argane, under his breath. They crawl down from the top of the passageway.

One crawls meticulously on all fours down the left side. The other hangs and drops the long way down, directly onto the trail. The blyssers appear fundamentally human, though they are not. They are distorted in comparison and stride predominantly on both hands and feet simultaneously. They have yellowed, slimy skin, large, sharp facial features and long, pointed ears. The blyssers are bald with but a few scraggly strands of hair atop their heads. They are frail and wear nothing but heavily soiled loin cloths and ragged goat leather vests. The blysser to Argane and Williams left, stays perched on the rock a few feet from ground level as the bolder and more daring one crawls closer to them.

"To pay a tax," hisses the blysser, now standing on two large feet alone and hunched over with his equally sizeable hands down along his sides.

"I highly doubt it. In fact, I am sure we will not," replies Argane.

"To payyy a taxxx…if pass you are to," snaps the blysser aggressively.

"We shall go around," returns the elder, nodding to the right.

"A tax is too for over there!" quips the creature.

"If we are to consider your fee…first I must tell you something," says Argane, motioning with his index finger, signaling the blysser to come to him. The blysser is hesitant at first but waddles over none the less, dragging his knuckles as he does. The elder man leans in close to the creature and whispers in his long, pointed, greasy ear. William leans over and looks Windimere in the eye as if just maybe his steed may enlighten him as to what he is witnessing. Rufus is fixated on the scene, from atop his hat.

The blysser pulls away quickly. "To pass! To pass!" he says in a raspy, loud voice. He motions forward assertively.

Argane kicks up his horse and William follows.

"Thank you, thank you," whispers the blysser, bowing his head as William passes. They trot through the underpass and when they are clear of it, William looks back to see the two creatures standing together on the trail beneath the pass waving them off with outstretched, bony arms.

"What did you say to it?" he asks.

"I told him that you and I are vampires and that our favorite delicacy is the thin blue blood of a blysser and that we are very thirsty…" Argane chuckles, "and with a snap of my fingers you would surely penetrate their scrawny necks your razor-sharp fangs and not leave a single drop left in their pathetic corpses."

William looking stunned, takes off his hat and looks at Rufus. Rufus nods yes and gives a thumbs up.

"Blyssers are a proud goblin race…but not too bright," adds Argane.

Later, down the soggy trail and with light rain dissipating, rays of sunlight shoot out from behind a large cloud causing everything before the travelers to glisten.

"Such wonder," says the elder, peering abroad. "I've been around for centuries and never grow tired of just how much beauty there is to behold in this world." William too takes in the sights of the landscape before them.

"It truly is something," he agrees. Even little Rufus of Kersius is in awe, from atop the boy's hat.

Dusk sets in with orange and pink smearing the skyline on the distant horizon, above the vast green plains.

"We shall arrive at Melancholy just before the days eve," announces Argane. They spend the next while of their trek riding slow and taking in the scenery as night falls. The ever-changing colors give way to deeper shaded skies of magenta and mauve. Soon, a soft breeze brings with it a deep violet that pulls the moon up among the clouds. The open fields again close-in to lush forestry and the trail narrows considerably as it is swallowed up inside.

"Just on the other side of the woods," affirms Argane. "Then we'll be there."

They travel the forest with ease only stopping briefly to water their horses. Once out of the woods, the trail leads them immediately to Melancholy's open front entrance. *As like Little Augustine, the forest seems to end near where the open threshold of the town's main passageway begins,* thinks William to himself as they pass through it.

Melancholy is a small village however, even smaller than Little Augustine. It has a single dirt road running straight through it. There are about thirty small wooden shacks on either side. They walk slowly through the shanty town. On the small porch of the first place to William's right is an elderly, heavy set woman, fast asleep in her rocking chair.

"We will take refuge at 'The Sleeping Sky Inn' toward the end of the village," says Argane, quietly.

A few doors down William notices another resident asleep on their porch, followed by another and then another. He observes the other side of the road to find the same. The residents seem to be sleeping every time he spots one…even their pets are asleep. The boy giggles… "Such a lazy place," he whispers to himself. He yawns big and wide. They soon arrive at 'The Sleeping Sky', They dismount and hitch their horses around the side.

William checks on Rufus to find, he too has fallen to slumber.

At the front of the building, a short log protrudes from the main doors frame above the top right side and a round sign dangles there from two rusty chains. It is branded with a yellow crescent moon, wearing a pale blue striped night cap, complete with a pom-pom on its tip.

Inside, the lobby has a bar to its left side and tables strewn about the room, filling the rest of the space. There are no windows, so the area is dimly lit by candlelight. The center of every table has one, each with a long blue flame, and there are also several candles spread out along the bar counter in a line.

"Curious," says William. Argane grunts and turns to him.

"The man at the bar, he is asleep."

"Aye?" inquires Argane.

"And there!" says William, pointing at a rather young man who is slouched over and sleeping at a table with his head buried in his arms.

"Everyone is sleeping," says William, in fascination.

"Yes…Yes, a very relaxing place this is…it is renowned for its tranquility." The elder motions the boy toward a nearby table and approaches the Bar. William seats himself with yet another yawn.

Argane sits down on a barstool opposite the keeper.

"Ahem," The wizard clears his throat to no avail. "AHEM!" and once again, but much louder.

"Oh yes kinsmen!" says the man as he snaps awake. "Aye m-my lord…back so soon? a pleasure," he adds.

"The pleasure is all mine Tristen…now for the boy and I," he says nodding over to William, who is now falling into a sleep of his own.

"Meat-rare, potatoes and cold-cream cake, with one keyetta tea and one-berry nectar."

"Certainly, my lord!"

"Argane, will be fine."

The young man then grabs two plates from behind the bar.

"There you are m'lord! Uh…Argane, sir."

"Thank you kindly," says the old wizard, as he looks at the two meals. The meat and potatoes are steaming, the side of cream cake is fresh and chilled as can be and even the tea is piping hot, while the nectar appears perfectly frosty. Argane reaches to take a platter in each hand.

"Allow me, sir!" says Tristen. They arrive at the table. As the nervous server sets down their plates, Argane shakes the table to wake William.

There is a large puddle of wax surrounding the candle between them. The long thin flame flickers as William comes to and examines the food before him. He is visibly groggy.

"My…how long was I asleep?" asks the boy before digging into his food. They proceed to eat in silence. Tristen takes his place, back behind the bar and resumes his position slouched on the counter. William finishes up after a short time and slides his plate forward.

"This place sure is cozy," he says while putting his arms on the table and burying his head into them, he falls immediately back to sleep. Argane clears the table and brings back the plates to where Tristan too has fallen back to sleep. He carefully carries William and Rufus to an empty room on the third floor.

After tucking the boy in, he carefully sets his hat with the equally asleep Rufus beside him on the mattress.

Argane then stands over the bed. He outstretches his arm and opens his hand pointing his palm down toward it. A pale green light begins to expel and shimmer just under his palm, the light source morphs into a small sphere and with a slight muffling sound, Argane releases it, and it instantaneously forms a large hollow hemisphere around the entire bed. The green energy is translucent and hums ever so slightly.

Argane taps it with his crooked index finger, producing a faint hollow sound.

"That ought to do it," he says before quietly exiting the room. Argane 'the immortal' makes his way downstairs and outside, to the front of the Inn. He sits on the floor of the porch cross legged, takes a small book from an inside pocket within his robes and begins to read.

Before long, he closes his book and his eyes, for he too is in need of rest.

The next morning William wakes underneath the forcefield and as the boy's eyes open, so do Argane's at the exact same time. With a rather perplexed expression, the boy sits up within the subtle green glow.

He looks at Rufus atop his hat. The frog is still asleep, so he proceeds to put the hat on carefully. He steps off of the bed and out of the bubble with ease. William feels incredible. Argane meets him at the doorway.

"Was that some sort of restoration or defense power?" asks the boy.

"The shield provides both, most definitely both," answers the wizard.

"Amazing," says the boy, turning back to take another look. "How do you?"—

Argane snaps and the green oval surrounding the bed disappears.

"You snap your fingers to dispel it, that's so great!"

"No…that was for effect…I usually simply will it away."

"Amazing," repeats William.

"Come, before we head on, I need to meet with my old friend, Wiley Bloodborn."

Back down at the empty bar Argane digs through his robes for a pouch. He sets a single, tiny, flawless white diamond down on a coaster where their plates were set the night before. They head outside, William makes a point of scanning all around to find out whether everyone he saw yesterday is still asleep or not. Most are. "Remarkable," he whispers, to himself.

"We will come back for the horses. Wiley is just across the road," says Argane.

They enter Wiley Bloodborn's cluttered shack, he wakes as they do.

Wiley is many centuries old with long white hair, sharp features and a steady subtle cough. He is wearing a long, flowing purple cloak with the hood up. The man rises from his chair, placed before a large, locked chest and facing his front door.

"You are back sooner than I had anticipated," he says.

"And so I am," agrees Argane.

"And you are William?" asks Wiley.

"I am," returns the boy.

"But of course you are! Well…right to it then." The host turns to a table behind him and picks something up from beside it. He hands it to Argane.

"Thank you, old friend," he says as he reaches for the invisible object. Before William can ask, a tall, thin staff appears in Argane's hand, upon him grasping it in his fist. "You encountered no issues to speak of then?"

"Not to speak of."

"You always provide such great interference…thank you, friend."

"Anytime, now not another moment! 'Til next time," says Wiley and with that, Argane and William leave the shack. They cross the road and mount their horses.

"Come William, we must pick up the pace now that we are well rested and this has returned to me," says Argane, as he straps his staff diagonally across his back.

"What is it exactly?" asks the boy of the staff.

"It is an ancient Narwhal tooth…it is my treasure, my comfort, my weapon…Many of my powers, spells and enchantments are locked within this staff…It is an extension of me…pure concentrated, complex power…but as fantastic as it is, there's always a chance it can be felt and sought after by the wrong people. Which is why we must ride quicker now and why I couldn't risk bringing it anywhere near Little Augustine, Khaprayelle or Selkirk."

"Amazing!" says the boy. "It looks quite harmless," he adds.

Argane smiles. "Let us hope it remains in that state for the rest of our venture."

12.
The Witch's Jar

As the rejuvenated travelers exit the sleepy forest village, the road soon winds toward yet another thick wooded area ahead.

"When we arrive at Old Crimsinth William, you will learn how to harness and apply your inner strength and power. You will meet the people of our circle, Be'wick of Senadell is our founder and the circle's headmaster. You will always have guidance from me but, Be'wick is steeped in the art of instruction and direction. There you will learn and absorb all we know about the magical arts as well as physical crafts also. You will further grow your heart, mind, body, and soul. We will divulge unto you all we can…and you will come to know all of it, through and through. Unlimited potential is within you, and you will be an apt pupil…rest assured, you were born with the gift."

"It seems like a lot will be expected of me, says the boy."

"Simply put, it is the way of life for us there…you'll see. No one is pressured to partake in anything they don't want. All of us there share a common cause and are working together to achieve it." A moment passes.

"That blade William, on your ankle? Have you ever wielded it?"

"My often blade? no, I have not."

"Could you…confidently use it if provoked?"

"Umm…Confidently? No…but, if need be, I sure would wield it," replies William.

"And what of your magic? can you use it precisely? in defense? or even in offense, if need be?"

"I am not certain," answers the boy, remembering the mysterious old woman from the roadside shack and the events that transpired there. He contemplates what he could have done differently.

They tread through the forest. It gradually gets dense and gloomy, as the sunshine above falls under cover. The trail narrows and turns to mud. Argane takes the lead and uses his staff for light. There is an oval shaped, polished stone embedded into the top. It begins to glow a brilliant, bright white and illuminates everything in their vicinity, encapsulating them within a large sphere. They trudge through the sticky terrain. William examines an interesting rock formation between some tree trunks on the right side of the path, as he gets closer to it.

"Oh my, it's a tombstone!" says William. "Oh no! They're all over!" he exclaims, as they appear, one after another.

"It is all right, William, the threat here is a minor one," claims Argane. The old wizard stops and so does William. An odd grinding sound begins to accrue from up ahead. The noise amplifies, then changes to a curious clacking sound.

"The un-dead?" whispers Argane to himself. Then he spots them.

"No," he says answering his own question. "Hmmm, well…not really," he adds.

"What is it? …what is it!" urges William in a panic.

"Calm down child, we are not in danger…they are only skulkers."

"Skulkers!" exclaims William.

Just then, a slow walking skeleton comes into plain view under the light. "Hold this," says Argane, turning back and extending the staff for William to take. He does so quickly. The wizard dismounts his horse and raises his left hand, grabbing the skeleton with a semi-transparent purple energy field, he then suspends it in the air above. With his right hand, he shoots a large, bright red blast from his palm underneath and past the skulker. It sends a second encroaching skeleton back with a jolt and into pieces. He then whips his left arm to the side, smashing the first skulker hard into a nearby tree trunk, smashing it apart and sending bones flying all over.

Argane stays still and silent, listening for any more skulkers that may be lurking or that may have been alerted…all is quiet, so he turns and mounts up onto Legacy. He prompts William to hand him back his staff. He does.

"You made short work of those skulkers," says the boy, in fascination.

"Yes, well…they are a brittle sort." They carry on.

"Wow," says William, as he and Windimere step over the separated bones of the second skulker. Argane leads with his light shimmering on high. William follows close by with his reins in his left hand and his often blade in his right. He scans his surroundings carefully. Soon after, they walk by the last tombstone. A few uneventful moments pass…so he tucks away his dagger.

The path begins to widen as the foliage thins out and they reach the forest's perimeter. Argane's staff light fades when daylight pushes back through the sparse trees. Soon the woods are behind them completely.

"What was that place?" asks William.

"It is a small forest called, 'The Dead Walk Woods.'"

"What!?…you could have warned me!" cries the boy.

"I could have…but then I might have risked putting fear into your mind…I thought if confronted, the occurrence would speak for itself, not so bad, eh?" asks Argane rhetorically, looking to the child, with a playful grin.

"But then how will I be able to trust you next time when there is danger afoot?"

"By then, how will you be certain whether I knew at all?" William appears unimpressed. "Oh, William rest assured, if there is any real danger you will know well in advance…so long as I do," adds Argane.

A time later, the riders are packing up from another roadside lunch.

"Soon, we must deviate from the beaten path to reach our destination," announces Argane, as they mount their steeds. "The road will take us to a fork, where there is a grand statue of Sonya Sage, where the fork breaks, we shall go due north, straight through."

Time passes as they steadily carry on. They ride all day and before long, dusk settles into the horizon once again. The moon is present, large, bright and full in all its glory.

"Let's make camp and fire off the trail in the clearing, back amongst the boulders," says Argane, pointing with his staff. William looks to see a cluster of giant quartz rocks strewn all over in a dark valley within the rolling landscape. "We should see danger coming from a distance, should it decide to come about," adds the wizard.

They set up their area at the center of three towering boulders as specified, so they are well hidden.

"We are amidst a trifecta William," says Argane, as he lights a small fire. "It gives us perfect defensive cover and a major vantage point if any are to intrude."

"Are we being hunted or some such thing?" asks William.

"I do not know if we are at the moment, but we must take extra care, if we are to anticipate the possibility."

William gazes into the flames as Argane sits down across from him. "What are you thinking about young one?"

"Nya," says William reluctantly. "The longer we wait, she could be killed! couldn't she?"

"Thayddeus, and his underlings keep the children they abduct for a while and when they prove not the ones they seek, they cast them out. We will get to her…in due time…and you two will be reunited."

"How do you know? How can I be sure?" urges William.

"The scroll speaks of your sister…years from now."

"Why didn't you tell me!" exclaims William.

"Some things must unfold on their own. You may not understand that now."

"I do not understand!" cries the boy.

"You will William, soon…you will."

"Who are they?" The ones that took her? the ones that killed my people? …Who are the high king's pawns!

"William…" Argane sits up closer to the fire. "They are more of a what to be precise…they are Moonrakers…half man, half demon…and they have the strength of ten men by night. In fact, it is the moonlight that gives them their strength. It acutely charges them."

William looks up to the pale blue moon, hanging over them.

"They are relentless and ruthless and only in their own demise do they rest. They are the epitome of merciless, unrelenting evil. The perfect senseless henchmen to carry out the evil ones twisted biddings."

"This is not the best bedtime story," says William, staring at the moon.

"Lad, you will take your just vengeance and through your revenge you will discover that you fight not only to avenge your family and your people but for the freedom of all the good and innocent beings of this land."

"There is much counting on my will," says the child.

"Aye, now how is that for a bedtime story?" asks Argane, rhetorically. William answers anyway.

"It is still scary…just in a different way," he replies.

"Tonight, could I sleep under your shields?"

Argane chuckles. "It is called 'The Green Squall', it is one of the only spells that the caster cannot use for themselves. I will teach it to you one day…when you are more accomplished, and you too can then lend it to others."

"I shall look forward to that," replies the boy.

"Lay back William," says the wizard as he rises to his feet.

William does and his elder casts the green squall.

"With this spell on-going, it takes plenty of concentration. I will meditate a while as to freeze it in time, then I shall sleep, and you will remain safe within it."

"Oh, Argane sir! I do not want to take away from your sleeping!"

"It is alright." He sits and takes out his little book of poetry.

"I would prefer that you feel safe…and if a centuries old mage cannot harness some magic for a night, then what good is he?"

William smiles, "Goodnight."

"Goodnight…and sweet dreams my young friend," says Argane.

Later, little William is sound asleep under the squall, as his keeper steadily works on sketching his map. He does so with a particular emphasis on Ergo's coastline.

The middle of the night comes with a breeze that seems to wipe clean the large, full moon, changing it from pale blue to bright white. The landscape before them, sounds of distant crickets and shimmers with the sporadic sparkle of scattered fireflies.

In the early morning, Argane is in a slight state of both meditation and sleep when the sun begins to show from behind the far away hills. Shadows stretch long and dark across the green fields by the large quartz boulders. The bright orange sun ascends and turns yellow, the shadows shorten and widen as they rotate gradually around the giant rocks.

The old wizard awakens first allowing the squall to fade as he marvels at the new day before him. He gazes ahead as if seeing the sunrise for the first time. He imagines countless other beautiful sunrises he has been witness to. The wonder never ceases to amaze him. The boy wakes shortly after.

"Good morning," says William as he sits up and rubs his eyes. Argane does not greet the boy.

He is consumed in the 'awe' of the sunrise.

"Good morning!" repeats the boy, this time the elder reacts, snapping out of his trance with a series of blinks.

"Good morning to you dear boy," he says in acknowledgement.

"Beautiful!" observes William of the sunrise, rubbing his eyes once more. The duo spend some more time admiring the particularly wondrous morning in silence, before gathering their things and heading through the fields of green and back to the trail.

"We shall arrive at Sonya's Fork before long William."

They cantor steadily and continue awhile before Argane halts due to a disturbance on the road ahead.

"It looks like a wagon has been plundered," suggests Argane as he squints his eyes.

In the distance is a horse drawn, wooden carriage. It is toppled over on its side. In front of it lay two dead or heavily wounded horses, also on their side. The animals do not move.

"There is no trace of the drivers," says the wizard.

"Should we go 'round?" asks the boy.

"I think not," replies his keeper. Upon closer watch, an old woman appears from behind the toppled vehicle. She is rummaging through the flipped wagon quite hastily.

"Let us proceed." Argane then kicks up his horse and William hesitantly follows.

They arrive before the wagon to find what appears to be three orange and smoldering piles of ash, just ahead of the carriage. There is one smaller pile, while the two ahead of it are significantly larger.

"They are dead…poor fellows," says Argane, of what can only have been a driver and two horses. At the wagon, the petite old woman is cursing in a foreign tongue.

"She is a maniacal hag," whispers Argane. The woman shrieks at the sight of the two travelers.

"Your fault!" she shouts.

The wizard laughs. "William, take a place beside the path…and stay low," he says, keeping his eyes on the woman. William leads Windimere carefully off the stony trail and down into the ditch. He trots away until he is underneath a nearby weeping willow.

"Your fault! Your aura…your…white energy has dissipated the riches within the vessel!" screams the woman from inside the hood of her black cloak. She finishes wagging her judgmental finger at Argane and climbs onto the carriage, on all fours. She takes her hood down, revealing long, scraggly, grey and white hair. Her face is heavily weathered, and she has a long, bent nose and horribly crooked, gapped teeth.

"Murderous witch!" yells Argane with deep and genuine anger. "Vulture!" he adds, as he pulls up his sleeves. The witch immediately jumps off the toppled wagon and snatches her broom from beside a black burlap sack.

Argane dismounts Legacy and points toward the willow tree. His horse then steadily canters to join William and Windimere. The witch begins shouting words that the boy has never heard. The corn brush end of her broom begins to emit blue sparks that sizzle and crack as she slowly turns it upside down and points it toward Argane. The wizard is not intimidated. She shoots a fantastic array of blue and white lightning at him. He lowers his head, showing only his hat and quickly raises his staff, deflecting the lightning off an invisible shield. It is somewhat revealed as it shimmers all around him upon impact. His defense sends fragments of electricity all over and outward.

"Blast!" screams the witch, who then quickly sends more of her lightening toward him.

This time, Argane crouches and positions himself just so. Some of the strands of electric current bounce back. They miss the sinister witch but only barely. Argane then drops to one knee, he briefly charges his hands and the staff before expelling a heavily pressurized shot of water at his adversary, at the same time the witch unloads her third offensive bolt of electricity. The water gushes forward, knocking the witch down and carrying her several yards. She shrieks and cries, while electricity envelopes her and courses through her body. Argane walks over as the electricity gradually dissipates, leaving the witch fried, twitching and exhausted.

"If you try another tactic, anything at all…you too shall be ash," proclaims Argane.

"So be it," gurgles the witch as water comes out of her mouth. She lays on her back trying to catch her breath. She fishes within the puddle, below her steaming cloak with her hands. Argane raises his staff. The end begins to glow bright orange.

"Okay, okay, I yield!" shrieks the witch. "I do not wish for this fate! I beg you!" she cries as she shows her hands and turns up her soiled palms.

"Wise," says Argane. "Go back to wherever it is you came," he adds.

The witch clambers to her feet. She takes two steps toward her black bag.

"I don't think so!" says Argane. She stops and looks at him sharply. She turns to pick up her broom.

"Not that either," he snaps.

"You can't mean to keep it!" she shouts. Argane bends down to retrieve the broom.

The witch quickly takes a crooked dagger from inside her cloak, she runs and swipes down hard at Argane. Just before the blade can plunge into him, an orange blast of energy shoots from his staff, hits the witch directly in her stomach and immediately sends a large mass of orange and grey bits into the air. They fall to the ground collecting into a scattered pile of orange ash. Argane grabs the broom and stands up. William comes running to the wagon from the willow tree.

"Indeed, the punishment should fit the crime," he says.

"I've never seen a witch before!" calls the boy.

"Not that you know of," suggests the wizard.

Argane breaks the broom in two and tucks the pieces into his belt.

"Check her bag, William. Witches are deeply steeped in black magic and the most sacred of arts. There may be something we can learn from, or at least properly discard of." The child picks up the bag and proceeds to look through it.

"Hmm…nothing much…some vegetables, fruit, silver pieces and just this…empty jar," he says.

He squats down and dumps the bag, sending the fruit rolling. The silver and vegetables collect in a small pile and the glass jar lands on top with a clank. It is a simple glass jar, bound with thin, black, wrought iron bars and a slanted cork. "Wait, there is a…bug or…something inside," he adds.

"Careful," says Argane.

He takes hold of the jar, raises it above his head and examines its tiny contents.

"It's…it is a girl! Uh, a woman, a blue haired woman with wings! I don't believe it!" exclaims the boy. "A tiny woman with wings! I think she is trying to speak…though I cannot hear her!" William is captivated. Argane approaches.

"Your first encounter with a fairy," he says.

"Indeed!" answers the boy excitedly.

"Poor thing, she was the ghastly witch's prisoner, no doubt…an ingredient, most likely."

"She is naked," observes William.

"Give her here, I will fashion the poor dear some clothing." Argane takes the jar and taps it on a rock.

It breaks into three pieces. He carefully puts the trembling fairy into his hand and walks to Legacy, he then sits the fairy on his saddle.

"You are safe now," he whispers. He puts the broken witch's broom into his saddlebag and takes out a small spool of thread and a needle. He searches a little more and finds a cloth rag. He tears a piece from it and proceeds to methodically stitch a perfect, tiny dress.

"Did you know that fairies were real?" asks William of Rufus, holding him in his hand.

Rufus nods yes.

"Ah, presentable now," announces Argane, showing off his handy work, as he holds out his hand with the freshly dressed fairy in his palm.

"Remarkable!" says William, astounded by what he sees.

"Do not be coy," says the wizard to the tiny woman.

"I am Argane, this is the boy William, and his little companion is the mighty Rufus of Kersius."

"Um, thank you…I am Appalonia," replies the fairy, in a soft, meek voice.

"That…that witch snuck up on me," she says, turning to Argane.

"And…and she swiped me up from inside a tree hollow, where I was simply minding my own business, picking lillaputions…I was minding my own business a bit too attentively I'm afraid and now I have no idea where I am…It feels like moons ago," she adds. "I must get back to my colony!"

"Where could your home possibly be?" asks Argane.

"Within a forest. I…I do not know where! It could be anywhere, I suppose. I have been in the dark for so long!" Appalonia buries her face in her hands.

"You should come with us. I know it must be extremely difficult…but I also know of some great fairian pockets where I am from. I will keep you safe until then and surely, they will take you in as their own and perhaps even help you locate your home."

"I miss my people dearly." The fairy wipes her tears. "But what other choice do I have…I am lucky to be alive. We know what evil witches do with our kind. I would have surely met my end…Thank you kindly."

"You are welcome, and fear not, no harm shall come to you now," assures Argane.

The adventurers get set and carry on around the plundered wagon and down the trail. Their newest companion flies just above William's left shoulder. She is across from Rufus who is at his favorite spot, front and center on the pointed brim of the boy's hat. Despite her sense of loss and, with her new-found freedom, Appalonia is radiant and aglow.

13.
Sonya Sage's Fork

Massive white clouds are suspended all over in bunches within the blue sky.

"All this traveling and you have not said a word, Rufus!" says the tiny fairy to the even tinier frog.

"Get used to it, little lady! Well, that is hardly pleasant," she replies.

Rufus squints his eyes and turns to her. She moves and flutters right in front of him.

"It is impossible for me to have heard you! Pish posh! Not impossible…though your mouth does not move. It is indeed a curious feat!" exclaims the fairy. William halts Windimere in his tracks.

"Argane!" he calls. The wizard stops his horse too.

"I am hearing your thoughts," says Appalonia. "I…I suppose I am! Unless you are using some sort of foolish trickery?" she inquires.

The pair observe Rufus and Appalonia, both are dumbfounded.

"It is no trick," affirms the frog. The fairy listens a few moments.

"You are an old fellow then and with such a sad story…That awful sorceress! My condolences for your hardships. They cannot hear you? He wants me to tell you both something," she says, looking to her much larger companions. "He says not to pity him, for he has been an amphibian for much longer than he was ever a man, and he is quite used to his form."

"Incomprehensible!" says Argane. "This is truly something!"

"It is wonderful!" shouts William, with glee. "You must stay with us for always," he adds.

Appalonia giggles playfully.

"What dear little friends I have made since Selkirk," says the wizard.

The group carries on toward Killik. They pass much of the time conversing with one another. Rufus speaks through his translator, telling stories to William and reminiscing with Argane.

They round a bend in the road and William is alarmed when the trails right hand side opens up to a gigantic, flat and wide-open space. It is not the way it opens or that it is so flat but the heavy swirling steam that snatches the boy's attention.

"What is up there, in the distance? It is like nothing I have ever seen!" he exclaims. The riders approach.

"This is the unending lake of black fog," says Argane.

They stop alongside it. It is easy to observe that the space within the valley is just that, a thick black fog that ripples as it agitates all along its surface. It excretes a faint, consistent vapor.

"What is down there?" inquires William, walking Windimere as close as he can get to the edge of the lake.

"It is a mystery what lies beneath," answers the wizard. "I have heard tell of people brave enough to descend below, but as the legend goes; no one has ever returned to speak about it. Whatever is down there is meant to be and that is a venture for another time."

"You are curious too," asks the child.

"It is our nature…there could be countless caches of useful or even vital components within this vast wonder. I've not seen anything like it either…not in all my travels or adventures," says the old wizard, "or…it could be desolate and empty, or worse still…a fatal endeavor for no such positive cause at all," he adds. William looks out at the entire lake of black, as it wavers lazily.

"It seems alive," he says, as he examines it. Soon they turn and trot back to the trail and head onward.

The group travels until dusk before Argane picks an area off-road and underneath a cluster of tall trees to make camp. He tells them to act natural as two men kicking up dust pass by in a horse and wagon. They nod and Argane nods back.

Later, they are set satisfied around the fire after eating a hearty meal.

"I know a great woman," says Argane to Appalonia. "When we get to Sonya's Fork," he says…as he turns to William, "we will journey north," the wizard then looks back at Appalonia, "through the woods to Ergo's Coast, at the Sea of Gods. Just before the forest gives way to the snowy shoreline, lives

Marple Weary. She is a lovely old friend of mine, and I am sure she can get you outfitted into something more…you."

"That sounds great…thank you," replies the fairy. "I shall look forward to that!" Appalonia is content above William's shoulder.

"There is no reason to keep you in such rags," says Argane with a wink.

Appalonia giggles and swipes her shiny, feathered, bright blue hair from her rose-colored eyes. Her lips taper to a smile and her perfectly fair skin begins to glow as her translucent, intricately patterned purple and green wings flutter just a little. She looks up to Rufus, who is peering down from William's hat brim.

"Rufus says, he would much appreciate some clothing of his own when we get to where we are going." She blushes. "A pair of short pants would be just splendid," adds Appalonia, repeating Rufus' request aloud.

"But of course, old friend," says Argane, smiling at him. "My apologies, it hadn't crossed my mind," he adds with a chuckle.

The group spends the evening talking and laughing. Appalonia is the first to fall asleep.

She is laying on William's hat near Rufus, who is almost asleep too. It is set beside the boy, near the fire-pit. The flames cast a subtle orange, flickering glimmer upon them.

"We shall come to Sonya's fork in the morrow, 'round midday, so long as there are not too many distractions. Get your rest child," says Argane.

"Aye, goodnight," the boy replies from under his blanket.

The next morning Argane is the first one awake. Upon fixing William's breakfast, he meticulously packs up his wares. Appalonia wakes up shortly thereafter. She looks around as she comes to and begins tugging on the boy's sleeve, waking little Rufus up in the process.

"Why, top o' the morning to you too," says the little fairy. The frog smiles.

"Hey, hey, hey little pixie, I am up!" cries the boy, as he slowly comes around.

"Excuse me, Mister William!" exclaims Appalonia all a flutter in front of the boy's face as he lays on his side.

"But I am no pixie. I am a fairy," she says pointing at his nose with her teeny tiny index finger.

"I…I do apologize, I did not know there was a difference."

"The young one has been quite sheltered," bellows Argane, from his place near Legacy.

"He knows not of such things," he adds.

"Well, I never!" exclaims Appalonia in exasperation.

"I shall not mix it up again," claims William. "Please…what is the difference?"

Appalonia huffs and puffs. "Pixies are manipulative and sinister and downright…not to be trusted! Fairies are wonderful! They are sweet, kind and helpful! We are nothing alike!" she proclaims in a matter-of-fact way of speaking.

"Alright, alright. I will never forget it," ensures William.

"Hrmp!" squeaks Appalonia with a sharp nod, prompting her bangs to fall onto her eyes. She sweeps her hair away aggressively. William sits up and slowly takes his breakfast in hand. Argane who has been observing from nearby smiles at the innocent banter. It is not the first time he has been witness to a fairy taking offence at being mistaken for a pixie.

Later on, down the path, the travelers enter a brisk chill within the air.

Not just any chill but a cold blast of thin air that does not relent but only grows more and more prominent as they go. The area thickens with lifeless trees and bushes. The landscape that William has grown so accustomed to is now turning baron and freezing. The trail elevates steadily as it winds through the colorless countryside. Shades of green and blue are replaced by tones of brown and grey.

"This is a cold I have never known," says the boy, as he pulls his hat tight over his eyebrows to block the wind. Soon after the sharp breeze carries with it tiny snowflakes that spin and dance all around the adventurers. "We are getting close," calls Argane, above the noise of the wind. The sky is dense with clouds and the sun is nowhere to be seen when it begins to snow harder.

They arrive at a part of the trail that turns hard to the left then right before it straightens out to reveal a miraculous and stunning statue of a lady. She is about a hundred yards away as she comes into view.

"There she is!" calls William. "I can hardly make her out within the snow but…she is beautiful!" he shouts. The large statue comes into clearer view gradually and grows larger as they approach. More and more the details present themselves. Sonya Sage shimmers.

The riders stand at the fork in the road and before her, looking way up. The statue is of white quartz and is intricately detailed. Blackened mildew streaks down her robe from her shoulders.

The giant version of Sonya Sage 'the Courageous' stands proud in a clearing, on a cubed base. She towers above the group. William scans the statue, head to toe. Sonya is adorned in a large cascading hooded mantle atop her long robe. She is staring straight ahead with determination in her eyes and her lips are formed to a subtle smirk. Her face beneath her hood appears smooth and very young. Long wavy hair frames her cheeks and chin as it flows down in front of her shoulders and along her chest. She is holding a long sword in each of her gloved hands and has the weapons crossed, upright and diagonal across her corseted torso making an "ex." Her knees are bent just so within her robe, exposing one smooth leg out from inside it, as they are set one in front of the other. An intricate pair of sandals completes her attire.

"She is so pretty!" exclaims Appalonia.

"She looks peaceful," adds William. "Who is she?" he asks.

"Sonya 'the Courageous' was a great young warrior of times past. She was an activist and a rebel. She was beloved by most, led armies of races and inspired generations…still does…and always will…it was truly something to behold," explains Argane who succumbs to the moment. A while passes while the riders examine the work of art.

Soon, they are off. "Stay close and tight," says Argane. They kick up their horses and disappear straight north into the tangled forest behind the relic, leaving the trail going left and right behind them too. For William, it will be the first time traveling off the beaten path. He quickly looks back and examines Sonya's shield. It is strapped to her back and embossed with a lynx in an attack position.

Eventually a broken path develops. It is narrow and winds as it steadily elevates. The majority of the snowfall is shielded by the dense woods, but the sharp wind finds its way through.

"We shall arrive at a clearing soon with some boulders throughout. We will stop there and indulge in hot drink and fire…It will be our last break before Killik!" calls Argane, clenching his robe closed around his neck and chin and from under his large hat, pulled way down low.

The wind rips violently through the woods, its frigid and relentless. William lifts Rufus from his place on his hat and drops him into his front pocket.

"Would you like to take shelter too, within my pocket?" asks William.

Appalonia shakes her head, "No, I am warm," she says within her glow. "Thank you, boy," she replies graciously.

The group continues on. The fierce climate lets up just a little, until finally…

"There! Just up there!" calls Argane, pointing to a small snowy clearing beside a large tree trunk to their right side. When they arrive, they dismount and tie their horses together and then around the tree trunk. William proceeds to gather fallen branches as quickly as he can and piles it up beside a large grey boulder, where there is shelter from the wind. The old wizard unpacks two cups, six tiny pouches of dried keyetta leaves and one canteen of water.

He begins meticulously concocting the beverages, using Legacy's saddle as his table-top and his body as a wind break.

"We are ready!" calls the boy, now standing before his pile of kindling. Argane hears the announcement through the 'whirring' winds but does not answer.

"Argane, sir! We are ready!" shouts William louder this time. His warm breath rolls steaming out of his mouth and into the cold. The boy waits a moment before holding out his two hands directly above the stack of wood. He concentrates for a moment and shoots a small fireball from his left hand. Then two from his right for better measure. The fire is ablaze instantly. William keeps his hands outstretched above to keep warm. The wizard hears the impact of the fireballs, followed by the crackling of the dead wood. He stops making their drinks and looks into the wooded distance ahead of himself and grins. Once the drinks are fixed, he squeezes one in each fist, allowing his hands to vibrate and heat up, until both are scalding hot and steaming. At the fire, he hands William his.

"Just hold it a while and warm up, soon it will be fit to drink," says Argane. "A great fire," he adds.

"I couldn't wait for you," replies William.

Argane winks. "How are you faring Appalonia?" he asks.

"I am perfect," she answers, from within her radiant, warm glow.

"And how about The Mighty Rufus?"

"He says he is comfortable and resting within William's pocket," relays the fairy.

"Curious is it not, William, we are two quite magical fellows and the fairy, and the frog are more naturally equipped to handle such elements?"

"Indeed, and they can communicate too," answers the boy, as he takes his first sip. "I cannot believe the weather here," he adds.

"We are traveling due north now and are elevating as well along an incline… as we come down the other side and arrive at Killik, the erratic weather and freezing temperatures will let up," says Argane.

"This is very good," says the boy, of his tea.

"Are you hungry."

"No, I am not, thank you." William studies Appalonia, as she hovers just beside him.

"Hey, Appalonia! I have not seen you eat…not even once since we had met. You must be starving!"

The fairy laughs gently from within her light. Argane chuckles too.

"What? …what is it?" urges William.

"Fairies do not eat," proclaims Appalonia.

"Here we go again," says the boy.

"How do you live without food?" he asks.

"Fairies naturally energize within their luminescence…and I drink water sometimes but that is all."

she answers. "When I am thirsty, a nice indulgence from a fresh morning dew drop is my absolute favorite."

"My! Extraordinary," whispers William to himself. "I am learning all the time."

"Get used to it, William. In this world, you will never stop learning for as long as you are in it."

Later, Argane leads them onto the narrow, broken path.

"I see smoke! Through the trees!" shouts William, over the whistling winds.

"Killik!" returns Argane.

The small mountain village is intricately placed within a deep valley among the tall trees and swirling snowflakes. Its brown wooden structures are camouflaged purposely within the dead forest. Tiny one, two, and three-room cabins are situated all over with narrow paths connecting many of them. Most of them have chimneys form which smoke gently billows and dissipates within the branches above.

The riders carefully descend the terrain and enter the Killikian territory. They are greeted by three children dressed in thick fur clothing and hats. Even their boots are bound with fur. They whoop, holler and cheer upon recognizing Argane. The old wizard smiles as he and Legacy slowly stride by, making further headway into Killik. Dusk is settling into the trees, and it gets dim as the group arrives at the community's center core. There is an extremely large fire pit with bulky tree trunks and crooked branches lightly aflame inside its rocky perimeter. Many cabins and shacks surround the pit in no clear order. With what is left of the days light, William observes the many structures high and low and among the surrounding hills.

Children run by joyously as a middle-aged man comes out of the front door of the shack nearest to Argane and the fire pit. He too is dressed heavily in fur and hide.

"Argane!" he says gruffly, "you are right on time and back successfully I see," says the man, looking at William. Argane nods. "Aye, this is the boy…William of Little Augustine. This is Appalonia and this my friends, is Shinoah Steelback."

"Hello mates," says the burly man with broad shoulders.

"Good day, sir," says William.

"Come, stew's on," directs the man motioning with his open arms, toward his home.

Inside a woman dressed in much less fur than Shinoah, is stirring the stew inside a large cauldron that is hung just so, over a small fire. The heat in the Steelback place is comforting.

"My wife…Yaria, as you know," says Shinoah to Argane.

"Hello," says William. Yaria turns around.

"Oh, my sweet little one," she says.

"Sit, sit," the boy does, followed by the two men.

"I see you have your very own fairy! Lucky boy," she says with a wink. Yaria then turns back to tending her stew, as it simmers.

"So old friend," says Shinoah. "How was your journey?"

"Good…very good," answers Argane, looking to William. The boy raises his eyebrows and smiles subtly, feeling a bit on the spot.

"Only one loss, one of the L.L.," adds the elder.

"Rabbit stew is served," says Yaria, turning around with two wooden bowls full. She places them in front of the welcomed guests.

"Shinoah, I am certain you can serve yourself?" says Yaria, suggestively.

The doting husband smiles as he rises to his feet to get himself some stew of his own.

"This is delicious, m'lady, thank you," says William.

"It is good to be back here," says Argane. The men spend a long-time drinking, talking and laughing. All the while the drone of celebratory noise gets louder and louder from outside.

"We had better get out there and join the festivities," says Yaria. "William, have you met my boys?"

"Nay…I have yet to meet any children formally," answers William. She looks to Argane. He smiles.

"They are a bit younger than you. Gunter is eight and Harrison is six. Our little girl Maddie is but four."

"Come!" directs Shinoah, rising from the table. When they exit, the cabin, the brightly lit fire-pit nearby is full and robust. Tall flames dance, wave and wobble. There are jovial people, young and old, sitting and standing all around. They are clearly having a lot of fun as they carry on in chatter and indulge in drink and smoke.

"Killik people are 'Sirks' William and are barbarians…notorious for working hard by day and playing even harder by night. It is a great privilege just to have welcome here and be among them," explains Argane, bending down and whispering in the boy's ear.

William observes everyone around the fire. The wizard leads him to a large, tree stump closer to it. They set down on it amongst the people. Appalonia is enjoying herself as evident by her ear-to-ear smile. Rufus is too, as he takes in the scene from his position back on William's hat. The Killikians join together in song and dance. Many of the ones closest to the heat shed most of their fur garb. Across the way through the orange light, Argane points out to William; two small girls who seem to be laughing and looking in the boy's direction. They are holding something, but the child cannot tell what.

Upon the boy spotting them, they slowly and sheepishly approach, carrying a polished oakwood bow.

Its frame glistens and shines by the fire light. The little girls without words but through mannerisms urge him to take it, as they nudge it forward into his chest. William stands up. "For me?" He looks to his guide in confusion. They further shove the weapon toward him.

"Go on...take it," says Argane...and so, the boy does. "Thank you," he says. As soon as William has the bow, the girls run off and disappear through the crowd from where they stood just moments before. The boy again looks to his keeper in confusion.

"The people here like you," says Argane.

The next morning William wakes to the muffled sounds of wood being chopped methodically outside. He lays on a straw mattress to find his bow and his hat laid out beside him. He gets out of bed and walks opposite the foot of it, to the window and stands on the tips of his toes to better see out.

Indeed, there is a Sirk man steadily chopping wood out back, with an axe. It looks briskly cold outside through the frosty window, though it is very warm inside. Just then he hears a familiar sound outside the bedroom door. Argane's laugher bellows. William quickly gets ready for another day. He exits the room to find that he is in the kitchen of the same small shack from the night before and that Argane is having a delightful conversation with Yaria who is preparing a wonderfully smelling meal.

"Ah, young one, let us break our fast, shall we? Come sit." William notices that Appalonia and Rufus are playing about the tables surface. "Just in time William," says the woman. She brings their plates. Yaria reminds the boy of his late mother.

"Chicken eggs, venison and potatoes...hope you like it," she says, as she sets down the food and turns back to her cooking area. "I am sure it is delicious," says William. He digs in.

As morning dissipates, the travelers make their way out of Killik to many nods, smiles, and waves as they go.

It's so different here this morning than it was last night, thinks William, as they weave along the pathway out. People who were so excited and merry then are all business now...serious...steadily working away on this task or that. They are fully focused and in deep concentration. Soon, Killik is reconsumed by the tall, dead trees of the forest and shortly thereafter, all traces of smoke from the village's chimneys are swallowed up too.

14.
Old Crimsinth. Just Past Killik, off of Ergo's Coast.

A while later they are back on lower land and with the weather warming considerably, the riders are stopped and watering their horses. William is admiring his bow.

"Why did they give me this?" he asks of Argane.

"The people of Killik are good in every sense. Not the savage barbarian types you may have heard about. They know you are with us. They respect you and feel for what you've been put through, as we all do…" Argane points at the bow. "Will you name it," he asks, "to match your Often blade?"

"I suppose I shall," replies the boy… "to carry on Calupa's tradition."

"Loyalty is a dying virtue," says Argane. "Do not ever forget Calupa and the sacrifice he made for you…"

William smiles softly.

"I shall name it then. Do you know the names of the girls who brought it to me?"

"I do, they are Delilah and Rose…first cousins, if I am not mistaken," answers Argane.

"It is settled then. It is Delilah Rose."

"A fine name, for a fine weapon young one, fine indeed."

"Do you like it too?" asks William of Rufus, from above, on his hat. The frog nods, yes.

"And you?" he asks Appalonia.

"I do indeed...it sounds like beautiful fairian name." With that, the travelers continue on. They arrive carefully at a clearing near the edge of a cliff.

"Wow," whispers William.

Beyond the treetops below, there is a large stretch of white sand beach at sea level that opens up to a massive ocean coast, there is a small bay, and a sandbar littered with ice platforms and tall limestone ruins all throughout the water's surface along the shoreline.

The group stands silent, in awe of the coastline, though it is cool and slightly foggy, it is beautiful still.

"Ergo's Coast," affirms the boy.

"Yes...and do you see...just down there?" asks Argane, pointing downward into the trees to a small black roof.

"I do," answers William.

"That is Marple's place. She is a loyal friend to our circle. Come, let us partake in our final stopover. Marple will get you outfitted," he says to the fairy. The voyagers veer left and carefully descend the rest of the decline in a single file, enroute to Marple Weary's shack. They arrive there shortly after. The one-room structure is sunk into the ground on one corner, extremely out of level and heavily bombarded by encroaching branches and bushes. The beach is just in view, through the brush from its main side. As they dismount and tie their horses off to the nearby trees, the front door opens, and they are greeted warmly by Marple herself. The woman is quite elderly. She appears as old as Argane. Straight, layered, white hair flows just past her shoulders. Her features are of medium size and are significantly symmetric. Her eyes are turquoise, and she is wearing a woolen beige cloak with pale-blue piping stitched around the neck and sleeve cuffs. The initials 'M.W.' are embroidered prominently with matching blue, into the back of the cloak, below the hood.

"A fine day!" she says with good cheer in her voice, she follows up her greeting with a big smile.

"Any hitches?" she asks.

"One, but it did not deter our objective."

"Fine! Just fine then...please...do come in."

The group does just that. William is floored. Upon entering, the place that seemed like a tiny shack on the outside, is a large, lavish haven on the inside, spacious and warm. There are high ceilings, many rooms and plenty of bookshelves lined with beautifully bound reading material. A cozy fire is ablaze below a stone mantle. They pass through the foyer to the lounge.

"William, dear boy, sit!" says the hostess, pulling out a chair. William sits down. Argane joins them at the large table as well. Marple stands there and examines the group.

"And who is this little delight?" she asks.

"I am Appalonia," replies the fairy.

"And so you are," says the old woman. Argane reaches into his robe and pulls out a pouch.

"You have the blue blades from Otterbrook."

"Indeed," says Argane, as he sets a tied bundle of about a dozen large blue blades of grass on the table.

"Wonderful, just wonderful," she says as she picks them up and holds them to her nose.

"I promised Appalonia you could clothe her better than I."

"But of course, I can! Come with me dear!" The fairy flutters beside the woman and they exit the room.

This place is so...full, says the boy of Marple's dwelling. Argane looks around the cluttered space.

Marple returns, rather quickly with Appalonia. The tiny fairy is stunning in a light green and pink dress, it has puffy shoulders, sparkling white frilly lace around the sleeve cuffs and at the base of the long, round skirt. The dress is complete with shiny satin white gloves cut just above the elbows.

Argane smiles.

"You look like a princess," says William. Appalonia blushes.

"Thank you again, so much," says the fairy to Marple in her tiny voice.

"My pleasure, love."

"Anything to report?" asks Argane.

"Nothing," answers the woman.

The wizard nods, "Perfection." A silent moment passes.

"Do you recall the exploits of The Mighty Rufus of Kersius?"

"But of course," says Marple. "Who could forget."

"Well...can you believe it? He is there," says Argane, nodding toward William's hat.

"He is where?" asks the woman, searching the boy with her eyes.

"A top William's hat."

"Oh, my gracious me!" she exclaims, of the little blue frog. "You are spinning a yarn!"

"I assure you, I am absolutely not," replies Argane.

"Well! pleased to see you again, friend…you know, the world believes you long dead!"

Rufus smiles. "He says he is pleased to see you too!" interjects Appalonia.

"He cannot speak for himself? how unfortunate." Marple listens attentively while the fairy brings her up to speed. "Aye, yes curses, eh? There must be a spell for that," says Marple.

"You really would think," affirms Argane, in agreement.

"Poor dear, poor, poor dear," says Marple.

Shortly thereafter, the group are all at the table eating twinkle-berry pie and drinking black currant cider. The elders watch while William and Appalonia chat and carry-on.

"Big changes are afoot," says Marple quietly.

"Indeed," concurs Argane, as he takes a sip of his tankard. "About time."

"Is the world ready?"

"It had better be."

Suddenly, a bird flies through a small, curtained hole, high in the wall and finds its place on a bookshelf in the corner of the room.

"Whoa!" cries Appalonia. "Frightened me nearly to dust!"

Argane chuckles.

"That is Odd Feather, my homing pigeon. He is a hard worker. William watches the pigeon curiously and notices his single black feather on his wing within all the other grey ones."

"No messages today it seems," says the woman upon searching her bird over.

"Well…we must be off…thank you, Marple," says Argane.

"Yes, the road was long to be sure…I shall see you all again very soon," she replies.

The boy follows the wizard's lead and rises from the table.

Marple leads them out and after they mount up, she merrily waves them off.

The group arrives at the white sands of the beach before long.

"It is beautiful," says William as they trot across the sand toward the shore.

The northeast coast is named after and old argonaut… "Ergo the Argo." A long time ago, he and his explorers discovered this land and frequented Crimsinth, even after its founding, when it was at the height of its prime and glory.

"It is wonderful! I have never seen sand so white and water so blue."

"It truly is. Crimsinth was once great, but it is a dead zone now. Catterbury's civil war decimated this poor city…it is all but ruins." They halt at the shoreline. A subtle tide rolls up some bedrock, along the sand bar and just past their horse's front legs. The water swirls around Legacy and Windimere's hooves and ankles before receding back again. There are large, fractured limestone partitions and columns scattered about and protruding from the ocean's surface before them.

"Do you see that giant wall? just yonder? more particularly the one that looks like a capitol L," asks Argane.

"I do," answers William.

"There is our entrance."

"Where is our entrance? It is just a wall."

"Things are not always as they seem…I thought you would have had that figured by now," says the wizard. "Watch your footing," he adds, as he steps out onto the water and steadily walks across to the 'L' shaped stone wall. William waits and watches. Argane turns Legacy around to face the boy.

"I am going with him," says Appalonia, she then flutters off ahead.

The boy waits and watches her until she joins up with Argane. He smiles.

"We cannot walk on water!" says William to Rufus.

"Just watch your footing! Easy does it!" calls the wizard, slowly. The distance between them leaves their voices sounding muffled. The boy inhales a big breath and exhales. He kicks subtly and Windimere slowly steps into the water. He is a few steps out when the boy begins to understand. He looks down to the large stretch of flat bedrock just under the water's surface. It leads to where Legacy and Argane stand in wait. William looks up quick to his mentor. The old wizard laughs and the boy nods yes. "Aha, alright…I get it," he says, shaking his head side to side.

"It is very slippery!" shouts Argane… "Easy does it!" he advises. Rufus and Windimere slowly and carefully make the short trek over the rock way. His horse slips just a little before reaching Argane and Appalonia at the wall. Argane steps Legacy further onto the platform at the 'L' shaped wall's base.

"I heard you laughing too fairy," says the boy.

"I was not!" returns Appalonia with a giggle.

"You were to," asserts William.

"Well…maybe so…but you thought Argane walked on water." She laughs again.

"Aye, I did…perhaps it is not as far-fetched as it seems," he replies. The boy prompts Windimere to join them on the platform which is protruding only barely above the water's surface.

The tall section of the wall faces the shore and runs north and south, with the short part facing south and running east and west.

"These might be ruins but they are solid stone," says William. He examines the two walls and the floor. "Where are we going from here? And where is the entrance? I don't see anything," says William.

Argane winks and taps his staff with a distinctive series of knocks on the floor at the inside corner of the L. The stone shudders to a thud. A moment of silence passes, until a large segment of the floor grinds open, slowly.

"I will follow you," says Argane. William peers down into the chasm. There is a wide and very long stone stairway. It gradually descends into the dark.

"It is quite dim," says the boy.

"It gets brighter, I assure you," insists Argane. "Besides, Appalonia will light the way." He out stretches his arm, directing William to lead them down.

The boy kicks up gently, slowly guiding his horse downward and into the tunnel. Argane follows and the thick, stone door proceeds to grind again, as it closes shut behind them. Outside the wind gains strength and a bit of lightning flashes within the clouds, illuminating the sky above the ocean.

Underneath, beside the staircase, there are a series of torches mounted every so often, lining the wall to their left; the right side of the stairway is open and poorly railed. *If one were to topple off the edge, it seems they would fall forever into the darkness, as if it were an endless abyss,* thinks William. He focusses ahead.

They reach the bottom to where it is much brighter. Torches and oil lamps are lit up and mounted everywhere. The group stands at the bottom of the stairs in a large landing area. There is straw strewn about the stone floor and there are chambers with no doors all over. A long corridor begins just ahead of them and continues way down into the distance. A man appears from the first room on their right and approaches. He is dressed in work clothes covered with leather armor. The two men greet each other but do not speak with the voices from their mouths but through the look in their eyes.

"William…I am Oren…it is my pleasure to meet you boy."

William nods.

"We walk from here," says the wizard. They dismount, and Oren takes their steeds. The elder leads toward the corridor. William looks back briefly. "To where do the horses go?" he asks, as Oren guides them into the room from which he came.

"We have underground accommodations just over there," answers Argane as he points in the direction where Oren is leading them. "And areas above ground too, that are well-hidden," he adds.

"Is he one of the circle's seven?"

"No…he is not, but very important to it, none the less." They walk awhile. The hallway takes a right turn, and they continue. Soon doorways leading into rooms begin appearing one by one on each side of the corridor. William studies them as they walk. The chambers are each close in size and the furnishings are similar too. They have lots of well stocked bookshelves. The boy looks them over, inquisitively. There are candles and tables with places to sit and there are mattresses to sleep on.

Most of the spaces are dimly lit. At the end of the hallway, they come to another staircase. This one, leads upward and gradually bends to the left. They ascend the stairway.

"This place is a stone-block maze," says Appalonia.

Argane laughs… "It surely is not," he says. They reach the top and the stairs open up to yet another long corridor, leading to the right. The hallway gets increasingly brighter as they walk through it.

More rooms. Thinks the boy to himself. They carry on until they reach the end which elevates to yet another staircase. It takes them up to another corridor.

"I think I will side with Appalonia," says William, as they go. Appalonia giggles.

"We are almost there," assures Argane playfully. Soon after they arrive at a dead end with another flight of stairs leading up to their immediate left. They climb the steep, wide stairway. They are flanked by blue-flame torches. A sound comes through the darkness from above.

"What is it?" asks the fairy.

William peers into the shadows. "It…it is a cat!"

A well-groomed, white cat comes prancing down the steps, as if to greet William with a series of meows.

"Ah, it is 'Hope'," announces Argane.

William kneels and pets the cat, while Appalonia flutters above, illuminating the feline's lustrous coat.

"She has pretty blue eyes!" exclaims the fairy. Suddenly the sounds of footsteps ring out and grow louder and louder, down the stairs toward them. An elderly woman appears through the darkness.

"Constance!" says Argane cheerfully.

"You have done it!" she exclaims. William looks up to see the elderly woman.

"Hello boy!" she says with glee.

"My lady," replies William, upon standing up straight.

"You have come acquainted with my little one, I see."

"She is wonderful," says the boy, as he bends down to pet her again. The elder woman is tickled.

"And what is your name lovely fairy?"

"Appalonia," she answers. Constance looks at Argane. He smiles.

"I have known many fairies in my time dear…you and I could be quite a pair," she adds.

"I look forward to your company," says Appalonia happily. Constance smiles warmly.

"Going for a book?" asks Argane.

"I was going to see Oren and the newest additions to our family," says the woman.

"William is a good lad and Windimere is a fine horse," affirms Argane. "They will fit in perfectly, as will our tinier additions, he adds."

Constance shakes her head yes and smiles again before passing the group and heading further down the stairs.

"I shall see you all again shortly." Hope bounds after her.

"One of the seven?" asks William.

"No…she is of a might all her own," answers the wizard.

They arrive at a landing atop the staircase, opposite a large, thick oak door with a bulky cast-iron handle and matching hinges. Large orange candles are mounted on each side of it.

"This is our main level; you will all likely meet everyone here. They have been waiting for you William…and for Rufus of Kersius…and for you Appalonia," says Argane, nodding at each one of them as he says their names…for all of us and everyone…This is where our story begins.

15.
The New Beginning

Argane takes a black key from inside his robe and opens the door, giving way to a large dining room with a high ceiling. There is a grand candle-lit chandelier at its center, hung by chain and pully above a large rectangle table, where four men are seated in twos and across from each other. The walls are consistent with the limestone William has become accustomed to seeing in the curious underwater fortress. Torches line the walls, oil-lamps are set upon tables and candlesticks stand tall and wide upon fluted quartz pillars, all over the room. There is luxurious red velvet and dark leather furniture in the chamber and an array of old, impressive oil paintings are hung about the space. William looks to the large, long, rectangle table and observes the men. Most of them are elderly, like Argane, and dressed similarly.

There is a lounge area to the left and what appears to be a kitchenette of sorts to the right with a small door along its back wall. He notices too, another large oak wood door beyond the table opposite to where he and his companions had just entered. The men seem to have just finished up eating a substantial feast and rise to their feet upon spotting the newcomers. William follows Argane's lead and heads toward the table. They do not speak at first but appear to be delighted.

"Men!" says Argane as they stand by. "I give you…the boy William of Little Augustine."

There are a couple of gasps followed by some uninterpretable banter until one of the men at the table speaks to William.

"Please boy…do sit…everyone…sit," he says, motioning to Argane and the other men.

The rest sit down as William takes a seat at the end closest to him. Argane remains standing.

"I am Be'wick," continues the eldest wizard.

"Nice to meet you, sir," replies William. "Y-you are part of the seven of the circle?"

"Indeed…we are all part. The man to my immediate left is Isla, across from him is Wezzton."

Wezzton nods. "And beside him is Luscious…Addly is probably at the surface or somewhere near it. Argane sit!" urges Be'wick. "You have been gone so long."

"I have business at the surface before I take rest. I shall do so. We will catch up soon, old friend."

With that, Argane disappears through the door that William took note of on the far side of the long table.

"Child…eat," says Be'wick of the large plate of food before him. William had not noticed it before.

"And your fairy…splendid! Constance is pleased, I am certain." "She was delighted," confirms the boy. "What is your name dear girl?"

"I am Appalonia."

Be'wick smiles at her, before setting his sights back on William.

"How was your venture here asks the head wizard.?"

"Well…quite educational," answers William. The men chuckle.

"Indeed," says Luscious. William begins eating his meal while the four men speak amongst themselves.

"You have a tiny frog upon your hat!" says Wezzton.

"Aye…I shall defer to Argane for his introduction, if that is acceptable."

The men laugh. "So adept in language," observes Isla.

"Surely," approves Be'wick.

Soon after, when William is full, he finishes with his plate and thanks Be'wick and the others.

"Pay no mind. You are fatigued from travel… yes?" inquires Be'wick.

"I am, sir. I imagine we all are," replies the boy.

"You must sleep…for as long as you need and awaken well-rested William…always keep in your heart and mind…that you are safe now, here with us and you always will be and so you are especially certain, know too, that all of us here are deeply sorry for your losses." The other men around the table solemnly agree. "Come now," says Be'wick, as he stands up. "I will show you to your quarters," he adds. William rises from the table, bids the other men farewell and follows Be'wick out of the dining room through the door that Argane had recently exited.

They take a right and start down another plain hallway lined with rooms with oak doors. William's quarters are the second last in the hallways left side. He notices, just past the last door that there is yet another flight of stairs that ascend upward. Be'wick opens his door after unlocking it with a black key.

William's room is quite small, but the space is utilized well. There is a goose down, single mattress with a thick wool blanket atop a four-post, cherry wood bed frame in the immediate left side corner, ahead of the foot is a small matching table set with two chairs and an oil-lamp, ready for lighting on its center, beside that is a sizeable chest with the key set on top, to its right is a bookshelf with a select few books on it, and in the last corner across from the side of the bed and to William's right, completing the space is a tall, open wardrobe full of clothes and out fits tailored to suit a small boy. There is a torch mounted onto the stone just between William's bed post and the door frame. Be'wick casually lights it with his crooked index finger. A steady stream of fire pours from it, as he holds it closely pointed toward the large wick.

"Well now," says the head wizard within the orange glow… "Get cozy, take rest…Marple has filled your dresser…with many fine things. There are books for when desire a passage to elsewhere, and in the morning, you'll meet the others at breakfast. After, you shall participate in some weeks end activities, then you will take a much-needed bath."

"Thank you, sir. Thank you very much."

"Be'wick…please lad, call me Be'wick. If you should find sleep elusive…someone is most always in the dining room studying."

"Thank you sir—um Be'wick. I am sure I will sleep fine. It feels like we had been on the road for a fortnight."

Be'wick smiles. "Not quite." He shuts the heavy door to a clank and disappears back down the hallway. William examines the room before digging through the wardrobe. He decides to go with a thick pair of bright red cotton coveralls.

"This room is very cozy," says Appalonia, as she flutters from William's shoulder and settles down on the bed. The boy carefully puts Rufus and his hat down beside her and proceeds to change into his red suit.

"Sooo comfortable," he whispers, with a quick shuffle of his legs.

He climbs into bed. Soon Rufus and Appalonia are fast asleep. William is almost asleep too, until Nya comes to his mind again. He is overcome with sadness and tosses and turns a while before getting out of bed to search the bookshelf. William opts for a shorter story than most. Something that would not take too long to read and that perhaps one that he can finish in a single session. The thin book bound in purple with gold print on the cover reads: 'The Ancient Mage and the Ice Dragon'. He retrieves the book and climbs back into bed covering himself with the thick, pure wool blanket.

The torch light casts a subtle glow upon the pages of his chosen reading. The flame flickers every so often. William reads attentively for a time, before rolling over and setting the book beside himself, his eyes are heavy…a moment or two later, he is finally sound asleep.

William and his little companions slumber through to the next afternoon, evening and right through to the following morning. William wakes last to the sounds of knocking and finds Appalonia and Rufus are steadily conversing playfully at the end of the bed. The persistent series of knocks at his door grows louder.

Not fully awake as yet and in a daze, he wonders; *If had he woken up on his own or was, he awakened by his friends atop the bed, or maybe the rapping on his door perhaps is what prompted him awake.* None the less he sits up and rubs his eyes.

"Good morning!" shouts the fairy merrily. The knocks continue from the opposite side of the door, followed by laughter…it sounds like young girls.

"Arntchya going to answer it?" asks Appalonia. William, not wanting to appear rude, jumps out of bed and opens the door. Standing before him are four children, similar to him in age.

There are two boys and two girls. The girls laugh again. This time at the sight of William in his bright red sleepwear.

William is still a bit too groggy to feel embarrassed.

"I am Leo," says the boy standing in front. "This is Hayden," he points with his thumb over to the other boy, an elf, who nods, "and they are Clari and Mila," he concludes, of the two girls set further behind. The girls are shy as they force smiles to greet him.

"Hello," says William.

"Argane has instructed us to fetch you for morning's breakfast."

"Thank you, I shall change clothes and join you there." William shuts the door and after he does the girls laugh yet again. He stops a second to better hear them, then quickly shakes his head side to side and opens the wardrobe. He proceeds to get dressed.

"Boy? are you happy there are other children?" inquires Appalonia.

William pauses to think… "I am," he answers. William looks of high-class in his fine outfit of choice. Overtop of a set of high-quality undergarments and a long sleeve shirt he is wearing a form fitting, black velvet, high collared, buckle fastened, overcoat. It is triple stitched with gold thread and gold braided piping lines the sleeve cuffs and front flaps. The lavish coat carries down to his calves and alongside it's matching black and gold pants. He wears a pair of black knee boots with the large cuff split at the front and folded over downward.

"Very dapper!" exclaims Appalonia. William motions to grab his hat from atop the bed.

"Oh no, no! She calls. It does not go! Silly," she adds before giggling.

"Sheesh!" he says, as he looks to Rufus and attempting to fix his hair with his hands.

"You shall take transport in my coat pocket then," he says, as he picks up his tiny blue friend. William stares at Rufus a moment. "How strange it must be for you with all your interesting history to have found yourself riding around in a child's pocket."

Rufus shrugs.

"He says it gets him much further along than hoping or swimming," says Appalonia.

"Well good then…here we go." The boy sets Rufus in his frontside, right pocket and the fairy hovers above his left shoulder. William takes a deep breath, and they start out for the dining room.

The chamber is well lit by way of the chandelier, torch light and candles, just as it was before. Though this time around, Argane's staff is set standing up-right at the center of the table. A fantastic sparkling sphere of bright white sets the whole room all that much more aglow. It is filled with a variety of delicacies, treats and beverages.

Argane is seated at the end closest to William with Be'wick at the opposite end. Constance and another four wizards are in the seats between them. The other chairs are filled with the children, Leo, Hayden, Clari and Mila.

There are other children present and a young woman to whom the boy has not yet been introduced. As he walks to the only empty seat beside Argane, he tallies up the kids, there are six in all, making him the seventh.

"You must feel rested by now?" asks Argane, when William sits.

"I do…very…It feels quite nice," confirms the boy. He sets Rufus down beside his plate.

"William, someone has returned to us," calls Be'wick. The young lady across from you, with the book in hand, is Whisspella, "The white witch." The young woman looks up from her reading and smiles. She wears a long, fitted, pale pink, satin dress with white long boots cut just below her knees and matching white gloves that carry-on up past her elbows. Atop her head is a long, conical, hard pointed hennin hat of matching pale pink with a veil pouring out from the tip and down along her back. On her neck is a thin, gold necklace with a small, spherical, polished sapphire at its center.

She is beautiful, thinks the boy, with her long, platinum blonde hair, deep blue pastel eyes and her soft features. She looks like she is in her late twenties...far younger than the other adults and elders he has met thus far, within the fortress.

"She is a good witch," adds Be'wick with a wink.

William smiles back as she adjusts her round, gold rimmed spectacles.

"I am Marple Weary's daughter," she says, "and Mila who you have met...is mine."

William looks at Mila who is steadily eating between Clari and another girl.

"Mila!" calls Whisspella, "you know we always thank the makers before we eat our provisions." Mila grins. She in fact does know better.

"Hello, boy William, I am Addly," says the only wizard whom William had not met before his long slumber.

"Good day Addly," replies William.

"We have all become acquainted?" asks Argane.

"No," says Be'wick... "It is just Poe and Sara who have not met William."

Poe, the only dwarf within the fortress says hello from across the table and little Sara, the youngest of the children and of Elven descent does too.

"Alright then...now, all have met! let us eat and be merry," says Be'wick.

He bows his head and the rest follow, so then does William. The head wizard continues.

"Thank the creator for all there is to eat.

Keep us safe from morning 'till sleep,

And through the night, while we dream.

Keep us near and in between."

He finishes and the group begins eating, William follows their lead. They consume their meals awhile in silence until Wezzton breaks it.

"So, young ones! It is still the week's end. What sort of fun shall be had on this fine day?"

"Hide and seek! on the surface!" shouts Hayden passionately.

"I was hoping we could fish again," says Poe.

"No, no, no, what about gardening with Constance?" urges Clari.

"I was going to practice spells with mother," says Mila firmly.

"What about the workshop—or lunging horses?" suggests Leo.

"Children! Children," interjects Be'wick, "try not to speak over each other and surely you will work it out to a happy medium."

"Like a compromise?" asks little Sara.

"Sort of child," answers Be'wick, "and what would you fancy doing?"

"To visit Marple would be divine," she replies, meekly.

"Well, I've an idea…why not let William decide."

"He is our newest member after all," agrees Luscious.

"Oh, I couldn't…I simply do not know," says William.

"I could use and do so enjoy company within my winter garden," suggests Constance.

"I am with you!" exclaims Sara, with her soft voice.

"Aye, me as well," says Clari.

"Okay then, why not the girls garden and the boys can…"

"Anything the boys can do, I surely can as well!" shouts Mila.

Addly pipes up. "Isla and I were busy at the surface, and we are going back up soon, all the rest sounds a bit too much like work for today."

"Yes, and a touch cold for fishing, I'm afraid," adds Isla.

Addly continues. "Why not, you boys and Mila play manhunt while we are topside…you rarely play it up there!"

Almost all the boys agree, with Poe opting to assist Oren in feeding the horses.

"It is settled then," affirms Be'wick.

After breakfast, Oren and Wezzton proceed to clean up and Sara and Clari take exit with Constance. William watches the girls as they go and grows curious.

"Please forgive me…but is Sara an um…elf?"

"Why do you ask?" answers Be'wick.

"It is just that we had a few back in Little Augustine…she is small, and her face appears as such."

"Well, you are correct; she is indeed an elf…We are an eclectic group, William. Do you know the meaning of the word?"

"Yes, like…having variety," answers the boy confidently.

"Yes…yes, you are bright young one…we have all sorts here." Just then Constance re-enters the room and approaches Appalonia and Rufus.

"I have set the girls up to prepare and we would be delighted if you two would join us."

"Sure!" exclaims Appalonia, without hesitation. Rufus climbs aboard Constance's outstretched hand.

They turn and leave the dining room.

"Where was I? Oh yes! Diversity, that was it! Hayden is an elf too, though his lineage is of the woodland elves, opposed to the northern ones, where we think Sara draws her ethnicity from. Poe is a dwarf from the lowlands of 'West Line,' Clari is a Seyus and Oren even has Mountain Orc blood." William looks surprised and scans the table.

"You look perplexed William," says Whisspella, handing her plate to Wezzton. She chuckles, "Well, I will retire to the archives," she adds, evidently not waiting for an answer.

"Always reading," claims Argane.

"No more than you?" she asks rhetorically.

He laughs… "I suppose it possible."

"Oh yes…also, William," says Be'wick, "can you keep a secret?"

"But of course," replies the boy.

"Constance has much she can teach your fairy Appalonia…she will keep her close. Encourage Appalonia to be open to staying here with us. Through lessons and training, her future can be brighter than she could have ever possibly imagined."

"I will certainly propose she stay."

"Yes…good…advocate for that," replies the elder. "But enough talk for now…there is much work for the coming week…do go and play. Argane and I will finish the clean-up," calls Be'wick to Wezzton and Oren.

"You are too kind," answers the much younger wizard.

"Yes, well do not soon forget it!"

"Unlike you to deviate from the rotation."

"I am sure we will all fare just fine with the change," assures Be'wick.

"Okay young ones, to the surface!" shouts Addly.

"And me!" adds Mila with a shout of her own.

"And Mila!" confirms Addly playfully.

The four children follow the men toward the door behind Argane.

"Have fun," he whispers as William passes.

"I will…this is some exile."

16.
All Work and 'Some' Play

Addly and Isla guide the children down the hallway past William's quarters, to the end. They take a set of stairs, climbing them to a narrower and darker corridor. Isla puts forth his open hands parallel to each other and casts a small bright white orb from his palms. It floats between them and expands, soon, shimmering colors of blue and yellow dance and shine brilliantly from within the orb. Addly then generates a similar light source of his own. They reach a dead end. There is a cast iron ladder bolted to the limestone; it ascends way up within a shaft.

"Young ones, I will lead," orders Addly, "then you all follow…Isla will take up the rear," he adds looking to William. The boy nods. He starts up the ladder followed by Leo, Hayden, and Mila. William then climbs on, followed finally by Isla. Both wizard's luminescent orbs have circled around and are now hovering just above their upper backs, as they climb. With the shaft lit perfectly, the group steadily reaches the top. As they get close to the ceiling Addly's light quickly fades. He stops and one by one they all follow suit. Isla prompts his light to fade as well. Addly grimaces as he pushes a round hatch open, just enough to see outside. Bright white daylight pours inside. He waits a moment for his eyes to adjust and squints while he scans the area. He then pushes the door completely open. It flops over and drops onto the ground above with a thud.

A solitary red leaf falls into the shaft and glides back and forth grazing William as it sways on by. Slowly, Addly climbs outside and helps each child up and out. When it is William's turn, Addly smiles at him.

"Didn't think you would be back outside so soon, did you?"

The boy thinks for a second… "I suppose I was not sure," Addly lifts William through the hatchway. The boy brushes himself off upon being set on the ground.

Isla is the last to exit and shuts the door. It is covered in foliage and camouflages perfectly within the ground. William breathes the cool air in deep and exhales slowly. He looks around and is captivated by the view of the ocean and the surrounding mountains. They are standing atop a cliff, grand in scale on the edge of the forest. Nearby, it drops off a long way down to the sea. Sparse trees and bushes of various species both alive and dead make up the area above the massive body of water below. William observes the great cliff in its entirety, as it bends around westward and…gradually to the north and forming a point around a bay. The stretch of land carries into the beyond and the peninsula curls and tapers off in the distance until it touches down into the blue water, exchanging its green and brown woods for white sands. Tiny snowflakes dance all around in every direction within the soft whirling winds. William's eyes avert themselves as he returns them back to his immediate surroundings. The snow is accumulating around tree trunks and boulders, but not so much that it will leave enough tracks to blow the cover of the children in hiding.

"Let all, the all, the oxen fleee!" shouts Mila as she runs to a large nearby tree stump. It is large in circumference. She immediately begins counting.

William had taken particular notice, of the hatch-door. As aforementioned, its topside is covered thick with leaves, grass and plants. It shuts level with the ground and is perfectly inconspicuous. It is so well camouflaged that the boy cannot spot it.

"William! You are looking for the door," says Hayden, "it is out of bounds for means of hiding oneself, just ask Poe, but if you ever need to find it in a hurry…it is precisely fourteen paces due south of that stump," he says, pointing to the one that Mila is bent over, laying on and hugging with her outstretched arms.

"Is it not…Olly, olly oxen free?" asks Leo, crinkling his nose.

"I think so," responds Hayden.

"And you're meant to say it, when a player cannot be found…right?"

"Yep." They laugh.

"You all know the drill…never too far, never out of sight…well *our* sight anyway," calls Addly.

"Our security measures are always high," says Leo.

William looks at him and nods.

"I'm counting!" shouts little Mila.

"We had better get on boys!" says Hayden. The three children scatter...

"The stump is home free then?" inquires William.

"You got it!" shouts Leo, as he clambers for a good hiding place. Hayden dashes toward some bushes and William bolts downgrade a little, to where Isla and Addly are set beside each other standing at a giant fallen tree. They are across from each other and using the side of it as a platform for a very large, very thick atlas. He dives underneath a nearby snowdrift and stays completely still. He is almost completely enveloped.

The men look at the drift. They get a kick out of William's quick determination to cloak himself, at any snowy cost.

"Fifteen...sixteen...seventeen," continues Mila with her face in her hands.

"Dear boy, you should know, they count to fifty," says Isla playfully.

"Thank you," replies William from under the blanket of snow, with a muffled voice.

Hayden crawls and squats under a juniper bush.

"Thirty-eight...thirty-nine...forty..." Leo chooses a spot behind a tall and narrow shard of white quartz that towers over him on a slant. He straightens his posture and leans his back against it.

"Forty-niiine... FIFTY!" shouts Mila. "Ready or not, here I come!"

She turns and canvases the area with slow quiet steps. She is very calculating in her process and stops now and then to listen to irregular sounds while on the hunt. Addly looks up from their book briefly and smirks a half smile at the sight of Mila and her cunning approach. Before long, she spots Hayden.

"Jigs up, Hayden! I see ya!" she calls before running back to the stump. The boy has no chance of beating her to home-free and gives up the race rather quickly.

"Gotcha, Hayden...you are finished!" she yells as she smacks home free with her palms.

"We all know you can run!" he shouts, in her direction.

"Aye, and catch yas! Alright! she calls out...I gotta get me two more rabbits!" she adds as she resumes her hunt.

Mila wanders a while. Hayden is sitting patiently on the stump. She stops when she sees the beautiful quartz stone protruding from the ground and up high.

"Well, that is just too pretty to be nothing," she says under her breath.

"If no one is behind that great rock! They 'sure' ought to be!" she calls. She gets close to the quartz…A moment passes.

"You ought not breathe so loudly silly!" she shouts.

"A race then!" yells Leo, as he bounds out from around the other side.

Mila narrowly beats him back to home free. Catching his breath, Leo proposes a question.

"So, you heard me breathing huh?"

"Nope," she quips… "tactics!" she adds, then laughs.

Leo looks to Hayden, "Do you believe her?" he asks.

"Alright…one more rabbit," she says coldly before starting out on her search for William.

She is careful at first. A while passes. Isla and Addly are always paying attention, though not always obviously. When she is only a few feet from the snowdrift and after stomping all around the woods, she huffs and puffs. "Fine! You win! Come out, come out wherever you arrre!"

William pops out of the heap fast, spooking Mila in the process.

"Ahh!" she screams, then shudders. "You were there?"

William laughs. "I sure was!"

"Impossible! You must be frozen, and you were right under my nose all the time!"

William brushes himself clean of the snow.

"Great job!" calls Leo.

"A boy will always win against a girl!" shouts Hayden.

"Do you two mean then, that you are girls?" she asks rhetorically. Hayden grimaces. "So, I am to hunt you three then?"

"Yes," answers Mila. In the next go round, William discovers all three of them rather quickly and handily wins the races to home free with the children with the exception of the one against Mila.

"It seems you and I are cut out for this," she says to William.

"Ah, you are full of beans," says Leo to the ever-boastful Mila.

After getting some tools together and taking an alternate route via a hidden passage in a section of stone wall, Constance, Appalonia, Clari and Sara ascend a series of long corridors until they too climb a shaft and are outside. They cross the beach into the woods far from where the other children are at play high up on the cliffs. Marple Weary's place stands between them and just about perfectly divides the two groups. The winter garden is hidden well, by dense bushes and tall trees. There is no clear-cut path to it and Constance keeps mindful to not walk the same route too often.

They stand just inside the garden patch. It is a perfect circle, large in circumference and though surrounded distinctly by a lot of dead forestry it is very much alive and robust with various colors and shades. Miraculously, the garden thrives. There are fruits and vegetables a plenty all around in a spiral. Soon, they are pruning the garden carefully with their bare hands and are moving steadily along. All three on their knees enjoying the work before them. Appalonia flutters through the garden and keeps close to Constance, while examining all the plants.

"It is beautiful…I have not seen so many colors since I was back home!" exclaims the fairy.

"Thank you, child," says the elder, graciously. Even Rufus is helping out with his tiny, webbed hands.

"Are your new short pants a good fit?" asks Constance. Rufus nods in approval of his little red loincloth.

When Constance and Appalonia get to the spirals center, there is a single flower there. It is tall, appears a bit aglow and smells better than any flower she has ever smelled before. Its petals are sky blue in color and shaped into a perfect five-point star. At the center is a small yellow circle; its stock is wavy, and it has but a single green leaf growing from it. The fairy gasps "I have never! Constance, what is this?"

"A star flower, quite simply…very rare…one could search a hundred years and not ever find one."

"They are our favorite!" interjects Sara.

"Indeed, it is divine," agrees Clari.

"It is an extremely useful flower for ingredients in elixirs and potions. There are many, many beneficial components to that little star…each part of it holds a different vital use than the next…the absurdity is," continues Constance, "that they absolutely will not grow near each other. You would have to plant one in the next town and that might be far enough away. It seems one could never have a whole patch of them, unfortunately.

"Wow!" says Appalonia in astonishment. "How is it that this can grow here at all? I mean, how can any of these things grow here, in such cold?"

"Well…winters turn is just a…a season, though very cold, yes and unrelenting at times due to the northern coast, one just needs to apply proper perspective…though the freeze proves many obstacles, it does not make growing a garden impossible…only…different. In fact, nothing is impossible. I can teach you how to plant a winter garden someday if you would like?"

"Oh geez, I don't know…my garden would be so small."

Constance laughs, "Maybe…maybe not."

Back at the fortress, down in the basement, Oren and Poe are in the horse stables. Oren is dressed in a casual, working outfit of boots, slacks, a hooded mantle and arm wraps. He is often the only one of the male elders that does not wear a long flowing robe and like Addly and Wezzton, appears not nearly as old as Be'wick, Argane, Isla, or Luscious. While the younger man is not part of the sevens circle, but an integral part of the group all the same. He brings two large burlap sacks to the center of the well-lit stables and stout Poe looking every bit of Dwarven descent in his highly durable blend of thick leather and iron trimmed attire, begins to dole out buckets of feed to each horse.

"This new one, Windimere is great in appearance," says Poe, looking up to him from outside his wooden box-stall.

"Yes, a fine steed he is, is he not," says Oren.

"Shall we lunge him outdoors?"

"No, it is week's end."

A moment passes. "Why did you not take advantage of the day and participate in manhunt?" asks Oren. "It is mostly work for us down here, with so little time for play," he adds.

"I like manhunt just fine, but I wanted to come with you and see our new addition."

"Aye, you do like it here among the horses, don't you and you are always a good helper," proclaims Oren.

Poe smiles and Windimere nickers. They proceed to tend to the horses and speak of this and that.

"This William," says Poe. "What people is he part of?" he asks.

"You wonder if he is of another race…like you or I?"

"I do."

"Aye, he is a human boy of pure blood but one of us none the less."

"Awful what the rakers did to his family," says Poe.

"Yes…he is safe here now…and one day, we will all be safer for it."

17.
The Curious Case of M.L. Higgins

That evening the group collectively thank Addly and Constance for yet another delicious dinner. The children are tasked with clearing the table and do so respectfully. Later, they are all seated back together at the cleared table, engaged in a competitive tournament of chess. The children play simultaneously on quartz slates with granite pieces.

Be'wick is the only elder left present in the dining room and is set comfortably reading a lengthy tome on a red velvet chair in the corner of the room. Beside him is a large blue candle with a long bright yellow flame atop a highly glossed round oak wood end table. Bookshelves line the walls behind him and along the wall to his left-hand side. The children are diagonal to him, at his right-side and in plain view.

In the basement in a spacious long room, aptly called 'the archives' sits Argane, Luscious and Wezzton at a well-lit, rectangle table. There are plenty of books stacked in front of them. The men are looking at a tattered map. Whisspella is nearby in a floral-patterned chair, heavily concentrating on her reading. She is radiant and brings a particular light of her own to any room.

"What does Be'wick think of the message?" asks Wezzton.

"He agrees that we should set out a dawn," replies Argane.

"And we can trust Marple's sources?"

"Of course, you know that."

"I suppose, I do know better."

"When did the pigeon deliver it?" asks Wezzton.

"Before dinner," answers Luscious.

"And who will join us?"

Two others…I was thinking Isla and Addly…ponders Argane.

"What did the message read exactly?" inquires Wezzton.

"It read that Morbit Len Higgins himself has been in hiding at Splendor and he is boisterously trading wits for drink…daily, that he seems adamant on nesting up there a while, has paid the inn keeper a foolish amount in advance for an extended stay and it also stated that he is alone."

"Perfect! What luck! Splendor is not far either…a day's ride northwest, at most," says Wezzton.

"Aye," nods Argane.

"This is our chance then. I will tell Isla and Addly. They are great riders," says Luscious… "and Addly will appreciate the education the trip will provide…I will have Oren ready your horses too," he adds.

"Wezzton, you know it is mandatory that Higgins tell us what he knows, why he double-crossed us and finally that he be removed," says Argane.

"I know it," replies Wezzton.

Up in the dining room it is evident that Hayden, Poe and Clari have been eliminated. They are set on the floor near Be'wick in front of a lavish mantle, on a lush carpet, playing jacks.

Sara and Mila play chess, while William and Leo play each other too.

"I always make it to the second round!" says Sara confidently as she moves one of her pawns forward.

Mila laughs… "But of course you do Sara! You are the youngest and therefore always get the bypass when our tournament is played with an odd numbered group!"

"Oh well, the fact remains."

Mila laughs again, "You are silly, a true feat would be to make it to the third, then you can boast."

Down the table, the two boys are silent and exchange very slow, calculated moves. Moments go by with the girls continually trading much quicker blows.

"Argane says that Chess is war encapsulated," says Leo, as he tucks his medium length brown hair behind his ear. He has well-proportioned features and brown eyes and could easily pass for his current adversaries' blood-brother.

"Encapsulated," repeats William… "Indeed…very strategic…each component working together under a commanding force to defend their territory and acquire more as well as conquer the opposing army and their king."

"Chess is my very favorite game…you seem well educated, as are we. Had you previously attended a school?" asks Leo.

"Sometimes, but…not a lot…not really…t'was my parents who taught us all the time," answers William.

"You're lucky, I did not know mine. I do not remember them at all."

"How did you come to be here?"

"Huzzah!" shouts Mila in celebration, down the table.

"One day, I will get ya," says Sara.

"Luscious rescued me from an orphanage in Red Rock. It had closed down when the town went broke, any remaining children were to be sold to slavery. Clari and I were the last two children left…he came through and saved us. I hear the town has come a long way but was an especially awful place when we were there."

"That story is both sad and happy," says William… "are you siblings?"

"No, we are close, but not brother and sister by blood."

Sara joins the game of jacks and Mila sits in wait watching the boys play out their game. It is close until finally William claims victory. Leo is gracious and the boys shake hands.

"A new champion then?" says Mila, as she climbs into Leo's former seat.

"Leo just about had me for a while."

"Well, he hasn't lost a game in quite some time. Alright then, here we go." The determined girl aggressively puts all their pieces into place. The competitors maneuver quickly at first and set up, until soon they must make their moves more carefully. Be'wicks's laughter bellows from his place in the corner from something he has read.

The children on the floor look at him oddly and laugh too. He does not seem to notice.

"You have been here all your life?" asks William.

"All my life!" answers Mila enthusiastically, as she takes the boy's knight.

"I have heard about some of your tragedies," she says, "more than any other child," she adds.

"I cannot begin to know your hurt and pain…but I do feel for you boy and I am happy you are here with us."

William looks into his lap… "Thank you Mila."

"Rest assured," she continues, "they will find her, but it will take time."

William's eyes widen and well up. He reluctantly looks at her and when he does, a single tear falls from his left eye. He breathes in deeply. Be'wick looks up from his book to observe the pair. Mila smiles at William subtly and then puts her hand on top of his briefly from across the table. He wipes his eyes and cheeks and moves his bishop.

Through the course of the game, it becomes evident that Mila is doing increasingly better…soon after she closes in on William's king with her queen and rook.

"Checkmate…I have done it! I am champion, I am finally champion!" she shouts. Clari and Sara rush over. Poe and Hayden look at one another with Leo looking on.

"Hooray!" yells Sara, "good show!"

After a bit more celebration, Mila turns to shake William's hand, they do so, and the girls run off in glee.

William promises himself, that for as long as he lives, he shall never tell Mila how he had let her win.

Later that evening Oren is busy taking large wooden buckets, one by one up the long staircase. He walks through the open hatch to where Whisspella stands on guard just outside. Oren dunks the bucket into the icy water near where Argane and William had made their entrance together into the bunkers for their first time together.

He then brings the full bucket down the steps and places it inside a room in the hallway just past the stables. He repeats this method with seven different buckets placing them in seven different rooms along the corridor.

When he is done filling the last bucket, Whisspella follows him inside. She reaches up and pounds the stone hatch in rapid succession with the side of her fist. It grinds shut behind them.

"Y'know, the young ones never fuss when made to fill their own baths and what's more, you know too that there are many of us here who can wield water," says the white witch.

"Yes, I know, but I do not mind now and then…I am down here so often, it is nice to get the exercise and fresh air," replies Oren.

"Yes, you certainly are a worker," she returns.

When they get to the basement level, Oren retires to the wood shop and Whisspella proceeds to heat up every bath. She holds her hand just above each bucket and emits a short wave of heat. When she arrives back at the dining room, she announces that their baths are prepared and to hurry or they will cool. The children make their way down with Leo leading the group as usual. They then separate one by one until they are all in a room of their own. All except Leo who waits 'till last with William and explains how to go about the bath and how summer evenings are better because they use the ocean. William is reminded of the lakeshore at Little Augustine and how so many villagers would often congregate there to partake in a variety of different activities.

Late that night, when all the children are asleep, some of the wizards are seated around the dimly lit dining room table.

"Then after he enlightens us, what then?" asks Isla.

"We have had Marple send word to Aleeso with the details and that his services would be appreciated," says Argane.

"What if he is not home? ...or it is too short of notice?" urges Wezzton, without waiting for the answers. "I say we handle him," he adds.

Be'wick interjects. "No, no Wez...we do not get our hands dirty on this. It is far too early to do something like that ourselves. We will not recklessly instigate any aggression on the high king's, informants or anyone who opposes our cause...not yet," he advises, from his place at the head of the table.

"Aleeso will be there...and we shall stop and confirm his acceptance personally on our way to Splendor," announces Argane.

"So, it is settled then," affirms Be'wick.

"We ride at dawn," says Addly. "Take good rest tonight men," he adds as he rises.

At dawn's break, Argane is in his quarters getting ready to track down M.L. Higgins. He is wearing a long flowing, black wool robe with a grey fur pelt layer lining his back and shoulders. It is fastened around his neck with a silver clasp. He has on a black, wide-brimmed, long pointed hat and black leather boots. He puts some rations of dried fruit and seeds into a small satchel, as well as some aubenite bits, emerald gems, a few red rubies and a handful of gold coins into a pouch, then places both small bags in an inside pocket. He takes a jagged, orcish dagger from his nightstand and tucks the blade pointing backward behind his belt and diagonal along his hip. He blows out the candles on his nightstand and exits the room, closing the door quietly behind him. In the archives Isla, Addly and Wezzton are quietly speaking amongst themselves when Argane arrives.

"Gentlemen," he says upon entering the room.

When the four arrive at the stables, Oren is already inside the wood shop across from it, tinkering with an object of some sort. Argane strokes Legacy's nose, before leading him out of his stall and climbing aboard. The others lead their steeds out of the stables too and mount them. Isla rides a dark horse called Solo. Addly rides a pinto called Junior and Wezzton rides a grey horse called Nitto. As they slowly take their left turn toward the stairs, Oren comes to the open doorway to wish them good luck on their mission. They make their way up the long staircase. Argane taps the hatch, reaching with the butt end of his dagger and the door grinds open. After confirming that the coast is clear, they carefully exit one after another. Wezzton who is the last, borrows Isla's staff, taps the door so it will shut, then hands it forward, returning the staff back to its owner. The weather outside is brisk and the sky is overcast…the sun is nowhere to be found behind the grey clouds. They cross the bedrock just under the icy water, cantor along the white sands of the beach and disappear into the forest's edge.

When they do, a significant gust of wind kicks up erasing any trace of their horse's hoof prints within the sand. They travel broken, narrow pathways inside the woods and along the ocean coastline. Not a word is spoken all morning. A time later, and with the sea well behind them, they reach a vast clearing. It gives way to pale yellow fields of grass. They are flat and lined with dead trees. They follow the tree line awhile until it runs parallel with a beaten path on the opposite side. They cross through an opening in the brush and onto the path. More time passes. They veer right, off the narrow trail and climb a large hill. On the other side is a small valley and at its center lies a single logwood hut. It is otherwise desolate in the valley of the hills.

"Been a while," says Isla, as they stop to examine the dwelling.

They stare for a few moments then kick-up and continue toward the bottom of the valley.

"It is nice to be out of the wind," says Addly, as they approach. The riders and the house are cloaked perfectly within the hills of the surrounding landscape. The four horsemen hitch their steeds on a post beside the structure. Before Argane can put his fist up to the front door to knock, it swings open.

"Still no horse, I see Aleeso," observes Argane.

"Oh please, no! A man is more agile on the legs he was given. After all your years friends, I am surprised you still have not figured that."

"Aye, but what about fatigue?" asks Addly. "It is for those very years the agility that you speak of somewhat dissipates, thus taking away from your position."

"Yes, and what of speed?" challenges Wezzton.

"Has it been that long in years?" Aleeso laughs… "You know me well, I am stubborn! But I'll yield from the debate. Come on in old friends, come on in."

"Did Oddfeather come to you?" asks Argane, as they stand just inside.

"Indeed, and I am delighted to accept, been a long time since I pulled a job for the seven."

"I have your payment in advance." Argane hands over one of his pouches.

"I thank you, so why not contact the assemblage for this?"

"No sense in dealing with them for such a man," answers Argane.

"An easy target, eh? so you believe me skilled enough then," quips Aleeso.

"After your accomplishments spanning more than a few dealings. I shall not humor you with gratuitous praise."

Aleeso laughs again.

"Besides…you are good enough to work on your own, why pay for the assemblage to appoint another we haven't done business with, just to have the poor bugger taxed before he even starts out," interjects Isla.

"Aye," agrees Aleeso. "So, any special requests?"

"Only that is done quietly," says Argane, "no unnecessary mess, no outlandish theatrics. Like it was stated in the letter…tonight after supper…he will likely be at the Inn above the watering hole called 'The Sleuth'. He will be drunk by then if not already."

Aleeso twists and bends over to remove something from his boot.

"This then shall do the trick."

He holds in his hand a small twig. He pulls the top end of the small, inconspicuous canister off and dumps a bit of black powder into his hand. "A wonderful combination of Seyusine and Arsenic!" exclaims Aleeso. "An odd combo yes, but I assure you there are few better concoctions and if your man is indeed a drunkard, it will be almost too easy! I will spike his drink, and the silly witless fellow will be finished fast. In, out, done."

"Good," says Argane, outstretching his arm and patting Aleeso on the shoulder.

The thin, white-haired, violet eyed, pale young man dressed in a fine black and orange satin body suit, tucks his chin length, wavy hair behind his ears and after smiling wryly, he caps the poison and slips it back into his boot. The men bid Aleeso fare well, wish him luck and are back outside.

"Ice elves," says Wezzton as the men turn out their horses and start out for the valley's hills.

They ride well and arrive at Splendor's boundary late in the afternoon. The quaint village is not guarded or fortified. Two story, run-down buildings line the main road. They are wooden and grey. It is obvious that the village is of little prosperity. The four men stop and converse briefly. Wezzton rides around to the far end of town and sets himself up near a large bush, not far beyond the perimeter. Argane and Isla then ride into Splendor leaving Addly behind. They hitch up and dismount right outside The Sleuth. It is rowdy within the tavern. Whoops, hollers and clanking cups and bottles emanate from the door-less front entry way.

"Happy hour," says Isla.

The pair enter and lean against the bar-counter. A few cheers erupt from some patrons inside the crowd upon recognizing Argane.

"Which room is Morbit Len Higgins?" asks Isla, of the barkeeper.

"Oh, that horrid fellow a friend of yours?" asks the big man behind the bar.

"Would not think you two to be a friend to such filth," he adds. Argane shoots the man a look of disdain.

"Just the room number," says Isla.

"Right…six," replies the man.

The two wizards leave and walk upstairs.

"An assuming man…they are the worst kind," says Argane. As they reach the top, they find 'six' at the end of the hall on their right. From outside the door, they can hear the voice of a woman.

"You can be a real creep! You know that?"

"I…m…m'lady…am a g-great man and will be a lord someday!" says M.L., drunk as predicted.

"A lord!" she exclaims before laughing loudly.

Isla knocks heavily.

"W…what, who is there? …I said I am busy!" yells M.L.

"You are too much, let me answer it this time! One might need something important. I'm getting it!" shouts the woman.

There is a series of thuds and the door swings open.

"Hello, fair lady, we have business with this fellow alone and it will take but a short while. You can wait right out here, yes?" says Argane before dropping a ruby into her hand.

"Wow!" exclaims the petite, inebriated woman, "what do you do? A smith? Oh, oh—carpentry!"

Argane chuckles. "I work a jinniwink," he says. Looking tired and confused she slumps down and sits on the floor cross-legged. "Now if anyone should come up and want in here, you holler…understand?"

"You got it mister," agrees the woman.

The men enter the room. They close and lock the door. M.L. is almost asleep on the bed. Isla shakes his head and leans back against the door. Argane goes across the room to an open curtained window and shuts it. He walks back and sits on a chair at the foot of the bed. The wizards stare at the disgraced ex-mayor and then at each other for a moment. Argane stands up and puts his hand over the now fully passed-out Higgins. He releases a plume of cloudy, white energy that slowly envelopes the bed, encapsulating the traitor in a milky oval orb, similar to the green squall, though it functions the very opposite. Isla then comes forward and drops his staff through the barrier and onto M.L.'s eye from above, poking him hard.

"What the!" shouts the man. As he jumps up, he bumps his head on the translucent oval's ceiling and falls back down grabbing his teary eye and his sore cranium. Argane sits back down. Higgins pulls himself up carefully. He rests on his elbows and squints pathetically as tears stream from his eye and down his sweaty, red, puffy cheeks.

"Ahh! Rubbish," he says, as Argane comes into view. "Bullocks!" he adds.

"You did not think you would really be able to hide?" asks Argane.

"M.L. grunts…did not think much of it at all!"

"Clearly," adds Isla.

"Ah geez, you too!"

"Aye," says Isla with a nod.

"Do not you old coots ever just die 'of old age'?"

Isla laughs and Argane grins.

"Just as soon as you die of overabundance," says Isla.

"Can I have my drink?"

"After," says Argane… "You will get your booze…but first…talk. What did you gain? …and what do they know?"

"They knew you would be near, to challenge their directive. That is all, I told them that and told you all nothing…a big deal," he says, with sarcasm.

"So, they knew all the time…the scroll was compromised."

"Yes, but you never got involved as such before, I just gave them a heads-up."

"But why?"

"Why else? …spoils! Money, riches…immunity."

"Immunity! But you had that through us."

"Did I? …The high king offers much more power with his security. Do not flatter yourselves!"

"So that's it?"

"No! I said money, did I not?"

"Typical of an old, snake oil hustling, failed warlock. That is all you care…money! don't dare speak of security."

"You're right, I care not for that or this land! You all can kill yourselves…destroy it if you must," says M.L. "Do not take me for 'Utzik Oddly'. I am far less glorious. My motives were simple ones," he adds.

"Aye, far less glorious and far less intelligent too," says Isla.

"Next to that name, you are but a parasite," says Argane. "You could have been positively important beyond your very comprehension to a cause greater than you'll ever know and yet you squandered it for riches and drink," says Argane.

"So be it," mutters Higgins.

"What I shared wasn't much of a tip anyway. You all were to stand by in wait. I disrupted little."

"But we could have saved people, saved the girl."

M.L. laughs. "Oh, yes the girl, the sacred little girl," he says sarcastically.

"Our savior was the girl, was it? Well, they have her and they too believe so strongly as do you all. Ha…fools, every one of you! Any intelligent being would have taken her before the fact…Your ridiculous plan was nonsense just the same! I got paid enough to disappear forever and you all can have your rebellion…your tomorrow war. Who needs it? My world is just fine. You characters are all the same…now let me be!"

Argane rises and opens the window. He peers outside onto the main road.

"If you got paid enough to disappear," he says before averting his eyes back to M.L. "you did well in that regard, to be sure and disappear you shall. Where is the girl?" he asks as he drops a gem into the white squall and onto his lap.

"He is disappointed in her. She is displaying little potential. He has her at his kingdom. If she does not start showing progress soon, they will sell her to Looka's bizarre in Sallinfell. Looka will then sell her to some baddies for slavery. That is the last I have heard of it…though knowing him perhaps he'll have her killed merely because he is annoyed."

"When would Looka receive her, if he did?" urges Argane.

"They turn out all their child slaves every waning gibbous… unless there is a disturbance for this or that matter, in which case the children are dropped under the following waxing crescent."

"Enjoy your 'spoils'," replies Argane before heading to the door. He then snaps his fingers, and the white squall vanishes.

"You know if you were not intoxicated all of the time you could use your wits to defend and ward yourself more clearly from such temptations."

"Yes, and if you were smart you would have killed me after you got what you needed and not paid me!" M.L. musters thunderous laughter that goes on for more than it should for a man in his position. "Are you that soft these days?" he adds. Argane turns to him and winks before exiting the room with Isla and closing the door.

Later that night, after supper down at the tavern below, M.L. retires, back up at room six and is doing even more drinking. This time he is alone and hiccupping profusely as he stumbles around, looking for yet another bottle of alcohol amongst his things on the dresser opposite the foot of the bed. The big man finds one, uncorks it and takes a long, steady guzzle, drinking almost all of it. He slams it back down onto the dresser and wobbles over to the bed. He begins to clumsily dump money from his pockets onto the mattress. Aleeso slowly appears at the window and quietly pushes it open further from the outside, within the shadows. The noise from patrons below is at an all-time high. His face is well hidden by the large, black hood flopped over his forehead. He climbs in through the window frame without a sound and strides past the drunkard, silently to the nearby dresser. He quickly and carefully dumps all the poison into the bottle of alcohol. Higgins still fumbling with his money is oblivious to Aleeso's presence. The elusive young man waits until

Higgins turns around and then spins alongside him until he is the one facing the bed. M.L. snatches the mead from the dresser and while he is steady finishing the poisoned contents of the bottle Aleeso glides back to the window and leans against its frame without a peep, he uses the curtains to further cloak himself. He watches closely while the man chugs, putting back every toxic drop. M.L. grimaces and looks at the bottle, stumbles hard and releases it, it falls to the floor with a clank. He stumbles again and backs into the bed prompting him to fall onto it in a seated position. After a moment, he begins to grab at his chest, followed by his throat. He then proceeds to cough and wheeze and froth at the mouth.

A few more moments pass until he stands up then falls to his knees. As he clutches his neck tightly, he begins grunting and gurgling violently. Aleeso releases the curtains. "Psst…fat man," he whispers from the window.

Higgins struggles to stand and falls down, forward onto his stomach. He turns his head up and looks his assassin in the eyes.

"Argane…" he musters before entering a fit of convulsions.

"You drink too much," says Aleeso, as he casually walks over to the chair by the bed and takes a seat. He crosses his legs and watches the big man die.

M.L.'s seizures dissipate slowly. He mumbles and drools a short while before the light leaves his eyes, they roll back in his head, and he is still. All is quiet in room number six. Aleeso collects the money from the atop the mattress and everywhere else the traitor had stashed any. Soon, without a sound, the assassin exits out the window from where he came.

18.
A Search for Nya

Late that evening Isla, Addly and Wezzton arrive back at Ergo's coast in Old Crimsinth. They park and water their horses and join up with Be'wick who has been sitting in wait. The three disclose what had transpired. They inform their headmaster that Aleeso was more than happy to formally accept their proposal, how they found M.L. Higgins and what he had said of his betrayal and furthermore how Argane had decided it best to carry on to Sallinfell to investigate Looka's Bizarre, in case there was any chance of bringing Nya to safety now and reunite her with her big brother.

"Looka's is only a day's ride south of Splendor, let us hope Argane's follow-up proves fruitful," says Be'wick.

The next morning at breakfast the children are inquisitive as to Argane's whereabouts.

Be'wick slyly plays down the issue by simply stating that he has traveled over to a small, nearby village and is visiting an old friend. The last thing he wants to do is initiate any false hopes into William's young heart and mind.

Across the land somewhere between Splendor and Sallinfell Argane is dousing a small fire. He pets Legacy a moment before giving him water and continuing down the trail. Later on, he passes a man riding a horse heading the opposite way.

He glares at the stranger closely, just in case he is a potential threat. He is not.

Argane arrives at Sallinfell in the late morning.

It is a much bigger community than that of its neighboring town of Splendor and the place is moderately fortified, however it lacks any official guards. Most of the buildings are made of wood, though there are larger stone structures scattered throughout.

Argane hitches Legacy to a cross-post set just inside the front entrance's threshold and starts out walking through the main road. There are Sallinfellian citizens all over. They seem pleasant and merry as they go about their business. There is a lot more hustle and bustle than expected. He had been there more than a few times before but back then Sallinfell was a drab and dreary place. A community, like most others, greatly affected by the evil high king's dark reign. It warms Argane's heart to see the town prospering, at least on the surface. It doesn't take much to notice that there is an annual festival underway. As the wizard mingles about, a boy tells him that they have one every other fortnight, on the number. There are jesters, circus acts, fire gobblers, men on stilts, a joust tournament and yes, exactly what Argane has come for…sales merchants. He walks slowly through the boisterous crowds, browsing vendor to vendor, looking for Looka and his stock of children. Soon he arrives at a merchant who looks more beggar than businessman. He sits alone behind a shoddy table. There is a boy and a girl both sitting atop a pile of hay beside him. They look bored, tired and in desperate need of a bath.

"Ye interested elder?" asks the skinny, grubby, toothless man as he stands up.

The vendor's leather armor helmet ear flaps are tattered and tangled up in his long greasy hair.

"Yes merchant," replies Argane.

"Oh good, now only the girl is available. A lovely couple put a deposit on the boy earlier this mornin.'"

"I see, they seem like good folks, boy?"

The boy says yes happily which immediately puts Argane at ease.

"Does she have a name?" he asks, returning his eyes to the salesman.

"Yes, she is called Ariel."

Argane nods. "How much?"

"Eight gold coins, fine sir."

He then takes his pouch from an inside pocket, counts the gold and drops it on the table.

"Come, child," he says warmly, and she does.

"Thank you, sir!" Argane neglects returning his expected, "you are welcome." to the trafficker.

"All good things, young one," he says to the boy before making his way back through the crowd.

"Where are you from Ariel?" he asks, putting out his hand for the tiny girl to hold as they walk.

I am from 'Truth and Promises', she answers, in a voice that matches her size.

"That's a longways off. Were you given up by your parents? ...or were you taken from them?"

"They died," she says, "the ones they call the 'night walkers' took me to the king after the fire."

"You mean the Moonrakers?"

"Maybe."

"You must have been scared?"

"At first," she replies.

"On our voyage home, I will speak of my other children and maybe you can talk of your experience in the kingdom?"

"Okay," she says innocently.

"Sir?" "Yes? my name is Argane dear."

"Argane dear...am I safe now?"

...The wizard smiles softly. "Yes, young one...you are safe now."

Back down the trail Ariel is set in front of Argane atop Legacy. They ride slowly.

"How long were you there, in the kingdom?"

"Not sure, felt like a long time, but I do not know."

"Were there other children?"

"Mhm."

"Several?"

"Yep."

"What did you all do there?"

"We were kept in cages a lot." Argane shuts his eyes in sorrow.

"We did not get food much and we had to clean the castle all the time. There were ugly giants who pushed and pulled us around and witches...awful witches. They would claim we knew special tricks and would yell and scream at us. They would try to teach us things...things most of us could not learn. The few girls that could, were taken to the towers."

"The towers?" inquires Argane.

"Yes, I know not why."

"Well, you are going to enjoy yourself where we are going."

"I am?" asks Ariel excitedly.

"Yes, there are many old souls like me, and we even have some children too. Boys and girls just about your age. How old are you, Ariel?"

"Six!" she exclaims.

"We have young ones from seven, all the way to eleven."

"You do? Boys and girls?"

"Yes, in fact a little girl called Sara, was six not that long ago. You will have your very own bed, lots of good food and you do not have to do chores you do not want to do…oh, oh and we only have one witch, but she is a good which."

The young little girl is left beaming as she stares off ahead of them.

"Can I ask one more thing?"

"Yes."

"Did you ever meet a girl at the kingdom whose name is Nya?"

"Umm, yes! She was nice…she was taken to the west-end tower, I think."

Argane rides steady and crosses the moonlit beach of Ergo's coast late that evening. He walks Legacy along the rock beneath the surf and disappears inside the bunkers. Most of the rooms are dark when they make their way to the dining room. They pass the basement archives to find Constance seated on a lavish cushioned chair reading a book, with Hope the cat nestled on her lap. Argane stops in to introduce Ariel and make some immediate arrangements.

"I am sure she is very hungry and if you can stay with her tonight, then in the morrow we will prepare her quarters."

"We would be delighted. Come child," says Constance. Argane carries on and arrives in the dining room to find Be'wick at his place at the end of the table drinking a hot beverage. He sits down in the chair closest to him and speaks: "Higgins' motive was money, Aleeso took care of him…Nya was not there…the slaver had two young ones however, a boy who was already accounted for and a girl…Ariel…she is with Constance."

Be'wick ponders a moment.

"We certainly are acquiring a rather large family." Be'wick's stated observation makes Argane laugh deeply, it prompts him to relax for the first time in days. His posture slumps. He crosses his arms and leans forward, resting them on the table… "We are indeed," he agrees. "There is a bit more," adds Argane.

"Aye?"

"Ariel had known Nya. It seems when a child displays a lack potential for that of wielding magic, they are sold off and if they do…the high king stashes them in the castle's towers. That is all she knew on the matter…whether put there to be imprisoned or killed I do not know."

"Perhaps they are kept and brainwashed…made to be allies…will broke by hand and wits twisted by word to be thereby used for evil biddings." After a few moments in silence, Be'wick announces his retirement for the night and takes his leave.

Argane chooses to remain at the table, until the last candle goes dim.

19.

Physical Education and Practical Magic

The following morning after Ariel has been introduced to everyone and breakfast has been consumed, most of the children are in the woods with some of their elders. They are practicing their archery. Constance and Whisspella have taken the youngest two, Sara and Ariel to Marple Weary's place. The ones outside are lined up in front of a distant row of targets. All of them are placed meticulously within some juniper bushes. It is clear that Leo and Hayden have the most experience. They shoot arrows well with their bows. Argane and Wezzton pace slowly behind the children, observing each one of them acutely. Isla and Addly are nearby and seated separately on two large tree stumps. They flank the group and evidently are keeping close watch for whoever might encroach upon their chosen training site.

"It is time to see what Delilah Rose is made of," says Argane, once he gets to William, stopping his stride with his hands behind his back.

"And how does the wrist guard fit?" asks Wezzton.

"Great," says William, looking to his right hand. "I owe Oren a great many thanks."

"Has she worked well?" asks Argane.

"I have not shot one arrow as yet."

"Do you mind?"

"Of course not…" When William is ready, he raises his bow, squeezes down on the grip and pulls back on the string, guiding his arrow just so. Suddenly Poe cheers from down the line, he has hit the bullseye of his target. William waits a few seconds to regain his composure then fires. His arrow hits the top right quadrant of the target, so close to the edge that had it been any further outward the arrow would have missed it completely and whistled off into the woods.

"Again," says Argane.

William takes another arrow from his quiver, sets the shaft onto the rest, guides the sight window up level with his eye and draws back the string. He squints, focusing ahead to the target, holds a moment and releases. The second shot is closer to the center but still well wide.

"Good young one, you just need get used to her," says Argane, before continuing his rounds.

After lunch at their indoor stables, Argane, Isla, Wezzton and Oren are focused on teaching the children the art of swordplay. They oppose each other one on one. William is the most inexperienced, but eager to learn. He concentrates as the men and other children instruct him their ways and enjoys himself when watching from the sidelines. Argane stays with him. The two lean against Windimere's stall as Mila and Hayden clash wooden blades.

"She is really something!" says William of Mila's skills with her short sword.

"She is," agrees Argane.

"Why do we fight within the stables?" asks William. Windimere neighs.

Argane smiles. He is happy the boy had asked.

"We do this not only for close quarter contact, but also so that our horses are used to commotion and chaos. They are being practiced just as all of you are, but we do head outside as well, to varying locations with more space from time to time."

William looks around studying the frightened faces of each horse. It is somewhat telling of what they shall one day experience on a much larger scale. For William, it seems so far away…a time when he will fight alongside his friends and elders with those very horses.

Later, Whisspella comes down to pass on Be'wick's message that dinner has been prepared.

Argane holds William back until all the children exit the stables. He guides him to a small, meticulously organized tool room. There is a large chest on a workbench. He opens it.

"You have your Often blade, Delilah Rose and now you have the 'Flaming heart'," proclaims Argane, as he hands William a flawless, shimmering and, razor sharp steel sword…It is almost as long as the boy is tall. He grasps the golden handle and marvels at the detail within it. There is a small heart engraved into the metal on the hand guard, it is surrounded by markings that he cannot decipher, and the handle is wrapped tightly in green cloth below the hilt. The blade starts wide at the base and is beveled at its edges, it narrows gradually to a diamond tipped point and gleams as he turns it over, further inspecting it.

"I do not know what to say. It is exquisite. I am over-whelmed…thank you."

"One day you will unleash it with an acutely applied expertise," says Argane.

The boy looks at the flaming heart again and this time it feels heavy in his hands.

"You are not big enough to use it yet…but you will be. We present all the children here with their own custom swords. None of you are skilled enough as yet, so don't take personally that yours too will not be wielded 'til your older."

"What are the inscriptions?" asks William.

"Spells…special spells…they coincide with the weapon. When you are ready, you will learn it's enchantments."

The next morning after breakfast, every soul within the underwater fortress with the exception of Oren make their way down to the lowest level, past the workshop and the stables. The hallway has no mounted torches and darkens considerably, prompting Be'wick to illuminate his staff as he leads the group to what seems like a dead end…He presses firmly upon an inconspicuous stone block just above the floor, within the wall. It and the five others stacked on top of it then slide upward disappearing further into the stonework above. He continues through the passageway into a large room. Inside, Addly begins to meticulously light the torches that line the secret space one after the other. He ignites them with flames that stream effortlessly from his fingertips. Wezzton makes his way to the center. There is a fire-pit in an impression in the floor. It is lined with large, raised blocks. He crouches to one knee and lights the stacked set of logs with two fireballs that he pushes easily from the palms of his hands. Quickly the room is revealed as it lights up brightly. The ceiling is very high, and the walls are distant and square to one another.

It is one of the largest chambers in the fortress and has no passageways other than the hidden one they entered through. There are long counters with stools lining much of the walls. There are varying tools and alchemy instruments strewn about their surfaces. There are potions and elixirs in glass jars, beakers of all sorts and colorful ingredients loose among the counter tops and pouring out of open burlap sacks. The elders and young ones alike fall in to form in preparation to participate in things that have come second nature to them.

"What are we doing here?" asks William.

"Magic!" replies Argane.

"Every day we work on certain skills…we alternate physical and magical just about every other day. At week's end, we enjoy leisure time and that is what we do here…we never deviate from those commitments so that when the time comes, we will all be ready. William's eyes scan his surroundings curiously. Some of the children are exerting colorful energy forces from their hands with the wizards while he sees that Constance and Whisspella are settling in at a long counter under a torch with Poe, Hayden, Clari and Ariel. Appalonia and Rufus are with them too."

"Why are Leo, Mila and Sara over with the men, while the others are with the women?" asks William.

"The ones with Constance and Whisspella are not capable of executing physical magic yet and may never be. We know little about Ariel…she is too new to us. Today they will work on other outward forms of which are equally important but where naturally occurring magic doesn't necessarily matter as much, such as casting spells from legendary texts or working on alchemy which is a study and procedure of mixing magical elements and ingredients to create powerful concoctions. The others, however, are going to focus on their given strengths, their inner ones so that one day they are able to use the might and magic within them to their utmost potential. What makes you so special is there may be no limit to what you can learn. Everyone else in our known history other than the high king of course, can only utilize as much magic as they were born with…what is engrained in them. They can hone it and make their internal arsenal stronger and faster. They can learn certain spells and such, but their range and potential are bound and limited…but yours may not be."

William deeply studies the children dealing their magic across the room, as if accepting his destiny further as he watches closely.

"Shall you show us what you have got?" asks Argane.

"Um…okay," says William, still watching the others. His mentor leads him towards them.

"Do you always practice in here?" inquires the boy.

"No, we have some areas we like to use up top but obviously, this is much safer. They reach the spot by the far corner of the room."

The other children stop what they are doing. William stands before them, and they back up to give him clearance.

"Well, I…I carry fire," says William. He then holds his open hands out, palms up and excretes two small fireballs from them. The spheres spin and crackle as they hover above each hand. They significantly brighten the space around him, as they dance and spark.

"I can shoot 'em hard," he adds before allowing them to slowly extinguish. "I have water power. I also have a form of thicker fluid that I can use. I can shoot it as well…sorta like my fire…I guess," he says, as two wobbly orbs gather above his palms.

"I am not exactly certain what this is made of," he says of the gelatinous, luminescent, blue liquid. The orbs bend and move as the boy holds them up for display. The other children gasp in awe. "It is definitely pliable," he says as he pushes them together into one. Just then Clari shouts out a series of words in which William has never heard before. He looks over to observe that she is trying in vain to accomplish a spell of sorts with Whisspella's guidance.

"We will experiment with this substance soon," says Argane.

William prompts the mysterious blue mass to dissolve and continues. "I have a light power that I will not do here as I am not confident that I could contain it in such a small place, and it can be blinding. There are magnetic powers, wind controls, invisible feats etc.…I have other types too, but I need much more space."

"We shall anticipate witnessing the water power, light, and any others you have another day," says Be'wick from the small audience.

"That is fine William…just fine," says Argane, as he approaches the boy.

"Great stuff!" William! exclaims Mila. "That blue stuff is incredible!"

Be'wick directs the others to continue with their practices.

Argane takes William to another part of the chamber, where Isla is shaking and knocking on a wooden wand. The table at which he is seated is covered in them.

"The children here have not yet succeeded in any, but I would like to give you a quick run through on enchanting...Do you know the meaning of the word?" asks Argane.

"No, not really."

"It is okay William, take a wand in hand...to enchant is to inject one's magical will into any thing or object outside of your own being. Enchantments can be given also through spells; however, the caster usually must be of expert level or better in that regard. Physically given enchantments can be accomplished by a lesser experienced entity, but this day and age both such occurrences are rare."

"Good show, boy William," says Isla, as he puts a wooden branch into the boy's hand. "Now, we do not expect you to accomplish such a feat for a while, but we will give you an introduction all the same...In many cases a wand or staff must be meditated on for a long time until eventually it begins to absorb and accept your will gradually. Lifeless things are of the most difficult than those of the living but are better controlled, much longer lasting and so much more useful. Close your eyes and focus on a power." Isla barely has the word out of his mouth when suddenly a stream of odorless green smoke gently pours out of the end of the stick. William raises his eyebrows a bit. Argane's eyes widen in surprise. He looks to Isla who appears shocked. The elders begin to cough within the small cloud. William prompts the power to fade. Isla waves his arms in the air to help better dissipate its leavings. "What was that young one?" he asks.

"I think it's a poison of some kind," replies William. "I'm sorry," he adds.

"Come, let us continue," says Argane.

"That is your wand now...and do keep it locked away in your chest when not in your grasp," says Isla, as they begin to walk away.

"Thank you," says the boy graciously. They arrive to Constance and Whisspella's area. Argane whispers to the older woman of the two, she then takes her children to join the others and hustles back.

"What are some of your standard spells?" he asks, of the young witch. She sits up on her stool and pulls a pile of books closer to her. She flips through them one by one, sliding most of them along the counter and back from where they came.

"Hmm, perhaps something elemental? maybe a size restraint? no, no...metal or mineral manipulation...either/ or..."

"Then either will do," says Argane.

"Are you doing good?" asks Appalonia in her small voice. She is hovering aglow above Constance's shoulder. William shrugs. The young woman goes through the largest, thickest book of her chosen stack.

"Ah, here are some," she says, turning it sideways so that Argane can better read it from where he stands. He bends over slightly and squints. Whisspella points to a small paragraph.

"Good," he says. He then takes a small, purple, tourmaline gemstone from his robe and puts it on the center crease of the open book. He takes it in his hands and lowers it so that William can better see the script.

"Can you read those three words? And when you do…feel them."

"Enok Sellemen Kelnum," says the boy. The little purple stone quickly turns into a shiny chunk of gold metal. Argane looks to Constance. She gasps in awe, just as the children had, when the boy displayed his undefined blue mass.

"Good going!" shouts the fairy, flapping her wings, excitedly.

"Come boy William, we have much to go over," says Argane. The pair exit the hidden room.

Late that night after dinner and everyone had cleaned up and done their share of reading, the only sounds to be heard in the fortress are the low voices of Argane and William. They speak by candlelight in the boy's quarters at the small table across from the foot of his bed where Appalonia lays asleep. Rufus listens intently.

"Obviously, your biological magic, your physical magic, are both extremely strong…you possess immense power on each side of the spectrum. You are pure natural," says Argane. The candle flickers. He continues, "The elders here will help you develop both and harness them…we will focus on many new things for you as well, so you become well rounded in every possible way. The uprising has been building in secret for a long time, but now that we have you, it will occur sooner than we had anticipated. We will notify our allies to form and train their armies now, not later. To accomplish this, some of our circle will ride and meet with various leaders. Oddfeather will fly for us, and Oren has six ravens who are excellent messengers, they will also take flight to spread the word ahead of our commute. In the time to come, you shall lead a rebellion William, a revolution…peasants, noblemen, the wealthy and the royal will rally in our cause. William stares at his mentor.

"What say you? ...young one?"

"We shall have a grand army," answers the boy.

"The masses William...all have been eager for so long. Great leaders at power points all over, lay patiently in wait to heed our call."

"How will I know I am ready?"

"Thayddeus must die by your hand...and die he will. When you are ready, we will know...both of us."

"And if I cannot tell?"

"You will...our good world depends upon it...When I went away, I found Mayor Higgins."

The boy perks up in his seat.

"He told me greed of money was his motive for double-crossing us and Little Augustine...and I was able to obtain a great piece of information. It led me to the place where I found little Ariel. She told a story we believe reliable. She said the high king has Nya captive within a tower in his castle."

Argane searches the boy's face for some reaction, but it is blank.

"Will she live? ...Will she be there when we arrive?" he asks, suppressing his emotions.

"If we do not find a means to rescue her beforehand and must wait for the strike...yes, I believe she will be, all the same."

"I do not understand his interest in her, perhaps it is to lure me and bait us into a trap."

"I do not think he knows for certain what he's after...though he was looking for a girl all along, remember? she may possess potential...may deem useful to him...after all she is your first blood sister, but that also means she is smart and resourceful, and knows how to preserve herself."

William lowers his head.

"He thinks she is the one," says William, in a low grief-stricken voice.

"I am sorry, William, but this is the reality upon which we have been given."

A moment passes until the boy brings his head up and wipes the tears from his face.

"Yes, I understand," he says. "At first, this all sounded unbelievable and was overwhelming but the more we are together, the more I have made peace with my destiny...with ours. I feel...anxious and...excited for our cause," says William, flashing a quick uncontrollable smile.

"There was a fire set inside you William…the day your family was taken…and it will grow and grow, until you are consumed with an undeniable need to make things right."

"I feel it," he sniffs… "I shall not tire, nor will I ever stop…until this is done."

20.
Another Annihilation

The next morning as dawn is breaking through the treetops, Oren is returning from the hills with a bucket of twinkleberries. He is near the beach on his way back to the fortress when he spots something moving about on the shoreline. Upon closer inspection, a white dove comes into focus. It marches and skitters as it paces back and forth in the sand. He wonders about the significance of the bird's presence as he carefully approaches.

A messenger perhaps? Maybe it is hurt? he ponders. Most anyone wishing to send communication has their flyers enter through a specified pigeonhole. Oren crouches before the dove. Bound to its leg is a small cylinder canister. He gently unties it. The bird flies off immediately. Inside, is a tightly rolled paper scroll, with a tiny wax seal that Oren does not recognize. He wastes no time hustling the message to Be'wick, who is reading in the main archives. He is the first one awake and never misses his early morning studies. The head wizard quickly sits up.

"It is Splendor, they are under attack!"

"Is there time?" asks Oren, without hesitation.

"Not likely. We shall soon see. They'll need immediate aid regardless. Alert Argane! Tell him to appoint another to go with him."

"Aye," replies Oren. He leaves post haste.

"Moonrakers," mutters Be'wick.

At ground level, Argane and Wezzton ride hard through woods enroute back to Splendor. They are hopeful they can arrive in time to at least assist any survivors the invaders may have left behind and learn something more about the high king Thayddeus' recent objective. On the journey, the courageous wizards only let up their gallop when absolutely necessary turning what is usually a couple days ride into one.

Finally, at Splendor, dusk has fully set in. The sky is dark blue with giant streaks of orange and pink smeared across it. The men slowly stop their horses and dismount by the main entrance to town.

"It is quiet as a tomb," says Wezzton.

"We are far too late," observes Argane. They tread carefully, guiding their horses into town. Within the main road, there are lifeless bodies strewn about. Men, women and children are dead and bloodied. Mangled in the streets, upon porches and staircases. They are on balconies and roofs. Some burnt heaps that once stood as proud homes, are still smoldering.

"Another massacre, courtesy of the high king," scoffs Wezzton in anger.

As they go, the men are meticulously roving the area keeping mindful as to not accidentally step on any bodies or in any puddles of blood.

"The moonrakers butcher with such unprecedented savagery," adds Wezzton.

They continue acutely sifting through the bodies with their eyes for any souls that may still have breath within them. At the towns threshold a small animal quickly runs by their horses. It's eyes glow red. Legacy grunts.

Time passes with the duo searching the scene on foot and as the stars slowly reveal themselves, their confidence dwindles and the hope of finding anyone fated to live all but vanishes. They circle back to the entrance.

"We shall ride on," orders Argane.

"Will we make camp on our way home then?" asks Wezzton.

"We are not going home," says Argane, as he pulls himself up onto his horse.

"To where are we going?"

"I have a feeling."

"A feeling? …Argane do enlighten."

"There are only two towns amidst this part of the northeast coastal region…after that you would be into a fortnight on horseback."

"Please proceed," urges Wezzton.

"Sallinfell," announces Argane.

The men ride fast under the starry night's sky, demanding peak performance from their horses once again as not to waste a second. Later after a brief rest and with dawn approaching, the dull light from orange flames can be seen burning holes into the landscape, far off in the distance.

"There!" shouts Argane loudly. They get closer to Sallinfell's perimeter and to another horrific scene.

This one however is not quite finished…within the smoke, fire and dead bodies are disturbing shrieks and screams of terror as some of the moonrakers still linger to carry out their last acts of brutality.

"Halt!" shouts Argane to Wezzton who is galloping significantly faster than he. Wezzton prompts his steed to do so, and he rears up hard, letting out a strong bellow.

"They mustn't see you! Watch your impulses, you know this!"

"Where are the moonraker's guards? They usually have hundreds! Where are they?" exclaims Wezzton.

"It has been a long night for them, perhaps they have headed on to let some youngers finish up."

The innocent victims' shouts sound off sporadically.

"There are but a few beasts! Let us go take them together!" urges Wezzton.

"You know what they can do!" says Argane in a stern voice. "You stay back, should I fall, it will be alone, and you will serve as witness and take our story home."

"But I can help!" shouts the younger wizard frantically.

"They are like iron and know not of fear. We cannot risk succumbing to fatalities in vain!" exclaims Argane.

"We have not challenged their kind in years, and they have never been so few! What about our studies?"

More screams ring out.

"They are still more than a formidable opponent!" returns the elder wizard.

He peers into the fires and at some of the struggling citizens.

"Do not make me regret this. Hyah" he says, as he kicks up his horse, directing him to gallop toward the burning town. Wezzton follows. The pair jump off their steeds just outside the front gates.

Argane whispers in Legacy's ear and the horse begins to trot away. Wezzton then instructs Nitto to follow. He does. The men peek around the stone columns of the open entrance way. Four moonrakers are stomping through the area and savagely bludgeoning to death anyone they come across who is not quite dead yet. They are very tall, extremely muscular and are lightly armored in leather and wear fur pieces. They lumber, carrying large melee weapons. Two hold steel maces, one a lavish brandistock and one has a rusty scythe. When not using their weaponry to finish their victims off, the rakers stomp them to death.

"We must make our move," says Wezzton.

"I will head straight up to them," adds Argane. "You maneuver along the rooftops and send down any force you see fit to help do them in with." Wez nods but before he can move Argane grabs his shoulder.

"Stay sharp," he says.

"Of course," replies Wezzton with a grin. He disappears behind a network of buildings. Argane takes his crooked dagger from his hip and proceeds to walk through the village weaving around the bloodied bodies. He grasps his blade in his left hand and holds it outward from his side. When he is close enough, he raises his right hand with his palm facing the stars. A large translucent purple orb of energy builds up and swirls just above. The subtle glow of burning buildings envelope the fight scene, causing everything along the lights' boundaries to silhouette in a black. He lets loose a loud, booming battle cry. It demands the moonrakers' attention. They stop what they are doing and turn to face their challenger. He shoots the ball at the closest raker. It explodes onto the left side of his torso sending countless sparkling particles of purple and white all over. The moonraker grunts loudly as the energy burns and twists him around, forcing him to fall on one knee. It drops its weapon with a thud as it grabs at the crater in its chest. Just then two teal streaks of light rain down one after the other from a nearby rooftop. They whistle as they fly fast and knock the unarmed raker further over and onto his side, taking chunks out of its body. Argane keeps the monster down with an unseen energy by his right hand and walks toward him. Wezzton continues shooting into the other three moonraker's vicinity.

As Argane gets close to the downed beast, it is able to break the wizards will with a mighty flail of his arms but before he can rise to his feet completely, Argane is quick to collect himself and bury his dagger deep into the slow-footed moonrakers temple. He begins to send fireballs from his free hand at the next closest raker, setting it aflame immediately. It manages to stay on its feet. Argane removes his dagger and runs toward it. The monster is disoriented when he sinks the blue blood drenched blade into its neck. It falls forward and continues to burn. Up above, Wezzton deploys vivid waves of red energy in which he does not stop emitting as he pounds the last two moonrakers into submission. The power appears frigid and is long pointed as the red streaks shatter upon impacting with the beasts. Argane squares off with the third moonraker, sending a series of white light blasts directly at him, blinding him for a moment. They quickly get close and engage in hand-to-hand combat. Wezzton drops from the roof to fight the fourth one directly. Argane's combatant swings and misses several times with his brandistock. Finally, the raker connects his weapon firmly with Argane's side. He cries out in pain and drops his dagger. The raker knocks off the wizard's hat, grabs him by his face and begins to squeeze, surely trying to crush it in his large hand. He easily lifts Argane off the ground by his head, displaying his gargantuan height. The struggling wizard sets his right hand ablaze and grasps the moonrakers face with a smuck. The raker releases him and takes hold of his melted face. He is blinded by the liquified grey-blue skin in his eyes. Argane collects and grips his blade, thrusting it hard into the rakers stomach three times in succession. The third raker falls. Argane observes that Wezzton is keeping his own nearby so does not hurry there to intervene. As he slowly retrieves his hat and walks toward the fight, the younger wizard's left punch is slipped and the moonraker upper cuts him with the blunt end of his mace splitting his chin wide-open. Argane shoots a fireball and sets the moonraker's upper body on fire. Wezzton recovers quickly and from point blank range shoots his teal energy straight into the raker's face, knocking him violently on his rear end. Argane now just a few strides away tosses Wezzton his dagger. Wiping the blood from his gash, he observes the last raker. It is critically immobilized and missing its jaw.

    He stabs the monster deep, right through the top of his head. The tip of the blade protrudes exposed out of the roof of the beast's mouth. It goes limp. Wezzton lets it drop over on its back before retrieving the blade.

    "Well," says Wezzton, catching his breath… "we did good then…eh?" blood drips steadily from the split on his chin.

    Argane looks at him plainly. "Aye…quite alright, so long as there are not anymore," he says. "Had not this been an ambush, we might have done much worse."

    Wezzton laughs, though nodding yes in agreement. He hands Argane his dagger. "They are colossal creatures! And certainly, do take a whooping."

    "We should scour for survivors," says Argane. The area has been growing increasingly warmer and brighter as the sun rises and the fires engulf the village. He begins searching through the bodies in the immediate vicinity until he notices a tall lanky man peering at him from around the corner of a building across the way.

"You there! It is alright now…come on out survivor," he calls.

"I am no survivor, and nor will you be when the high king hears of this!" shouts the mysterious watcher. Wezzton instantly shoots an invisible bolt of energy in his direction, smashing the corner of the tattered building to pieces. When Argane gets to the busted corner, he is surprised to discover that not only is the man still there in one piece, but he has turned semi-transparent.

"You cannot kill me fool!" snaps the being. Instinctually, Argane proceeds to plunge his dagger into the specter. His weapon including his hand and forearm go right through it. The blade sticks into the wall of the building. Argane's eyes widen. The strange phantom simply stares at him… "You will all die," he says before walking straight through Argane and heading out of town. He glows pale blue in the dark and before long he is out of sight. The wizards watch him glide eerily into nothing.

"A ghost?" asks Wez.

"Nay…afraid not, he says, of the apparition. I have not seen a ghost in years…and when is the last time they did anyone's bidding but their own."

Later, the pair are steady rounding up the wounded. They have saved three souls, all men. Two are unconscious while the other man is wounded heavily at his elbow. Wezzton loads up the two unconscious while Argane takes the man injured badly at his arm. He struggles to mount his horse. He has a large laceration on his side and broken ribs, so he takes his time to tightly wrap and tend to his and the survivors' injuries. Soon, they are riding fast through the morning light.

"I have not seen magic wielded with such precision," says Argane's passenger.

"What is your name Sallinfellian?"

"Kinto Redfield elder, and yours?"

"Argane of Abraham."

"Not Argane the Immortal!" The wizard remains silent.

"Unbelievable…it is you! I have heard of your legend friend!"

"Have you?"

"Aye, yes…I certainly have…and so, you shall be fine then," says Kinto, referring to Argane's wound.

"Indeed," replies the wizard. The men must shout above the racing winds and the monotonous clip-clop of Legacy's hooves.

"Why would those…things attack us so? …our whole village…decimated!"

"I am not certain, when we arrive at our safe-haven, answers shall present themselves."

"Thank you for saving us."

"Have you lost family on this day?"

"No…not in this onslaught…I am alone in the world."

A time later Wezzton calls for Argane to stop.

"One of my men…he is dead," says Wezzton. "We have lost him."

"Great sage!" exclaims Kinto, "who is it?" He winces as he climbs down from Legacy in agony to closer inspect the deceased. "It is Jory Selpa!" he cries… "That other man, I think we are losing him too," says Wezzton regretfully. "He is Octavio Crane," he says, through his pain.

"We will do our best to further save your man," says Argane.

"What of Jory?" asks Kinto.

"Let us set him up against a tree. We cannot do much more if Octavio is to make it. The men set Jory seated and leaning with his back to a large tree trunk."

"With all this absurdity, I had forgotten how cold it is," says Kinto with vapor rolling out of his mouth. He shivers. "Let us go now," says Argane. "I regret we could not have come to know this man," he adds.

"He was of good people," says Kinto sincerely.

The four ride as quickly as they can and arrive on the beach at Ergo's coast at sunset. Before Legacy's first hoof can break the water's surface Wezzton calls out. "No!"

"What is it?" urges Argane.

"It is Octavio…he has made passage I'm afraid."

"I had just recently checked him. He had a pulse!"

Argane turns around holding his bloodied side. The lower half of Wezzton's face, his neck and chest are soaked deep red from the blood loss of his chin. Argane lowers his head.

"We were so close…set him afloat."

Kinto and Wezzton follow his orders and carry Octavio's lifeless body to the shore and lower him into the icy water. Kinto pushes him gently outward.

"Kinto of Sallinfell...you are the sole survivor," says Argane. The men stay put in silence a moment watching Octavio's body float away and sink before entering through the hidden passageway. They hurry to find Be'wick alone in the archives.

"This is Be'wick, the headmaster of our circle and main councilor," says Argane to Kinto.

Be'wick rises and goes straight for his wound.

"Argane, you are hurt badly," he says. He opens the soiled robe and carefully rifles through the layers of bloody wrappings and under gear thereby exposing Argane's side. It has an extensive tear in it and three snapped ribs poke out from the shredded flesh.

"You are sweating profusely, and you are white...You are lucky to have made it here old friend, you have lost a lot of blood."

"Moonrakers," says Argane. Wezzton puts his head down and shakes his head in shame for his eagerness to quarrel with them.

"If not for our altercation though, Kinto here, would have met with unjust demise, adds Argane." Be'wick then puts his open palms onto the large wound and presses his hands down hard. Slowly but surely the wounds recede, close together and seal beneath them. He releases his friend's side.

"Great sage!" exclaims Kinto. "You...you...you are a god!"

"I am no god," says Be'wick...He examines his arm. I am knowledgeable, I'm powerful...a healer but not a god. He then takes hold of Wezzton's chin, and his injury too is almost instantly gone.

"There are many wounds in which I can heal," says Be'wick, turning back to Kinto "but when an appendage is as nearly severed as that arm is, there is nothing I can do for it...it will not fuse correctly, not even close...so it wouldn't function properly, as well an infection could develop and fester and poison your blood...it could kill you.

"And...so...what of it then?"

"These men have saved your life...risking their own in the process. Be happy you are of the living and accept peace in that...the arm however...must go."

"I am grateful sir and indebted to these men," says Kinto graciously, with a slight bow of his head.

"Wezzton," orders Be'wick. "Wake Oren and tell him he has a duty to fulfil."

21.
Tyrant

The sunlight shimmers within the rustling grass of the uninhabited green hills. Beaten paths slash and divide the plains into uneven sections. One in particular, cuts straight to the enormous castle. The morning sun's warmth melts away at the previous evening's snowfall. A large moat encircles the super-structure. There is a series of drawbridges that lay open all around it.

    The castle is made of limestone blocks and its many pointed towers scrape the sky. Black and yellow striped flags fly proudly from poles atop their peaks.

The castle belongs to high king Thayddeus 'the evil' and it is the biggest in all the land by ten times at least. Crows circle the peaks and call out from on top of dormers and in valleys within its great network of roofs. There are several stained-glass windows all over and there are numerous open doors at ground level. It is an altogether pompous dwelling with very little fortification. A blunder of arrogance. However, there are ample guards. Inside, Thayddeus himself sits upon a lavish throne of solid gold with black velvet cushions, fire-breathing dragons and slithering snakes are meticulously embossed within the soft metal of the throne's high back, arms and legs. The King is adorned in the colors of his house's banner. He wears a long, thick, black, hooded cloak with yellow piping along the edges. It shrouds what appears to be intricate, gold-plated armor and long black boots. The hood of the cloak is pulled down low, underneath his crown and masking his eyes. The pure gold crown above his hood is a simple band with only its long, outward bent, points giving it flare. The bottom of Thayddeus' face is exposed revealing more gold metal plating, that make up his smiling mouth, perfect teeth, and sculpted chin.

Two guards stand, shrouded plainly, in all black and with full masks, flank their king's throne. A beautiful woman with a black and white, flowing silk dress and black wimple paces in front of him. It is Jezella 'the Nefarious.' She appears young, with clear skin, a radiant complexion and symmetrically set, well-defined features.

"Why!" demands Thayddeus in a deeply menacing, mechanical voice… "has not my pathetic phantom creation not stood before me and spoken of Sallinfell as yet…why…have I not been given confirmation of its falling?"

"How should I know!" snaps Jezella. She stops quick from her stride.

"He is a bumbling fool, but he is never late with word," claims the high king.

"Guards! Fetch the rat!" screams the sorceress. The two guards bow in unison, before taking the steps down from beside Thayddeus and across the empty space, exiting the giant throne room. It has high ceilings, wall-mounted torches and red-carpet lays overtop a black and white checkered marble floor, leading from the ironwood, double-doorway to the infamous throne.

"Why? My king…Do you insist on having those disgusting children sold when deemed useless?"

Thayddeus perks up, takes off his crown and turns back his hood, fully revealing a gold plated, shiny bald head and a menacing, robotic, skull-like, face. His empty eye-sockets are filled with dark matter and his mouth is locked in a beaming smile.

"Tell me witch…what type of child makes more profit…a dead child or a free child?" asks the king through his gritted gold teeth.

"You are mad! We should be permitted to just ring their grubby little necks and toss them into the boar pen!"

"A child set free makes his way. A child set free…grows to be an adult…an adult works his hands to bone, marries has more children who do the same and by the time my henchmen have raked a city clean those 'free children' have accrued so much more money than ones long killed and digested within the pens would have."

Jezella laughs wickedly, "Thade, you are rich beyond reason! What do you care of money?" she shouts. "And to pretend that you care for lives, young or grown! Is preposterous!" Her continued, shrill laughter bounces off the stone walls.

"Hold your tongue woman. You are the only being in this kingdom and likely all the land that I let keep their power."

"The only way to take mine would be to kill me!" she shouts. Thayddeus stares at her with His dark eyes, the matter within gently swirling.

Jezella scoffs. "You would never! I am your longest serving and most powerful ally by far!"

The large wooden doors fly open from across the room with a bang that reverberates within the space. The two guards have returned with the king's phantom. Their footsteps echo as they walk aggressively to him with the wraith in front of them.

It fades when passing through the bright sunlight beaming onto the carpet through the windows that line the room high up at its backside behind their leader. Thayddeus stands.

"What say you!" he snaps. "What of the problem in Sallinfell?"

"How did you know master?"

"Spirit, I am your maker! Do not undermine my intelligence!"

"There were two men there…th-they killed the last four rakers as they were finishing up. All the times I have been witness to your minions I have not seen anyone fight back like that…not ever…let alone wield m-magic!"

"Magic!" shouts Thayddeus. Jezella smiles wryly at his display of frustration, as she watches the altercation attentively.

"Describe them!" he demands.

"One appeared...much older than we...long cloaks, big hats...I do not know...they, they wielded power without effort and in fantastic arrays of color."

"Did you oppose them with the power I infused you with?"

"I—"

"Did you fight them? at least!" yells Thayddeus.

"I was frightened, your grace! I did my best to...intimidate."

"Frightened!" shouts Thayddeus loudly.

"I gave you emotions to better kill...not cower...you fool!"

Thayddeus raises his hand, and his creation begins to rise off the floor and glow blue then purple and finally red. Its suffering heightens with every change. The phantom's anguish reaches its precipice when it turns black. The wraith explodes with a bright white flash of light and disappears into thin air.

"My king, who now will watch the Moonrakers carry out their—"

"Choose your words carefully woman or you will be next," quips Thayddeus. The sorceress suppresses her smile.

"Of course, my king," she replies, calmly and continues...

"Now that Sallinfell has been handled...what of Smeed? The sad little town has not been properly addressed in quite some time. When shall we have it crushed again?" A moment passes.

"Today," says Thayddeus.

"What about the rakers?"

"They can take their rest. We are due for an obliteration...would you not agree?"

Jezella's eyes widen, as a big smile overcomes her face. She releases her signature, sinister laugh.

A fortnight passes with High King Thayddeus and Jezella the Nefarious wreaking havoc across the land. They reach their destination when they enter the village of Smeed under a blood red sky of dusk. Several people are out and about, many finishing up their workday or making their way home to their families for dinner. They ride through the open threshold on pitch black stallions with piercing eyes of crimson. The horses gallop to the nearest citizens and rear back before boxing them down with their front hooves and trampling them to death on cue. All the town folk in the vicinity begin to yell and scream in horror. Thayddeus jumps off his stallion and proceeds to push a yellow light wave from his palms that glides incredibly wide through the entire town, severing any in half, whom it passes through. The light source effortlessly kills nearly a hundred people. Buildings and homes are sliced all the way through by the immense power as it passes through the village, before disappearing beyond the end of the main road. Jezella is using a silver staff to electrocute anyone able to evade the light power and make an attempt to scramble to safety. With loud and mighty, crooked bolts of blue, she screams with a high pitch as she downs one innocent group after another. Thayddeus, unchallenged, easily holds his position on the road while Jezella climbs up to the roofs. He uses invisible forces to push energy all around at large crowds of people as they scatter. Many are caught within it and drop dead instantly. The evil duo spare none, not the children, not even the animals. When just about every living thing is destroyed completely, Thayddeus gathers the clouds above together, guiding them with his hands before pulling lightning out of them sending it down hard onto the damaged buildings and broken homes. They burst into flames upon impact. Jezella joins in, torching the structures near her with streams of blue and red fire from the top end of her staff.

When every last thing is dead and the town has crumbled and is burning, they mount their stallions.

"Thade, what of killing the children?" calls Jezella, as she scans the bodies of the levelled village.

"You did not seem to mind," he answers. "I believe we have whom we've been looking for."

He kicks up his horse and cantors over their victims and out of the ruins. Jezella shoots fire balls onto the dead with her staff as she follows, setting them ablaze too.

Days later, when they arrive trotting back to Thayddeus' castle, it is dark outside, and little is going on.

A few slaves are doing the last of their duties within the orange glow of surrounding torch light and are preparing to pull in the final drawbridge.

There is a man, an elf and a dwarf speaking there by it when Thayddeus and Jezella reach the main area. They are still hidden within the shadows.

"His moonrakers obviously are not what he thinks they are, otherwise why bother to get off his 'high horse' to get his own boots dirty?" says the man.

"I will not speak ill within a thousand yards of this…palace," says the elf. The third one, the dwarf stays silent. Upon over-hearing, Thayddeus gallops across the bridge to where the three stand and halts.

"Who spoke in criticism of their ruler!" he snaps. "All your heads will find the end of a pike!"

"What say you!" The elf shakes his head, no.

Then the man pipes up. "It was I your highness, I do apologize," he says peering up to Thayddeus.

Jezella laughs with her high pitch from behind him.

The high king dismounts and steps to the slave, staring him straight in the eye.

"You have saved your companions peasant…wise choice…is this 'off my high horse' enough?"

"Yes, master…I mean…no…well it's—"

Suddenly the king grasps the man by the neck. "You don't think I knew who spoke before I asked? your admission won't save you, nor will your groveling." He squeezes tight as he lifts his newest victim clear off his feet. The man struggles significantly before he stops breathing. Thayddeus then pummels his lifeless body into the ground with merciless, brute force.

"You two idiots will have his head on a pike and out front before the bridge is turned in. I want it there for morning and let it be a lesson to all."

"Yes, your highness," confirms the elf.

"Is it clear for you too dwarf?"

"Certainly sire."

"It talks! Splendid…certainly indeed," says Thayddeus with his deep voice. He mounts his stallion and heads inside. Jezella follows. She laughs and shoves the elf with the butt end of her staff as they stride by.

The two stand in the castle's grand dining room.

"My phantom spoke of two elderly wizards."

"Please continue m'lord," says Jezella.

"I know who they are…aside from you and I, there are but a handful of souls capable of such magic."

"Who do you presume?"

"Argane the Immortal and his lesser cousin Luscious is a start."

"You do not think!" exclaims the sorceress.

"Oh, but I do woman."

"Old Argane and Luscious of Abraham?"

"Have you happened across any other two wizards called Argane and Luscious?" asks the king with obvious sarcasm.

"I do apologize, my king. What to do Thayddeus? We had combed all the lands for those two vermin and their friends years ago."

"I do not intend to waste time and resources now…I will wait for them to come to us. Now witch…leave me," says Thayddeus, dismissing Jezella with a flick of his wrist.

Over at the Seven's circle's submerged fortress Oren brings Be'wick and Argane a message. They are seated in the dining room alone in deep conversation. "Oddfeather has couriered a letter from Mayor Rimpod at Khaprayelle. Marple has deciphered it and forwarded it to us."

"What is it then?" inquires Be'wick.

Oren continues, "It seems a group of travelers from the Double 'L' have passed by Smeed to find it in smoldering ruins."

"Another community lost," says Argane.

"Terrible…just terrible…anything else?" asks Be'wick.

"Well, it seems there were murdered children there, within the rubble...of both genders." Be'wick looks Argane in the eyes. Argane returns the glare.

"Thank you, Oren," says Be'wick.

A moment passes.

"He thinks he has found the one," affirms Argane.

"You know what this means?" asks Be'wick rhetorically.

Argane answers him anyway. "It means we are ready to take the next step…it means we must get to her…must prepare for our attack."

"Yes," says Be'wick. "It means our allies must be alerted at once, it means they must accelerate their preparation…The armies must strengthen, stand and be rallied for the common cause…The people must know that we will be taking back our freedom and when the time is right, we will all have our war."

22.
Seven Years Later

The warm summer breeze stirs gently as long, green grass rustles above the cliff that overlooks the sea of gods. William is alongside its massive wall. Near the top, it is soft and slanted enough to traverse, though care must still be exhibited in order to maintain good footing. The teenager is steadily searching the soil in front of him. He has developed into a very fit young man and displays his agility, maneuvering the cliff-side effortlessly. He has a large pack slung over his shoulder.

"What does Constance use 'sharp root' for anyway!" calls Hayden from his spot further below.

"She uses it in cooking," answers Poe from nearby.

"No, no, it is for a potion or something," calls Leo from above, "is it not William?"

William is preoccupied stuffing some of the sharp root into his pack. He scans the blue sky above and continues digging around in front of himself. Loose soil gives way and slides a long way down toward the water. "Uhh, no actually…she makes rope with it," he replies finally.

"What!" exclaims Leo. Hayden laughs.

"She is getting very old and cannot climb out here anymore that is all that matters," comments Poe.

William stops again and looks up, then resumes his search. "I'm certain there are more uses…and even more certain they send us out here to learn."

"Learn what?" inquires Hayden skeptically.

"Whatever there is to, I suppose," answers William.

"How many have you all gathered?" shouts Leo.

"Three," yells Hayden.

"Three here!" calls Poe.

"Well, I got myself four here! What about you William?" shouts Leo.

William again has stopped working and seems to be concentrating on something above the cliff within the forest.

"I have seven," he says still keeping his senses acutely focused above.

"Let's go," he adds, we have plenty.

The group ascends the cliffside. When they reach the top, Leo peers back over the edge to the water.

"That is a long way from here!" Waves crash into a cluster of boulders at the bottom.

"It sure is," agrees Hayden.

"It is all perspective, is it not?" proposes William, who seems to have tracked something and is looking beyond, into the trees.

"We—"

"Shh!" urges William…he motions his friends to crouch, and they do. He too gets low to the ground.

Suddenly some brush and plants begin to stir. Twigs snap and pop. The sounds grow louder as they come ever closer to them. William unsheathes the flaming heart. Just then out of the bushes comes a man appearing in his early forties or so, adorned in shiny, polished, silver armor and riding an extremely rare animal. He is mounted atop a big, deep blue Pegasus. It rears up and spreads its wings at the sight of William and his flaming sword.

"Whoa, whoa," says the rider to his grand steed.

"Who are you?" demands William, as he stands up.

When the foreign man and his Pegasus gain their composure, he scans the group and speaks.

"I shall guess then that you are William. I am a friend, I assure you…I am Sebastian of the Netherwhere."

"How do we know you are a friend? Just because you say it is so!? I have not heard your story."

"No, no, William he is!" says Leo. "Argane used to tell us his tales…he is a great warrior from time's past." William lowers his sword. "You are certain," he asks while keeping his eyes locked with Sebastian's.

"Aye," replies Leo.

"Well, any friend of Argane is a friend of mine."

"Thank you," says Sebastian. "The pleasure is mine, to be sure."

William puts away his sword. Its flames extinguish as he does.

"I must commend you four on your spotting an encroacher and furthermore your collective readiness to defend your territory from an intruder."

"T'was not us entirely sir, it was William alone, who was alerted to your presence," says Leo.

"Bug off! I could tell something was afoot," says Hayden.

Poe laughs... "Yes, yes like when that clan of vampires ambushed us!"

"Or that run in with the kirndornst," adds Leo. They share a good laugh.

"Sir, up to now we have never seen a Pegasus in person, only in illustration. It is wonderful. What do you call it?" asks Hayden.

"His name is 'True' and in the Netherwhere, which is where I am from, there are a great many things that mainlanders have never laid eyes upon."

The five arrive down at the shore on the beach and Leo begins to step onto the submerged flat rock that leads to their secret hatch in the floor by the 'L' shaped wall.

"Wait," says William. "This man can lead us there."

"Oh William, he is on our side."

"Just wait...proceed please Sebastian," orders William.

"I do admire your grit young man," he says before stepping upon the rock. He then rears back, and his Pegasus takes flight. With just a few flaps of his giant wings, he soars and turns, landing by the hatch. William's expression remains unaltered. He and the boys follow along the flat rock. Sebastian then prompts his steed to tap the door with his hoof in succession. He stands back and the stone block door grinds open.

"Not bad for not having done that in fifteen or so years, eh men?"

When they arrive at the stables, Sebastian and Oren exchange pleasantries. After a short time, they head on to the dining room. The group enters to find Be'wick, Argane, Luscious and Isla set around the table.

Argane is the first to see Sebastian. He lights up and rises from his chair.

"You are early!"

"Ah...and so I am the first to arrive! Wonderful!" exclaims Sebastian excitedly. "Just as I had hoped."

The others greet the much younger man and while within the commotion Argane requests that every teen with the exception of William, deliver the cache of sharp roots to Constance. "He is a great protector of yours," says Sebastian. "It was difficult to gain clearance."

"I do apologize," says William.

"No, never! One must always look out for their family."

"A proper introduction is in order fellows," directs Be'wick.

"William…Sir Sebastian of the Netherwhere, is a gifted knight and one of our dearest allies. He is eager to fight at our side."

"It is an unprecedented testament of loyalty…King Thayddeus has no direct adversaries in the Netherwhere," adds Argane.

"It is simple. The enemy of my friends is my enemy," says Sebastian.

"This man has fought for many a cause with us William," continues Be'wick.

"Something we have always lacked where I am from, are great battles," interjects Sebastian.

"Too much ice," says Isla with a chuckle.

"It is just too far away," laughs Argane.

"In all seriousness friends," says Sebastian, as he looks to William. "No journey is too far when your family is in need…besides the Netherwhere can be such a bore, devoid of any magic or excitement," he adds, looking to Argane.

They too share a laugh.

"So, am I to believe, I am the very first?"

"Aye," confirms Argane.

"We had sent word long ago to every allied city, town and village. Their armies have been preparing in secret, for quite some time now. Everyone is eager to meet in Shallowlake at the plains of Nevermore as soon as the first leaf falls at the turn of the upcoming season. We hope to catch Thayddeus off guard and ram our assault straight through to him."

"Regarding the revolt…we will have superior numbers then?" inquires Sebastian.

"Yes," answers Argane… "but we'll need ten to their one…at least. All of our rebels…the resistance, is represented by those of the living…Thayddeus has un-dead at *his* disposal."

"Is Khaprayelle still your strongest allegiance?"

"Strongest, biggest…aye, they and the double L are great warriors," says Argane… "I have been trying to communicate with the league…they are critical to our revolution, assistance from them will prove pivotal to our goal."

"Has it not been fruitful? …the attempts …the outreach?" asks Sebastian.

"No…not as yet."

"Do you remain hopeful?"

"I absolutely must," confirms Argane.

After dinner, some of the younger ones are in the main library studying. William and Mila are in a chamber of their own, rearranging some books into better organized categories, as Constance had requested of them earlier. They speak in low voices to one another amidst dim torchlight and flickering candles.

"I have never seen a Pegasus before, have you?" asks William, while he hands Mila a book from the high stack on the floor between them.

"Me? …gosh no…I had heard stories though and have seen illustrations and paintings. I just love them and True is particularly beautiful. The Netherwhere is full of things uncommon to the rest of the lands, ice people, minotaurs…dragons! They say that even some of the foliage and the trees will speak to you!"

"Wow!" exclaims William.

"Yes, and apart from Sebastian, the Netherwhere territory has never been in battle! Not ever…apparently, it is extremely cold there and quite far away," she says, as she adds some more books to the shelf in front of her.

"How far?" inquires William.

"It took Sebastian over half a year to arrive here."

"It did not!"

"It most certainly did! The desire to give freedom back to the people stretches to all corners of Primera…This Sebastian, as goes the legend is absolutely good in every way…selfless…he fights without obligation, to defend the oppressed and any injustice. The legend goes that he was knighted at only fifteen and though does not admit it easily, he rules the Netherwhere due to unanimous urging by his kinsmen. He does all these things and none for self-gain…Be'wick says this type of man is mostly extinct in these times."

"Boy, an honor that he lays his allegiance with us, to be sure…what an expert he must be with blades and bows," says William.

"And with his heart…does it make you nervous that a man like him comes in rally behind your lead?" asks Mila, as she lays her hand on his heart.

William smiles… "When you put it that way, I do feel nervous, yes…it is overwhelming, this…prophecy says…so little about anything after the very time we live in now…our time…our uprising. Once my seventeenth birthday came to pass, the future was no longer written. It is merely…speculation. I feel a bit unstable…insecure even…soon I will not be able to count on anything."

"You can count on me," says Mila. William appears solemn.

"Nya still lives," she says as she puts her finger to his lips and brushes it over them. "She does William and soon you will reunite with her."

"Thank you," he whispers.

She places the last of the books on the shelf, then turns back to him and kisses his cheek gently.

"Soon…we will all be free."

He looks around her to the doorway to see if anybody saw them…no one did.

The next day after breakfast William waits around until most everyone disperses from the dining room to sharpen their skills. Kinto is the last to leave but before he does, William speaks with him briefly.

"Has Isla's newest prototype proven superior?"

Kinto looks at his stub. "No…but it seems he is onto something this time 'round…It has been so long without the arm, I have sort of gotten used to it," he says, with a shrug.

William smiles…he waits a while there until like clockwork Be'wick enters to sit in his coveted chair.

"So, William what is on your mind?" Argane enters and seats himself at the table too.

The young man is somewhat agitated. He sits on the edge of his seat and fidgets with his shirt sleeves.

"Nya…we need to get her out first…before the assault on Thayddeus' castle…I do not trust that she will be found unharmed amidst our great battle." Appalonia hums gently above Rufus who is perched just so on his left shoulder.

"You know we have been watching her through outlaying monitors, and you know there are two main reasons in which to wait. If we sent a rescue team in, you would need to be there. We cannot risk sacrificing you in a scenario such as that. Without you our rebellion is moot…it will be nothing. You are more powerful than all of us here…also, if we launch any sort of campaign at that castle, any chance of catching them off guard in the future will be lost." Be'wick continues….

"Even if we did attempt something, what do you intend to do? Just walk in through the front door?"

"I do not mean to attempt her rescue separate from the battle. We can get her out first and by that very action, we reveal our declaration of war," replies William.

"Sirs!" says Appalonia loudly from within her glow. "Rufus has something quite important to say." The frog then leaps off William's shoulder and lands on the table. Appalonia flutters down and lands beside him. Appalonia speaks… "He—he would like me to talk for him, not just in halted translations but freely, repeating his words as if I were him."

"Speak freely," says Be'wick. He nods at Rufus.

"I have been pondering this proposal for a long, long time…what about a diversion?" says Appalonia on Rufus' behalf.

"Please continue," says Be'wick.

"If Appalonia and you all are willing and I know she is, she could fly me above Thayddeus' castle and lower me onto the roof. We all know the high king despises fairies and that if anyone there spotted her, she would surely be squashed but not frogs, we are generally unassuming…I will find a way inside, scout the castle and when I arrive at the right spot, I will use my cursed three words and blow the west tower sky high. We shall have a group close to the tower, within the woods and as soon as the tower is opened up like a broken bottle. The ones in hiding can storm the west-wing, locate Nya and bring her out. It would have to be a fast rescue. The explosion of the tower could serve as our army's signal, prompting immediate attack." Appalonia finishes speaking and looks to Rufus. His eyes are locked upon Be'wick's.

"Rufus…my dear old friend, I praise you for your bravery, but I could not let you give your life," says William sincerely.

"I have lived almost two and a half centuries young William," says Appalonia, as the frog turns and focuses on his friend. "I will have no regrets and would be honored to play this part in our grand story…to initiate the great battle that ends the dark reign."

"But—"

"I offer this with my whole heart, William," says Appalonia for Rufus.

"I know Rufus well and believe his plan to be pure of heart," says Argane.

"What say you? Will you let this be the way of it Be'wick?" asks the fairy for the frog.

"He looks to Rufus of Kersius and sees not the blue amphibian he has become but the young warrior he once was." He then looks to Argane, who raises his eyebrows and keeps them up. He then looks to William who still appears stunned by Rufus' courageous proposal.

"Forgive me friends…but do let me sleep on this one…I need to be certain about some details and how we might best execute this plan if we are to utilize it. I commend you…Rufus 'the brave', your offer of sacrifice for freedom and the greater good of all has left me devoid of certain words…even after all this time, you still truly are great."

William retires to his room early this night. He does not read of magic or sharpen his blades. This night he speaks with Rufus and Appalonia. Mila has retired early too and has snuck into his room as she often does.

"I am numb at the prospect of re-uniting with my sister…what if she is not what I expect? what if she does not remember me?" he says to Mila.

"She is your sister…she will."

"I feel awful at the thought of you doing it," he says to Rufus.

"Do not feel as such," says Appalonia. "He says it will be perfect and that it is his choice alone and will be happy if Be'wick allows it to be so."

"I did not know fairies can fly that high," says Mila, with a soft chuckle.

"Me neither!" responds Appalonia. "And carrying Rufus to boot," she adds. It will take practice.

"You can do it…fairies are notoriously strong," communicates Rufus to the second guessing Appalonia.

Soon after, William and Mila are in quiet conversation. The young lady is laid out on the bed on her back while William is seated upon it and facing her with his back to the wall and his legs crossed. Appalonia and Rufus are fast asleep beside each other on a satin pillow.

"I have been here seven years…learning and preparing for a battle with the evilest of beings…all the while not a moment has gone by where I have not thought of my sister…and the one who took her. Anxious only begins to describe how I have felt about pursuing these two ends…and now that we are drawing so near them…I am afraid…I fear I will miss life as I know it now and the things left behind."

"To feel fear is natural, William. It is our nature to feel things within our hearts…you must use it as a strength and a power, not as a weakness or an inadequacy…to feel the fear and to respect it, is to respect the situation in which you will be dealing…free from any repression or restraint. The day you do not feel…that is when you need worry." She sits up and joins him along the wall. They embrace.

"Do you remember years ago when I spotted that pink feather up in that tall tree on our way back from grandmother's."

"Aye?"

"Do you remember climbing up there for me because I was so upset and sad that I could not get it for myself?"

"You were a very tenacious child. Continue…" says William, suspiciously.

"Were you scared?"

"Yes."

"Yet you retrieved the feather and gave it to me."

"Yes."

"Why?"

"Because I did not want you to get hurt and I wanted you to have the feather, because it meant so much to you."

"Yes, I depended on you for it, and you got it for me because I was incapable."

A few moments pass…

"As bold as I acted…I would never have climbed that tree," admits Mila.

"I loved you so much, even back then…I just wanted something from you, to feel united and I knew you could do it…"

"I was always drawn to you as well," says William.

Mila then digs into the front pocket of her brown leather tunic to reveal an old flattened pink feather.

William is surprised and deeply touched. He smiles warmly. They stretch out and embrace a while more…

"I must go…if anyone discovers me missing from my chambers and finds me here, I do not know what we would say…especially with the battle so quickly approaching."

23.
Michael and the League of Archangels
From the Third Dimension

Argane is down shore from the ruined columns of the circle's hidden fortress.

He scans the bright, early morning sky, then the perfectly flat surface of the sea and finally the rickety, wooden, two-man vessel at his feet within the sandy shoreline. The bow sways slightly, causing an insignificant ripple to generate around it and carry outward. He slowly slides the canoe further into the water, steadies himself, steps inside and sits down. The old wizard takes the oar in hand. Dawn is breaking and as it does, the warm summer climate pulls a thin haze out from the cool water. It lingers just above and disperses gradually as the boat slowly glides through it. The vessel creaks while Argane rows, back and forth, from one side to the next. He soon arrives at a small mountain island and carefully ties off the boat to a decrepit wooden dock. He proceeds to ascend the rocky terrain using his staff for leverage as he climbs. Near the top of the precipice Argane sets himself down on his knees within some long grass in front of a large fragment of glimmering white quartz protruding from the ground behind him. He then sticks his staff into the soil, crosses his legs and leans back against the rock.

The view is magnificent from where he sits…He looks down into the distance at the old, fortified school's ruins by the beach and imagines it as it was centuries before…It towers way up above the sea of gods and its enchantments sparkle in shades of blue and pink in front of the mountainous forest behind it. Citizens of Crimsinth carry on about their day, happy and full of life. Slowly, the stone building fades and vanishes from Argane's mind and the beach. The clear water of the sea looks like a sheet of glass. It is stunning.

The blue and white, smeared oil painting that is the sky reflects perfectly...infinitely pointing back at one another. It is challenging to differentiate between the two and where they meet. Argane breathes in deep, taking a piece of nature's beauty in with him as he does. He closes his eyes and slowly exhales.

"Why do you neglect us?" he says softly. "This was your home for a time too...you loved these lands...and our people." With eyes still closed, he waits a few moments as a breeze passes, then continues, "You fought with us, you fought for us, time and time again...for causes primitive to this."

He waits some more and breathes deeply. "We need you now...I fear the ones here cannot accomplish our task without you." He exhales slowly. "You must not turn your back...the people here are not through...not finished."

With that, he bows his head and meditates. A long time passes until the smooth, shiny, oval, white stone embedded into the top end of his staff begins to glow. He remains there for a while. Finally, he raises his head to scan the nearby area. The orange light of his staff fades. The wizard rises, removes it from the ground and starts out back down the rocks, to the boat.

He arrives at the dining room in perfect time for breakfast. When he sits at his end of the long table, he notices Be'wick watching him. They share a blank stare. While everyone is dug in and eating Be'wick explains how the young adults with magical powers will sharpen only those from now on and those relying on their prowess with physical weaponry will focus their efforts on them.

"All except William," he says. "You will work exclusively with Sebastian."

"I look forward to working with you until our battle," says the knight.

"The pleasure is mine," returns William.

After breakfast, William, Sebastian, Be'wick, Whisspella and Constance are seated around the table.

"His alchemy is thorough," says Constance. "His potions and elixirs are wonderful," she adds with a smile.

"Whisspella?" says Be'wick.

"Yes, his knowledge in the magical arts both historical and modern are well rounded," replies the young witch, upon looking up from her book of notes. "And Argane tells me your manipulation of naturally occurring elements are unprecedented and that your 'defy magic' is perfect as are your wards and general defenses."

"Thank you," says William.

"His common spells are flawless as well and his complex ones, adept," interjects Constance. "Little Hope can surely attest to that!" she adds with a gentle chuckle, stroking her cat's white fur, as she lay there peacefully on her lap.

"Well young, William, we agree your ability to wield magic is more powerful and robust than any we have ever seen at your age. I know your skills with melee weaponry are great too, but you will learn even more from Sebastian. Once our armies penetrate their border and attack…you will need the most abundant repertoire possible of various offences among your arsenal…to fully utilize your power against Thayddeus. We will cut a path to him, but it will just be you and he…and you must be ready to deal in whichever tactics are necessary," proclaims Be'wick.

Later, William and Sebastian are outside within a clearing by Marple Weary's shack. They are engaged in the art of swordplay. Sebastian has on his trademark polished silver armor, while William is wearing a much more crudely designed, mammoth bone armor.

"Do you find the gear you wear to be cumbersome?" asks William, as their swords clash loudly.

"I did at first…to be honest. I preferred to dress down in battle, but being a knight, I am expected to dawn the outfit and so have become accustomed to its weight and mechanics. Although I'm certainly more agile without its restraints, I used to think it possible that wearing it would in turn kill me rather than save me but of course that was not a proper mindset, says Sebastian."

"Will you wear it on our day of uprising?"

"I shall," he says, as he swings his sword.

"I find armor of any kind restricting…it seems I will never get used to it," says William. "And I change types all the time."

"You will do what you feel is right…for you."

They clash blades again.

"Why do you fight?"

"Easy, people are in trouble!" replies Sebastian. They stop dueling.

"Let me ask something of you William…are you confident that you will destroy the evil king and send his broken soul into every hell?"

"I must be, mustn't I?"

Sebastian snickers slightly... "well you will...you will come to know that as your fate and your legend will be bigger than all of ours, mine, Argane's, Sonya's, Beauregard's, Aiden's...all of them," he says firmly.

"How are you so certain?"

"Will," answers Sebastian... "with everything you were born with and all you've been taught, ironically you need no more than the will to do it...and I know you have it." The knight points the tip of his blade to William's face... "It is how it is there...in your eyes. I see it...and 'there'," he says, lowering his sword to his chest... "in your heart. It is evident in your aura your will burn like fire—true! Because of who you are and, who I see before me...that is why I am certain."

After midnight, in the forest below an endless ocean of cascading bright white stars. William is carefully maneuvering through the thicket. He crouches low as he sneaks quietly through the cool night's air. He wears a thick, dark green cloak of wool. The hood is large and pulled over his head to just above his eyes. He arrives at the forest's edge before long. It gives way to vast and gradually rolling fields. In the wide-open space in the distant valley is High King Thayddeus' gargantuan super-castle.

Slaves, workers, henchmen and guards can be seen stirring within dim lighting from William's vantage point within the edge of the bushes. Torches are lit sporadically atop poles all along ground level. They are around the castle's moat, near doorways and mounted in iron sconces below stained-glass windows. William tries but cannot hear the ones carrying on outside the castle. He is too far away. A big, bright, full moon hangs low, suspended within the stars above the castle, spot lighting it to perfection. William stands upright and walks out of the forest's perimeter and into the open field...he continues his stare, down to the castle. Suddenly the atmosphere gets cold and crisp as he watches. His sword within its sheath begins to subtly glow yellow, orange then gradually it turns pink and finally red. He takes it out and holds it by his side...thick, flames begin to slowly excrete from its blade...it is lit up, brilliantly from the hilt to the tip with slow moving red flames crawling all over it. William's eyes stay fixed upon the castle until finally he looks down at the flaming blade. He raises it out in front of himself and looks to the castle again. There is a rustling from the bushes behind him. He spins around and out lumbers the illuminated white bear.

It is Indigo! William is stunned at the sight of the great beast as he saunters out into the field and in front of him. William is astonished, he wants to but cannot muster a word.

"We wait…with you," says the bear in his breathy deep voice. Vapor rolls out of his mouth as he speaks, within his cool glow.

William is bewildered but manages to respond. "Who does? …who…waits? I…I thought I would never see you again…that maybe…maybe I had dreamt you."

"No boy…I was there then, and I am here now…our kingdom…of the animals are in waiting."

"I…I do not understand."

"We have known of your coming for a long, long time…more than even your fellow man…"

"The synergy amidst these lands has been tilted heavily for quite some time…harmony suffers and has endured enough. When the first leaf falls to the ground and your people align…we will all be here…waiting and watching…if your efforts seem in vain and appear bleak. We will be there."

"Are—"

"You must keep your eyes open…always and he will come to you."

"Who? …I—"

"When he comes…you will know," says Indigo firmly, before turning and receding back into the forest. William is wide-eyed as the great bear disappears into the darkness of the woods and his white light fades. He blinks fast a few times, then spins back around to observe the castle…it is gone. He blinks again and awakens in his bed.

24.
The Meeting of the Minds

While the youngers are training outside on Ergo's coastline. There are seven elders seated around the infamous dining room table. Be'wick and Argane make up the two ends as Isla, Luscious, Addly and Wezzton are along the side nearest the lounge area. Marple is on the side by the kitchen and in her stead, Whisspella is keeping watch at the Weary shack.

Be'wick begins, "I have sent word to the six major city's leaders…they are to meet here and further discuss strategies and confirm the readiness of their armies in preparation for the leaves fall."

The younger wizards gasp upon hearing the announcement.

Uncharacteristically, Addly interrupts his headmaster. "Surely it cannot be here?"

"What if any have turned coat! Our plan could be sabotaged," adds Wezzton.

"You men have come a long way from promising mages to official wizards of our circle, do trust your elder," says Marple of Be'wick.

"These six men have been corresponding with us for years," says Be'wick, firmly.

Marple nods her head in agreement. "These are leaders, former kings of the righteous…tried, true men. They are our people and believe in this cause…just as much as we do," she says.

"I apologize," says Addly.

"And who of us is to be present on this day of counselling?" asks Wezzton.

"We here in this room now," replies Be'wick.

"Once we are all confident in our alignment, all we need do is lay in wait…for natures signal."

"A great many will die," says Luscious.

"Well over three quarters of our projected numbers," adds Isla.

Marple looks at Be'wick, then back to Isla. "A quite insignificant statistic...although a great many more have died under this tyranny and the dark reign will never stop without our intervening. It is a just sacrifice in exchange for peace...these lands have not been free for over two centuries...the people know the time has come...few will waver, nor fear death, for that their children may live free and their children's children...and so on and so forth."

Several uneventful weeks come and pass. It is mid-summer, during week's end, and William has just finished escorting Mila to her grandmother's shack. They share a secret kiss outside the structure and bid one another farewell. It is a warm, calm day. William is taking particular time within his steps to enjoy the scenery, enroute back to the fortress when he notices an unusual sparkling bush up the mountain side to his right in the opposite direction of the beach. After some thought, he decides to investigate.

Too bright for twinkle berries...or fireflies, he thinks to himself. When he arrives at the bush, he is surprised and wary to witness the sparkles as they swirl and merge into a swarm. They are magnificent and bright...like an array of tiny gems, though these seem to have life, driven together by a mysterious force. It allows them to leave the bush and ride the small breezes that push by. They dance and twirl between the trees. William follows carefully as they travel, deeper into the wild.

They take him all over, around bushes, under tree branches, and over narrow winding creeks. Finally, they stop near the mountain's base, where suddenly they drop quickly out of his line of sight and descend down a hill. William hurries toward the edge of the slope cautiously and looks downward. The mysterious cluster of shimmering dust circles around the mane of a big, beautiful lion before dispelling into thin air and re-appearing as a tiny fairy. She hovers above the grand animal's head and giggles. The lion is fitted with a bridle, reins, a saddle and stirrups.

William carefully descends the grassy hill. "Are you a fairy? ...or ...a pixie?" asks William, hesitantly.

She giggles again.

"Why I am a fairy, silly!"

"Are you friend? or foe?"

She laughs aloud. "William, we are friends," she replies. "This is Kalyden. He is one of the princes of our land. The one for whom you have been foretold by Indigo 'the extraordinary'. He would be honored if you would accept his guardianship for your assault upon the 'evil ones' liar. The world around William never ceases to amaze him and yet again has rendered him speechless."

"I…um…"

"All of us would be honored," she says as she looks all around the forest, gesturing with her outstretched arms… "forgive me but…you do not have much say in this…we want him with you…for your protection." William pulls himself out of his funk. "The honor would be mine."

The fairy giggles in delight and begins to fade. "No please, do not go yet!" urges William. "I know the lands are vast, but…we have a lost fairy in our group…could you know her perhaps!"

"Boy…If not for our common cause, I likely would not…but because of this…we do…but you see, she is not lost and therefore not meant to be taken home yet…she, as we all do…has her part to play."

William pauses. "Oddly enough…I understand," he says.

"Goodbye friend."

"Fairy, what is your name?"

"Call me Lydia," she replies before disappearing.

The lion stares at William and bobs his head twice in succession. William walks toward him and pets the bridge of his nose.

"What am I gonna tell the others about you?" he says before climbing aboard the big cat.

"Do you know where we dwell, Kalyden?" Without hesitation, the feline bounds back up the hill and in the direction of the beach.

William holds on tight.

More weeks go by slowly with plenty of anticipation to go around. The group of teenagers stick to their training as always. Even the youngest ones, Sara and Ariel, have come a long way in their development. Sara has become quite a tenacious wielder of magical artistry, while Ariel is a brilliant young archer and fierce too with a sword. Mila Weary is the most talented in tactical arts, while Clari's talents lie in melee' weaponry.

Leo is advanced in practical magic and is a fierce swordsman. Hayden is great with the bow and favors it heavily. He has matured greatly as elves often do within these adolescent years of their life. Poe the dwarf's strength lies with blunt weapons and has become a revered alchemist within the circle's elders. They all work hard together. Not one of them slacks or wavers.

The young ones this night, are in the archives reading up on the land's long history, when an open conversation springs up.

"It just occurred to me," says Hayden… "not a one of us have ever engaged in real warfare."

"That just occurred to you?" asks Leo, sarcastically.

Poe laughs.

"Well, the thought has always been there but…we are approaching the leaves fall and none of us are battle hardened," returns Hayden.

"They say you must run before you can walk," says Clari.

"That is a good point but, I do not fully agree with the context," says Poe.

"We have been running for years!" exclaims Sara.

Ariel laughs at her friend's display of exuberance. "While on one hand, battle experience would likely help…perhaps on the other, it could instill fear in going forward."

"I'd like to believe our years of competitive sparring against each other has amounted to something we can apply," says Leo.

"The only truth," interjects William. "Is that we shall invest all of our hearts and souls, as we always do…with everything we do…into this fight…such speculations matter not."

Mila smiles as she watches from beside him as he speaks.

Throughout the next day, the six former kings arrive at Ergo's coast for the unprecedented summit. First both King Heinridge of Khaprayelle and King Blackurn of Redrock. Then King Elroy of Trillingham, followed by King Magnes of Xirn, King Rafferty of Artillin and finally King Irongrab of Selkirk. The dining room table is almost full. The twelve men and Marple sit eagerly around it.

"Thank you all for coming. I appreciate the risks involved but also the necessity," says Be'wick from his seat at the end of the table. He continues…The six cities that you all represent are the biggest players in our uprising. Other cities, towns, villages, communities and outlaying factions have their part…we know that…we trust that, but it was important for us to have you six here to personally ask and answer any queries.

Argane then speaks from the table's opposite end. "We have corresponded for many, many years since the first days of our proposed campaign…and so here we are, and no more messages will be sent as the leaves fall draws closer."

"First, we would like to ask the questions, we will go around the table," adds Marple.

"So, men…are your armies prepared to their very maximum?" asks Be'wick.

Unanimously five men say yes and nod their heads positively.

"Aye, never more," says Irongrab of Selkirk, completing the answers.

"Do any of you men choose to join in the battle physically when we invade?"

Heinridge, Blackurn, Rafferty and Elroy decline the notion while expressing that if the army shall waver, they will certainly join. Magnes and especially Irongrab enthusiastically express their desire to be in the field.

"I will be keeping track of my kills!" says Irongrab, in his gruff voice.

"Aye, now that is an idea!" agrees Wezzton.

Irongrab laughs under his long brown beard and adjusts his horned, iron helmet. "I like your grit young man! And I will see you in the grass," says the dwarf as he points at the young wizard with his outstretched index finger.

Wez nods and grins.

"Alright, alright. Men…and lady, for today, we would like to speak generally and after dinner, before our ales and wine, we shall speak strategy," says Be'wick.

"Who among you shall fight?" asks Irongrab. Be'wick answers quickly. "Most of us, I and Addly will not. He is my understudy…the women shall not."

"With the exception of my daughter," adds Marple.

"Pardon my being bold but is your daughter a necessary part…to be put into this?" asks Irongrab.

"Aside from William, Whisspella, Marple's daughter is among the most powerful of all of us," says Be'wick.

"Aye," replies Irongrab… "I am just looking out for the young woman, is all."

"I understand," says Marple sincerely.

"Are the young ones ready?" inquires Heinridge.

"Yes, as ready as they will ever be," says Argane.

"What is your confidence level for our efforts…all of us…collectively?"

"If we didn't believe we were ready, we wouldn't do this yet…so, long as we can clear through the initial enemy lines and William can get to Thayddeus…Then victory will be ours…it is imminent. The death toll we will incur? for our efforts? collectively? Will be great…All that matters however, is that they face one another."

The group goes silent.

"That shall be it for now, we would be honored if all of you would make yourselves comfortable. Let us enjoy each other's company without talk of war or the oppression in which we all live under but in celebration of our campaign for freedom and peace."

All six agree to Be'wick's directive without hesitation.

For the remainder of the day, everyone loosens up and enjoys their time talking, playing games and eating. They find themselves in different places within the fortress and as the evening draws in and night falls, the party find themselves back in the dining room after a fine feast and attentively discussing important strategy options for their day of reckoning. When every possible decision has been made, Constance introduces a crate of her divine brew. Most of the men spend the rest of the night indulging themselves on it before retiring to their allotted quarters in the mid of night, with a few more of them following suit within the early part of the morning. Amidst the irregular distractions, William and Mila are able to stay together in his chamber, undetected.by the elders. Irongrab, Magnes, Wezzton and Sebastian are among the last to sleep. They whoop, holler and enjoy themselves merrily with Oren and an unlimited box of bottles in the wood shop. All of them manage to eventually pass-out in the most interesting of places and positions. Irongrab and Magnes sleep in the stables in the hay next to Windimere, Wezzton is buried within his long-robe on top of a large bookshelf in a small library, Sebastian is curled up on a table next to a cross-cut saw and Oren is nearby, laid out well atop a large pile of wood chips.

The next morning after breakfast the six former kings prepare to start out for their territories. Irongrab is the brunt of jokes as he is clearly the most affected by last night's over-indulgences. He plays along and is a rather good sport as he is aggressive with the chalice and knows it.

The following weeks come and go. The weather gets brisker by the day, especially in the early morning hours where frost is becoming more and more prevalent.

25.
Contact

Under yet another beautiful sunrise, Argane walks slowly across the sandy shoreline and launches the small, rickety, boat. It is a cool, calm, clear sky morning. As he closes the gap between himself and the island, tall, early autumn daisies pop into view anywhere that there is grass within the grey rocks and boulders of the mountain. When he arrives at the base, he docks the vessel and climbs up to his choice spot. He sinks his staff into the island and sits crossed legged before it. Its top end lights up orange immediately. Birds can be heard all around as the wind kicks up. He watches as a small southbound flock of starlings fly together overhead. He closes his eyes and speaks:

"Many moons have I spoke to you…I fear you will leave us to our darkness…please do not. Our people have a vast union of armies…invasion is afoot. With your people…we will crush the high kingdom…please come to our aid. Please join us, stand with us and fight." A breeze begins to rush, and it swirls around the wizard as it passes. "We need you now." More wind stirs and grows stronger as the staff-light fades. Down the mountain in front of the surf a young man slowly appears out of a split fragment of skewed landscape. He has wavy, pale yellow, feathered hair. It frames one side of his face, hiding half of his black eyebrows and the bluest of eyes. He has a fair complexion and perfectly symmetric features with a pointed nose, chiseled jaw and square chin. The man wears a deep red, high collared long sleeve, puffy chested blouse with frilly cuffs underneath a thick, dark blue, duster jacket that flows down to just below his knees. Bronze metal buckles line the front flaps of his jacket, up to its lapels and line the forearms as well. He wears white slacks tucked into long, black, cuffed boots and has on matching black leather gloves.

The man appears elegant and rugged all at once. A thick layer of dust coats his shoulders and tapers off.

Argane sees him but does not react.

The mysterious man shakes himself off and displays effortless agility as he ascends the hill to the elder, who does not budge.

"You still have not given up on these people?" states the much younger man.

"They are good people…there is still hope here," affirms Argane.

"The ones here…in this place…have not been righteous for more than two millennia."

"You are wrong Michael, you know yourself…you have seen it! Your people lived here in the fourth dimension for so long and you loved it as your own! It is yours who taught ours the language, that is still our native tongue…and as for your claim…well…all the bad I have seen in my time here, I have been witness to unprecedented goodness, ten-fold! They just need this chance. They are shrouded in evil which is not of their doing! You must remember you all loved this world once."

"Yes…we did…but slowly and surely, they proved us wrong, proved us foolish! Time and time again. We saw too bloody often, how there can never be peace here…not in a world so filled with people that think only of themselves, always toiling to gain and stay ahead of all others within this world they share. I see why there is injustice, ignorance, and corruption here …murder and unending war! There can never be peace!"

Argane stands up and snatches his staff from the ground. "You are wrong …and you will see that! Do not turn your back! And to lay claim that where you came from now is any better than ours here is…preposterous!"

"We turned and left a long, long time ago!" says Michael.

"Aye! But give us this chance, this is not a lost cause, help us and you will see it is not just wickedness here…that the people of this world are good and yearn for righteousness…now more than ever. It is an evil that we did not birth and one that we cannot break away from alone…help us to be free…you owe us…because you owe me."

Michael flashes a condescending smirk and looks down and then all over. A single bird flies up high and cries out.

"Please, you were our brothers…you are our neighbors," urges Argane.

"In our dimension…the third…right now there is peace," says Michael.

"There certainly was not always…and do give it time."

Michael's smirk changes to a subtle smile as he stares off deeply into the distance and recalls the pivotal assistance Argane had so graciously supplied he and his people in times past. "Upon notice of the first leaves fall…we will see you in the valley of the Shallowlake, at the plains of Nevermore…as your circle and the six kings have planned and worry not…we will be ample, and we will be ready."

Argane is stone-faced and remains so. "Thank you," he says. Michael bows his head, turns and walks back through the wind, down the mountainside and toward the sea of gods. Argane has a glint in his weathered eye as he watches his old friend fade and disappear.

The next morning it is William who is the first one up before dawn. He quietly gets dressed in warm attire and takes a moment to watch Appalonia and Rufus who are both fast asleep within a small crevice in the sheets atop his mattress. He wonders if they would be interested in going for a short ride with him but decides against it, so as to keep his secret morning venture just that. He tucks his 'Often' blade into his boot…It is much smaller now in his hand than it used to be.

Before discreetly making his way down to the basement stables, he stops briefly in the forge to sharpen his dagger and then visits with his old horse Windimere and Sebastian's Pegasus 'True' before climbing onto Kalyden. The lion has quickly become guard to the stables and all the horses therein and has since become a great companion to Oren. William calls a direction out to the majestic animal, and it works effortlessly…the feline understands every word of the language, though does not speak it himself, or perhaps chooses not to. They appear at the beach and disappear into the forestry, behind the sand.

William has grown to thoroughly enjoy his early morning travels with the lion prince and though he only does it once in a while, he recognizes the risk of being detected by the wrong kind but doesn't let it faze him or distract from indulging in the tranquility that it brings. He has grown immensely powerful and knows it and feels even safer atop his newest friend.

Even Marple, from within her lookout, must feel he is safe from danger too, as she sees him every time, but has never told the other elders. It is their secret. She even gives a little wave through her small window.

The bright sunshine beams into forest with various sizes of rays between the trees. *Mila would love this*; he thinks as he looks at all the colorful leaves.

She had been with him before on his morning rides but for some reason, felt he should go alone on this day. The atmosphere in the woods is silent as he takes in its beauty. Many of the birds have migrated to warmer climates so it is mostly the nocturnal dwellers that have taken up ownership of the forest. They creep the woods with incomparable agility, after all Kalyden may be royalty but he is still a cat. Soon he crouches slowly and waits...he hears something. William grows anxious as he begins to growl deeply out of pure, irresistible instinct. Upon the heightened emotion, William immediately scans the forest and quickly spots a large human-like beast moving behind the trees directly in front of them. The giant begins to look around as if he can smell them. "I will handle this but if I need you...you know what to do."

The figure comes closer and into view.

"I...I don't believe it...I think it's a...moonraker," whispers William.

"They travel in numbers and never in daylight if they can help it...it must be lost," he ponders aloud. Suddenly the raker focuses in on the pair and begins to stomp faster through the forest towards them.

The young man nods positively to himself. "Aye, c'mon," says William, under his breath. The raker is almost double the size of William but seems to struggle as it moves. Their power is quite diminished when not under the moonlight. William dismounts Kalyden. He growls louder and digs his claws into the ground deep. The monster stops and snorts. His blue skull-face is raw and menacing. William and the moonraker face each other and square off.

"Go on, make your move then," says William. The hulking raker's large hands are empty and the creature seems even less intelligent than his counterparts usually do.

He digs around beneath his hooded fur pelt mantle then around to his back and pulls a large Warhammer from his belt.

"Yes...that's it...bring it," says William calmly. Suddenly, the moonraker lunges forward and raises the weapon.

William quickly blasts the raker with two large snowballs and the beast is frozen solid, instantly.

Kalyden eases up.

"Search the vicinity! Make certain, there are no others," orders William. The lion takes off like a shot.

The young man walks slowly around the frosty creature and analyzes it closely. The ice exudes a slight water vapor, and tiny snowflakes begin to gingerly fall all around them. An after effect of his sub-zero blast. The towering moonraker is paralyzed with its big arms raised above its head and the deadly hammer stuck straight upward within its large, clenched fists. William stops in front of his challenger, looks at the beast's massive, muscular build and giant, thick, fur clothes and shivers. The forest goes silent again and still, until he speaks.

"So, you are of the ones that murdered my parents," whispers William, as he stares up into its frozen eyes, their red glow extinguished. "And took my sister!" he says with anger mounting.

He circles around again, inspecting the beast up and down. "Daft, senseless minions," he mutters. "Existing for nothing other than to accomplish pure evil."

When he comes around in front of the raker a second time, he stops again and looks it in the eyes once more. "When we are finished with your kind…every last one of you…will be DEAD!" he announces coldly. He unsheathes his flaming heart. The blade turns red as it becomes engulfed in flames. He squeezes it in his hand as tightly as he can. The sound of his calloused skin grinding on the sword's handle can be heard well and his knuckles turn white. William's eyes go dark. He quickly jumps backwards into the air and launches a heavy backhanded swing as he does, taking off the monster's arms in process of decapitating the frozen moonraker. The arms and head fly off backward from the strike and land with hard thuds onto the firm ground, the hammer still clenched inside the severed arm's fists. The rakers body is off balance and teeters slightly as it sways. William approaches and presses the tip of his sword against the raker's frozen chest. It sizzles as he pushes hard against it. The carcass falls backward slowly at first then faster upon building momentum. It lands on the ground with a loud thump and breaks into several large chunks. The flames distinguish slowly. William turns and begins to walk from where he came. Kalyden reappears immediately from the thicket. He jumps on and sheathes his weapon. He gives the lion a firm pat on his powerful shoulder. The lion looks at the dead raker for just a second, before walking smoothly back to the fortress.

26.
The Fall of the First Leaf

The last days before the fall had been spent with all the teenagers polishing their skills to their utmost plateau. The youngers have also been training together without the supervision of the elders and are therefore governing themselves. All of them are together in a clearing on the small mountain island opposite the ruins in front of the beach. Several boats float in a bound cluster, docked along the shore. The impending invasion being so close has loosened everyone up within the fortress…even the members of the great circle have been a lot less serious of late and even if it were to a fault, not many of them would care. It is midday on the forgotten edge of northeast Regalian coast, and the sky is significantly over-cast above. The clashing of swords rings out below the grey clouds as they all battle in an up-tempo frenzy. Each frantic, accurate offence blocked and countered by the other with precise fluidity.

"Alright, Alright!" shouts Leo as he finally bests Poe. "Let us not tire ourselves before the tournament!" he shouts…They gradually stop what they are doing. Leo continues… "rounds of one on one, as per usual…Ariel…draw straws," he orders. She takes out eight smooth, tiny wooden sticks of varying lengths from her pack and fans them out within her hands, conscientiously hiding their bottom ends.

The group gathers around her.

"Pull!" she says loudly, as she catches her breath, and so they do. She herself is left with the shortest straw. "CHEATER!" shouts Sara.

"I am not!" replies Ariel. Sara laughs, signaling that she had been intentionally teasing her. Ariel gives her a playful shove. The combatants stand, sit and crouch on the flat, grey slate rock of their chosen battleground. There are a few boulders strewn about the area and long, thin, dead trees flow straight through many wide cracks in the giant rock. William looks out beyond the endless ocean to the massive collection of dark clouds. A bolt of lightning briefly illuminates them as it crashes into the sea. Ariel gathers the sticks from each person, sorts through them and officially appoints the matchups for the first round of the fencing tournament.

"It is Leo vs. William, Hayden vs. Poe, Mila vs. Clari and Sara will take me on. Sara will particularly need good luck to advance from her round," adds Ariel. She does her best to not laugh.

"You say that every time Ariel," returns Sara.

"I do not!" she exclaims.

"You are in fantasy of the day that you may once best me!"

"It is right around the corner!" claims Ariel with a wry smile.

"Pish-posh," replies Sara.

Leo gets set and William faces him in readiness. Leo makes his move and with two quick counters, William bests him. The spectators belt out some jeers to the quick and unsatisfying duel.

Hayden and Poe square off and though Hayden has claimed victory over Poe more often, it is Poe who is victorious this day.

Mila and Clari's sword fight does not last too long either and what was close at the beginning ends up heavily in Mila's favor. The last quarrel of the first go 'round has also become the main event, what with all the back-and-forth razzing between the ambitious competitors.

It is a lengthy contest. Sara has more to lose with Ariel, determined as ever to take down her closest friend. The miraculous fight has all the tricks, and, in the end, Sara wins again with a clever and swift combo. They shake hands. Sara willfully collapses to the slate rock, while Ariel bends over with her hands on her knees. The rivals are spent and the on-lookers cheer.

"One day!" says Sara as she catches her breath from her back. Ariel shrugs. "Aye...the day is coming soon," she states with confidence.

In the second round, William makes quick work of Poe too, as he did with Leo in the first.

Mila beats Sara after a well fought battle, setting up a face-off between the two secret lovers.

"Do not take it easy on me!" shouts Mila as they get ready. William smiles subtly. The girls call and cheer for Mila, as they circle one another. She knows better than to make the first move on William.

A few moments pass until he steps up to her quickly and easily disarms her. She looks down to her sword and then back up at him, he flashes a slight grin.

"Boo!" call her supporters in the audience, before sharing in good natured laughs.

Later, everyone is tired from yet another long day and are gathered around the dining room table, enjoying a robust feast. They talk, laugh and share stories.

"Our group certainly has grown, has it not?" observes Be'wick.

"In more ways than one," says Isla.

"Here, here!" interjects Addly. "I would like to make a toast…to the best bunch of people I have ever known and a perfectly fine family too!" They all raise their glasses and shout in merriment.

In the late evening, amidst a typical night within the fortress, the elders are scattered about studying this or that from a book of their choosing. Whisspella is reading in the archives with Constance. Hope the cat as always is curled up on her lap. Oren and Sebastian are tending to the horses and the youngers are settling in for sleep. William enters his quarters and is about to get into bed with a book, called 'King Beauregard.' He looks to Appalonia who is snuggled up beside Rufus.

"Constance asked if you would meet with her and Whisspella in the archives."

"She did? …but it is so late…"

"Yes, I do not know why."

"Okay…I will not wake you when I arrive back."

"I should think not, you are pretty tiny."

"Very funny!" she says, before flying to a crack in the door and exiting through it.

William laughs as he gets under his layered wool covers. "She is great, is she not?" he says, looking beside himself to Rufus. He nods, in agreement. The fairy arrives in the archives where the women are seated. "You wanted to see me?" she asks.

"Oh, little deary…I did! Come, sit upon this book," says Constance, as she carefully shoos Hope from her lap and lays a large, blue book upon it. Whisspella is in a chair nearby them and closes her reading material. Appalonia flutters and lands on the book's cover.

"What is it?" she asks.

"This is an important issue regarding a very serious proposal...one you are really going to have to give a lot of thought to."

Appalonia appears worried. "Um...okay?" she responds in confusion.

"And you cannot tell a soul...We have been patiently waiting for the right time to offer this to you...a time after you'd been with us awhile and after the plans for the war were set." adds Constance.

Appalonia is perplexed.

"This might seem odd but...do you...like...being a fairy?"

"Whaaat...? Well, yeah...I do not understand...what are you talking about?"

"Dear girl, as to spare the mysterious theatrics, I will just come out and say it. We have the power to make you human." The fairy's eyes widen.

"You, you are not serious!" exclaims Appalonia.

"Believe me, I am...I was a fairy myself," says Constance.

"Oh, oh my...I-I need to sit down," says Appalonia and she does. She drops fast from her feet and onto her rear-end. "I-I don't believe this!" She holds her head.

"I know, I know, it is a lot to take in. That's why I requested that you sit." Constance giggles and continues... "It is easy...a simple spell would be cast. And it is painless, but what's more and the most important thing for you to understand, is that...it is irreversible."

"Oh wow! Oh wow!" repeats, Appalonia, as she allows her hands to slump limp down beside her from her head. She is thoroughly overwhelmed.

"You need not answer us now. Take as long as you need...We are always here and now you know it is an option...just something to think about is all," says Constance softly.

"I'll say!" exclaims Appalonia. "You were a fairy! This is a lot to take in to be sure."

"Yes, I understand and yes...a long, long time ago." The elder woman nods slowly.

"Do you...have...any regrets?"

"No, but we are all different," replies Constance. "And obviously...if you should decide to do this...you must wait until after our uprising."

"Rufus' plan depends upon you having your wings," says Whisspella.

"Oh my, Rufus! Cannot such a spell be cast unto him? like in a reversal, of sorts?"

"Rufus is under a wicked curse…we have researched for years about that…there is simply nothing we can do for him unfortunately."

Appalonia appears visibly wounded.

"I'm sorry," adds Whisspella.

"Yes, but of course. I understand. Forgive me but it is awfully late, and I do need to take a rest. This news has made me feel…a tad dizzy."

"Indeed," says Constance, she smiles warmly.

Early the following morning Oren has come to the surface to fetch a large bucket of water. He crouches down at the edge of the stone block floor, bucket in hand and continues with his chores. He submerges it into the icy water and looks over onto the beach as it fills up. He notices a small billow of white smoke coming from the area among the colorful trees above Marple's shack. It is a long, thin streak that seems to have smudged the sky and is barely moving within the thin air. There is a short, slender tree that stands alone out in front at the forest's edge where it meets the sands of the beach. It is just slightly ahead of the rest and positioned just so. Oren's eyes meet with it after scanning the plume of smoke and array of colorful maple trees within his direct line of sight, in front of Marple's shack. He studies it… A single red leaf suddenly detaches and sways side to side as it gingerly drifts to the ground. He drops his bucket, never taking his eyes off of it and walks out onto the giant rock beneath the water's surface. He marches up the beach takes the leaf carefully in hand, hurries back along the rock, takes the bucket into his free hand and disappears back below. The door grinds shut above him. Oren hastily descends the long staircase and upon arriving at the bottom he drops the bucket without breaking stride. The water sloshes violently within. He walks through the corridors and up the stairs to the dining room and enters rather loudly to find Be'wick just where he thought he would, in the corner, in his favorite red chair, reading a book. He stands before him.

"What is it?" Oren? asks the circle's headmaster.

He holds the red leaf out in front of him and his words are firm. "It is time."

27.
They Come from All Around

The fortress is a buzz with everyone preparing for the journey to Shallowlake. They are dressed warmly and steadily stuffing their packs with necessities and laying out their choice weaponry. William is in his chamber. He dons an immaculate, thick, white, long-robe with grey linings over top of a dark green leather tunic with white laces down the front. His pants are matching green, and his boots are also grey with folded down cuffs around their top ends. He wraps his neck and shoulders with a grey fur pelt scarf and tucks his chin length hair behind his ears before putting on his green hat and pulling on his hood. He slings an arrow quiver and Delilah Rose over his shoulder, onto his back followed by a small pack. He then puts on his arm guard, slides Often into his boot and straps his flaming heart around his hips. "I am ready," he announces.

Appalonia flutters over and joins him, hovering above his left shoulder.

"Have you told Constance of your decision?"

"Yes, I told her as soon as we woke up."

William smiles.

"Rufus!" he says, putting his hand out above the mattress. He hops on.

"I will put you in my pocket for now and when we are enroute, I will put you up on my hat…just like old times," he says. Rufus nods. William then holds him up in front of his face… "Are you nervous?"

Rufus shakes his head 'no' without hesitation.

"He wants to know if you are?" says Appalonia.

He thinks a moment before answering… "I am."

The group gathers outside on the beach. Marple meets them on the sand.

"There is no more need for you out there anymore," says Be'wick of Marple's shack, as he looks down at her from his horse.

"Aye, change is afoot," she says.

Be'wick looks like a force to be reckoned with. He wears a bright white, long-robe and, his equally white beard flows long and wavy along his chest and down to his belt. Black leather boots match his black gloved hands. He clutches a long, golden trident vertically in his fist. The eldest one has a fire in his eyes. Everyone is on horseback except William who is atop the lion and Sebastian is on his Pegasus.

"Constance and I will anticipate your word of victory," says Marple, before turning and facing everyone else on the sand. She raises her arms, "Good grace to you all!" she shouts. The group collectively holler and cheer. Marple lowers her arms and heads toward the fortress.

With Be'wick following closely by…Argane and Luscious divide the gathering, as they make way into the mountain's forest.

"Fall in," shouts Be'wick. The group forms two lines side by side and gradually disappear into the woods behind their leaders.

"I would like to stay by you…before the fight," says Mila to William.

He looks at her lovingly… "And I you."

The convoy travel for several days and nights, always carefully scanning the area as they go and watching one another's back when camped. The group attentively follows Be'wick's commands accordingly all the while.

They arrive at Shallowlake late in the daytime. A few armies from smaller towns and communities have already rallied there at the center of the dry lake. There are at least one thousand people preoccupied among makeshift tents of varying colors, shapes and sizes all over the massive camp in the hidden lakebed. Be'wick and Argane share a smile upon the sight of it as they observe the action from the grassy perimeter and witness more people file in from the surrounding tree lines. They climb down to join the rebels. Calls of glee ring out from the crowds upon receiving more fighters. Most of them can't yet know the prowess of the particular group that just arrived but word travels fast within an excited mob. Shinoah Steelback and his men from Killik are among the camp and appear ready. When the fifteen trot deeper into the crowd, they are greeted with yet more cheers of admiration and joy. Soon after, as the young warriors set up camp for themselves and the elders of the circle, the Khaprayellans accompanied by the infamous 'Double L' file in. The people of Redrock led by King Blackurn enter shortly thereafter and join up inside the barren lake. King Heinridge and Mayor Rimpod seek out Be'wick and Argane to confirm setting up Orion and Bix Jingling at the perimeters' only obvious hard path to intercept any passersby.

"Splendid!" says Be'wick. Almost simultaneously the gargantuan stone man enters the area. He bursts through the trees before reaching the clearing. About twenty more 'Double L's' are surrounding him in escort.

"As if he himself is not security enough," chuckles Argane.

"And the plan for the second wave is still a go," says Be'wick.

"Aye," replies Heinridge.

The growing crowd gasps and cheers in awe when Orion approaches. People pour in almost constantly, be it from small communities or large cities.

"We are already close to five thousand men, by the look of it!" says Mayor Rimpod, with delight.

"Oh, and there is more good news!" he adds. "During our venture here, everyone we spoke to was in pure ecstasy at the news of the impending war against the high king and many are here with us now, eager to bring the fight to Thayddeus! People have come from all over to join in our efforts. It truly is a revolution!" he exclaims.

Be'wick and Argane look at each other with expressions of pride on their faces and determination in their eyes.

"Though our numbers are still rapidly growing, send word within the crowds that the attack will be in mere days, so as that everyone is in a state of readiness. Tell everyone you see to pass the word on," orders Be'wick.

Rimpod nods.

Throughout the rest of the day and into the early evening, many more allies arrive, including King Irongrab, with drink in hand and the small but mighty Selkirkian army behind him, King Magnus is back from afar with his Xirn people and even more from smaller communities and independent rebels from undocumented factions arrive looking to partake in the uprising.

At dusk, up a hill near the east side of the lake, on the end of the path that joins with the only road by the lake, stands Bix, in front of the gargantuan stoneman, Orion.

They are flanked well by tall trees on each side of them, cloaking the stone behemoth from random travelers who may happen by. It isn't long before a man comes into view, riding a mule. He is heavily intoxicated. His transport zigs and zags, back and forth along the road and when he finally gets close enough, the drunkard calls out.

"Who goes there!" he shouts with a slur.

"Bix Jingling…and Orion…the titan of Khaprayelle."

"Never heard 'a ya'! Go on then!" yells the man with a hiccup.

He clearly does not notice the giant, enchanted statue behind Bix due to a combination of casted shadows and binge drinking.

"Also!" says the gnome as he stamps his short staff. "We do not go anywhere…we stand on guard!"

"Aye, yes…well, I would like to pass."

"Orion take hold of this imbecile!" orders Bix. The titan then swoops his arm downward and snatches the man from his mule, who spooks and skitters off.

"Whoa!" yells the man as Orion hangs him from his ankles and upside-down eye to eye with Bix.

"Are you a Thayddeus minion? you fool!" asks Bix.

"What! Absolutely n-not!" cries the man. "I am a drifter and no more…a tr-transient…I despise the high king! Who does not hate his…highness!" The man wreaks of booze.

"Let him down!" calls Bix. Orion sets him down softly, on his back.

"We have a large party with the intention to take his head. Why don't you join them? hmmm?"

suggests Bix.

"Now? …when…will we be taking the…bastard's head?" asks the drunk.

"A matter of days."

"I will be happy to help…in the…doing of that…great thing!" says the man.

"Go on then, follow the noise. You cannot miss them…just through the trees there," says Bix pointing to his left. The man seems confused. "This is not a yarn?"

"Oh, go on man! Before I have you squashed!"

"Just…through there?"

"Yes," replies the gnome, rolling his eyes.

The man struggles through the bushes on his way to the valley.

"And try to sober up eh…find some…red tea or…something!"

The elders of the seven and their young proteges each have their large tents at the center of the lakebed. There are old banners from a bygone era atop their peaks and accompanying those too, are the Double L's current ones. Below, inside, there are flame lamps inside allowing easy visibility within the voids. Be'wick, Argane, Luscious and Isla are stood up and leaning over a table, studying a large map. Mayor Rimpod enters. "King Elroy of Trillingham has arrived with his men!" he announces.

"Good," says Be'wick.

"But that is not all…others have come to fight! So many communities have arrived that I have lost count. Among them are dwarves, Seyus people, elves, and even the Ilken Falls orcish clan have shown up for the cause."

"Remarkable!" praises Luscious.

"Thank you, Mayor," replies Argane.

Kinto enters too. "Have you heard the news!" he shouts.

"Indeed, just now," says Argane.

"How is your arm amidst the commotion of the day?" asks Isla.

"Great! Perfect in fact," he answers, of his mechanical arm. "Thank you, thank you both," says Kinto looking at Oren.

Allying rebels continue to pour in throughout the night. Many men and women of all kinds of races spend the early morning hours, mingling, singing, and drinking by bonfires. Most everyone is genuinely enjoying themselves. There is no evidence of any fear about what's to come.

The teenagers are also in their tent.

"I cannot believe how the masses behave as our war draws so near," says William, of the over ten thousand merry fighters.

"We are young and have been raised to adhere to a strict and disciplined schedule, but these people know what they're doing," says Clari. "It is good William…everyone is at ease and excited for the chance to finally change things." adds Mila.

"Shall we tour the grounds a bit William?" asks Leo. "Hayden, Poe and I thought we might."

"I would love to…I really would, but I thought I would spend time with Mila this night."

"But of course, c'mon boys," says Leo. The trio exit the tent.

William is seated on a cot. Mila joins him there and puts her head on his shoulder.

"Ha! Gotcha!" exclaims Ariel. She has finally bested Sara in a game of chess, at a small table, opposite the young lovers.

"Ah, bugger!" exclaims Sara.

Clari is methodically sharpening her blades under a flame lamp in the corner. She looks up to William and Mila... "Do you know how many times I have sharpened these very blades in anticipation of our uprising?"

"Countless," says Mila.

"twenty-seven," answers Clari, as she holds up her long sword... "it is a wonder there is any blade left."

Back next door, Sebastian enters the circles tent after a lengthy traipse around the busy camp. He walks to Argane.

"Out there, the people's morale is at a peak, but they are beginning to stir over William."

"In regard to what?" asks Argane.

"Well, they want to hear from him and honestly...so would I if I were in their boots. They have rallied for this cause and, they are here backing his lead as well as ours...but they have never even seen him, let alone heard from him...to a lot of them, William is a myth, an urban legend...simply a promise."

Argane ponders a moment and looks to Be'wick. The headmaster nods. "We will remedy something, spread word that the young one will speak at dawn, of the morning before we set out, thank you Sebastian." The young knight exits the tent to address the concern.

"What of Michael's league of arc-angels," asks Luscious.

"They will be here," confirms Argane. "I expect, they will appear at precisely the right time."

"Wezzton...send for William, I would like to see him please," orders Argane. The younger wizard does so and returns quickly. William promptly follows.

"It has come to our attention that the camp would like to hear from you." He instantly gets anxious. "They would?"

"Yes, and we think they should, it is honorable to do as such. We are indebted to this alliance for their supporting us."

"I understand...only...what do I say?"

"Whatever comes to your heart and mind. These people have united here to follow us into battle...to follow you. Every one of us within this dry lake needs one another if victory is to be realized. They need to see you and hear you and believe in you...and you need to see them and hear them and believe in them too."

"An enormous weight bears heavy on my shoulders," says William.

"And you are becoming just the man to carry it," returns Argane.

He looks to his elder.

"I will tell you when its time…just let it flow, you'll do fine," advises the young man's old mentor.

"Aye, thank you, Argane," says William. Argane smiles. He then turns to leave the tent and stops.

"Are you…the ones of the circle…are any of you nervous…scared even?" he asks, facing the flap door.

"Every single man in Shallowlake is scared," answers Be'wick, lifting his eyes from the map. A silent moment passes. Just then Irongrab barges through the entryway.

"Aye, what festivities, chaps!" he says loudly… "Such a great time to be had! Wezzton you dirty beggar. Let us go outside together in merriment! There are people to meet…and lots to drink!" Irongrab spots Whisspella…She is glaring up from her book at him with sharpened, squinted eyes.

"Apologies, m'lady…I'd not meant to interrupt."

Irongrab and Wezzton exit the tent.

"Every single man except one," says Addly.

Be'wick continues…

"Fear…William, simply shows that you have heart…it is a good thing…to succeed in life one must truly feel throughout, and the key is knowing how to control such emotions."

Later on, in the middle of the night, the last of the rowdy ones within the camp are finally asleep in their tents or passed out by small dying bonfires and soon all is quiet…even Bix Jingling is curled up on Orion's giant toe, snoring away as the titan guards the camp, slowly and meticulously scanning the area for potential threats. His security is a constant. Much of the time in the camp at Shallowlake is spent the same way. A few more days go by with new arrivals coming less and less. When a full day passes and no more arrive, it is decided that evening by the senior members of the circle's seven that the invasion is officially on for the following day.

William wakes up just before sunrise. It is cold. He carefully and quietly puts on his robe; He is the first one awake within the entire dry lake valley. He creeps around Kalyden and silently walks outside.

He is surprised to find the whole place silent. William is fascinated by all he observes…an endless network of tents, as far as he can see in all directions.

He averts his eyes to the sky. It is an underlit, washed out, pale shade of blue as the sun, still hidden, approaches the horizon. The trees are a blended, black silhouette, atop its faint blue backdrop. William studies the spectacle...

This is quite possibly the last serene moment I will ever have; he thinks. He stares into the light blue abyss, reveling at its ever-impressive beauty. He spots something above...moving...a thing he has never seen before. He has become used to that, but this is different. It looked like a small piece of the trees had detached itself from the rest and within its own silhouette it spins, swirls and dances in the far away distance...he squints his eyes in disbelief. "It cannot be," he whispers. "It is a dragon!"

It seems to be playing as it twirls through the sky, then...as quickly as it appeared, it is gone...enveloped within the blackness.

A time after, with the sun fully exposed above the distant treetops that surround the valley, everyone is bustling about. They all have left their tents assembled, as ordered. Some of them are eating for stamina and some preparing their packs for the last time.

"We have fifteen thousand brave warriors, I'd wager," says Argane, from atop a stack of crates, as he surveys the crowd.

"Most everyone seems to have awakened," notes Be'wick. The men climb down. "It's difficult to imagine how many of us, will find our way back here...once it's over, says Argane."

"Imagine well, old friend," replies Be'wick.

They enter the younger's tent.

"Argane!" shouts Ariel. He smiles in acknowledgment. William has just finished dressing for battle. The wizard puts his hand on his shoulder...

"It is time my friend," he says.

"And you two, are you ready to do your part?" asks Argane, of his tiniest companions.

"Yep," says Appalonia. Rufus nods yes, as always.

William lifts the frog to his favorite place atop his hat, the fairy joins with them and hovers at hers, above his left shoulder.

They exit the tent with the others in tow. William proceeds to climb the tall stack of crates, where his mentors had been monitoring the vast gathering. He breathes deeply as he gets to the top and stands above the enormous crowd. It is a feeling that he has never felt. He is overwhelmed. Chills run along the surface of his skin as he observes the people below. *How ever will they hear me?* he thinks.

"Um...We do not know each other!" he shouts.

The ones at ground level, nearest him take notice until quickly, more and more have their eyes fixed toward his direction. "We cannot hear you boy!" calls a man from in the distance.

"We do not know each other!" yells William, even louder. "You do not know me! And I do not know you!" he says. The people around the hub of the camp where William stands are silent. Only the sounds of the odd horse can be heard here and there. He raises his voice even louder and as he shouts, more and more people pay attention, until many of the ragtag army is transfixed upon him. He continues...

"I am William...we know our common cause...for equality and for peace! and for freedom! and through it, we will come to know each other well! It is this! that brings us together now...and will keep us together forever!" William looks at the people all around him. Many of them are dirty and they wear soiled clothing. A repercussion of life amidst the dark reign. He looks closer at their faces and sees pain in their eyes and heartache. He is overcome with the feeling he had that terrible morning at Little Augustine, years before. He envisions the destroyed, levelled village in front of him...only he sees himself ...standing there...alone, bewildered...lost. Suddenly the people before him appear, surrounding him there within the decimated town that was once his home...his everything...and he sees his parents. His eyes avert back to the lakebed, he notices a young man amongst the people that looks like he does.

"We are all brothers!" he shouts. A large part of the crowd cheers. He envisions Nya, there beside him on the crates. "And sisters!" he shouts even louder, as he points out a young girl in the crowd. "And no matter what happens today! You are with me, and I am with you!" Now almost all are cheering... "and we are one!"

He calls out to thunderous cheers of excitement and elation. "No matter what unfolds today, we are united! and we shall *always* be! and we will defend our freedoms...for righteousness...and good and for prosperity and long lives that we all deserve! For all our ancestors and the ones that have been taken from us! For us here now, together...and for our children and our children's children! and their children!"

Everyone is inspired and cries out and cheers in triumph as William gazes upon them.

"For all of us!" he shouts. He jumps off the crates. Argane smacks him firmly on the back.

The crowd is reborn in unification. Out from the gathering of people applauding William's speech comes Wiley Blood-born from Melancholy.

"You have come a long way lad," he says.

"Well now, I thought you too old for this!" says Argane, playfully.

"Never!" says Wiley. "Wouldn't miss it for anything."

Mila latches onto William and hugs him tight. She whispers terms of endearment into his ear. Even Appalonia drops down onto his hat, squeezes her eyes shut and embraces Rufus. He must hold on to William's hat as to not fall off while Appalonia squishes him in her grasp. The crowd too continues to buzz, exchanging pleasantries, motivating gestures and encouraging words.

The group maneuvers through the exuberant army. Several people call out to William. Many to shake his hand or pat his back. He is cordial as can be. They finally arrive back inside the elder's tent, to find Aleeso analyzing the map.

"Inspiring words young one," he says, without looking up.

"Aleeso!" calls Argane, in delight. "I knew you would be here."

The assassin grins. "Any reconnaissance work for me?"

"No, just plain old battle," replies Argane.

"It will have to do," jokes Aleeso, with a wink.

A short while passes. Sebastian and Oren enter the circle's tent.

"The consensus is that all the people are ready…and eager," announces Sebastian.

"Send word as fast as you can and address all you tell to do the same, that we are mounting very soon and to do so too and follow us to the last hill's valley, where we will halt there in wait. When everyone has fallen in together…we will have further instruction on travel and our attack," orders Be'wick.

"Yes," says Sebastian.

"Addly, Wezzton…assist them please!" adds the headmaster.

The four leave to spread the message within the crowd. The word spreads like wildfire.

"The rakers powers will be more than halved under daylight," says Be'wick, to Aleeso and Wiley.

"Remember, go for their throats." He continues to divulge the plan of engagement, explaining Rufus' part, then Orion's. Next-door, over in the younger's tent Jon of the 'Double L' enters looking to greet William. He is delighted.

"I had to see the boy, who has become such a sensation!" says Jon as they shake hands.

"You sure were an important delivery. I am glad I did not mess it up."

William smiles. He is happy to see Jon after so much time.

"So, this is it huh?"

"Aye, I will see you in the field Jon," says William, respectfully.

Jon takes his exit. The young ones quickly gather their weaponry and proceed out of the tent.

They mount their horses. "Stay beside me," says William to Mila.

The elders of the circle arrive outside and do the same. Be'wick raises his trident, signaling everyone else who has a horse to mount up, as previously instructed within the crowd by Sebastian. He waits a moment and kicks up his horse with his heels. The fifteen from Old Crimsinth follow his lead. Slowly, the fifteen-thousand-person army does the same and intricately funnels in behind. The massive convoy pour out of Shallowlake in tight formation and to the path in an enormous train. No one is left behind. Orion is in front of Be'wick and Argane and begins to walk when they arrive to him at the edge of the dry lake. The people are in awe as they observe the Khaprayellan titan. Bix falls back and climbs aboard with Mayor Rimpod atop his horse. The group is a grand spectacle as it cuts through the countryside. They are marching directly to High King Thayddeus' super-castle.

28.
The Mighty Rufus of Kersius Seals His Fate

Later the army begins to arrive in front of the last hill in Nevermore before the clearing where Thayddeus is located. The leaders halt in the valley below and consistently order the group to feather out and assemble parallel in rows, one behind the other along the vast hillside. It is extremely wide across. Tens of thousands of yards at least and provides ample coverage for the invaders. The army faces the grassy hill where the circle is set up and giving directions. The incline ascends gradually upward about fifteen yards to where it levels out flat before descending gradually back down on the opposite side where there is nothing but wide-open plains that lead right to the super-castle. The top of the hill will be an ideal area to command from. Be'wick orders Addly to creep up the incline and keep close watch to ensure no one at the castle is alerted by their presence before is necessary. Orion is tucked into the trees, way behind them, crouched and well-hidden. The riders look at him in fascination as they trot by on their horses. Slowly but surely the army of rebels gathers and keeps quiet as they do. The people merely whisper but only when they must. Addly scans the castle through a small telescope. It is about three hundred yards away. Guards, slaves and creatures carry about as usual.

Idiot! thinks Addly of Thayddeus' arrogance in not fortifying his palace with ramparts and parapets.

Gradually, as the army appears from the forest and align, so too does Michael's archangels, though they appear not out of the colorful bushes but right out of thin air.

Be'wick nudges Argane with the butt of his trident and nods toward them as they emerge one by one. Argane grins at the sight and watches the angels simultaneously appear more clearly. The people begin to stir as they look on. The angels add another five hundred to their overall count. Michael seeks out Argane and another is with him. He has mid-length dark brown feathered hair, parted at the side, brown eyes, a dark complexion and perfectly symmetric facial features.

He wears a grey, thick collared, long sleeve shirt and a duster jacket with silver buckles along the front flaps and along the forearms. The jacket flows down to just below his knees and deep red pants that are tucked into his long, black cuffed boots. He, as does Michael, looks rugged and elegant all at once. His clothes and especially shoulders are extremely dusty from his passage through the dimensional void.

"A tad late, but we'll take it," says Argane, with a wink from atop his horse.

"How is the outlook?" asks Michael, from below.

"Better than we thought, but still…it will be a serious challenge. William must get to the king and face him directly if we are to succeed."

"Too bad we can't move between the voids indoors, eh?"

Argane chuckles. "Can't be too easy for us."

"We'd have brought our horses through but…we anticipate enough of our share of loss for today."

"Let us hope not."

"Well, we are at your command…This is Adam…he is my number two. If I fall, he will pick up my lead and if he should meet his demise, well then, may our God cross the spaces between to show himself here and help us all."

"Thank you, friends. Please, fall in…somewhere near the front lines," says Argane.

The angels exchange pleasantries with the wizards before leaving to set themselves up accordingly.

"They all look very much alike," says Be'wick, of the angels.

"Indeed," agrees Argane. "And they still carry those rather curious arms at their hip too I see."

"Well, their swords are exquisite," observes the circle's headmaster.

Every archangel has a long, silver, glimmering sword strapped to their hips and an equally shiny, single shot; flint-lock style hand pistol holstered to the opposite side. Their jackets are slung around the ivory handles of their guns, exposing them perfectly for easy access.

A while passes until all the invaders have fallen into a very wide and deep set of rows before the hill. They are as still as can be. Nothing moves but the odd horse's hooves and the banners and flags in which some of the bigger community's appointed bearers are carrying. Addly remains near the top of the hill, he is laying on his stomach with his elbows in the grass, meticulously keeping watch. William steps out of the row that is the furthest one back from the castle to work his way towards front and center.

"I will be back," he whispers to Leo on his left and then repeats the whisper again to Mila on his right.

He and Kalyden quickly walk by the dark blue and orange flag representing the 'Double L'. He observes it briefly as he carries on, to meet up with Be'wick and Argane. Appalonia is above his shoulder and Rufus is on his hat's brim as usual. He hands his hat to Be'wick and the fairy approaches when he does. The five wizards of the circle and Whisspella the white witch pass it around from one to another, bidding Rufus farewell.

They each do so in their own personal way. When the hat comes back around, Argane is the last of them to say his piece.

It has been the utmost pleasure, dear friend and history shall never forget your bravery here today. "You will be a legendary hero, for all days." He hands the hat back to William.

"You are my best friend," he says, with tears forming in his eyes…"you saved me…all those years ago…I would've have never made it through those dark nights without you…and while we live free and in peace, we will always remember you and how your ultimate sacrifice helped to make it possible…how you saved…all of us…I love you and will miss you always." Rufus grins his signature grin.

"He says thank you…he says he loves you all," says Appalonia softly…she too is choked up.

Be'wick carefully raises him in his hand from William's hat and holds him in his open palm. Appalonia flutters to Rufus and puts her arms around her friend, squeezing him tight under his scrawny arms and locking her hands around his torso. She lifts off and starts out toward the west tower. William slowly analyzes the bycocket hat…he drags his fingers along the front of the brim, before pulling his hood up and over his head. He hands it back to Be'wick. "Please keep this safe for me."

Be'wick nods yes. A moment later, the circle's headmaster raises his left arm signaling Sebastian and Whisspella to surreptitiously ride the long way around through the woods and stake out the area opposite the army, behind the castle's west tower where Nya is presumed to be. They do so without hesitation. He then sends Oren in search of Bix. "On your way, tell everyone you see to spread word, down the lines in both directions that after the explosion the titan will lead us into battle and to stay in position. When he reaches the castle…that is when we will charge at full speed ahead. Oren leaves the area with purpose. Bix arrives at attention shortly thereafter.

"Bix Jingling," says Be'wick.

"At your service," he replies, as he stamps his staff onto the ground. From Bix's perspective Be'wick is a very long way up, on his horse.

"As soon as there is action at the west tower, send Orion in to do as much damage to the castle as possible, have him start at the east side and work his way to the center…the army will be atop the hill and when he starts in on it, we will charge that instant."

"Got it!" says the gnome and with another quick stamp of his staff, he runs to Orion's hiding place within the tree line. A time later Sebastian and Whisspella arrive at their rendezvous point. They are well hidden and there are little to no threats from where they wait. Soon, all the pieces are in place…all except Appalonia and Rufus who are still high up in the air…

Everyone waiting is in formation, still and silent, collectively holding their breath.

"You sure are heavy!" says Appalonia.

"Do tell me you are not going to go down?" says Rufus.

Appalonia laughs nervously. "Oh no, no, no…we are okay in that regard."

"Of this flight, I am quite terrified you know. At least, you are not stuck looking down!"

"Good point," agrees the fairy.

"Me falling to my death during the commute is much less glorious than the intended outcome."

"Rufus, be serious!"

A moment passes… "I'd like to know in confidence…how do you feel about this? …your…end?"

"Rest assured, I am excited! And my dear Appalonia…please, do not ever forget…it was my idea. I have lived long and what better way to take part in all this? I can fight! This way…I can fight. It is a great honor. I fear too that there is no other way to finally achieve freedom for our people and to give William a real chance to save Nya…also do not forget, I knew her…and I knew him when they were both but tiny children…I was witness to what they did to their family and my home…my keeper Dora…I was with her for almost two hundred years…these atrocities must be avenged."

"Let us go over the game plan…" says Sebastian, as he strokes his Pegasus' nose softly. Whisspella is leaning on a tree and watching the westside of the castle closely, from their spot nearby, among the trees. She begins,

"When the tower opens up, like it's supposed to, we move…the directive is to get in and out fast, take care of any who oppose, and bring Nya to William without leaving any witnesses or tails," says the white witch.

"Right," confirms the knight.

Whisspella continues. "So, we gain entry, we kill anyone who is not a child, and we find the fourteen-year-old girl. If we do and she comes willingly, graciously, then good! All the better…and that is it!"

"And if not?"

"Then she is made to…whatever means necessary."

"Well, I do hope it is the not the latter, for everyone's sake."

"If Thayddeus has not warped her mind and broken her will, she will thank us, especially when she sees her brother."

"Should be quite a spectacle to behold…the tower blowing open, should Rufus be able to execute as planned…I'm hoping we are far enough away and under sufficient cover."

"That Rufus certainly is courageous," says Whisspella upon looking up at the sky above the super castle.

"Aye…he was a hero of mine you know, growing up," says Sebastian.

"The history is impressive…I know Argane regards him very highly also."

"Indeed, I have read *all* the stories written about his escapades when he was a man."

"And soon his legacy will be even greater. According to Argane, the old city of Kersius diminished significantly when Jezella bested him. Had that not happened the way it did, his reputation would not have been crippled and the leadership there would likely not have crumbled."

"I have read *her* stories…now there was one wicked sorceress," affirms Whisspella. "Interestingly enough, she disappeared from the history books shortly after Thayddeus came about but no one knows to what end, there has only ever been vague speculation and rumor," she adds.

Over at the hill, tensions are high, as everybody waits anxiously for the signal. Bix stands by his massive companion and stabs his staff in and out of the ground in nervous repetition. "It has been a long time since you and I have been immersed in such a fight, old boy," he says with a hint of rare vulnerability. He is eager to hear the blast and get it over with, knowing all too well the chaos that will ensue. "It's always the lead-up, that is the worst is it not?" Orion looks down to him, expressionless, stone-faced.

Up ahead, within the militant lines, Leo looks to Hayden and forces a smile. Hayden exhales slowly. A bead of sweat slowly rolls down his cheek from his temple.

Way up in the sky, Appalonia's eyes well up as the castle's peaks have gotten overwhelmingly close. They enter the airspace directly above. Rufus surveys the tile roofs carefully to identify the tower that is at the western most point. He briefly observes the large amount of people scattered around, below…Funny, he thinks, of how oblivious they are to what they will soon encounter and be thrust into. Rufus continues to analyze the intricate network of roofs. They are large and tall with many pitches and accompanying runs. There are several hips, valleys and dormers. It is an architectural marvel. "Keep on going," he says to Appalonia. "There…it is the furthest tower," he adds…

"to our left, that is our stop." A few moments pass, Appalonia lands near the tower roof's edge and releases Rufus. The tiles are corroded and made of thick, dark ceramic and shall provide good footing. She looks to him, wipes her tears and exhales heavily.

"It will be okay," says Rufus.

"Will it? ...You are my best pal," she says sniffling.

"All will be better off after it is over."

"Yes, 'sniff'...I know...I do," she says, reining in her emotions.

"I must go now," he says.

"I will miss you...and...I love you," she says, displaying relief as she tries to gain her composure.

"I love you too...bring yourself to safety and wait for William." Rufus hops further down the roof and crawls to the very edge.

Appalonia watches him go before reluctantly taking flight and heading back to safety.

He walks around a section of the roof's perimeter searching for entry and discovers a potential spot underneath the over-hang. He carefully crawls under the roof's edge and upside down along the wooden soffit. There is a space where the limestone meets the wood where the mortar has given way to a gap. He crawls through about a third of the way before coming to a dead end and backing out. He searches the towers outer wall further until he finds another crevice. A small bird has burrowed it fully on through. The small space leads right to the other side of the block. He crawls through the void and into the tower. The top floor of the shaft is a prison cell, with an elevated concrete slab and straw all over the floor. There is an empty bucket. To Rufus' surprise there are only cobwebs inside of it. It seems that this particular cell has not been used in a while. There is a closed iron hatch door in the floor near the exterior wall. He crawls down through another void and to the next part of the tower. It is wide open and leads all the way down to the bottom, where there is another cell. He cannot be sure as to its occupancy. A long, narrow, stone staircase spirals downward, along the wall of the shaft to the chamber floor. He takes the shortest route, crawling down in a straight line along the wall. Rufus gets to the cell at the castles main level to find its barred door open...and the space furnished. It is carpeted and has a mattress, sheets and pillows on its stone slab. There is a dresser with jewelry on top, shelves lined with various wares, and ample fresh water in a bucket. He finds nothing else of interest and starts out searching the castle further, moving in the shadows within the hallway beyond the cell's open doorway. The short corridor takes him to a large, lavish great room with an extremely high ceiling. There are lit candles all over large wooden tables and there are varying pieces of weaponry strewn about. At the space's center is a grand chandelier, hanging from the stone ceiling way above by thick chains. Hundreds of small candles light it up brightly. It is quiet until the sound of tapping footsteps begin to ring out, growing louder and louder and more aggressive as they draw near. A woman starts yelling assertively.

"I said for you to ready the guillotine annnd the gallows! Not just the gallows…in fact, I will have your head today too! I have had it with your incompetence!" shouts the voice.

The angry and evidently irrational woman enters the exquisitely furnished chamber. She is followed by a man very thin in stature.

"You shall stay in Nya's room and when today's show is *almost* over with, you will be the last to give your life!" she says coldly.

Rufus is excited and inspired upon hearing the name of his old friend and for the first time ever since her disappearance, it has been confirmed…Nya is alive. He wishes he could see the face of the woman who speaks so harshly up and around the bend but chooses to remain still and hidden.

The shrill voice continues. "If you cannot follow simple orders," she snaps. "To simply ready the guillotine *as well* as the gallows, then you will be the last one hanging from it on this day!"

"This is an atrocity," says the man.

"Excuse me!" screams the woman. "I will take your sorry life, here and now, without a crowd!" she says before spinning him around to face her.

"Please, I am sorry I did not mean anything by it…please Jezella," he pleads.

Rufus' eyes flick wide open. He is in utter shock at what he has just heard. *How could I not have recognized her wretched voice?* he thinks.

The woman grabs the man's arm and hustles around the corner, into the corridor by Rufus and toward the cell. Rufus clambers mentally to stay calm. He cannot believe his luck…emotions within him swirl.

"Jezella, your grace, what will happen when Nya gets back to be in her room?"

"She is at the castle's center on Thade's floor, doing my biddings for the day…you need not worry about that!" she barks. She shoves the man into the cell then slams and locks the door. "Ugh!" she exclaims. "You are a disgrace …despicable," she adds before quickly starting back down the hall and back past Rufus.

Most of his emotions stop at once. All but one. He is elated. He revels of the very thought…The chance to not only blow the tower sky-high for William and the rebels while Nya is out of harm's way, but to be able to deal revenge to his old nemesis in the process is a fate beyond his wildest dreams. Amazing, he thinks…Rufus studies the sorceress. He grins, steps out from the shadows and follows behind her. He is grateful beyond measure for his good fortune. Jezella sits down forcefully in a chair at the end of the room's largest table and slumps into it. She snatches a small book from her black dress and starts to read it, with the fingertips of her free hand steadily massaging her forehead.

She is a sitting duck! He thinks in disbelief. He watches her. If only he could have done it when she was within the tower…how to get her back over there? He ponders his strike.

"My grace! My grace!" calls the man from Nya's cell.

"Ugh, what is it? You fool!" she shouts. She slams down her book and stands up. Her steps ring out again as she walks quickly back down the hall and by. Rufus is stunned. He follows.

"This had better be important! You imbecile!"

"My grace, I-I am not confident anyone else could oversee the…"

"Silence!" she snaps. "Your job was an easy one…now! Not another word or I will murder you where you stand…Imp!" The man stops talking and nods compliantly. Jezella turns and stomps back down the corridor yet again.

Rufus hops to the center of the hall into a streak of daylight that shines diagonally across the floor through a small, barred window. As she gains ground, he braces himself. He speaks two words loudly and clearly. "MEZZO! TONKUS!" Jezella stops cold in her tracks and glares down sharply at the brave little invader. Her eyes focus in on him. "It cannot be!" she shrieks. "You! It is you!" she screams. "No!" She starts running toward Rufus. He smiles wide… "TUKK!" he shouts. After the third word is spoken, the mighty Rufus of Kersius instantly glows brightly. Jezella the Nefarious is blinded. Rays of ultra-violet light and white heat, shoot out of him in every direction singeing the stone walls and the sorceress. As they burn her, she continues to run and scream, frantically. She knows very well what's about to happen. Her sad attempt to trample Rufus is amiss on her way down the hallway. Just before she enters the large room to take cover, the bright white frog explodes obliterating the corridor, sending large parts of it sky high. Jezella is sent flying through the room, over the table at which she was reading and crashing hard into the far wall. Fragments and debris pin her to it.

Miraculously, Nya's cell is virtually unscathed, though the shaft above has a large fracture and most of its roof is gone. The room's iron door is dented heavily inward, with large chunks of stone block pressed against it, other than some bits of rubble and toppled over items, the interior space itself is intact, but the floor has slouched. In the great room there is stone dust everywhere and visibility is low and getting worse. The sorceress is badly burned all over her body, she is bleeding from several lacerations and missing her left arm below the elbow. She is certain her left leg is fractured in several places as she struggles to free herself from the rubble. The corridor is gone, and the tower is ruined, it has buckled at its foundation and has critical, structural damage to its base, leaving it heavily slumped and leaning away from the castle.

Outside, the rebels, behind the hill, stir after hearing the thunderous explosion and watch in awe as a large stack of dust fills the air like a cloud of smoke. The ground immediately begins to rumble and shake as Orion takes off running with massive strides out from the forest and toward the compromised castle. Some of the army below shout in awe as he effortlessly strides over them, the hill, and across the plains.

"Men!" yells Be'wick. "Forward slowly...halt!" he shouts as they reach the top of the hill. The sight is incredible as it comes into view. The titan is sprinting with reckless abandon, straight toward the castle. People and creatures alike run in a frenzy both outside and inside the castle. The ones on the outside have a much better idea of what is happening. While the ones inside are much more confused about the commotion. The rebel army whoop and holler with excitement. Their adrenaline ramps up at a rapid pace.

Thayddeus is alone in his master's quarters at the center of his castle...the oakwood door is being pounded on by a panicked castle-hand. He orders his guards to stay put and answers it personally.

"What is the bother?" he asks, agitated. "The earthquake has you fools startled, has it?" he comments.

"This is no quake—your excellency. The southwest tower has been struck! We are under attack!"

"You are mad," says Thayddeus in his calm, deep voice.

"Look westward out a window in the southeast wing, you will see m'lord!" says the peasant, urgently.

Thayddeus shoves him further into the hallway and slams the large door behind himself. He walks vigorously through the castle. Residents are scurrying all over. It is pandemonium. He gets to the southeastern wing and marches through an elegant lounge area to a large, open, stained-glass window, facing outside. He looks out in front of the castle. He sees the stone giant coming straight for it. He is in disbelief but remains composed. He backs up quick when Orion stomps through the front courtyard and over the moat. The ground quakes evermore.

He grabs the castle and proceeds to punch massive holes in it with his huge fists. He rips chunks out of the walls too as he dismantles it. The building shakes as he unleashes awesome, destructive fury. Several flattened, bloody men and creatures alike lay embedded within his giant footprints in the ground below. Residents scramble as large stone blocks and debris fall, crashing hard to the ground. Some are crushed as they hustle in vain to flee and gain clearance from danger. Pieces fall violently into the water and onto the main drawbridge destroying it easily. Huge plumes of dust billow from the ruptured building.

From the north side of the western tower, Sebastian and Whisspella do not hesitate to stash their steeds and get inside the castle. They help each other over large piles of rubble and through the thick atmosphere to gain entrance, through the opening in the corridor that Rufus had created.

The army on the hill are stunned as they watch Orion relentlessly smash the castle. He is nearly as tall as the structure itself. The sight is incredible as he steadily deals his devastating blows. Not only as a declaration of war and to cause carnage, but to create a diversion whilst the rebel army closes in, and Nya of Little Augustine is sought after.

29.

At the Height of Battle

Be'wick raises his trident. "Men! women!" he shouts loudly. "Steady…steadyyy!"

"Here we go," says William to Mila… "Stay close."

"Charrrrrge!"

Everyone on the front line takes off as fast as their horses will allow. Each lined up row follows the other in quick succession. Many members of the army shout varying battle cries as they ride across the green frontier. Be'wick, Argane, Addly, Oren, Heiridge, Rimpod, Elroy and some of the league of angels are among the only ones left on the hill. King Thayddeus spots the invaders and quickly descends the castle. He grabs the first man he sees and shouts for him to order the moonrakers out from their underground bunkers and to tell all the commoners inside the castle to get out and defend it.

Michael turns to Argane. "If you don't mind…I've ordered a few of my most trusted men to stay up here and lay witness to the outcome of this."

"You are the best warriors I have ever seen; you do what you feel is best, I would not question your judgement in battle."

"Thank you, we shall do all we can…I will join those there, in the eye of the hurricane soon, once it is established."

"Good luck and thank you again…I will see you down there," says Argane.

In the field in front of the castle many bewildered defenders have quickly gathered and formed varying sized crowds. They are under-dressed and under-armed. Some of them clamber to find anything they can pick up to use as a weapon or a shield before they fall in within the groups. They collectively brace themselves as the whirlwind approaches.

Thayddeus makes his way back up to the higher levels of his castle. He stands at a high window and watches.

The determined, rebel army of over fifteen thousand collide with the king's henchmen who make up barely a third of their attacker's number. Some rebels stay mounted, hacking and slashing the inadequate defenders with ease. The ones met with a challenge and knocked off their horses from offensive impacts, wipe out their adversaries from their feet with even more accuracy. Orion continuously ravages the structure all the while, adding to the dust and debris flying all over. Michael enters the battle and instantly makes advancements for his side. Upon arrival, the wizards of the circle waste no time taking out their enemies in groups with miraculous displays of magic. Their young proteges also do well against the king's men. The ones using melee weaponry are flawless in their executions, while the ones wielding magic are also precise as they dispatch of their foes.

In frustration, Thayddeus runs up through the castle even higher, ascending the staircase floor after floor at an unbelievably quick pace. He is flying into a mad rage more and more as he goes. He reaches the top and jumps through a stone slab door and walks fast to the edge of the low sloped roof. By now, most of the center section of the front of his castle is destroyed and crumbling. The roof quivers as Orion pounds the structure again and again. Thayddeus watches the titan deal his devastating damage below. He follows him, walking carefully several rooves over, one after the next…steadily closing the gap on the unwitting stone giant until finally he is directly above him. He looks over the edge. His dead men are everywhere within the grass and muck. His people are extremely outnumbered, and it shows easily from Thayddeus' vantage point above the battlefield. More archangels have appeared again, this time within the fight and they quickly proceed to turn the tide even more in the rebel's favor. They dominate the king's men, slicing them with their swords and shooting them with their guns. The defenders are terrified as the invaders collectively dole out their blend of magic, physical might and bullets. Thayddeus averts his eyes back to Orion, he puts his hands out and beams of yellow light pour out of each of his palms. They penetrate Orion's head for a few seconds…until the titan shatters into countless small pieces. An enormous pile of rubble falls loudly to the ground, joining the grey stone debris that had collected in piles in front of the castle during his onslaught. Underneath, members of both sides are killed by the falling stones and gravel.

A giant stack of dust is left hanging where Orion was standing only moments before.

Be'wick and the others examining the battle from the hill gasp at the sight.

Almost instantly, thousands of moonrakers flow out from the castle and all around through hidden, under-ground passageways and into the battlefield. Thayddeus watches as his rakers integrate themselves into the fight. His hooded cloak whips around as he turns to leave.

On the hill, Be'wick feels a cold wave consume his immediate vicinity. Indigo, the great bear lumbers there and stops beside him.

"Our union is at your command…if need be," says the bear deeply.

"We were not certain whether you would involve yourselves, old watcher," replies Be'wick.

"The dark reign…affects all things."

"Stay here with us and we will give you word."

"And your champion?"

Be'wick extends his telescope.

William is atop Kalyden, blasting moonrakers with a power, unseen to most. The lion prince is a remarkable force too. He tears and shreds venerable combatants with great strength. "Untouchable thus far," answers the head wizard.

"Good…very good," drawls Indigo.

Thayddeus has added ebony dragon-scale armor pieces to his attire and assertively descends the castle to an underground tunnel. It is pitch black. He uses his eyes to light the way. They glow bright white, illuminating the pathway before him. Bats and swillers alike flutter clumsily as he marches through.

On the battlefield, the rebels begin to suffer their share of casualties. There are fallen combatants from just about every represented faction on the ground. There are bloodied bodies all over. Some are bashed, others are dismembered. It is a grisly sight, as they get trampled on, below heavy steps.

Inside, Sebastian and Whisspella grow increasingly anxious as their immediate search for Nya within the west wing has turned up nothing. Through excruciating pain, Jezella keeps still and quiet as they pass.

"There is no one!" calls Whisspella. "She must be out there fighting!"

"We have to go further!" urges Sebastian. "We need to scour the castle deeper!"

"Thayddeus would devour us without effort...are you mad?"

"I shall not fail my objective!"

"It is not *failure*...failure would be dying without effecting anything for the greater good! We must join the fight!"

"We are in it! and you are of the most powerful in all the land...could you not challenge him if you must!"

"William has power unseen! The prophecy names him...and him alone! You do not understand Sebastian 'of the Netherwhere'! There is a secret to William that we had not dare tell him...a power no one else could possess! Let alone wield!"

"And what is that? What good could a power possibly be? If you do not even know you possess it?"

"If we told him...It could corrupt and distract its natural course...his power has been growing in him all his life! Not only does he wield magic more powerful and vast than any other ever has, but as his strength grows unbound, so too does his heart...this very battle is bringing it to a peak."

"I do not understand!" urges Sebastian.

"He is becoming invincible! shouts Whisspella...if he gets up to the top of this castle, he cannot be stopped...will not be stopped...not by anyone. You see, it is him and him alone that can cut the head off the infernal snake so the rest can wither away and die. It is the innocent, passionate, pure-heart that only *he* possesses that can wipe away this evil from our world...and restore the good that has been shrouded in darkness for so long. William is the only one capable of killing Thayddeus and Thayddeus likely knows just what is coming for him...he knows he must face William; he knows now the truth...that the one whom he has been seeking all this time has arrived to fulfil his destiny."

Behind the super-castle the high king jumps up through an inconspicuous hatch under the grass and onto a massive graveyard. There are thousands of tombstones. Most bear dark traces of baked on mildew within their illegible embossing's and along their edges. The white, washed out, faded markers lean crooked this way and that. He looks back one hundred yards away at least, up gradually rising, empty fields to his palace. Its rear-side is virtually unscathed. It stands there almost peacefully.

Within the battle Clari has positioned herself high up on a pile of rubble in the inside corner of a fractured castle wall, near what was its main entrance. She is unloading arrows into her enemies from an advantageous vantage point.

She was tenacious to set herself up there and does well, heavily wounding rakers and every so often fatally killing the odd one she that she manages to shoot through the neck or temples. Unfortunately, she is running low on arrows and a couple of rakers have spotted her.

Inside the castle, Sebastian and Whisspella have left the great room. Jezella finally, painfully Manages to dig herself free. She dusts herself off and takes a few awkward steps forward before a bone snaps, in her already broken leg. She stumbles and falls to the floor in agony…grimacing and clenching her teeth, a stream of drool rolls out from her mouth and hangs there from her bottom lip. Her eyes are crimson. The sorceress struggles to get up. Soon she does and drags her leg behind her as she heads for the blown-out hallway. She falls again and lets out a blood-curdling shriek. "Jezella! Oh Jezella! Is it you! Please! Let me out…please, help me…I can fight!" The jaded woman ignores her captor's pleas and carefully climbs out of the demolished corridor and down the large pile of debris.

"Please!" calls the trapped prisoner, in a disturbing tone of voice. He is desperate.

Most of the fighting is around the front and on the opposite side of the castle. No one notices as she hobbles to the nearby forest and disappears.

Within the battle, Wezzton and Irongrab are a powerful duo. Together, they enthusiastically cut down their foes with ease. They utilize their combination of magic and brute strength with impressive fluidity. Irongrab cries out in excitement, as he drops his adversaries. Wezzton is more candid but smiles and even laughs in triumph upon besting his.

At another area within the chaos, Aleeso maneuvers the crowd with an unnatural speed as he quickly dispatches of his enemies, often before they know what hit them. He jumps, ducks and spins around them, slicing their heels, stomachs, and necks with unprecedented agility. Isla is a powerhouse too, managing to use space and time to his utmost advantage. He destroys the moonrakers with varying elemental powers. A seasoned veteran of wizardry, and it shows. He is composed and focused, as he works with his hands and wands. Sara and Ariel are paired up and performing well, maneuvering the fierce crowd and blending their strikes wisely, all the while attentively watching each other's backs. Both are a cunning force. Poe had been fighting well too, though finds himself on his back. A raker towers over him and raises its brandistock to deal a devastating blow but an orc tackles him, knocking him off balance and down to one knee. Kinto, however, was not so lucky. Poe sees what is left of him on the ground. When he gets to his feet, he notices many rebels dropping all over the battlefield, including their horses before snapping out of his trance and running to join the orc's efforts in finishing the much larger raker. It is not an easy task. The rakers are slower in the light of day, but do not tire like common men do and they maintain their strength well, however diminished.

    Back at the center of the castle, Clari has shot her last arrow. The two rakers flank her and close in. She scrambles back and forth and unsheathes her sword. With her back up against the wall, she decides her only chance is to swipe at the encroaching rakers once they are in front of her and jump over them in an effort to escape down the pile of debris and rejoin the battle at the bottom. When she does, one of the rakers raises his arm, stopping her in her tracks and sending her back down hard into the rubble. The other bends down and pulls her arm off. She screams, before taking a fatal blow to the chest from the raker that had thrown her down. The monster holds up his battle-ax and analyzes its sharp, blood-soaked blade. Clari's death seems to mark the impending change of battle. The tide of war has been gradually turning as countless members of the rebel army meet their demise at the hands of the infamous moonrakers and the castle's various defenders. The ground has been churned to mud, within it, Luscious is eventually overcome and mobbed. He suffers several axes blows to his body and falls lifeless to the ground. Time has allowed the core of Thayddeus' moonraker army to congregate around the smashed super-castle's many voids and they remain there, guarding it with the full intention of protecting their king. A large group of defenders have also asserted themselves around the destroyed corridor's opening.

    At the mass graveyard, Thayddeus looks on to all the slouched, tarnished gravestones, he spreads his arms apart and raises them. He appears to be pulling up with great effort on a weight unseen. The ground in front of all the headstones begins to form mounds…they split and separates into chunks. Dusty skeletons fight to break free from the dirt and climb up out of their holes. Most are wearing rusty loose-fitting, chainmail armor with ragged surcoats over top and all of them are armed.

    Back at the battle, Mila is in trouble as moonrakers and resident defenders close in on her.

She stands there holding her ground, blasting fire at all who surround her, keeping them at bay. William, who is never far and still atop Kalyden tears through the group. He circles around her and lifts her onto the lion before quickly breaking free from the cluster.

Wiley Bloodborn is surrounded by rakers and defenders too, he is swallowed up and suffers a similar fate as Luscious had.

Up on the hill, Argane has seen enough from afar and hands over the telescope.

"I will see you again, old friend," he says to Be'wick. He does not wait for a reaction and takes off on his horse, arriving quickly onto the battlefield.

The archangels are among the only faction doing particularly well of late. They are highly skilled swordsmen who rely primarily on their superior steel and though their guns take a moment to load, they still use them at the right times to instantly kill a great many of Thayddeus' minions.

Leo and Hayden, who fought well together for a good while, have since been split apart. Leo is holding his own by himself. Hayden has merged with a group of fellow elves who are thick inside the chaos. He holds ground with his bow for a good long time alongside his kinsmen, before surrendering to fatigue and succumbing to death. About fifty yards away thousands of skeletons are walking towards the warzone. Thayddeus has returned to the castle.

Argane strides around the area with Legacy and utilizing him when he can within the fight. Whisspella and Sebastian have exited the castle and do very well immediately, allowing lots of space from which to deal their collective damage.

Wezzton and Irongrab's kills continue to multiply, however…they are growing tired and the rakers are everywhere. Rebels are dropping all around them, leaving them outmatched against the monsters. Wezzton uses his defenses and fires off all the magic in his arsenal valiantly, but it is not enough, for he is swarmed by rakers and killed. Irongrab is bludgeoned continuously by a pair of them but is able to break free and gain back control over some of the enemies within the area, before escaping to a less threatening area.

In the woods near the northwest side of the castle, Jezella is slumped over a boulder. The sorceress has been slipping in and out of consciousness. She winces and wheezes as she analyses her severed arm, then hops on her good leg. After several attempts, she is stable. Jezella proceeds to blast the stone in front of her with her only hand. Fireballs explode onto it and burn. She fires at the same spot on the boulder several times, over and over until the rock's surface burns to a scorching orange glow. Sweating profusely, she stumbles closer and smacks the stub of her arm onto it. She screams incredibly loud, as she presses it there and holds it down. The large wound sizzles and smokes. Her voice echoes throughout the forest and all around the castle. Thayddeus hears it faintly. He ponders on the fate of his companion and the origin of the scream. The ones embroiled in battle hear the echo as well. She finishes searing her wound and looks it over. It is sealed well, and the operation has stopped most of the blood loss. She hopes it is as disinfected as can be under the circumstances. Whisspella's horse Olivia spooks and snorts at the sound of the sorceresses' whimpers. Jezella looks sharply to her and is wickedly ecstatic, as not only has the white witch's horse given herself up, but she has blown Sebastian's Pegasus' cover too, in the process. Jezella hobbles towards the steeds with her fused stub still steaming.

She climbs onto the Pegasus in agony. He moves side to side and is considerably nervous of his strange passenger. She pets his shoulders above his grand wings. Olivia, who is visibly uncomfortable, steps sideways as to widen the gap between her and Jezella. She cautiously looks over through the side of her eye.

The irritated sorceress looks quick at the frightened horse and slowly stretches her arm outward with the most sinister of looks in her piercing, bloodshot eyes. She puts the palm of her hand beside Olivia's head. The horse's eyes are filled with terror. A soft, blueish, wavy light source drifts out of her temple and into Jezella's hand, when it dissipates Olivia collapses lifeless to the ground with a muffled thump. Jezella grabs the reins then kicks True with all her might, letting out a bellow as she tries to suppress her pain as best, she can. He snorts in discomfort before champing down on his bit and leaping into a forward trot. She leads him through the forest to just outside its boundary, then into a clearing by the back of the castle and pulls back firmly on his reins. The Pegasus takes flight. The sorceress cackles as they ascend higher and higher up into the sky above the enchanted graveyard. Her laughter turns maniacal as she guides herself to safety. True soars, revealing his giant wingspan. She flies him way above the treetops and looks back briefly at the smoldering castle and blood-soaked field of the commencing battle below in the distance before turning and heading further northwest…they soon begin to fade within the blue backdrop. Jezella does not look back.

The army of skeletons arrive at the field with swords and shields in hand.

"You must let me down there!" urges Addly, regarding the arrival of the new warriors and their armies ever declining numbers.

"You are my understudy…I will not allow you to risk your life," replies Be'wick sternly.

Amidst the battle, Bix Jingling is bravely fighting from a very different perspective. The gnome barely comes up to the raker's knees and takes advantage of the slow-witted beasts by stabbing at their feet with his dagger and shocking their ankles with electric sparks that he effortlessly emits from his small staff. He is cautious to not be stepped on or kicked and is very much enjoying himself, laughing proudly of the injuries he inflicts. Across the way, the first archangel finally falls from a long sword through the heart. There is no blood and once fallen he fades and vanishes slowly. The 'L.L.' warrior's numbers, though fighting well have been cut almost to half. Jonathan is covered in sweat and mud as he hacks and slashes with precision, proving that he has become something much greater than a chaperone.

As the battle rages on, fatigue mounts. Sara and Ariel each quickly guzzle a vile of Constance's elixir. They seem rejuvenated shortly thereafter and full of energy. They are among the first ones of the rebel army to take on the newest additions to the field. The skeleton's might is strong but they collapse dead for a second time at the smallest of efforts. Poe is again fighting well. He is using his heavy weaponry to ward off rakers and kill skeletons rather quickly with strong, direct blows. The circle's rebel army is almost halved now too and equal to Thayddeus' and the warzone is less condensed as there are so fewer alive as time wears on. This allows the surviving combatants to spread out, enlarging the battle grounds thus giving most of the rebel army the advantage. They can better use their spacing against their foes for short rests, taking medicines, factoring long-range striking strategies and for casting magic. Leo, however, who has been fighting courageously and combining many styles has found himself at odds. He has strayed far away from the main battle within a series of unfortunate events and is embroiled within a solo fight against four rakers at once. They stalk him relentlessly as they approach and continuously engage. Leo cannot get in close enough for proper melee attacks and had run out of arrows a long time ago. Finally, as he is steadily backing up, two of them briefly drop their guard, in desperation, he musters the strength to instantly flash two large ice spikes at them, killing them both simultaneously. The other two dash at him. He lunges backward into a large unforeseen thorn bush, that sticks him all over his body. The two surviving rakers are able to take a hold of him. They mercilessly pull him apart. The view from the clouds shows the thorn bush...it is only one of few within the entire battlefield. The relentless brutes drop Leo's limp body parts among the bush and lumber on back to the heart of the battle. They are met by Shinoah Steelback and some of the Killikians and are dealt with well.

By the castle, more angels are destroyed and vanish. Aleeso is still proving deadly. He takes down men, skeletons and rakers with uncanny precision. The skeleton's total numbers are particularly significantly depleted. The rebel army have had plenty of success with them. Michael blasts a raker between the eyes with his pistol, while effortlessly cutting another in half with his longsword. The lead angel's speed is impressive. Adam does much of the same style of fighting where he is. The archangels are especially proficient in the art of war and extremely dangerous. None of their challengers are a match for their firearms.

Be'wick and the rest of the men, along with the great bear on the far hill continue to monitor the field closely. Indigo looks up at Be'wick...he returns a telling glance, before peering back out upon the battle. There is constant scrambling within the quarreling combatants. Flares of color splash throughout the chaos. The noises of exertion are ever present...sounds of pain and of triumph. There are explosions and the clash of metal on metal is always ringing.

Whisspella and Sebastian have separated. They both display just why their reputations are that of legend. Whisspella fights with an ease of flow incomparable as she effortlessly harnesses space and time.

The white witch stays well clear of her adversaries and whips a matching pair of solid orbs about. They are the size of grapefruits, a translucent pink shade and look like crystal spheres at first glance but are in fact something so much more divine. She manages them fluently with unseen forces as she flings and throws them, crushing the rakers skulls as they fly around with remarkable synergy, always coming back to her hands before she aggressively slings them again and again. She dances and spins as they deal their brutal damage. Her pink silk dress flows like liquid as it twirls around her perfect physique.

Sebastian's offence is also great, though much different. He slashes and impales any that he crosses with a swordsmanship elite to any on the field…and barely breaks a sweat doing it.

Within his chamber, Thayddeus has grown impatient and is pacing the floor. He ascends back to the roof-top to where he had obliterated the stone titan.

The circle's army is finally able to not only take back momentum but to hold on to it, thereby gaining control and the advantage in number odds as well.

Argane and Isla have partnered together and are an extremely powerful duo. Argane who is always calculating the battle and surveying his surroundings spots Thayddeus way up on the roof.

"It is time, I must find William!" he calls.

"Go, go!" shouts Isla, while engaging the enemy.

Argane and Legacy bound into a gallop and take off. They weave around dead warriors and fallen horses…He sees William in the distance after a short search. He is dominating with his distinctive style of magic and unusual vehicle. Argane rides quickly toward him, through various obstructions.

He cannot delay his course to engage with any of them. Everything they have been anticipating has fallen into place and aligned. William must now confront Thayddeus. When the elder arrives, the young man is handily killing all the rakers he can atop Kalyden. The lion is covered in thick dirt and blood spatter. The bottom of William's white robe is heavily soiled too. Mila's attire is no better.

She clenches her arms and locks them around his chest as he works impressively and covers his back when necessary. Argane aids them in clearing out the rest of the nearby opposition. "Your time is now! We have them where we want them. He is on top of the castle, at the center!" shouts the wizard.

"What of Nya?" cries William.

"I do not know!" answers his mentor.

He is disappointed to hear it but remains focused. "I will go inside and send Kalyden back to the hill when I get there. It is not his fight! See that he does so, see that he gets to safety!" shouts William, before starting out toward the castle.

"Mila should mount up with me!" calls the Argane. William halts briefly and looks Mila in the eyes.

Her passion exudes from them. "We shall not leave each other! I made a promise!" he shouts and begins again to run toward the fractured southwest corridor by the crumbling westward tower. Argane watches them go…it finally dawns on him, what they mean to each other. He recalls all the times throughout the past that the pair were closer than friend's ought to be. He smiles warmly.

"They are enduring and fighting gallantly…and are slowly winning this revolt," says Indigo to Be'wick, from their position on the hill. A handful of men from the circle's army miraculously begin to unleash magical might…even common men who were reluctant at first, display their crude secret wonderfully as they grow confident. The colors attract moonrakers and skeletons alike, but it matters not, now. The rebels are winning. Rainbows of color shimmer and gleam throughout the battlefield. One man, a seyus, does particularly well divulging his newly revealed tactics. "Mylo!" shouts a dwarf from nearby.

"You do not need to target yourself!"

"The balance of the scales are tipping to our side, my friend!" returns the seyus man, as he blasts towards their adversaries. "Unleash fury upon them! He cries out. The formidable Magnus of Xirn is nearby, he has been fighting well and is among several who add their magic into the fight."

Be'wick and the others watching atop the hill are elated and proud at the sight of the numerous rebels lighting up the crowd. "It is beautiful!" shouts Mayor Rimpod.

Addly calls out. "The perseverance…the will of the people is truly something to behold!"

"A wonderful sight indeed," agrees Be'wick. Moments pass… "They marvel at the battle before them. It seems those of the wilds will not need lay their lives on the line this day," adds Be'wick. Indigo nods.

30.
The High King

William, Mila and Kalyden with his superior agility, climbs the pile of rubble at the base of the west tower's corridor effortlessly.

When they are through the opening and inside, they hop off the lion. Mila examines the blood smears all over the floor.

"Go on my friend…you have fought admirably but we need you not where I am going." William thanks Kalyden and sets his eyes on the large room ahead. The lion prince takes his leave.

"Help! Help me, please, I am trapped and am but an innocent prisoner!" cries the man from inside the blocked-up cell. "Who are you?" calls William. The two cannot see one another. The heap of broken stone blocks divides them.

"I am an innocent man, is that not all that matters?" says the captive desperately.

"I have business here but when I come back, I will let you free, so long as you are not vicious towards us…if you are indeed a friend, I will know but if you are a foe…I will see to that too and will treat you accordingly," affirms William.

"But what if you forget me?"

"What is your name?"

"Marcus," replies the man.

"I will see you Marcus," says William. He turns and continues further into the castle with his love close by his side. Kalyden runs through the battlefield and back to Argane, who is waiting with Bix Jingling near the front of the castle. They are holding off enemies with ease.

"Kalyden!" shouts the wizard. "Bix will accompany you to the hill! You two must deliver word that William is in the castle and hunting down

Thayddeus!" He reaches down with his staff and Bix stamps his then wraps his arms and legs around Argane's. He clings there. The elder lifts him to the lion's back.

They take off like a shot, weaving through the battle. As they go, they pass Irongrab who is steadily fighting with some of his army by his side. He is filthy and breathes heavy, as he helps fight off the last of the moonrakers.

A skeleton from behind him sticks him with a short, crooked dagger. He yells out in pain, gruffly as the knife sticks out of his shoulder blade. He swings around and shatters the skeleton with a close-fisted back hand. The circle's army collectively envelope and constrict the high king's defenders even further.

In the castle, William and Mila maneuver quietly as they make their way upward. They keep their guard up and search for Nya all the while. Most front-side staircases are blocked off from the fallout of Orion's onslaught, slowing their progression considerably. The southeast section is almost all closed off.

Bix and Kalyden arrive to Be'wick, Addly and the rest there at the hill.

"The lad...he is inside!" shouts Bix.

"Bold Bix Jingling, you have fought valiantly today, thank you," says Be'wick. The lion prince lines up beside Indigo and lays down panting. The great white bear looks over at him and grunts, the feline returns a small roar and bobs his head up and down slightly. Bix, still catching up with his breath as well, allows himself to fall backwards off of kalyden, and into the grass.

At the battle, Argane continues to fight the enemy. He meets back up with Isla again, who is maintaining his positive impression, as any who oppose him is not much competition.

"Isla, fall back!" shouts Argane.

"Ah...I have come this far!" he yells confidently, shrugging off the order. He drops his arms and takes a brief break before resuming his offensive.

William and Mila continue to carefully navigate the eerily quiet castle. They are at about the middle level...

"When we get to him, I want you to stay well clear," says William.

"But I can help you."

"I know you can...but these are my wishes...alright?"

"Yes," says Mila with a hint of dejection in her demeanor.

"Promise me."

"I do, I promise."

Argane notices Sara and Ariel deeply embroiled in battle. He rides to them and helps finish off their challengers. "Get on!" he orders, as he jumps from Legacy. They mount up without hesitation.

"You two have done enough," he says. "Take him and head back to the hill."

The two muddy, fatigued girls do not reply, they are exhausted. Sara takes the reins and starts out over the ever-shrinking battlefield toward safety. Argane begins firing combinations of differing powers into the opposing crowds. The skeletons are scarce now and even the moonrakers numbers are dwindled down to a minimum. Up on the top floor, William and Mila quietly scour the level room by room. The first few doors they open reveal nothing of significance. He opens another one. Mila is close behind. All seven years could not prepare William for this moment. He looks inside and there she stands. It is Nya. She has doubled in age…a fourteen-year-old girl now but William recognizes his sister all the same. She raises her hands, and wobbly blue masses emit from them and hover. It is the same power William had first shown Argane so long ago.

"Nya!" he shouts with excited compassion. "It's me! William!" he adds, with conviction in his voice.

"William?" she extinguishes her power.

"Your brother…it's me," he says. His eyes well up…

"It cannot be…you died…my brother died!" she says in shock.

"I did not die that day! I was asleep in the cellar and when I woke, our home was destroyed, and you were gone! It is true, our parents were killed but I live. We are here to save you! Finally!"

"Save me?" she inquires, as William slowly approaches.

"Yes! Yes."

"I…despise life here…it is awful…but how do I know you are really my brother? How do I know it is really you?"

William pulls back his hood further exposing his face. He attempts to wipe the dirt and blood from it with his soiled hands.

"The same way I know it is you."

Nya's eyes also well up with tears as she looks at her brother's face closely.

"It is me…ask me anything, oh how can I prove it to you?"

"Speak of our young childhood," she says tenderly.

"Our father is Merrick...our mother is Elsa. We lived in Little Augustine on Big Trout Lake! You love Dora the baker and her little pet frog Rufus," he says, with an uncontrollable, joyous laugh. Tears flow down his cheeks.

"A great family took me under their wing and for seven years we put together this army to come here today...I thought of nothing but you all the time!"

"Oh brother! It's as if the more you talk, the more I can see into your eyes and through to your soul. It is you! It is!" she exclaims, quickly stepping forward and hugging him with all her might.

"I presumed you dead all this time and yet...I often wondered and then yesterday, I dreamt I was outside alone, in front of the castle and an old white bear came to me and spoke! He told me of your coming...Oh how I had hoped the revelation would come true!" she cries. "And it has!" They release from their hug.

"It is true! sister...it is! I am here now, and you are finally safe." They embrace again. "Soon we will be truly free my dearest Nya...but first...I must find him...I must find Thayddeus." They release again.

"He is on top of the castle in the middle. He ordered me to stay here and destroy any intruders that wish to pass...but I could not...I wanted to believe you would come."

"I love you Nya. Wait here with my Mila and I shall be back soon." William turns to leave.

"You are going to kill the high king...aren't you?" she asks.

He stops briefly in his tracks before starting back out for the door... "Yes."

Outside, the rebel army is doubling the defenders in total numbers. The men of the 'double L' and the league of archangels band together, while the wizards, Aleeso, Irongrab and Magnus align themselves with the more common combatants of their side to close in on what is left of the moonrakers. The skeletons are almost all but destroyed as well as most other defenders of the once super castle.

William enters Thayddeus' main chamber and quickly finds a winding, iron staircase at the back of the quarters within the shadows. He aggressively ascends them. They spiral to the ceiling where there is an open hatch door. He moves through without hesitation and stands on the roof. It is nearly flat and very large. William scans all around but cannot find Thayddeus. He walks forward along the ceramic, all the way to the front edge. The evil king is down one level on a terrace. It is a lengthy drop to the flat, stone block run. It is spacious there below. The platform is symmetrically positioned between two tall dormers that flank the space, far away on each side. There are wooden barrels and crates, long dead, potted plants all over and there is a large, meticulously detailed black and gold, stained glass window in the wall just underneath where William is standing. The dark figure is set down below, way ahead of him at the front of the castle watching the dwindling battle.

He stands as master of all he surveys, with legs, wide apart and arms wide too aa his black-gloved hands lay resting casually on the railing of the tarnished, black wrought iron fence in front of him. Each baluster has a sharp spear head at its top end. The fence is short, and only barely reaches Thayddeus' hips. It is missing sections here and there. He leans forward against it. He cannot be pleased by what he sees before him. His army substantially depleted and losing the fight below, significantly.

His long cloak flows back and sways in the breeze, revealing part of his shiny, golden, armored body. Not his castle, nor the battle is as important as what he knows is coming. He stands there not only to witness the events of the day. The high king is waiting. He adjusts his matching gold, high pointed crown above his hood. William lowers himself down and hangs on the edge of the roof. He stays there suspended a moment then drops silently to the washed-out, grey limestone. He rises and pulls his hood on. William is not surprised when he discovers the large window behind him and how it is in fact a grand stained glass, portrait of Thayddeus himself striking a menacing pose on his throne in his signature black and gold garb. William looks into the face of the portrait and furrows his eyebrows when he notices some of his own hooded reflection staring back at him from Thayddeus' face. His bright eyes, filling the dark voids of that of his counterpart's. He is paralyzed there a moment…He shakes the strange feeling, turns slowly and begins to walk toward the evil high king.

At the hill, Indigo looks up to Be'wick. His horse whinnies. "The ancients of our land are proud," says the bear.

"Aye…though more is yet to come, old friend."

William gets close. Thayddeus is in delight and turns around revealing his sinister smile. He speaks:

"Nya is dead then?"

"Oh no…my sister is very much alive," returns William.

Thayddeus pauses, then continues… "And so, it is you who comes for me."

"I am here Thayddeus, it is time for our revenge…it is time to give the power back to the people."

Be'wick leans forward to look over at Heinridge, who is down the line between Rimpod and Oren… "When this is all over…we will summon Halen to come and finish the task Orion had started."

"This is an evil place, and it shall be wiped away…completely…so as no man, woman or child shall ever know what once stood here and they can finally have their peace," says William.

"Come and take it for them then," says the high king.

William continues toward him. Thayddeus quickly throws out his yellow wave of destruction magic. It is paper thin and very wide and glows as it floats forward. William crouches and emits a shield of blue. It covers his front-side in a concave hemisphere that starts above his head and ends down below his toes. This is Thayddeus' most relied on weapon. The one he has wiped out hundreds at once with. It breaks William's shield, but the light passes through him to no ill-affect.

Thayddeus is amazed that it did not phase the courageous young man before him. He dispels the energy wave, then dispatches a series of offensive powers in all shapes, sizes and colors. William blocks and dodges them in precise succession. The few powers that do elude his defenses are insignificant and drift through him, again to no affects. Thayddeus runs toward him in a fit of frustration, firing lightning bolts from his hands. William repels them with timely placed defensive wards and braces himself as he is tackled. They rise to their feet. Thayddeus conjures a translucent, golden long sword from the out of the air. William quickly unsheathes his 'flaming heart,' and they engage in rapid sword play. The evil king is strong and backs William up a long way, right to the stained-glass portrait. William is relying heavily on defensive tactics to hold ground as best he can with his infamous sword in one hand and a conjured shield in the other. Thayddeus keeps coming at him, William tries to counter in vain. It seems every move he makes; his nemesis is one move ahead. The high king raises the golden sword above his head and swings it down over top of William. He blocks it and attempts to counter again. Thayddeus kicks him hard in the chest with the tread of his big black boot, sending him through the window and shattering it. William lands on his rear end inside the room below and instantly springs back up onto his feet. He dispels his shield energy, sheathes his enchanted sword, and bounds back outside, colliding with Thayddeus, knocking him to the ground. He is able to go on the offence and unloads a blended series of fire balls and blue mass shots from where he stands. They disappear in front of Thayddeus. The evil king calmly rises. William unsheathes his sword again and they re-engage with their blades, this time much quicker. They move in a circle, and it is Thayddeus whose back is to the window, as William presses him fiercely. Gold and red flashes fly all around them as they clash their swords.

Thayddeus charges and pushes him back further and further. The high king's speed and strength appears too much for his young challenger and ironically, magic is almost futile for either of them to rely on. They continue to battle as they crash into the iron fence by the roof's front edge. The war in the field has wound down to a halt as any remaining defenders have surrendered. Both sides stop and look way up to the fierce fight between the archenemies. Nya and Mila arrive at the upper roof and look below in nervous anticipation. William and Thayddeus are toe to toe trading sword strikes, furiously until suddenly they stop. They are tired and face to face, searching one another's eyes closely as they lean on each other. Thayddeus' head butts William hard, splitting his forehead and throwing his hood back. He is overcome and loses grip of his sword as he stumbles backwards and drops to one knee. His weapons flames die out.

"Nooo!" cries Nya. She jumps off the roof in front of the broken window. Mila follows her. Thayddeus snatches the 'flaming heart' with his free hand. It turns black…He tosses it back onto the stone further away and laughs deeply from the pit of his stomach. He conjures a second, identical gold sword and slowly circles William. He finally stops and stands in front of him with both swords crossed below William's chin, in front of his neck.

"An execution then," says Thayddeus calmly, with his deep voice. He begins to laugh again from his diaphragm. William stares up at the sky for a moment in disbelief and closes his eyes tight…without warning, and with lightning-fast speed, he quickly grabs his 'Often' blade from his boot and instantly plunges it deep into Thayddeus' stomach.

His golden swords vanish.

William grits his teeth as his adrenaline spikes. He pulls away, holsters his dagger, and retrieves his sword. It lights up bright red and bursts into flames as he stands up. He spins around behind Thayddeus and wrenches his head backwards as he impales him through his back and out his chest. The evil high king's jagged, gold crown falls down as his hood comes off and it bounces on the stone behind them before rolling away and settling to a stop, upside down, near the edge of the roof. Sparks emit from Thayddeus' chest when William slides his bloody, steaming blade back out of his body. He puts the flaming heart around to the front of Thayddeus' neck and effortlessly cuts his head clean off. The small amount of rakers and skeletons that are left, fall to the ground lifeless. William lets his body go. The knees buckle as it slumps over forward and onto the wrought iron fence. He push-kicks it all the way over. Thayddeus' dead body falls through the air, all the way down, landing hard in front of what's left of the circle's army.

William walks through a nearby opening in the fence where there is a stone block overhang lining the edge of the castle roof. He stands there with Thayddeus' golden head in one hand, the severed wires below the neck still sparking and his flaming heart in the other, its fire still raging. He is winded and breathing heavily. Nya and Mila slowly approach and stand one on each side of him. All is silent, but his breath. He drops the head. It falls a long way, splashing into the castle's blood red moat. All the survivors of the rebel army cheer in unison and raise their arms. William looks down at them with eyes wide open. His whole life flashes before them. He feels shocked as reality sets in. He looks off into the vast green landscape and to the distant horizon. He is covered in blood and sweat. Appalonia flutters there above his shoulder and lights up. He looks back down to the people below with tears in his eyes and slowly raises his flaming sword, they cheer even louder in mass celebration.

"High King William!" shouts one of the noblemen.

With his chest pounding and piercing eyes, he looks over to his left at Nya and then over to his right at Mila. "What do I do now?" he asks.

She answers wholeheartedly. "William…The kingdom…It's yours."

W.D.R.